LANA KORTCHIK grew up in two opposite corners of the Soviet Union – a snow-white Siberian town and the golden-domed Ukrainian capital. At the age of sixteen, she moved to Australia with her mother. Lana and her family live on the Central Coast of New South Wales, where it never snows and is always summer-warm. She loves books, martial arts, the ocean and Napoleonic history. Her short stories have appeared in many magazines and anthologies, and she was the winner of the Historical Novel Society Autumn 2012 Short Fiction competition. In 2020 she became a *USA Today* bestseller with her debut historical novel, *Sisters of War*.

Also by Lana Kortchik

Sisters of War

Daughters of the Resistance

LANA KORTCHIK

ONE PLACE. MANY STORIES

HQ
An imprint of HarperCollins*Publishers* Ltd
1 London Bridge Street
London SE1 9GF

www.harpercollins.co.uk

HarperCollins*Publishers*
1st Floor, Watermarque Building, Ringsend Road
Dublin 4, Ireland

1

First published in Great Britain by
HQ, an imprint of HarperCollins*Publishers* Ltd 2021

ISBN: 9780008364878

'As the sun sets and hills grow dark,
as the birdsong ends and fields fall silent,
as the people laugh and take their rest,
I watch.
My heart hurries
to the twilit gardens of Ukraine.'

Taras Shevchenko

January 1943

Chapter 1

A hundred kilometres from occupied Kiev, lost in the snowdrifts and evergreen pines, a freight train crawled through the Ukrainian countryside, carrying Lisa Smirnova to a certain death. As she huddled in the corner, feet numb and hands trembling, she could feel other bodies pressing into her with every motion of the train, enveloping her in a putrid cloud of sweat, urine and worse. Her face damp with tears, she thought of her family, who would never know what had happened to her. She thought of her life before the war, of sunshine and happiness, gone without a trace. But most of all, she thought of a small piece of stale bread she had left on the kitchen table of her communal apartment that morning, with a smear of butter she'd managed to find at the market. Having forgotten what butter looked, smelt and tasted like after a year and a half of occupation, she had been more than happy to part with the silver bracelet her father had given to her for her eighteenth birthday just to hold the tiny white ball in her hands. To Lisa, it was more than dinner for one night. The butter was a sign. God had sent this miracle her way to tell her she no longer had anything to fear.

But, of course, there was plenty to fear and now the bread remained in the kitchen in plain sight of her neighbours. How long before someone noticed it and claimed it for their own? Not that it mattered, because Lisa wasn't coming back. As she stared into darkness that was alive with sound – groans, sobs and occasional laughter – she berated herself for being so short-sighted. She should have devoured the butter right there, at the market, instead of taking it home and trying to pretend she was a regular girl living a regular life in a place that hadn't been twisted and torn by Hitler's Army Group South. At the very least, she should have hidden the bread in her pocket when she heard the hated Nazis knocking on the door of the apartment she shared with five other people, young and afraid, just like herself. Had she done that, she wouldn't be so mind-numbingly hungry right now. Everything looked different on a full stomach. Maybe if she'd eaten the bread, the future wouldn't appear so grim to Lisa.

Stupid, stupid, stupid, she repeated to herself to the chug-chug-chug of the train as it carried her away from home, from everything and everyone she loved; the streets of her childhood; the happy memories; her parents, brothers and sister.

Lisa had always thought she was meant for great things. Ever since she was a little girl, her father had told her she was his little princess, and she believed him. He told her she could do anything she wanted, be anything she wanted. And she believed him. And then, on the 22nd of June 1941, the day Hitler bombed Kiev for the first time, everything had changed.

War was the last thing she'd expected as she was finishing school and preparing for university and the rest of her life. In a matter of weeks, her grandmother, her best friend and her fiancé had been killed by the Nazis. Her beloved papa was gone, lost in a prison camp somewhere. And here she was, on a train of death, too scared to even think about what the rest of her life would look like.

Lisa closed her eyes, wishing she was as far away from here as possible. In her old bedroom, perhaps, eating an ice cream and reading a book. Not a serious book her older sister preferred, like *War and Peace* or *The Count of Monte-Cristo*, but a romance, light-hearted and hopeful, or her favourite poems by Pushkin and Lermontov that never failed to make her heart soar because there was hope and anguish and love in every line, in every word. She wished she was on the bank of the mighty Dnieper, swimming with her sister and brothers, splashing in the water with the care-less abandon of a childhood barely gone.

The train had no windows and she couldn't see the places they were passing, couldn't see her old life as it faded away, perhaps forever. All she could do was imagine the majestic woods as they gave way to villages, burnt out and abandoned, the town squares and people haggling for food. Exhausted, she wanted to sit down but there was no space, with people packed like wood into the narrow carriage. Instead, she was forced to stand in the dark, shivering in her threadbare coat and old woolly hat. What wouldn't she give to feel warm! With the train moving and the wind howling outside, the icy air seeped through every nook and cranny, and the cold was almost as fierce as the hunger.

Snippets of conversations reached her. '*They killed them all, shot them right in front of me . . . A tough winter for the Germans . . . Bloodbath at Stalingrad.*' Lisa squeezed her fists tight and put them over her ears but she could still hear. There was no relief. There was no sleep, either. Even when she managed to doze off standing up, the voices slithered their way into her nightmares.

Finally, some light. Someone lit a kerosene lamp. Now she could see the bodies closing in on her, like an inferno. She could see a bucket by the wall, a foul smell emanating from it. In the far corner of the carriage was a bit of hay where a young woman was sleeping soundly, covered by a thin blanket. Pushing people out of the way and giving the bucket a wide berth, Lisa made her way to the girl.

'Hey, can you hear me?' She shook her and the girl cried out, opening her eyes, her face white from fear. 'Move over, let other people get some rest. My feet are killing me.'

The girl muttered something and rolled over. It was clear she was determined to go back to sleep. But Lisa was determined not to let her. She shoved the girl again, harder.

'What's your problem?' the girl cried, no longer looking afraid but angry. 'What do you want from me?'

'You've been sleeping since we got on the train. Others are tired too. I've been standing for three hours.'

'Leave her alone,' someone shouted.

'Just want things to be fair, that's all. It's selfish of her to have all this space to herself.' She turned to the girl. 'If you move a little, I could sit down too. Please!'

The girl's expression softened and she shuffled into the corner with a sigh. In the dim light Lisa saw her face. It was covered in bruises. When she moved, she did so with great difficulty, as if every little bit of her hurt. 'Be my guest,' she said. Even her voice sounded bruised, hoarse and defeated. The girl was small and chubby, though maybe a few years older than Lisa. With her blonde hair and large freckles on the bridge of her nose, she looked as if she'd spent too much time in the sun. Lisa wondered where she'd found sun in the middle of Ukrainian winter when it perpetually rained, or snowed, or both.

The girl stared at Lisa, who was now sitting next to her. Then she turned away, reached inside her string bag and pulled out a small piece of dry bread, breaking it in half and handing the bigger piece to Lisa. 'Want some?'

Eagerly, Lisa nodded, feeling a warmth spread through her, trying not to show how much the gesture touched her and how desperate she was for something to eat, even if it was the German bread that was hard like brick and crumbled under her fingertips, leaving a bitter aftertaste in her mouth. 'Thank you,' she whispered, shoving the bread in her mouth. 'I haven't eaten since yesterday.'

'You are welcome.'

'What happened to you, anyway?' asked Lisa through a

4

mouthful of bread, appraising the girl and her blue and purple face and her bandaged leg.

'What happened to all of us, I suppose. The war happened.'

'They beat you? Why?'

'Let's just say, I wasn't too enthusiastic about their all-expenses-paid holiday to Germany. Don't worry, it looks worse than it is. I'm Masha, by the way.'

'I'm Lisa.'

'How much longer, do you think?'

'On the train? Days. Germany is a long way away,' Lisa replied dejectedly. She couldn't imagine continuing like this for another minute, let alone days of crouching on the cold floor, of smelling the unwashed bodies, of the wheels thumping, taking her away from home towards her own personal hell.

'Do you speak any German?' asked Masha, appraising Lisa in turn.

'A little bit. Enough to get by.'

'That's good. If they know you can speak their language, you might get a better job. I hope I get to work for a nice family. You know what happens to those who end up in factories or labour camps.'

Over the last few months in Kiev, Lisa had done her best not to hear the terrible rumours that reached her about the Eastern workers. As she sat on the floor of a moving train next to her new friend, still hungry after the bread she had eaten, her back sore, her feet aching, she imagined operating machinery at a factory all day, without ever seeing the blue skies. She imagined scrubbing someone's toilet, washing their sheets and ironing their clothes. From dawn to dusk, day after miserable day. It didn't bear thinking about. 'I don't think I'll ever make it back to Kiev alive,' she said, closing her eyes wearily.

'I guess you're a glass-half-empty type of person,' replied Masha. 'I try to see positives in every situation.'

'What's so positive about going to Germany as slave labour?'

'At least they haven't killed us.'

'Yet,' muttered Lisa.

The train came to a sudden stop. It didn't slow down gradually but the brakes screeched and the clunky machine halted abruptly, as if hitting an invisible wall. Masha fell on Lisa, who was propelled to the floor, hitting the legs of a small boy who was napping while standing up with his head on his mother's hip. Lisa cried out in pain, rubbing her sore ankle. 'What's happening?' she exclaimed.

With no windows they had no way to see out of the cramped carriage. Lisa could hear a dog barking and angry German voices.

'We must be at one of the villages,' said an old woman wrapped in a woolly kerchief. 'Finally, they will feed us and we can stretch our legs.'

'Hell will freeze over before they feed us,' grumbled an old man with bandages on his face.

'They want us to work for them. We can't work if we are hungry.'

'The Nazis have ways to force you, hungry or not.'

The old woman said something in reply. Lisa saw her lips move but her voice was lost in a gunshot. Something exploded nearby, followed by machine-gun fire and many more gunshots. Lisa crawled into a corner, trying to make herself smaller, less conspicuous. With her hands over her eyes, she prayed. *Dear God, please help me! I will never be bad again. I will never wear my sister's shoes without asking. I will never tell lies. I will never be selfish or greedy or unkind.* Lisa had never been inside a church before but, as she hugged her knees in fear, shuddering at every rifle shot and every explosion, she prayed as if her life depended on it.

Suddenly, all was quiet again, as if they had imagined the chaos of only moments ago. An expectant silence fell over the train. Two men tried to force the metal doors open but it was no use. They were locked in like animals inside their dirty, smelly cage. 'Anyone there? What's going on?' they shouted, knocking loudly. Lisa wished they would stay quiet. She imagined the door opening slowly to reveal German machine guns pointed at them. She imagined the bullets raining down on the people gathered inside the carriage, with nowhere to run and nowhere to hide.

After five minutes of waiting for something to happen, Lisa was ready to faint. But a realisation made her open her eyes with hope. The voices she heard now were not German. Even though she couldn't make out the words, Lisa could swear the people outside were speaking Russian.

Somewhere, a horse neighed. Lisa thought she was imagining it. Footsteps resounded through the narrow corridor that led to the compartment where two hundred people were huddled together in fear. Lisa rose to her feet and stretched her neck.

'Can you see anything?' demanded Masha, her eyes frantic.

Lisa shook her head. There were too many people in front of her. She stepped from foot to foot impatiently and bit her lip.

The metal door slid open with a screech and two men appeared, wearing uniforms Lisa hadn't seen since before the occupation. The colour had faded and the threads were coming apart in places but there was no mistaking it – they were Red Army uniforms. The taller of the two had two golden stars on his epaulettes. He had a commanding presence about him, and Lisa found that she couldn't take her eyes off him. She wasn't the only one. The man might have been wearing a threadbare uniform that was falling apart but he carried himself like a general. At his feet was a dog, a black wolf-like creature the size of a small bear. The other man was shorter, his eyes shifty, as if he was uncomfortable being the centre of attention. He seemed to fade into the background next to his taller, more imposing companion, who saluted the expectant crowd and said, 'Comrades! This train is not going any further. You can all return home. Outside you will find trucks that will take you back to Kiev.'

The train that had been silent but a moment ago erupted. Everyone had a question for the two men. *What happened? We heard gunshots outside. Is it safe to come out? Will we be transferred to a different train? You mean, we are free to go? What about the guards?*

Trembling with anxiety, Lisa stood on tiptoes to see the taller man's face.

'You don't have to worry about the guards. And yes, you are free to go,' he replied.

'Who are you?' asked a man with a broken arm and tears of relief in his eyes.

'We are the partisans.'

Lisa had heard of the partisans, a group of selfless warriors hiding in the woods and fighting till the last breath to rid the Soviet Union of the greatest evil it had ever encountered, even as the government and the army had given up. Her fist on her chest, she watched the two men. All around her, people scrambled to their feet. They didn't wait to be asked twice but collected their meagre belongings and rushed towards the exit.

'Did you hear that, Miss Negativity? We are free to go,' Masha said to Lisa, leaning on her arm. The girls hobbled slowly towards the exit. Lisa jumped off the train, breathing a momentary sigh of relief, and helped Masha down. After the near-darkness of the carriage, the whiteness of the snow and the brightness of the pale winter sun blinded her. After the stench and the staleness, the fresh air made her light-headed and a little dizzy. There wasn't a building or a man-made structure in sight. Nothing at all but snow-capped pine trees as far as the eye could see, stretching their branches towards the sky as if in prayer. In between the pine trees, a narrow unpaved road weaved its way away from the train tracks. She could see a dozen trucks parked on top of the hill and hundreds of people trickling from every carriage of the train of doom that now stood motionless and defeated in the middle of the forest. On the snow nearby, Lisa could see lifeless bodies in German uniforms. She shuddered and looked away.

Lisa's gaze searched for the partisans who had come to their rescue, but they were nowhere to be seen.

Shielding her face from the sun, Masha pointed somewhere behind Lisa and said, 'What is happening? The trucks are leaving.'

'Wait here for me. I'll see what's going on,' said Lisa.

Waving and shouting, she hurried in the direction of the trucks but it was too late. One after another they disappeared in a cloud of white dust. She ran as fast as she could but her foot lost its grip on the ice and she tripped. She would have fallen if a strong hand didn't catch her. Turning around, she recognised the taller of the two partisans, who was now leaning over her, helping her up. 'Careful,' he said. 'It's treacherous today.' Through a veil of snow, she watched his face. She had never seen eyes like that before. They were not just dark but black. Black like the night, like the winter sky at dusk. His dark hair, what she could see of it from under his fur hat, was longer than was conventional for a man. There was something unusual in his features, something exotic as if inside his veins ran Mongol blood. The blood of kings and conquerors. 'Are you all right? You look a bit lost,' the man added.

Lisa blinked and looked away, her cheeks burning. 'I think we missed our truck.' She wished she was dressed better, wished she wasn't hidden under an unflattering kerchief. When he turned around to look at the trucks, she pulled it off her head, tidying her auburn hair with the tips of her fingers.

'You might be right,' he said, turning back to her. 'Put your kerchief back on or you'll catch a cold. It's twenty below today.'

Reluctantly she put her kerchief back on, blushing at the familiar way this stranger told her what to do.

'I'm Maxim and this is Anton,' he said, pointing at the other partisan, who was holding two horses and pacing on the spot as if to keep warm.

'I'm Lisa. My friend Masha is still by the train. She can't walk by herself.'

Anton happily agreed to help Masha. When he was gone, Lisa asked, 'How will we get back to Kiev now? The trucks are gone.'

'They will come back eventually but you are going to have to

9

come with us. It's not safe for two girls alone in the woods. The German presence here is too high.'

'Come back with you where?'

'Our settlement is twenty minutes away.'

He smiled and despite her exhaustion, hunger and uncertainty, she smiled back. The dog approached Lisa with his tail wagging and sniffed her hands. She wanted to stroke it to impress its owner but didn't dare. She had never seen an animal this big or this ferocious-looking. The dog suited Maxim. It looked like it belonged to a fearless warrior.

Anton reappeared, leading a limping Masha up the hill. 'Your carriage awaits, my ladies,' he said, bowing comically and pointing at the horses. He had a broad face with thin lips and a large nose. He wasn't just shorter than Maxim, he was smaller, too. His shoulders were not as wide, his legs and arms thinner but his smile was kind. With the two partisans by her side, Lisa felt safe for the first time in months.

'I've never been on a horse before,' she said uncertainly. The animal was the size of a small mountain. Involuntarily she took a step away from it. 'There's no saddle. How do we hold on?'

'Just hold on to me. You'll be all right,' said Maxim, suppressing a smile.

He lifted her up and Lisa sat straight on the chestnut giant's bare back with her eyes shut tight. She was certain that the moment she opened her eyes and saw how high up she was, she would fall off the horse out of fear. Thankfully, the horse wasn't moving. It was as if it could sense how nervous she was and decided to go easy on her. Anton struggled to help Masha, who with a broken leg couldn't stay up on the horse. Finally, with the help of Maxim, he managed to sit her up and climbed behind her, supporting her with his left arm while holding the reins with his right. Maxim leapt up in front of Lisa as if he was born in a saddle, like a cowboy or a drover. Slowly they set off, with the wolf-dog running a few steps ahead.

The forest sounded like the sea during a storm. Lisa's throat was parched from the icy air and the skin of her face felt raw. As they rode through the woods, she held on to Maxim. Underneath his uniform, he felt wiry and strong. He smelt of soap and smoke, like he'd been sitting near a campfire for too long.

The snow was a white whirlwind all around them. Lisa couldn't make out anything, not even Anton's horse only a few steps ahead. All she could see was the rider in front of her. The wind made it almost impossible to speak, but she was desperate to talk to him. 'How do you know where to go in this weather?' she shouted.

'I don't, but Bear does. I follow him.'

'Bear?'

'My dog. He's my eyes, ears and nose. My best friend. He's saved my life more times than I can remember. I couldn't do what I do without him by my side.'

'And what is it that you do?'

'We oppose the Nazis every step of the way. Destroying their lines of communication. Laying ambuscades. Mining roads and bridges. Killing their high-ranking officers. Even stealing their food and cattle whenever we can.'

'That's incredible.'

'This week alone we blew up two bridges, cut two hundred kilometres of telephone cable and took two villages from the Nazis. And today we stopped a train transporting people to Germany—'

'Thank you for that.'

'You're welcome.' He whistled to Bear, who had strayed away from the path, perhaps to follow an animal trail. Instantly, the dog's ears sprang up and he leapt through the snow back to his owner.

'How many of you are there?' asked Lisa, leaning closer to hear him better and hoping he wouldn't notice.

'Six battalions around Kiev, two hundred people each. Over a thousand of us scattered around these woods.'

Lisa held her breath, her chest swelling in admiration. 'How long have you been a partisan?'

'Since the occupation. We've given them a hard time in the last year and a bit.'

'So I've heard.'

Despite the snow and the piercing cold, she didn't want the ride to end. Suddenly Maxim emitted a bird's cry, startling her. A similar sound was heard in reply. If Lisa didn't know better, she would have thought the birds were real.

'We are here,' said Maxim.

The trees had receded. In front of them was a wide meadow that looked deserted. Lisa could see small hills scattered here and there. Maxim got off his horse and helped Lisa down. She found herself knee-deep in snow, with his arms around her. In the light of the setting sun she examined the clearing. 'Two hundred people live here? But I can't see any buildings.'

'That's the whole idea. If you can't see us, neither can the Nazis.'

She heard voices and saw Anton's horse appear from behind the wall of snow. Masha looked pale, as if she was in great pain. If it wasn't for Anton's arm holding her tight, she would have slipped off the horse.

'You two must be exhausted,' said Maxim when Masha was safely on the ground, leaning on Lisa. 'Let's find you something to eat and a bed to sleep in.'

As they walked through the camp, Lisa saw men and women emerging from underground like bears from their caves. She realised the little hills were not hills at all but dwellings. The partisans smoked, laughed and exchanged greetings. A few men stared openly at the girls and Lisa shivered, moving closer to Maxim and wishing she was invisible.

Maxim and Anton took the girls to a dugout, hidden away under a metre of snow, with a small wooden door and an opening large enough for them to crawl through. Inside, the little lodging was made of wood – everything except for the little stove that was made of clay. A fire was burning and it was warm and humid. By the light of a candle Lisa could see half a dozen tables and a small bed in the corner. On this bed a round woman was sleeping, covered by a large cardigan with holes in it.

'Yulya, wake up.' Maxim shook her lightly. 'We have guests. Do you have any food for them?'

The woman stirred, rubbed her eyes, then sat up and glared first at Maxim, then at the newcomers. 'More mouths to feed! Do I look like I have a magic tree that grows bread?'

'Let's be hospitable, shall we? The girls have been through a lot.'

'Hospitable,' grumbled Yulya, getting up slowly, as if her limbs were an old rusty mechanism in need of oil. 'What is this, a luxury hotel?' Still muttering, she walked outside and soon reappeared with two chunks of dark bread and two glasses of milk. Maxim and Anton said their goodbyes, promising the girls Yulya would look after them. Seeing the unfriendly face across the table, Lisa found it hard to believe.

After the girls finished their food, Yulya gave them more bread wrapped in a towel and took them to another dugout – a narrow room with five wooden beds covered with straw. Four of them looked untouched. The fifth had someone's personal belongings all over it – books, clothes, even a dirty plate. It smelt damp and unclean but Lisa was too exhausted to care. Thanking Yulya, she fell into the nearest bed and closed her eyes, wishing she was in her childhood bed back home, under a warm blanket with her head on a soft pillow.

After Yulya left, telling the girls breakfast was promptly at six, Lisa sat up in her uncomfortable bed made of straw and whispered, 'Masha, are you awake?'

'I'm awake.'

'I don't want to go back to Kiev. No one is waiting for me back there.' Lisa thought of her mother's face as she told her to leave and not come back. She thought of her sister's quiet resentment and of the cold and soulless apartment, overrun by rats and dirty dishes, that she called home because her family had turned their backs on her. If she could help it, she would never go back. Anything was better than the loneliness and fear of the past year.

'What choice do we have?'

'We could stay here.'

'Stay in the partisan battalion? Are you out of your mind? Do you know what the Nazis do to the partisans and their families?'

'The minute we get back to Kiev, they will pick us up again. I don't want to end up back on that train. I'd rather die.'

'I don't like it here, Lisa. In the dugout, I mean.' Masha sounded like a little girl, lost and afraid. 'It's so damp in here, and cold. I don't like small spaces. I feel like I'm suffocating, like I can't breathe. It feels like . . .' She hesitated. 'We are not dead yet but we are buried alive. Do you know what I mean?'

'I feel safe here. Even I barely know where I am. How could the Nazis ever find me?'

In a small voice Masha said, 'I don't like the dark, either. When the candle burns out, it's going to be so dark in here.'

'We'll light a new candle. And I'm right here. You don't need to worry.'

'Will you hold my hand till I fall asleep?'

'Of course.'

Soon, the sound of Masha's breathing from the bed next to her own became deeper, but Lisa continued to hold her hand while she lay on her back and watched the candlelight twirling on a small table in the corner. For the first time in months, hidden away in a burrow like a forest animal, among trees and snowdrifts, she didn't feel afraid. Nothing bad could happen to her here, among the partisans – the giants of songs and fairy tales who would protect her from all evil.

Chapter 2

Ever since she was a little girl, Irina Antonova had loved painting. For others, memories were triggered by scents, tastes, places or perhaps old photographs. For Irina, it had always been colours. Marrying the love of her life was the golden hues of late-autumn trees, the golden wedding rings on their fingers and the golden specks in his twinkling eyes. The day her daughter was born was the green jungle of flowers in her room, her green hospital gown, the green pines stretching their arms to her window as if in greeting to the new life nestled in her lap. The first summer they had spent at their dacha as a family was the azure of the sky and the turquoise of the river. Capturing colour had always been a passion of hers. When she was younger, she never left the house without a sketchbook and some pencils. Dozens of those sketchbooks were stored away in a box under her bed, each hiding happy recollections of days long gone.

But since the Nazi soldiers had marched through Kiev, scorching, terrorising and killing wherever they went, Irina's pencils had remained forgotten in a drawer somewhere because, as far as she was concerned, war had no colour. It was grey, just like the uniforms that seemingly overnight flooded her beloved city. Her artist's fingers, so skilled at drawing flowers, fruit and seascapes, were incapable of rendering the faces of the condemned walking to Babi Yar – grim, lifeless and resigned. They were incapable of capturing the expression on old women's faces as they were about to be shot for selling their produce at the market – in broad daylight, in front of dozens of passers-by who averted their eyes as if nothing out of the ordinary was happening. Her pencils couldn't convey the distress of twelve-year-old children as they were wrestled from their mothers' arms and put on trains bound for German factories, where they would be forced to work until they collapsed. They couldn't capture the mothers' soul-destroying anguish.

Although the horrors were not in Irina's sketchbook, they were etched deep inside her mind and she was afraid that for as long as she lived, she would not forget.

The war had split Irina's life in two. On one hand, there was her pre-war self: carefree and in love, certain that nothing bad could ever happen to her. On the other hand, there was her present self: haggard and hungry and afraid. She had become someone she didn't recognise, and yet, she could barely remember herself before the war. The happiness of only two years past seemed like a lifetime ago.

But today everything seemed different. For the first time since the war had started, Irina noticed the bright orange of the sun at dawn and the fluorescent white of the snow. The pencil in her hand never stopped moving as she sketched cradles and dummies and tiny dolls, while her left hand remained on her stomach, where a new life was forming, as if in defiance to death all around her. This new life made Irina temporarily forget the nightmare of the occupation and notice the beauty that still remained, as if to spite the enemy who did their best to eradicate everything beautiful they came in contact with.

In her tiny office on Priorskaya Street, Irina was having lunch. The clock above the door was mocking her, playing games. All she wanted was for the hours to fly so she could go home, cuddle her daughter and read her a story. But the silver-plated arms refused to move and it felt to her that they had been stuck on midday for hours. She tried not to think of the queue outside her door that wound its way down the corridor and onto the street, the queue of people waiting to register the death of a loved one. People were dying at an unprecedented rate in Kiev. Young and old, death didn't discriminate in times of war. There had been some births and marriages this week, like a brief ray of sunshine on a stormy day, but she could count them on one hand.

Her job was a parade of human suffering, never-ending and unabating. It was a showcase of what the Nazis had done to Kiev, to Ukraine, to all of the Soviet Union.

'It's my mother, she was walking home one day, then a building collapsed.'

'My sister never came home one evening. We found her three days later, brutally murdered.'

'I lost my whole family. My parents and brothers, all gone.'

Tears, anguish, twisted faces.

But today, she refused to think of death and darkness. With a smile on her face, she imagined walking hand in hand with her husband under an unblemished summer sky with not a Nazi aeroplane in sight. The sun on her face, his arm around her shoulders, his lips on hers. She thought of everything they hadn't done but should have, if it wasn't for the war, like buying her daughter her first ice cream or taking her sledging.

If she moved her chair slightly to the left, through the window she could see the old school building where she had worked as an art teacher before the war. As she wrote down the names of the dead in her register and dreamt of a better life, she often wondered what had happened to her pupils. She liked to tell herself that they had been evacuated and were safe, away from the front line and the Nazi atrocities. But one day she had come across a name she recognised in her list of doom. It was a girl she had taught three years previously, an eager little thing with pigtails and a

17

wide grin. That night, Irina held her daughter close and cried until dawn. Since then, she went through the lists on autopilot, not pausing to think about the people behind the names.

Suddenly queasy, she pushed her boiled potato away and watched the thick wall of snow that hid the burnt-out school and a bomb crater in the middle of the street. The snow was white, shimmering, magical. It created an illusion of beauty, as if she had been transported to a different reality where there was no war and no fear. What wouldn't she give to run through the snow with her daughter, build a snowman, throw snowballs and not feel afraid. Such little joys and yet, even that was denied them.

Irina poked the pitiful-looking potato with a fork, her hunger battling with her morning sickness. Finally, the hunger won. She placed a tiny morsel in her mouth and chewed slowly, fighting a wave of nausea. As she was finishing her tea, the door creaked. Irina was going to tell whoever it was to wait until one when the registry office would reopen but the large woman with a hard face standing in the doorway looked familiar. Her grey hair was braided like a little girl's, giving her a peculiar look, like a jigsaw puzzle with a few pieces out of place. Her teeth, or what was left of them, were yellow. Her shoulders were large like a man's. Irina recognised her neighbour, Katerina.

'I hope it's all right,' mumbled the woman. 'Your mother-in-law said I could come and see you on your lunch break. I couldn't possibly stand in the queue with all those people. My leg's been bothering me.'

'Of course, please come in.' With a sigh Irina packed what was left of her lunch away, placing it in her bag. 'What can I do for you?'

'It's my husband, Valery. He died from a heart attack last night.'

Irina remembered the softly spoken man who waved to her every morning as she walked past. That simple gesture had never failed to put a smile on her face, even on the days when she didn't feel like smiling. Her heart heavy with sadness, she said, 'I'm so sorry for your loss.'

'Don't be. The old bastard used to beat the life out of me. I've been dreaming of this day for years.'

Irina studied her neighbour. She couldn't imagine the quiet and petite Valery raising his hand to loud and big-boned Katerina.

'Now I'm all alone,' the neighbour added softly, covering her eyes with her hands and bursting into tears.

'What about your daughter?' asked Irina, feeling sorry for the old woman and on the verge of tears herself.

'Larisa volunteered to go to Germany for work. Valery and I took her to the train station a week ago. I don't think he got over saying goodbye to her. He saw danger everywhere.'

'Why didn't you come to see me?' Irina lowered her voice, even though the door was firmly shut. 'I would have figured out a way to keep her in Kiev.'

'I know you would have. You help everyone. You have a kind heart.'

'If we don't help each other, the Nazis might as well have won.' Preventing able workers from travelling to Germany was Irina's way of defying the Germans. Yes, she worked in a German organisation and because of that many friends and former colleagues looked down on her. What they didn't realise was that she risked her life every day to help her people. It didn't compare to what her husband did at the partisan battalion. But it was a contribution.

'Larisa wanted to go to Germany. Because she went voluntarily, she'll have better living conditions and more food. She's working at a munitions factory over there.'

'Making bullets to be used against our soldiers? She volunteered for this?' Irina tried and failed to keep shock and disapproval from her voice.

Katerina's lips were a thin pale line on her round face. 'She'll be safer there. And that's all I care about,' she said in a haughty voice. 'Her safety.'

Irina opened her mouth to tell Katerina about the stream of Ukrainian workers trickling back from Germany to Kiev over the past few months. Sick, exhausted and barely able to walk, many of them came home to die. And they were the lucky ones. Not everyone made it back. She wanted to say all of that to her neighbour, but didn't. There was little point. Katerina truly believed she did her best for Larisa by encouraging her to go to Germany. She had hope for a better future for her daughter, even if that future involved making bullets for the enemy. Who was Irina to take that hope away? She understood only too well a mother's fear for her child's life in the chaos of war. 'All done. Here are your documents; you can have them back. If you ever need anything, please let me know.'

As she opened the door, Katerina turned around and asked, 'And how is that handsome husband of yours in the partisan battalion? Is he still every German officer's worst nightmare?'

Irina looked up from her records with a start.

'Don't worry. I won't tell anyone.' Katerina smiled. It wasn't a kind smile. She looked triumphant, like she had just won an important battle.

Irina, who didn't know they were fighting a battle and didn't care for one, shuddered. How could Katerina possibly know their secret? Irina often saw the neighbour sitting on a porch outside her house with a few friends, whispering and pointing. One word from her to the Gestapo and Irina's family would disappear, never to be seen again.

The human river outside her office soon swallowed Katerina, pushing her out of the way, but Irina remained in her chair, trembling.

It was already dark when she left work. She had fifteen minutes before the curfew to make it to the market, barter some food for dinner and walk home. Anyone found on the streets after the curfew imposed by the Nazis could be arrested and thrown in jail. A neighbour had gone missing once and returned two weeks later badly beaten, with a broken arm. He swore he was arrested before the curfew. The German officer who had stopped him had a watch that was a few minutes too fast.

Irina couldn't afford to go to jail. Her little girl was waiting for her.

Because no one bothered to clear the snow on the street, it took her twice as long as usual to walk a few hundred metres to the market. With every step she fell through the snow up to her knees and soon her boots filled with slush. On the corner of Berezhanskaya and Lugova Streets she slipped on the ice and fell. A handsome young man helped her up, a sad smile on his face. She barely noticed, even though smiles were as rare as bread in the Ukrainian capital.

Occasional grey uniforms walked past Irina, not smiling and not even glancing in her direction. After fifteen months of occupation (how could it only be fifteen months when it seemed like a lifetime?), she still felt like she was caught in a horrible nightmare. It was baffling that the beloved streets of her childhood should belong not to her people but to the Nazi hordes.

Shivering at her thoughts as much as the cold, Irina crossed the road to the market, where villagers brought their meagre produce – wilted potatoes, carrots, beetroot, sometimes eggs, very occasionally meat of unknown origin – and exchanged them for gold and other valuables. In her pocket was her most precious possession, a pair of golden earrings her husband had given her on their wedding day. It broke her heart to part with them because just looking at them brought back so many wonderful memories. The way his eyes lit up when he saw her in her wedding dress. The way he spun her around the dance floor, whispering that she was the most beautiful woman in the world and the only one for him. The way she felt dizzy and disorientated, intoxicated with love.

She'd never imagined giving the earrings away. But then, she'd never imagined living in an occupied city, enslaved and ravaged by war. She'd never imagined what it would feel like to have no food to give to her two-year-old daughter. As she prepared to exchange her husband's wedding present for some old potatoes and, if she was lucky, a couple of eggs, Irina told herself the memories were not in the earrings but inside her heart. They would always be with her. No one could take them away.

When Irina arrived at the square, she found nothing but a few empty stalls hidden under a pile of fresh snow. The market that only yesterday was bustling with life was abandoned. For a few moments she stood as if frozen to the spot, uncertain what to do next. She couldn't return home empty-handed. She couldn't bear the look of hunger and despair on her daughter's face and the way she cried through the night for something to eat. There was another market in Podol but it would take her twenty minutes to get there. It was unlikely she would make it back before curfew. Was food for one night worth the risk?

'Irina, wait!' she heard as she was about to start walking in the direction of Podol, praying she didn't stumble on a Nazi patrol.

She turned around and found herself face to face with her best friend. Tall, ballerina-thin, with her blonde hair hidden under a large hat and her eyes dark with worry, Tamara wrapped her arms around Irina. Pleased to see the familiar face of someone she had been friends with since they were little girls, Irina hugged her back tightly. For a few moments the two women stood still in an empty town square with their arms around each other.

Finally pulling away, Tamara said, 'Were you looking for the market? It's not here anymore.'

'I can see that. I was about to walk to Podol.'

'No point walking anywhere. Every market in town is gone.'

'What do you mean, gone?'

Tamara shrugged. 'Everyone's been arrested. The sellers and the buyers.'

'That's impossible!' exclaimed Irina. What she wanted to say was: *How are we going to live now?* They couldn't survive on what the Nazis were giving them. The market was their lifeline.

'They rounded up everyone they could get their hands on. I was just around the corner when the Nazis arrived. Another minute and I would have been arrested too.' Her friend crossed herself, looking up at the sky as if in gratitude.

'But why? Why now?'

'Haven't you heard? The partisans stopped another train bound for Germany. The Nazis are furious. This is payback.'

For Irina, living under the Nazi occupation was like wading through a minefield. No matter what direction you took, you could trigger an explosion that would rip you apart. At the same time, you couldn't remain in one spot forever. You had to move through that field, come what may. Irina knew she could be arrested at any moment – as she was making her family's breakfast for having a husband in the partisan battalion; as she sat at her desk at work for helping a hapless soul escape the threat of German mobilisation; as she was walking home for breaking the curfew; as she was leaving the market for trading some jewellery for a small piece of bread. She had been lucky so far, but she couldn't help but feel that sooner or later her luck would run out. 'We have no food left at home. Nothing at all. What am I going to do? Sonya is always hungry. And I feel so helpless.'

Tamara reached into her carry bag and handed her friend half a loaf of white bread. 'Here, take this. For Sonya.'

Irina stared at the bread in amazement. It wasn't the Nazi-issue bread they received on their ration cards every week – bitter, cardboard-like and difficult to chew. This bread had a golden crust, was soft on the inside and smelt delicious. Irina hadn't seen bread like this in fifteen months. 'Where did you get that?'

'The German officer staying with me gave me two loaves, right before he left for the Stalingrad front. This was his parting gift.'

'That's kind of him.'

'He enjoyed the meals I cooked and the laundry I did for him. What more does a man want?'

Irina shook her head with regret. 'Thank you, but I can't take your bread. You need it as much as I do.'

'Nonsense. Of course you can. I'll be fine. I don't have a child to feed.'

Irina broke the bread in two and handed half back to Tamara. 'Here, why don't we share?' When Tamara took the chunk of bread and placed it in her bag, Irina added, 'Sonya will be so happy. How can I ever thank you?'

'There *is* something you can do for me.' Tamara seemed to hesitate, looking around cautiously. The street was deserted. But in Nazi-occupied Kiev, even the walls had ears.

A piece of paper appeared in Tamara's hand, trembling in the wind. Irina took it. It was an order for Tamara Semenova to report to the train station for compulsory mobilisation to Germany. The two of them stood in the empty market square, snow falling between them. 'I can't work for them, Ira. It will be the death of me. A friend of mine just returned. They sent her home because she got sick. I didn't even recognise her when I saw her. Where was the bubbly young girl we said goodbye to at the station? Her hair is completely white. You won't believe the stories she told me. They don't let you have any food or water on the job. They work you like cattle, twenty hours a day. They beat you for making eye contact with your supervisor or for moving too slowly.' There was horror in Tamara's eyes, as if these things were already happening to her.

Irina pressed her friend's hand gently. 'Don't worry, I'll help you. Come by my office tomorrow and bring your passport. I can stamp it to make it look like you are married.' The Nazis weren't taking married women yet. It was a loophole many Kievans were exploiting. Who knew how long it would last? At the rate things were going, Irina suspected not too long.

'A fake marriage? Sounds perfect. I'll be there for my fake wedding first thing tomorrow morning.' Tamara beamed with relief and looked her friend up and down. 'I've never seen you more beautiful. Your skin is glowing. And your hair . . .'

Self-consciously, Irina tucked her long dark hair under her hat. Now that she was pregnant, it was shinier and curlier than usual. As much as she wanted to, she couldn't tell her best friend her secret. She had to tell her husband first. 'Maxim is coming home next week. I'm happy, that's all.'

'How do you even get through the week without seeing him? I remember when you couldn't last a day without each other.'

Still can't, Irina wanted to say.

'Remember when he walked twenty kilometres from his parents' dacha one summer to give you a bunch of roses?'

Irina sighed. 'Not quite what we imagined our life to be when we were young and full of hope, is it?'

'No, not quite.' Tamara looked up and her eyes twinkled. 'I'm seeing someone too, you know. I think he might be the one. I'm in love, Ira!'

Irina laughed at the serious expression on her friend's face. 'How long have you been in love this time?'

'Laugh all you want. It's easy for you, married to the love of your life.'

'I'm not laughing. I'm happy for you. Who is this man? Someone I know?'

'I can't tell you yet. I don't want to jinx it. Once I know for sure that it's serious, I'll tell you everything.'

'But you just said he's "the one". Make up your mind!'

Teasing one another, while glancing nervously at their watches, with only five minutes to spare until the curfew, the two young women walked briskly home through the quiet streets, averting their eyes from the German soldiers and Nazi flags with hated swastikas swaying from every building. When they reached Tamara's house, Irina said, 'Remember to bring your passport. And don't worry about anything. We'll fix this.' She was glad she could help Tamara. To save her friend's life, to deceive the Nazis, if only in this small way, made her feel more in control.

As she walked the short distance home, she savoured the

metallic taste in her mouth and the queasy feeling at the back of her throat that reminded her of the wonderful change taking place inside her body. In her pocket she still had her earrings and suddenly she was glad she didn't give them away for a few potatoes that would be gone tomorrow. For the first time since the occupation, Irina's heart beat faster with hope.

Hope for a better life, a new beginning.

*

Home was an apartment in a dilapidated building on Kazanskaya Street overlooking Berezovyi Gai Park, shared by Irina and her daughter, her parents-in-law, Zina and Kirill, and Zina's nephew Dmitry, who had moved in a week after the occupation had started when the Nazis had forced him out of his apartment in Podol. The place was too small to fit all of them but somehow it did, even when Maxim came to visit from the partisan battalion, which to Irina's sadness wasn't very often. Opening the door with her key, she called out to her daughter, her breath catching. This was what she had been waiting for since she left that morning – to see Sonya's face light up at the sight of her mother, to hold her and feel her weight in her arms.

Her eyes on the dining-room door at the end of a long corridor, Irina placed her bag with the precious bread in the corner and removed her shoes. Any minute now a small voice would cry for Mama, little feet would pitter-patter across the floor and a tiny head would appear through the doorway. Irina took her coat off and undid her scarf. The house remained quiet. Fighting a strong feeling of unease, she called out again, imagining a knock on the door, German boots clomping through the house and the arms of a stranger reaching for her daughter. She tried her best to chase away the terrible vision but it hovered over her like a ghost.

A faint sound of static reached her from the dining room. On unsteady legs Irina followed it, fearing the worst. When she walked in, she saw Dmitry hunched over the table, a radio receiver in his lap. His glasses askew, his blond hair messy and long, he had the look of an absent-minded professor about him.

Dmitry looked up from the radio and smiled. Anticipating her question, he said, 'Zina took Sonya to play with Oxana's little ones.'

Irina almost groaned with relief. She should have known her mother-in-law had taken her daughter to the neighbour's apartment upstairs. Zina often did that to give herself a break and have a cup of tea with her friend. Irina's job was getting to her, she realised. She saw darkness everywhere she looked. Not that she had to look far. 'Any luck?' She nodded at the radio. For the last few days Dmitry had been trying to catch news from the front.

'Not yet, but I'm not giving up. If we know what's going on out there, we can spread the word. We can boost morale.'

Just like her husband, Dmitry was a partisan. Unlike Maxim, however, he didn't blow up bridges or cut telephone cables but worked closely with the local population, trying to find Ukrainians who held important positions in Nazi organisations and were willing to commit acts of sabotage. In a way, his job was more dangerous than Maxim's. One word from his contacts, and the Gestapo would march into their little apartment and whisk him away.

The radio coughed and fell quiet, finally coming back to life with a distorted male voice. 'Stalingrad . . . Heavy German losses . . . The Red Army is gaining . . . Victory.' Irina's hand flew to her mouth and she trembled with joy. It had been a while since they'd heard the words *Red Army* and *victory* in the same sentence. The German-controlled *Ukrainian Word* wanted them to believe the war had already been won by Hitler. But here was a snippet of truth in the sea of lies that changed everything. Not only had the Red Army not been destroyed, as the despicable newspaper insisted, but it was also fighting and gaining ground. This was the first piece of good news they had had since the occupation. The first piece of good news in fifteen months.

There was a loud knock and Dmitry flipped the switch on the radio. The voice died away, leaving an unfamiliar feeling behind, a hope that one day in the near future something in their lives would change. Dmitry hid the radio under a pile of clothes Irina had been ironing the day before, while she walked to the front door with a smile on her face. 'Did Zina forget her key again?' she wondered out loud, eager to embrace her daughter.

But when she opened the door, it wasn't Zina standing outside with her granddaughter in her arms. Instead, two German soldiers glared at her through the doorway. Irina recoiled from them with horror, unable to look away from their square faces and the terrifying swastikas that adorned their armbands. The taller of the two watched her suspiciously, while the shorter pushed his way in. 'Blankets, towels, sheets. We'll take everything you have,' he said in broken Russian. Irina nodded uncertainly, backing away, and they followed her to the dining room.

Here was something else that contradicted the propaganda they read in the newspaper every day. If the Nazis were winning, why did so many wounded German soldiers come back from Stalingrad front? Why did they need so many blankets and towels for their hospitals? But as Irina shivered under the Nazi soldiers' glare, all she could think about was the radio receiver hidden under the clothes. If the Germans found it, the whole household would pay. A week ago, a family of four was arrested for hiding a radio. They were taken away and shot in public, the children first. Then the Nazis returned and burnt their house down. Nothing was left of the place that had once housed four souls with their hopes and joys and fears. Nothing but a pile of black soot.

Dmitry was nowhere to be seen and Irina tried with all her might not to glance in the direction of the radio. 'We don't have any spare blankets. Only enough for the family. But plenty of towels.'

'*Wunderbar*,' said the shorter soldier. 'We need towels. But blankets too. All your blankets.'

'If we give you our blankets, we will freeze. The nights are cold. I have a baby.'

There was something resembling pity on the shorter soldier's face. But Irina wasn't looking at him. The taller of the two made an abrupt movement in the direction of the clothes that concealed the radio. He picked up a sheet and a pair of trousers. Irina froze, unable to speak. The soldier reached for a pillowcase. Underneath the pillowcase she could see the outline of the radio receiver. She felt a chill run through her, a shriek of sheer panic forming at the back of her throat.

'Here you are,' said Dmitry, suddenly appearing from the bedroom and handing them half a dozen towels and all their blankets.

The German turned away from the radio and took the towels and the blankets. Nodding, the two soldiers disappeared through the front door.

For the few seconds it took for them to close the door and walk away, their footsteps resounding ominously down the corridor, Dmitry and Irina didn't speak. 'That was close,' said Dmitry finally, clearing his throat. 'With the number of patrols these days, it's not safe to keep the radio here. I'll find somewhere else to hide it.'

Irina leant on the wall and closed her eyes, counting to ten. She couldn't speak.

'Are you all right?' asked Dmitry. 'Do you want anything? A glass of water?'

'I'm fine. I just need a moment.'

'Don't worry. They won't be back. They got what they wanted. And I'll find a blanket for Sonya tonight.'

'Thank God she wasn't here.' At first Irina was annoyed at her mother-in-law for taking her little girl away just as she was returning from work. Now she was grateful. 'I feel so afraid sometimes, I don't know what to do with myself.'

'It's war. We all feel afraid.'

'Ever since I had Sonya . . . I'm just so scared for her, Dima.

I'm afraid that the minute I turn my back, she'll disappear. That when I come home from work, she won't be here. That someone will take her away or she'll get sick or I won't have enough food for her. I can't stop the what-ifs running through my head, driving me crazy.'

'I don't have any children, but I suppose the fear is part of being a parent.'

'I can't stop the terrible scenarios in my head. When she was born . . . they brought her to me, all wrapped up, only her tiny face visible. And what a face it was – bright red, scrunched up, screaming loudly. No one could calm her. But the minute I picked her up and started singing, she stopped crying and looked at me sideways, as if wondering who I was. That was the moment I fell in love with her.' Irina smiled at the memory. 'She brings me so much joy. I feel like no human being deserves this much joy. But it could all be taken away at any moment. If anything happens to her, Dima . . . She's my life.'

'Nothing is going to happen to her. We'll make sure of that. You heard the radio. Our army is gaining ground. The Germans won't stay here for much longer.'

Her hand on her chest, Irina breathed slower.

'Dinner is on the stove,' Dmitry added. 'Eat before it gets cold.'

'You made dinner?'

'A vegetable stew, your favourite.'

'I thought we didn't have any vegetables.'

'Yesterday we didn't have any vegetables. But today I went to the village and got three potatoes and four carrots. And . . .' he paused for dramatic effect '. . . a whole onion.'

'What would we do without you?'

'Without me you wouldn't have an onion for dinner.' He waved and dashed to the door, the radio wrapped in a towel under his arm.

'You are not eating? I have some bread.'

'I have to run. I'm meeting someone.'

'Is it a date?' She winked at him, cheerful now that the red mist of fear had cleared.

'Yes, a date with an old official who seems loyal to us.'

'Seems loyal? Or is loyal?'

'That's what I'm trying to find out.'

'Be careful,' she muttered but the door had already closed behind him and he didn't hear. As she waited for her daughter to return Irina had some stew but didn't touch the bread Tamara had given her – she was saving it for Sonya. She made herself a weak cup of tea, using yesterday's tea leaves, and sat at the table, watching it grow cold.

Finally, half an hour later, she heard her little girl's excited voice. 'Doggy,' cried Sonya as the front door opened. 'Doooggy!'

'That's right,' came Kirill's voice. Irina's father-in-law sounded tired. Although he loved looking after his granddaughter, lately Irina was noticing how old and frail he'd been looking. 'Doggy says woof. And what animal says neigh?'

'Horsey,' cried Sonya. 'Grandpa horsey!'

Irina leapt to the front door and when Sonya saw her, she cried, 'Mama, Mama!' She was in Kirill's arms, her small body pressed into him, her dark eyes – her father's eyes – sparkling, her dark hair long and curly. Behind them, Irina's mother-in-law, Zina, was unbuttoning her coat.

'I'm back, little one, I'm home,' whispered Irina, picking up Sonya and showering her with kisses. The deaths, the fear, her long day, even the visit from the Nazis that had scared her so much – suddenly it all fell away as she inhaled her daughter's baby smell. All she could see was her little one.

'Good thing, too. This old horsey needs a rest. My back is killing me.' Kirill stretched and groaned. 'You are back later than usual. Have you eaten?'

Smiling affectionately at her father-in-law, Irina nodded and carried Sonya to the kitchen. When the little girl tried the bread, her eyes lit up. She had never had bread like this before, with a delicious golden crust that melted in your mouth. Even though it was the bread of Irina's childhood, it was now reserved for the Nazis. 'More,' cried Sonya, 'More, more!' Irina held her on her lap, happy to give her more. At this rate, the bread wouldn't last as long as she had hoped but it didn't matter. It was worth it to see a smile on her daughter's face.

Later, in their bedroom, while Irina was breastfeeding Sonya to sleep, she thought that despite her fears and the enemy on her doorstep, she was the luckiest person alive because she had her little girl. As she held her close, a feeling of extreme joy rushed through her, unconditional love unlike anything she had experienced before she became a mother.

And soon she would have another baby. She could hardly wait.

The lights were low and the sounds subsided. She was holding her daughter close, her face in her hair, listening to the endearing noises she made with her lips while she fed. At times like this, Irina could almost forget there was a war, could almost pretend death and desolation hadn't come to the streets of Kiev, if it wasn't for the harsh German shouts reaching her through the window and the German planes buzzing incessantly in the air. She could tell by the soft breathing that Sonya was falling asleep. The little girl had once slept in her cot but when Maxim left for the partisan battalion, she'd started waking up in the middle of the night, screaming. And Irina started taking her to bed with her. Now Sonya would cry whenever anyone tried to place her in her cot because she knew it meant sleeping on her own, when all she wanted was her mother's protective arms around her. Irina was happy to have Sonya by her side at night. She too longed for the comfort of her daughter's warm little body next to her.

She felt herself drifting, a smile on her face, when the door flew open and the room lit up. Reluctantly, Irina opened her eyes and the joy of only moments ago evaporated as if by magic. Her mother-in-law stood in the doorway, holding an old kerosene lamp. Although Zina had a motherly look about her, with her eyes set deep in her round face, her hair grey and her body heavy, it was an illusion, one that evaporated the moment she opened her mouth. Her voice was whiny and shrill, always demanding something or complaining or admonishing. 'She's in your bed, again. You need to stop that. It's not normal.'

'Please, Zina Andreevna. Not now. You'll wake Sonya.' After Irina and Maxim had first been married, Zina had insisted that Irina call her Mama, as it was custom for daughters-in-law to address their mothers-in-law. But try as she might, Irina couldn't force herself to do it. Her lips refused to form the correct syllables. It felt unnatural, wrong even, as if she was betraying her real mother. And so she addressed her husband's mother by her first and patronymic names, as if she was her superior, a teacher at school or a supervisor at work. Zina hated it but there was nothing she could do about it.

'It's not fair to us. Kirill spent two hours trying to settle her for her afternoon nap today. She was crying and crying, asking for her mother,' said Zina, her brow furrowed in disapproval.

'I'm just breastfeeding her,' Irina said, thinking, *Why am I defending myself to this woman? Isn't it up to me as a mother what I do with my child?*

'That's another thing. It's not healthy for a two-year-old to still be breastfed.'

Sonya stirred in her sleep and her face twisted. Irina felt the familiar anger wash over her like a wave. 'It's perfectly healthy. It's the healthiest thing in the world.'

'At this age? I don't think so. Why don't you ask your friends if they're still breastfeeding their children at two. It's unheard of.'

'I don't care what other people do. I only care what we do.'

'It's not normal—'

'It's normal for us!' Irina interrupted, her voice rising.

'She won't start sleeping through the night if you continue to breastfeed. I'm tired of being woken up five times a night because the baby is screaming.'

'So you are thinking of what's best for you, not what's best for her?' Irina pretended to sound surprised, even though she wasn't.

'It's best for everyone. Better for the baby to sleep.'

'How will she sleep if she's hungry? Stop breastfeeding and then what? We don't have any other milk to give her. Hardly have any food to give her at all.' Irina felt her cheeks burning. It was always like this. Zina provoked her and when she got the response she desired, she twisted the situation to make it look like Irina was the bad person, disrespectful and rude, raising her voice to someone twice her age. Zina was an expert at playing the victim. Firmly, Irina added, 'I respect your opinion but I am Sonya's mother, not you. It's up to me when to stop breastfeeding. It's not your place to tell me.'

'While you live under my roof, it *is* my place to tell you. And if you still want us to babysit while you are out working, I suggest you listen to me.'

'I'm grateful for all your help but if it's too much trouble, I'll ask someone else to babysit.' Despite her brave words, Irina's heart sank. Who could she ask? Her friends had problems of their own. Who had the time and energy to look after a toddler all day while she went to work?

Zina sniggered. 'You'd let a complete stranger look after your daughter when she has loving grandparents at home? What kind of mother would do that?'

'Just to make your life easier.' Irina could see her mother-in-law was desperate for a fight. But Irina wasn't up for it today, like most days. She longed for the serenity of a few minutes ago. 'Did you want anything?'

'My reading glasses,' barked Zina, pointing at the bedside table. 'I spent an hour reading to Sonya at lunch before Kirill took her for a nap.'

After Zina left, Irina couldn't get to sleep for a long time. More often than not, Zina would lure her into an argument and leave her frustrated and upset. How she wished she could tell the

34

woman to mind her own business. But she knew she couldn't, not while she was living in Zina's house, married to her son, so Irina kept quiet, even when Zina had insisted she wasn't cut out to be a mother and when on the day of their wedding she had said she wasn't good enough for her son.

When they had first met, Irina and Maxim dreamt of a little apartment of their own. All they wanted was to have their own nest where they could live and dream and love each other, a place that was just theirs, where no one could tell them what to do. Even if it was just a communal apartment, nothing but a room that belonged to them and nobody else. They had joined a queue for accommodation and waited. And waited, and waited, together with tens of thousands of others who'd been in that queue for many years. Apparently, there was a shortage of housing in Kiev. And now, with the Nazis in the Soviet Union and so many buildings destroyed by fire, with so many homeless wandering the streets with nowhere to go, Irina was lucky to have a roof over her head for her and her daughter. She knew it and, what was worse, Zina knew it too.

And if Irina did decide to leave and stay with her friend Tamara in her tiny apartment, with barely space for one person, let alone two adults and a toddler, what would she tell her husband? How would she explain why she had shunned his parents' hospitality? His parents whom he revered, who could do no wrong in his eyes.

Maxim had come into Irina's life three weeks after she lost her grandmother, the only family she had left. The feelings of heartbreak and black despair weren't new. She had experienced them before, when her father left and her mother took her own life, unable to go on without the man she loved. What was new was the crippling loneliness and having no one in the whole world to turn to. But Maxim changed all that.

When a friend introduced them, Irina thought he was the most handsome young man she'd ever seen. No one expected their relationship to last, least of all her. He could have had any girl

35

he wanted. There were certainly enough of them buzzing around him like bees around honey. But night after intoxicating night that summer, he strummed his guitar for her and read poetry to her and nobody else. He looked at her like she was the most beautiful woman in the world. Like she was the one. She remembered the feeling with longing, of her head spinning with happiness, of floating through time and space as she watched his lips move as he talked, of her heart leaping in her chest. Of falling in love.

If living with her husband's cruel mother was the price she had to pay to be with him, so be it.

Chapter 3

Lisa dreamt she was onboard a ship, lost in the dark, while all around her the sea and the wind roared in anger. When she woke up, she felt like she was still trapped on that ship – someone was shaking her and not letting go. Opening her eyes a fraction, she saw a white face framed by a red scarf. Groggy and confused, for a moment not knowing where she was, Lisa sat up and rubbed her eyes. When she looked up again, the face was still there, smiling brightly. It belonged to a girl with waist-length dark braids, long and thin like a crane, with birdlike features. She seemed awfully young to Lisa. Too young to be in a place like this. She wouldn't look out of place in a brown school uniform with a red Young Pioneers tie around her neck, except for her eyes that, despite the smile, seemed anxious and on edge, as if she knew too much. She had an old person's eyes on a young face.

When the girl saw that Lisa was awake, she gave her one final shake and cried, 'Get up right now! What do you think this is, a holiday resort?' To show she was only joking, she winked at Lisa and pinched her arm.

Lisa blinked and pulled herself up, so the girl's beaming face wouldn't be looking down on her. Her feet were numb from the cold and she had a bad cramp in her arm after sleeping on the uncomfortable bed. She rubbed it, hoping to restore the circulation. When that didn't work, she clenched her fist a few times and when that didn't work either, she placed her arm on the bag of clothes she'd been using as a pillow.

'What are you doing?' asked the girl, staring at Lisa as if she had grown a second head.

Lisa yawned and attempted to hide under her thick winter coat. Maybe if she pretended to go back to sleep, the girl would go away?

But the girl didn't look like she had any intention of going away. She tried to pull the coat off. Lisa held on and for a few seconds they played tug-of-war, which the girl finally won. 'Papa told me to make sure you were awake and I'm not leaving here until you are.'

'Who is your papa?' asked Lisa, shivering. She wished she could have her coat back, but the girl had thrown it on one of the other beds. Lisa felt damp and unclean. Bits of moist soil had fallen on her during the night and when she touched her face, there was mud on her fingertips. She wished she could see herself in the mirror. With her hair matted and her skin dirty, she suspected she looked like she belonged in the forest.

'He's in charge here. Unfortunately, you two sleepyheads have missed breakfast. It was especially delicious this morning. Just kidding. It was vile as always. Yulya has many talents but cooking isn't one of them. I don't know why Papa made her cook.' The girl wrinkled her nose in disapproval. 'Here, I brought you some snow.'

'To eat?' Lisa glanced inside the bowl, hoping to see some porridge. Her stomach rumbled.

'No, silly. To wash with.'

Lisa wondered how one could wash with a bowl of snow. She looked around. Masha was still asleep, curled up under her old woolly kerchief with only the top of her head visible. What time was it? It felt early. She could swear it was still dark outside.

'I'm Anna, by the way. We are roommates. There were two

more girls sleeping here. But one of them went back to Kiev and another . . .' Anna's cheerful face dimmed for a moment and she stopped talking.

'What's happening?' Masha was awake and sitting up in bed.

'What's happening is that there is a big assembly outside. Everyone must attend. And you two are still in bed,' said Anna.

'What's an assembly?' asked Lisa, stretching.

'It's where we exchange information and receive orders for the day.'

'We don't need to attend it. We are not staying here. We are going home today,' said Masha, slowly getting up and wincing as she placed weight on her bad leg.

'That might be so. But for now you are here. And if you're here, you must follow the rules.'

Lisa rubbed her face with snow, then passed the bowl to Masha. She had to admit, it did feel refreshing. She no longer felt drowsy, just dirty and extremely hungry. She thought with longing of the borscht her sister used to cook before the war, with beef and beetroot and a spoonful of sour cream, of her mother's blinis hot off the stove, laden with strawberry jam and a tiny bit of honey. Of her brother Nikolai's cheeky face as he would snatch the last blini out of Lisa's hands and laugh. Suddenly she missed her family with a sharpness that took even her by surprise.

The Smirnovs lived on Tarasovskaya Street in Central Kiev, a stone's throw away from the famous Taras Shevchenko University. There were two boys – Stanislav, the eldest, and Nikolai, the youngest. And two girls, Lisa and Natasha, only a year between them. Lisa was her father's favourite, a fact she never tired of reminding her siblings. Papa had always showered her with gifts and praises. No matter what she did, he was proud of her. Mama was more equal in her affections but sometimes in the evening, when she brushed Lisa's long red hair before bed, she would tell her how beautiful she was, how big she was getting, but that she would always be her baby girl, no matter what. Lisa didn't have many memories of her early years but when she closed her eyes sometimes and thought back on that time, she remembered a feeling of warmth and unconditional love.

They were a close family, until war had torn them apart. Stanislav was fighting on the Eastern Front somewhere. Grandmother was gone, shot by a German officer on the second day of the occupation. Papa had been taken away by the Nazis one day, never to be seen again. And Lisa and her sister were no longer talking.

Masha asked, 'Can we get something to eat first?'

'You can ask Yulya but I don't think she'll give you anything.'

'Why not?'

'Because everything's already been eaten. You'll have to wait till lunchtime.' Anna looked at her watch. 'That's five hours from now.'

Sighing, Lisa put on her coat, her boots and her hat that covered half her face, and then followed Anna outside, where it wasn't dark but shimmering white. All she could see was a thick curtain of snow falling to the ground. Nothing else was visible, not the trees, not the meadow, nor even the sky. 'I hate snow,' muttered Lisa. 'It makes everything so difficult.'

'Yes, it makes it difficult for anyone to find us,' said Anna. 'It hides our footprints, hides all traces of us. It's a good thing.'

'I just want to feel warm again. I miss summer.'

'True, in summer it's warmer and there's more food, but we are also easier to spot.'

Lisa shrugged, thinking to herself that she would take the risk if it meant there was no wet icy-cold slush inside her boots and under her scarf. With Masha leaning on her arm, she could barely walk through the snow. Every step was a struggle as she fell in knee-deep and then had to pull herself and Masha out and make another step and pull herself out again. After two minutes of this she was out of breath.

In silence they hobbled a hundred or so paces through the forest until they reached an open space where a few dozen people were gathered in anticipation. Mostly men, either past their prime or barely out of school, too old or too young to have been conscripted into the Red Army, and a few women here and there, wearing Red Army uniforms that were falling apart at the seams, faces dirty and cheeks hollow, with kerchiefs tied around their heads to protect them from the frost. They shuffled from foot to foot to keep warm, smoked, shook hands, spoke and laughed. These were the brave warriors instilling terror in the Nazis, destroying bridges and blowing up trucks, removing telephone cables and stopping trains.

While the partisans watched the girls with curiosity, Lisa surreptitiously glanced into every face in the hope of spotting Maxim. She couldn't wait to see him again, so she could thank him for saving her from certain death in Germany. When she thought of him, her heart was warm with gratitude. Pointing at a hundred or so people gathered around the meadow, she asked, 'Is this all of you?'

'Almost. A few men left in the middle of the night to mine a bridge at Dermanka. They should be back soon.'

Was Maxim one of them? Lisa wanted to ask but didn't want her new friend to think she was interested in him.

A small, stooped man stepped in front of them and raised his hand. They could barely see him behind the falling snow but instantly everyone fell silent. For a few seconds nothing was heard but the partisans' heavy breathing. 'That's Azamat, my papa,' whispered Anna proudly in Lisa's ear.

Azamat spoke quietly but confidently. Everyone around seemed to hold their breaths to hear what he had to say. 'First and foremost, I wanted to congratulate you on a job well done. A train to Germany was intercepted yesterday; three high-ranking Nazi officers and thirty soldiers are dead. Hundreds of our people were free to return home. It's a great achievement but there are many lessons to be learnt and many ways in which we can improve.'

'What's there to improve? One hundred per cent losses for the enemy, and we haven't lost a single man,' cried out a burly man

41

in a sheepskin coat. His voice resonated loud and clear through the woods.

'That's Danilo,' whispered Anna. 'You don't want to get on his bad side. He kills the Nazis with his bare hands.'

Looking at Danilo, Lisa could easily believe it. The man was built like a bear and looked angry like one, his eyes bloodshot and mean.

'I don't think I've ever seen him smile,' said Anna.

Lisa could believe that too. Danilo looked like he had swallowed a handful of sour grapes.

The leader glanced at Danilo before replying. A shadow of something resembling annoyance passed over his face but a second later it was gone. 'It is true, we haven't lost any men and that's commendable. But we wasted ammunition. We need to be more conscious of that. Once we run out, what are we going to do?'

'I'll fight with rocks if I have to,' exclaimed a withered old man to Lisa's right.

'I know you will. You are all brave men. But it's best if we don't let it get to that. From now on, we act in small groups. Seven people maximum.'

'Seven people! That's insane,' grumbled Danilo. 'If we come across a big regiment, they will destroy us.'

'That's why we act from ambuscades. We make every shot count. We don't fire unless we are assured of success.'

The woman who Lisa recognised as Yulya said, 'I suppose it has its advantages. A small group is easier to hide. A small group can retreat without being spotted.' Danilo glared in her direction but she didn't seem to notice.

'Yulya and Danilo are married,' whispered Anna. 'They never agree on anything.'

'Apart from that, well done, partisans! Our fight is not over until every single Nazi is out of Kiev and the Soviet Union. Now that the rail communication has been disrupted, our next mission is to regain the German-occupied villages.'

'I like the sound of that. The villagers will feed us and give us clothes,' cried a young boy who was so thin and dressed so poorly, he seemed in desperate need of those things.

'Yes, the villagers will be very grateful. But it's more than that. The news will travel all over Kiev and raise morale. People will see that the Nazis are not as invincible as they think. They will know partisans are leaving the woods and occupying the villages. And you know what they'll think? If the Nazis can't beat the partisans, how can they ever beat the Red Army?'

Danilo stepped forward. 'The Nazis are no longer using main roads to move their troops and ammunition. They use smaller trails, which slows them down. Do you know why?'

'The roads were snowed in?' someone shouted from the back.

'They are afraid of us. We inconvenience them, lower their efficiency. It's only a matter of time before they are gone from our soil for good!'

As the partisans cheered and threw their hats in the air, Lisa felt a strange sense of displacement, like she was living someone else's life. One minute she was in occupied Kiev, counting down the days of the occupation, waiting for the war to end and her life to resume. The next, she was on the train to Germany, her worst fears realised. And now she was here, among brave and selfless warriors who had put their country first, who risked their lives every day as if they meant nothing. But she wasn't brave, nor was she selfless. What was she doing here?

*

In the early afternoon, the sun peered from behind the clouds and the little settlement sparkled like a diamond. But inside the dugout that served as a cafeteria, it was dim, damp and cold. Bent over a narrow table, straining their eyes to see in the near-darkness, while a candle burnt on a shelf above them, Anna, Lisa and Masha were mending uniforms. The old fabric fell apart under Lisa's fingertips and she had to stitch it over and over again. Lunch had come and gone and still the girls were hungry. Lisa could barely concentrate due to the ache in her stomach. She couldn't possibly be expected to work while feeling like this. And yet, the partisans didn't complain. Nor did they remain seated on a bench inside a dugout but organised themselves into small groups and went out to fight the evil forces that had occupied their city.

There was still no sign of Maxim.

The material Lisa was holding smelt of sweat and blood. 'Shouldn't we wash these first?' she asked, wrinkling her nose.

'In this weather? They'll never dry. And wash them with what? If you can find some soap, by all means, wash them,' said Anna, the needle moving swiftly in her hand. She didn't seem to mind the work. If her fingers were stiff from the cold and her head light from hunger, she didn't show it.

'How did you end up here, in the battalion?' asked Masha, who was already on her third uniform.

'I followed my papa,' said Anna. 'Like many people here who followed their loved ones. I didn't want him to be all alone and I wanted to do my bit for the country, so I came here. Papa is an old warrior. He was a partisan during the Great War and the Civil War. He knows these woods like the back of his hand. He was never going to sit back and watch the Nazis take our city. He was the one who organised everything, rallied everyone together, set up food and ammunition stores.' There was pride in her voice. And love.

'What's it been like?' asked Lisa, wondering how long they were expected to do this. She'd never been good with her hands. Even though she had a younger brother, Lisa was the real baby of the family. Her mother and sister cooked food for her to eat. They sewed clothes for her to wear. Lisa never had to do anything for herself and it showed.

'It feels good to know we are making a difference. We are not taking this lying down. We are resisting, making their life difficult.

But we are hungry all the time. We can never get warm. And the Nazis are determined to wipe us out.'

'How can they ever find you here, in the woods?' asked Masha.

'We don't stay in the woods. We go out to find them. Besides, we are not as well hidden as you might think. A few months ago a local guide brought a Nazi regiment right to our camp.' Anna shuddered at the memory. Her habitual smile was gone and she looked even younger, like a little girl, vulnerable and lost.

'The locals did that? But why?' asked Lisa, putting her sewing down.

'Some people would sell their own grandmother if it meant they could have a better life. They go out of their way to suck up to the Nazis,' said Anna, not looking up from the uniform she was mending, as if she didn't want the girls to see the fear on her face. 'The Ukrainian policemen are often worse than the Germans. At the start of the war, a Nazi officer came to our house with a Ukrainian interpreter. They were looking for radio receivers and weapons. When I saw the Ukrainian pig with his self-satisfied greasy face, I couldn't help myself. I told him exactly what I thought of him. I called him a traitor, said he should be ashamed of himself turning his back on his own country like this.'

'I wish I was as brave as you,' said Masha, wide-eyed. 'I wish I had the courage to say something like that to someone's face.'

'Brave and reckless,' said Lisa. 'What did the man do?'

'He was furious. Slapped me hard across my face and would have hit me again if the German officer didn't stop him. He shouted at him for hitting a woman. I couldn't believe my ears. When the Ukrainian pig told him what I'd said to him, the officer laughed so hard, I thought his pants would split. And then he said, "But the young lady is right. You are a traitor. Why are you punishing her for telling the truth?"'

'Did you say the Nazis came to your camp?' asked Lisa, shivering. 'What happened?'

'They came in the night. I was sound asleep. Gunshots woke

45

me. It was terrifying. Luckily, our camp was on top of a hill. Although we were surrounded, that gave us a strategic advantage. We managed to break through and escape. Lost all our food supplies though. Since then, I never go anywhere without my rifle. I even keep it under my bed when I sleep.' Anna pointed under the table. When Lisa glanced underneath, she saw an outline of a long-barrelled rifle half-hidden under a pile of old blankets and uniforms.

'Even if I had a rifle, I wouldn't know what to do with it. Where did you learn how to shoot?' asked Masha, watching Anna with admiration.

'Maxim teaches everyone. Why don't you ask him?'

Lisa felt her cheeks redden. Suddenly she was desperate to learn how to shoot. The war had broken her heart in so many ways. As she watched her friend Olga taken away with the other Jewish people in Kiev, never to be seen again, as she clung to her fiancé Alexei's lifeless body, killed by the Nazis for nothing more than being in the wrong place at the wrong time, she had felt so helpless and small. Since then, all she wanted was to make a difference. And maybe now she could. The fact it would be Maxim teaching her how to shoot was an added bonus. 'Where is Maxim from?' she asked carefully. She was dying to learn more about the man who had saved her life but didn't want to appear too eager. 'Is his family in Kiev?'

'I don't know,' said Anna. 'He's a very private person. Never talks about himself. But what I do know is that he's one of the best snipers in all of Ukraine, possibly even the Soviet Union. The Nazis are terrified of him. And I can't say I blame them, with the number of high-ranking officers they have lost because of him. He's been learning how to shoot since he was a little boy. I think he was a national champion when he was at school. It's a passion of his.'

'A good passion to have in times of war,' said Lisa, wishing she had an interest like that, something to take her mind off the war and the heartbreak. As a little girl, she had enjoyed ballet. As a teenager, she had played chess with her older sister because she wanted to be closer to her. And she had enjoyed school tremendously – something not many of her friends realised. She loved learning new things. In September 1941, she was supposed to start her history degree at Taras Shevchenko University in Kiev. Her dream was to become a history professor like her beloved grandfather. She had grown up listening to stories of kings and heroes, of bloody battles and royal balls, of loyalty and valour, not made-up stories one read in novels but things that had really happened, thus making them even more precious. These stories had captured her imagination and all she wanted was to share them with others.

But Hitler had other ideas and in June 1941 her life had changed forever.

'My passion is music,' said Anna. 'Quite pointless during the war but sometimes I play the guitar or accordion for the men and they like it. It cheers them up.'

'My mama is a piano teacher. I can play a little bit too,' said Lisa.

'I thought you said you had no family left,' said Masha.

'I didn't say that. I said I had nowhere to go. I don't talk to my family.' Once, before the war, Lisa and her sister Natasha had been inseparable. Whenever she liked a boy or had an argument with her parents or received a bad mark at school, Lisa would turn to her sister for support. A year younger, all Lisa ever wanted was to be more like Natasha. Her sister liked chess, so she learnt how to play, even though it gave her a headache. Natasha liked Tolstoy, so Lisa stayed up late, reading *War and Peace*, even though it bored her senseless. In her last year of school, at a piano recital, Lisa met a handsome boy named Alexei and they became sweethearts. It was Natasha who covered for Lisa every time she snuck out of the house to meet him. And it was Natasha who had convinced their parents Lisa wasn't too young to marry after Alexei proposed.

But then Hitler's hordes had arrived. Natasha and their grandmother were walking home one day when a Nazi officer confronted them. He shot her grandmother and would have shot her too if a Hungarian soldier didn't step in, killing the officer. The murder of an officer in bright daylight in occupied Kiev wasn't something the Nazis could overlook. They rounded up two hundred Soviets and hanged them, making an example out of them. Lisa's fiancé Alexei was one of them and Lisa blamed her sister. With hindsight she could see it wasn't Natasha's fault. It was the war. But back then, heartbroken and alone, blinded by grief, she did her best to come between her sister and the Hungarian soldier she had fallen in love with. She had finally succeeded but somewhere along the way, through her hatred and anger, she lost her whole family.

Lisa hadn't seen her sister for eight months. The last thing Natasha had said to her was that she hated her, that Lisa was no longer her sister, that if she ever saw her again, she was going to kill her. At first, Lisa was angry. Then she was hurt. And once the anger and the hurt subsided, the heartache remained. She missed her sister and the rest of her family with a fierceness that left her short of breath.

The two girls stared at Lisa with horror and curiosity. They watched her expectantly, as if waiting for her to tell them more. When she didn't, Masha said, 'I can't imagine not talking to my family. I miss my mama so much.'

'Is she here, in Kiev?' asked Lisa, happy to change the subject.

'She evacuated to Novosibirsk before the Germans arrived, to stay with her sister. At first, she refused to go without me. I had to threaten to volunteer for the front if she didn't.'

'You didn't want to leave?'

'My husband was staying to protect the city, and I felt needed in Kiev. I worked as a nurse. When wounded soldiers began to arrive from the front, I felt like I was helping with the war effort. Now I wish I'd gone. My husband left with the Red Army soon after and life in Kiev without him and without Mama became unbearable.'

'Where is your husband now?'

'I wish I knew. On the Eastern Front somewhere, fighting the

Nazis. There have been no letters from him or Mama since the occupation started. Sometimes I feel so alone.' Masha paused for a second, as if gathering her thoughts. 'I've never been away from Mama before. When I was younger, she would wait for me on the porch every day to come home from school. That's what I think about when things get tough. The expression on Mama's face when she saw me walking down the street.'

Through the small opening in the ground Lisa could see the setting sun. It tinted the tops of the pine trees red and soon it was gone but the pile of uniforms in front of them didn't diminish in size. While the girls sewed, Lisa stared into space, daydreaming. Outside, all she could see was darkness. Inside, there were rickety tables and dusty floors. There was a small wood-burning stove in the corner but Yulya had forbidden them from touching it. 'To save the kindling,' she said. Lisa wanted to point out they were surrounded by kindling. They were in the woods, after all. But she said nothing. She was a little intimidated by the large grouchy woman.

All at once, the forest was no longer silent. Someone somewhere was screaming for help. The voices were too loud, the noises too sharp in the woods that until now had been tranquil and quiet. Without a word the three girls looked at each other and jumped to their feet, leaving the half-finished uniforms on the table. Anna ran outside, not pausing to put her hat or scarf on, and Lisa would have run too if Masha wasn't leaning on her arm and hopping on her one good leg, making it difficult for Lisa to walk.

The wind was howling like a pack of desperate wolves. The trees were no longer motionless but swaying from side to side like the masts of a ship caught in a storm. Lisa shivered, trying to shake off a feeling of dark foreboding, when she saw five men moving swiftly towards them. One of them held a torch and the other four were carrying a stretcher. The torchbearer was grim and silent as he led the way. The reflection of the flame danced on his face. His uniform was torn and muddy. Not muddy, Lisa realised, but covered in blood. With horror she recognised Maxim.

Her horror receded a little when she realised he didn't look hurt. It must have been someone else's blood. From where Lisa was standing, she couldn't see who the man on the stretcher was or whether he was all right, but she heard Anna take a sharp breath and cry out, 'Anton,' dashing through the forest and ignoring the branches that were lashing her face like sharp razors. When she got to the stretcher, she took Anton's hand in hers and kissed it.

With her heart beating painfully in her chest, Lisa remembered the jolly young man who together with Maxim had helped them get to the settlement and cheered them up with his jokes. When she approached, Masha still hanging on her arm, she saw red blotches of fresh blood on Anton's uniform. He lay still on the stretcher and his eyes were closed. Feeling queasy and unwell, her legs trembling at the sight of blood, she wondered where they were taking him. Did they have a doctor or a hospital at the battalion? For Anton's sake, she sincerely hoped so.

'What happened?' cried Anna, her eyes frantic. 'Is he going to be all right?'

'He's been shot,' replied Maxim. 'We need to get him to the hospital and quick.'

So they did have a hospital, thought Lisa, following the stretcher and dragging Masha behind her. All she could hear was a buzz of voices. A large crowd gathered and everyone wanted to know the details. 'Where was he shot? Is he conscious? How much blood did he lose? Damn Nazis, one day they'll pay for everything!' The men carrying the stretcher ignored the questions, so intent were they on whisking Anton to safety.

The opening to the hospital was too small to fit the stretcher. Maxim and a man Lisa had never seen before lifted Anton gently and carried him in their arms. He groaned and opened his eyes. Anna sprang forward and took his hand, shaking him lightly. He didn't respond, closing his eyes again.

The hospital was nothing more than a large dugout, as damp and cold as the dwelling the three girls shared but much more spacious. Lisa was able to stand without hitting her head on the wooden beams of the ceiling and walk around freely between the beds without risking stubbing her toe on a piece of furniture. She marvelled at the ability of the partisans to create something like this in the middle of nowhere, among birches and pine trees and wild animals, something so well camouflaged and at the same time so well equipped, with every detail thought out and every need provided for. There were medicine cupboards and shelves with old books and magazines, dog-eared and battered with use. There was a small camp stove, a kerosene lamp and a kettle, a dozen wooden beds and a narrow table in the middle, a chair and a bedside table next to every bed. There were blankets on the beds but no sheets or pillows.

The men placed Anton on the bed nearest to the entrance. For a moment everyone watched him without a word. Then Anna pushed her way forward and said, 'He needs a nurse or a doctor. We must take him to a proper hospital.'

'No proper hospital. Every Nazi in Kiev knows his face,' said Maxim. He looked helpless and sad. Lisa wanted to reach out and touch him.

Masha hobbled forward and said, 'I'm a nurse. I can take a look at Anton.'

Suddenly all eyes were on Masha, who blushed. Anna cried, 'You're a nurse! Thank God! Just what we need, after our nurse was killed last week. What are you waiting for? Do something.'

As Lisa helped Masha across the room where Anton was lying on top of a dirty blanket, Masha asked, 'Do you have sulphur powder here? Anything for the pain?'

'We do have sulphur powder. For the pain we have vodka,' said Maxim.

'Vodka will do. Where was he hit?'

'Just above the knee. He was unconscious in the truck. The few times he woke up, he was delirious, screaming that he didn't want to lose his leg. He seemed in a lot of pain.'

Masha leant over Anton and placed her hand on his forehead. 'Can you hear me?' she asked softly. 'I need to examine your leg. I will have to cut your trousers open, so that I can see the wound. Is that all right?'

Anton's eyelids flickered, his face twisted in pain. 'Yes,' he said, his voice strained, as if talking cost him what little energy he had left.

'Find a comfortable position and try to relax.'

'Easy for you to say. It hurts like hell.'

'I know.'

One of the men passed Masha a small knife and she cut open the trouser leg, exposing Anton's thigh. Lisa gasped when she saw the large wound. Once again, she felt light-headed and dizzy. But Masha didn't seem to mind the sight of blood. 'We need to elevate the leg. Is there anything we could use to put underneath? A pillow or a rolled-up blanket?'

'What for?' demanded Anna.

'To stop the blood flow. It's harder for the blood to flow upwards than downwards.'

Nodding, Anna fetched a sack of old clothes. Masha positioned Anton's leg on top of it, putting on a pair of gloves and examining the wound, gently probing around the opening. Anton groaned.

'The good news is, the bullet has exited. See here – there's an entrance wound and an exit wound. I will need to disinfect them. It will hurt. Do you want to have some vodka before I do so?'

Anton nodded. Masha handed him a shot of vodka and once he'd taken a swig, she cleaned the wound and disinfected it with more vodka. Anton's face went white and he clasped his fists but didn't make a sound. For a moment he looked like he had passed out but then he opened his eyes slowly, looking dazed. Masha whispered encouragements to him as she applied some sulphur powder and a bandage. 'I need to make a tourniquet. It will apply pressure and further stop the blood flow. What I need is a belt and a long stick.'

Someone went out to find the items she had requested. When

they returned, she wrapped the belt around the leg, two inches above the wound, then used the rest of the belt to tie the stick tightly to the leg. Slowly she turned it to apply pressure. 'Now, we can't leave it on for too long or you might lose this leg. Let's hope it stops the bleeding quickly and then we can remove it. How are you feeling?'

'Good as new,' said Anton, wincing.

Anna declared she would stay with Anton all night, so she could be there if he needed anything. She whispered conspiratorially to the girls that he was her sweetheart. 'I followed my papa here and Anton followed me. I'm all he has in the world. His parents were killed by the Nazis a few months ago. If anything happens to him, I will never forgive myself.'

'Nothing is going to happen to him,' said Masha, hugging Anna. 'I'll make sure of that.'

That night, when it was just the two of them in the dugout, after they had brushed their teeth with baking soda Anna had lent them and washed their faces with snow, Masha said to Lisa, 'I am going to sleep for two hours and then I'll go back and check on Anton.' She looked like a different person, thought Lisa. Her eyes were burning with purpose.

'You were a hero today. Without you, what would Anton have done?'

'I don't want to go back to Kiev anymore. I want to stay here, Lisa. I want to help. The partisans need a nurse and I could really make a difference.'

'They'll be lucky to have you,' whispered Lisa, happy she wouldn't be alone at the battalion, that she would have her new friend by her side, but a little jealous too. She wished she had a calling, something to give her life meaning, to make her feel like she wasn't just wasting away, waiting for the war to take her like it had already taken so many others.

Tomorrow, she would ask Maxim to teach her how to shoot. She could hardly wait.

Chapter 4

The upside of Irina's pregnancy was that she could sleep anytime anywhere. Gone were the sleepless nights when she would fret and stare into space, the terrors of her day whirring through her mind. These days she could doze off at her desk at lunch and in her bed while breastfeeding her daughter, the kicking and tickling of the tiny hands and feet notwithstanding. The downside of her pregnancy was that no matter how much sleep she got, she was excruciatingly, overwhelmingly tired. Every morning she would wake up and think, *I can't do this. I can't get out of bed and go through another soul-destroying day at work, only to come home to another soul-destroying evening with Zina.*

There was nowhere for her to hide, nowhere to go to avoid the German soldiers on the streets of Kiev or her mother-in-law in the kitchen. It was easier in the mornings, when she was out of the door as the rest of the house was waking up. But evenings were a different story as they cooked and ate their meagre dinner and waited their turn to use the bathroom that had no running water, only a bucket of thawed snow Irina would bring from the street. Every evening was a battle that was neither won nor lost but dragged on with no end in sight.

'You won't believe what the Germans did yesterday,' Zina said one evening in the middle of January as she stirred some old vegetables in a pan. Irina could swear her mother-in-law saved her horror stories for when Irina came back from work. As if her day wasn't horrifying enough. 'Do you hear me, Irina? Do you hear me, Kirill? I know your book is interesting but I'm trying to tell you something. I don't want to compete for your attention with Dostoevsky.'

'I'm sorry, dear,' Kirill said softly, putting his book away and sitting up straight, with his hands folded together, like an obedient schoolboy.

Irina didn't look up from her cutting board and didn't acknowledge Zina. Maybe tomorrow, when she had more strength, she would fake politeness and respect, if only for her husband's sake. But today she was done pretending.

Zina continued, 'They opened a cinema in Podol and invited young people to a movie. Everyone was so excited. What an unexpected treat! But as soon as the movie started, they locked the doors and arrested everyone. They are all on a train to Germany as we speak.' Kirill shook his head in disgust. Dismayed, Irina continued to grate a carrot for her daughter, who was in her highchair, playing with her dolls. Zina continued, 'They didn't even have a chance to say goodbye to their families. I heard it from Marta who heard it from her friend, whose brother went to see this movie and never came back.'

'The Nazis have killed half of us in Babi Yar, and now they are trying to enslave what's left of us. They are not going to get away with it, mark my words,' grumbled Kirill.

'And who is going to stop them?'

How could Irina stay quiet now? Defiantly she raised her head. 'Our partisans are doing their best. Maxim—'

'Hush, child. Don't say it out loud. The walls have ears,' cried Zina, who was petrified of having a son in a partisan battalion and what it could mean for her.

'Our army is doing well,' said Kirill. 'The Nazis don't want us to know this, but the tide is turning for them in this war. The first Ukrainian towns are being liberated by the Red Army. Soon they'll be here—'

'Don't talk such rubbish and get our hopes up unnecessarily,' barked Zina, interrupting him. Irina could see Kirill's face deflate a little and felt sorry for the old man. Suddenly, Zina turned sharply around and pointed an accusing finger at Irina. 'What are you doing, grating that carrot? That's ridiculous. Let the girl chew on it. She needs to learn how. At this rate she'll never know how to use those teeth.' Zina's left eye twitched, a sure sign she was looking for an argument.

Irina felt her cheeks flush. She almost groaned out loud. *Please God, not today*, she thought. 'Carrots are quite hard. I don't want her to choke,' she said calmly, while inside she was seething.

'Nonsense. When Maxim was a baby, he chewed on everything. Apples, pears and carrots. Never did him any harm.'

Trembling, Irina lowered her eyes, leant close to her daughter and whispered an endearment in her ear.

'You are overprotective, to the point of being harmful. You do everything for her. It's not right. At this rate she'll never learn how to be independent,' added Zina.

'Independent? She's two. And what do you mean, not right? Isn't it part of being a mother? Being protective?' *Here I am again, defending myself to Zina*, she thought. *As if I have something to prove.*

'You are too soft on her. You shouldn't rush to pick her up the minute she starts crying. Before you know it, you'll have a spoilt brat on your hands.'

Irina felt her knees shaking. In a moment, she was going to tell Zina exactly what she thought, then pack what little belongings she had, take Sonya and go . . . where? That was the problem. She had nowhere to go.

To Irina's relief, Kirill came to her rescue. 'You can't spoil a child with love. Leave the poor girl alone. Let her find her own way as a mother.'

Irina smiled gratefully at her father-in-law, who never defended himself against his wife but here he was, defending Irina. She felt a tremendous affection for the older man who had been like a father to her ever since she'd met Maxim. Zina rolled her eyes in an exasperated manner that suggested her husband was in big trouble for daring to side against her.

'Don't pay any attention to her. She just wants to help but doesn't know how to go about it,' Kirill whispered to Irina when Zina was out of earshot.

'I understand,' said Irina. That was a lie. She didn't understand why Zina enjoyed being horrible to everyone around her. Did it make her feel more important? Did it cheer her up and brighten her day?

Later, as the rest of the house slept, Irina sat at the kitchen table, her fingers wrapped around a cup of tea for warmth. Every bitter sip, for she made it as strong as possible, brought the memories of evenings with friends, of home-baked cakes and biscuits, of laughter and happiness. Now there were no cakes or biscuits or laughter but, to Irina, tea was comfort. And comfort was even harder to come by in times of war than food.

This was her favourite time of day, when everyone was in bed and she could enjoy a few rare moments of solitude. Outside, a wall of snow was falling. Beyond the snow was darkness. Her hand on her flat stomach, she sang softly to her unborn baby and thought of her husband, hidden in the woods somewhere, risking his life to rid Kiev of the Nazis. How she longed to see his face, to put her arms around him. Was he thinking of her too, wherever he was? Was he missing her, just like she was missing him? Every time he left, her heart broke a little bit more. How did she live day after day, not knowing if he was safe?

Whenever he came to visit, which wasn't nearly often enough, she asked him to describe his daily routine, so that when she was alone, she could close her eyes and picture what he was doing at any particular moment in time. *He's having breakfast*, she would say to herself. *He's back after a long day, having dinner, relaxing and playing his guitar. He's asleep, safe in his dugout.* And she would feel closer to him and a little less lonely.

She tried not to think about what happened in between, after breakfast and before dinner.

Somewhere, a door screeched open and a floorboard creaked. Irina froze, her fingers curled around the cup. She hoped it was Kirill, craving the last cigarette of the day, but feared it was Zina coming in for a glass of milk. For as long as she'd known her, her mother-in-law had been a troubled sleeper. If someone breathed loudly on the other side of the house, she would wake up. A fake smile plastered on her face, Irina turned to the door, praying whoever it was would soon go away, leaving her alone with her tea and her bitter thoughts.

When the door opened, it wasn't Zina or Kirill she saw in the light of the kerosene lamp. Instead, a tall man stood in the doorway, shaking snow off his coat. Irina squealed in excitement, leapt off her chair, knocking it to the ground, and ran into his arms. Laughing, he caught her and lifted her up in the air, showering her face with kisses.

'Maxim! What are you doing here? We didn't expect you till tomorrow.' She felt giddy and excited. The skin of her cheeks felt raw from his stubble but she didn't care. Here he was, alive and well and looking at her with such love, it made her heart ache. Thank God!

Carefully he placed her on the ground. He looked thinner than she remembered and his eyes were darker, as if he too had terrible fears keeping him up at night. 'I couldn't wait till tomorrow. I had to see you and Sonya.'

'Are you hungry? Let me make you something to eat.' Reluctantly she wriggled away from him and made a move towards the stove.

He took her hand and pulled her to him. 'Later. Let me look at you.'

She relaxed into his arms and inhaled his scent. Forget tea, this was comfort. 'Why don't you take your coat off? Look at you, all wet from the snow. Do you want me to wake your parents? They'll be so happy.'

'Later,' he repeated. 'I want to see Sonya first.'

Without removing his coat or his hat, dropping snow on Zina's pristine floors, Maxim followed Irina to the bedroom where Sonya was asleep, splayed across her parents' bed, her mouth slightly open, her arms tucked under her little dark-haired head. He watched her with a tender smile, while Irina couldn't take her eyes off him.

'She looks so grown up. I can't believe it's only been three weeks.' He wrapped his arms around Irina and nuzzled her ear. 'Tell me everything that happened since I saw you last. What have you been doing?'

'The usual. Work, home, then work again. Now there are no markets in Kiev, we have to go to the village just to get some food. We all take turns. Oh, and I went to see a doctor on Wednesday. The poor man looked like he could do with a visit to the doctor himself. He could barely speak. So many people are starving in Kiev . . .'

'Wait, why did you go to the doctor?'

He sounded worried and she couldn't help but smile. She couldn't wait to tell him. 'I haven't been feeling well.'

'What's wrong?'

'Let's see. I've been feeling queasy for days. I even threw up a few times. My breasts are tender. I've put on weight. And I'm constantly craving pickled tomatoes.'

He looked into her face with wonder. 'What are you saying? We are going to have another baby?'

'We are going to have another baby!'

There were tears in his eyes as he held her close and whispered how much he loved her. 'How far along are you?'

'Not long. A few weeks. Maybe six.'

'You have no idea how happy I am. It's a good sign. Now everything will be all right. God wouldn't let this happen if He didn't have a plan for us.'

'I hope so,' she whispered, grasping him. 'I really do.' She didn't want to tell him about a pregnant girl she had seen earlier that week, trapped under a collapsed building. A dozen people worked to set her free but when they finally succeeded, she was dead. Nor did she tell him how many young people had died in Kiev this month alone. She didn't tell him because she didn't want to upset him and because she, too, wanted to hope for the best and believe that God hadn't forgotten about them in occupied Ukraine.

But he kissed her so intently, she soon forgot all about her fears as she kissed him back, while he undid the buttons of her cardigan and then her nightgown and pushed them off her shoulders and onto the floor. Soon she was naked in front of him, while he still had his coat on. Ever since he had joined the partisan battalion, she saw him so rarely and their meetings were so brief, she had spent every night in between dreaming of holding him in her arms. And now he was here, with her, only to disappear the following morning as if this was nothing but another wonderful dream. Irina wanted to cry but she gritted her teeth and forced herself not to. She wouldn't cry now, in front of him. She wouldn't ruin what little time they had together.

He took his coat off and placed it on the floor, then laid her down gently. They made love quietly, careful not to disturb their daughter or wake his parents. Irina bit her lip to stop herself from crying out. Even after five years together, he still took her breath away.

Afterwards, she snuggled into him and put her head on his chest. She felt drowsy, drifting off then forcing herself to stay awake because this night was all they would have together for a long time.

'We are drowning in snow,' he was saying. 'Can never get dry or warm. Frostbite is a real problem. The other day one of the men lost a finger. Everyone is desperate for winter to end.'

'Oh, no. Promise you'll take care of yourself.' She stroked his fingers affectionately, then brought them to her lips and kissed them one after another. 'I think about you all the time, out there without us. It's freezing here too. There's no heating or electricity. Sometimes I don't know how to keep Sonya warm, how to keep myself warm. But then I imagine how much harder it must be for you and I just get on with it.'

'That's what we do too. We just get on with it. What choice do we have?'

Irina pulled herself on top of him and wrapped herself around him. They were whispering into each other's mouths, lips millimetres from each other. Irina realised she'd spent her days perpetually in darkness, walking through occupied Kiev, registering the dead, searching for food, worrying about Sonya and trying to placate Zina. But Maxim filled her soul with light. When she was with him she felt alive again.

'Tell me a memory,' she whispered, her fingers touching the stubble on his face, the soft skin of his lips, his strong arms.

'What kind of memory would you like?' She could tell he was smiling in the dark, a teasing smile she loved so much.

'The happiest you can think of. When we were young and in love.'

'You mean we're no longer young and in love? I can't choose just one. There are so many happy memories. Let me think. I remember when we first met and you came to see me at my parents' dacha. I think it was the hottest summer on record. I wanted to have a picnic, to play badminton. But you had other ideas. It was too warm to do anything, you said. Too warm for clothes. I remember you stripping off and running to the river. That's my happiest memory. You, stark naked, diving into the water.'

'I remember.' She sighed with longing for peace, for warmth, for his hungry eyes on her. 'It was the first time we made love.'

'And when we finished, we heard my mother, who decided to surprise us with some lemonade. I've never seen anyone dress so quickly.'

'I'm glad she didn't show up five minutes earlier.'

'She wouldn't. I bet they could hear you all the way to Kiev.'

'That was my first time,' she said quietly.

'I'm going to tell you something I never told you back then. My nineteen-year-old pride didn't allow me to.'

He fell quiet, as if lost in the past. Irina pulled him by the arm. 'What is it? Tell me already.'

'It was my first time too. Now, why are you crying?'

'I love you.'

'And that's making you cry?'

'I'm just so happy. So glad to have you home with us where you belong.'

'It's good to be home. And I love you too. Here, put your clothes back on or you will freeze.' He helped her into her nightgown and old cardigan and wrapped her in a blanket Dmitry was able to find in a village. 'I hate being away from you and Sonya. I already missed her first step and first word. I don't want to miss anything else.'

'We hate being away from you. Why don't you come home?' That was all Irina wanted. For her husband to come home.

'I wish I could. But I need to be with the battalion. I can't be a half-hearted soldier, a soldier when it suits me. I'm in this with all my heart. You know that.'

'Then take us with you. We can live in the woods with you. I'll help out at the battalion. I know it will be hard but we'll have each other.' Even as she said it, she knew it was impossible. If it was just her, she wouldn't care about sleeping in snow and risking her life. All she wanted was to be with Maxim and away from Zina. But it wasn't just her. She had to think of Sonya and her unborn baby.

As if reading her mind, Maxim said, 'Partisan life is not for a woman with a small child. Especially now you're pregnant. It's not a life for anyone, really.'

'It's difficult for me here without you. Your mother . . . We don't get along so well. Sometimes she says things that upset me.'

'Don't be silly. My parents love you. They are so happy to

have you and Sonya around. Just the other day Mama said what a great help you were to her. I know she can be harsh sometimes, but she has a kind heart.'

'Of course she does,' Irina said, trying hard to hide the sarcasm in her voice.

'You are like a daughter to her.'

Of course I am, Irina wanted to say but didn't.

*

Irina woke early the next morning and watched Maxim for a while, observing his chest rise and fall, and the winter sun playing on his face. She forced herself to memorise every little detail of the face she loved, so that when he wasn't there, she could close her eyes and see him in her mind. Sonya was curled up next to him and they looked so adorable together, so peaceful and content. Irina longed for her pencils. She longed to draw them like this, sleeping with childish unconcern, as if there was no war, no hunger and no danger in their world.

She wished she had more time to watch him sleep. Once, they had nothing but time. She missed the lazy mornings they had spent together when they were first married. Unlike Maxim, Irina had always been an early riser. Before they had Sonya, on the days when Maxim's parents were away at their dacha, she would often wake up before dawn and sit in front of her canvas in nothing but her nightie, picking up a brush and losing herself in the imaginary world she was creating. Hours would fly by and then she would turn around and see Maxim standing behind her, watching her. She could still see the expression on his face – his hunger and love for her and a mute fascination as he watched beauty emerge from under her paintbrush. She would smile and turn back to her painting, only to feel a pair of arms embrace her, his lips in her ear, whispering how much he loved her, how irresistible she looked, dressed as she was, absorbed as she was in her work. And he would make love to her right there, in front of her painting, with the windows open and the morning breeze playing on her skin, while the brush was still in her hand, leaving streaks of colour on his naked back.

Later, they would go out and explore Kiev's hidden gems, the markets, the cobbled alleyways and stunning buildings, as yet untouched by war. And some days they would stay in, enjoying the luxury of being in the house alone and undisturbed. For months afterwards, when the summer was over and his parents were back, she wouldn't be able to look at her canvas, at the brushes, at the palette without blushing.

It seemed like a lifetime ago, a distant and almost forgotten dream. Now there was no laughter without a fearful glance over her shoulder, no smile that wasn't tinged with heartbreak. Her parents-in-law no longer went to their dacha and Maxim was hardly ever home. Where there had once been joy was now sadness. Where there had once been hope and love and happiness, now there was a numb feeling of emptiness and dread. Sometimes, when she was desperate, when she didn't know where the next meal was coming from or whether they would survive the next Nazi patrol, these memories of the two of them together when they were young and carefree were the only thing that kept her going.

She lived every moment with him as if it were her last. Did it make their love more intense, their desire for each other stronger? She didn't want that. All she wanted was to spend her days cooking his meals, cleaning his house and looking after his children. She longed for the boring and the mundane, for the luxury of taking him for granted.

Reluctantly she got up and, glancing at the two of them one more time – Maxim and Sonya, her little family – got dressed, brushed her long dark hair, threw on a coat and a hat, stuck her feet in a pair of felt boots, the only footwear that kept her feet warm enough in this weather, and walked outside with a bucket, filling it with snow. Then she carried it to the kitchen, boiled their kettle and cooked some oats. Maxim loved his porridge for breakfast. Before the war, Irina would make it with lots of milk and a spoonful of honey. She would add some blueberries if it was the season for them, or chunks of crunchy apple. Today it was nothing but oats and melted snow but she knew he would devour every bite like it was the most delicious thing he'd ever tasted.

'I brought some butter and half a dozen eggs. Check my rucksack.'

She twirled around at the sound of his voice. He was standing in the doorway with Sonya in his arms. Her breath caught at the sight of him. He was the tallest man she'd ever met, the kindest, the smartest and the most handsome. He was the most of everything. And she was the luckiest girl in the world to have him. 'I haven't seen butter since before the war. Where did you get it?'

'Some German soldiers were kind enough to share it with me.'

'That's nice of them.'

He laughed as if it was the funniest thing he'd heard all week. 'To be honest, they didn't have much choice.'

Sonya wriggled out of his arms and ran to her mother, hugging her leg. Reverently Irina unwrapped the butter and gave a spoonful to her daughter, putting another spoonful in their porridge. Maxim brushed a strand of hair away from her face. 'You are so beautiful. Look at you, you are glowing.' He placed his hand on her stomach and drew her and Sonya close. For a moment they remained still. Irina wanted to stay like this forever, just the three of them, a happy family, together and unafraid. She wanted to stop time, freeze it like a photograph.

'You are up so early,' murmured Maxim. 'I was hoping to have you all to myself a little bit longer.'

'Maxim!' cried Zina from the doorway, her hand at her mouth. The illusion of togetherness was gone. Irina felt something inside her deflate a little. Maxim pulled away and turned to his mother, who ran to his side, shouting, 'Kirill, come here this instant! You won't believe who I found! What a wonderful surprise!' Zina pushed Irina out of the way and pulled Maxim into a hug, not a mean feat, considering her son was twice as big as her and two heads taller. 'I can't believe I'm seeing you. I can't believe you're here. For how long?' Zina dabbed her eyes with a handkerchief.

'I have to go back this morning. Mama, please don't cry.'

'How can I not if we haven't seen you for three weeks? We haven't heard a word. We didn't know what to think. And now you are telling me we have moments before you have to leave again.'

'Hush, woman. He has better things to do than sit by your skirts and listen to your moaning.' Kirill had appeared and took his turn to hug his son, holding him tight for a moment and not letting go.

Suddenly, it felt like there was a wall between Irina and Maxim. He didn't look at her and didn't touch her as he talked to his parents. Zina was glued to his side, as if afraid he'd disappear the minute she strayed too far. She was sweet like sugar this morning. Where was the disdainful smile, the narrowed eyes, the shrill voice? All she had for her son was loving smiles and affectionate tears. Just like Irina, she didn't take her eyes off him. She insisted on serving the food Irina had cooked and then sat by his side, stroking his hand and repeating, 'Eat, darling, eat.'

Maxim reached for his spoon, smiled at Irina and said, 'Finally we have something to celebrate. The Red Army is getting closer every day. They are liberating East Ukraine as we speak.'

Kirill glanced at Zina triumphantly, as if to say, I told you so. She didn't seem to notice. 'That's wonderful news, darling.'

Sonya chatted in Maxim's lap as he ate, while three pairs of eyes watched his every move, and three pairs of ears listened to his every word. He was their only son, beloved husband, the one shining light in their dark universe.

'Will you join the Red Army with the other partisans?' asked Kirill.

'Our orders are to help them from within. Destroy the enemy infrastructure, lower their morale. A couple of days ago we blew up train tracks and disrupted the trains taking people to Germany. Yesterday we blew up a bridge.'

'You did an incredible thing for our people,' said Irina, her adoring eyes on him, thinking of the relief on the faces of young Ukrainians in her office as she told them about the temporary reprieve from Germany.

'But the Nazis are furious,' said Zina with a frown and a roll of her eyes. 'They are threatening hell to everyone responsible. There are notices about it all over Kiev. Promise you'll be careful.'

'I promise,' said Maxim, his gaze not on his mother but on Irina, whose insides were numb with fear. 'Don't worry. They'd have to find us first.'

She looked into his breath-taking face, longing to touch him. Yet, on his left was his mother, her hand on his arm, her eyes red from tears. And on his right was his father, watching him with a proud smile. 'But you are not always hidden. Sometimes you come out. To attack trains, for instance.'

'We attack when they least expect it. By the time they realise what's happening, we are long gone.'

'That's right. It's the Nazis who should be afraid,' said Kirill, nodding his approval.

The Nazis *were* afraid, thought Irina. And that was the problem. She never read the articles in the *Ukrainian Word* describing the horrors inflicted on the partisans caught by the Germans. She couldn't bear it. But there was no escaping the gossip at work and in the village as she bartered her valuables for food. Sometimes she wished she was blind and deaf, so she couldn't see or hear what Hitler's hordes were doing to her country.

Zina said, 'I don't think you should stay with the partisans anymore. It's too dangerous.'

'There's a war on, Mama. No matter what you do, it's dangerous. And I want to make a difference.'

'One man can't make a difference.'

'If everyone thought like you, we would have lost this war a long time ago,' said Kirill.

'Don't tell me how to think.' Zina glared at her husband. 'I just want my son back. I didn't stay up nights with him when he was little and hold him in my arms when he was sick only to lose him in this war.'

'You didn't bring me up to sit back and do nothing,' Maxim said quietly but firmly. This wasn't the first time they were having this conversation. And it wouldn't be the last.

So many emotions passed over Zina's face – the debilitating fear for her son's life, the mind-numbing loneliness of long days without him and the desperate desire to save her child the only way she knew how, by keeping him close. As a mother and a wife, Irina understood perfectly. She couldn't believe it, but she felt sorry for her mother-in-law. Her heart was breaking for her. For all of them.

Zina pulled on Irina's sleeve. 'Can I have another cup of tea? And can you bring my glasses from the bedroom, please? I need to tie them around my neck because I keep losing them.'

Irina was about to get up when Maxim said, 'I'll get your glasses, Mama. Let Ira relax. In her condition, she needs rest.'

'In her condition?' Zina's face darkened but she quickly recovered and smiled at Maxim. She wore her smile like a mask over her face, while her eyes darted from her son to her daughter-in-law.

'Yes, we are having another baby. And I want you to look after Ira for me.'

'I'm so happy for you both.' Kirill jumped to his feet and hugged Maxim and Irina.

After breakfast, Irina watched with her heart in her throat as Maxim gathered his belongings, getting ready to leave. It seemed like he had just walked through the door five minutes ago. And now he was going. And she was staying here, alone with Zina and the terror on the streets and inside her head. 'We shouldn't have told them yet. In case something goes wrong,' she said quietly, uncertainly.

'Nothing will go wrong. Can't you see? After everything we've been through, this baby is going to bring us luck.'

'Still, we should have waited.' She didn't want to share their secret with Zina. She wanted to keep it to herself, if only for a few more weeks.

'Didn't you see how happy they were?'

The four of them crowded into the narrow corridor to watch Maxim put on his coat and boots and walk away from them. Sonya was crying, as if she could sense something sad was happening. Zina's lips trembled. Kirill was grim and mute. And Irina could barely hold herself up, leaning on the wall with her hands to her chest.

'Can't you stay a little bit longer? Just another hour,' she pleaded.

She wanted to say how much one hour with him would mean to her but didn't get a chance. Zina hugged Maxim and wailed, 'Yes, stay. And not for an hour but for good.'

'Mama, we talked about this.' He turned to Irina. 'I wish I could stay but it will be just as difficult in an hour.'

'Please, be careful. Keep yourself safe,' said Kirill.

After what seemed like a thousand kisses and a river of tears from his mother, Maxim was finally leaving. 'I will walk you out,' said Irina. 'Kirill, would you mind looking after Sonya for me, please?' She desperately needed a minute alone with her husband, away from prying eyes, so she could tell him that he was her whole world, so she could hear him say it back to her. She needed those words to pull her through the next few weeks without him.

'What a great idea! I'll come too,' said Zina.

'I need your help with the candlesticks, woman,' said Kirill, coming to Irina's rescue as she stood with her boots in her hands, unable to speak.

'What candlesticks?'

'The candlesticks I'm taking to the village to exchange for food. You said I could take some of your jewellery too. You need to show me what to take. I don't want to hear your crying later if I give away the wrong thing.' Kirill winked at Irina.

'Can't it wait?'

'If you want me to get back before curfew, we need to do it now.'

Zina complained loudly but stayed home. Before she changed

her mind, Irina dashed through the door after Maxim. She couldn't wait to feel his arms around her. She didn't have to wait long. The minute they were alone together, he drew her to him. German shouts filled the air. Somewhere, a car honked. Nazi planes were buzzing overhead like a hive of angry bees, the indifferent observers to the misery of Kiev. Irina barely noticed. All she could see was Maxim.

He kissed her face, her eyes, the tip of her nose, ran his hands through her hair. 'Where is your hat?' he whispered, his voice hoarse. Irina shrugged. She was in such a rush, she completely forgot. Her ears felt numb from the wind and her hair was wet with snow. 'Here, wrap my scarf around your head. You need to start taking better care of yourself. You have our baby to think about.' He enveloped her in his scarf and lifted her collar to protect her neck from the cold. Instantly she felt warmer, and not just because of the scarf.

'I'll look after myself, and you need to promise to be careful. Our baby needs its father. So does Sonya.'

'I promise I won't do anything reckless.'

Their arms around each other, they meandered through the back streets to avoid the Nazi patrol and stopped at the corner of Rezervnaya and Avtozavodskaya Streets, where the truck would pick him up. To delay the inevitable goodbye, she walked as slowly as she could. 'What do you have planned this week? Wait, don't tell me or I'll worry. I just want you to know that I think about you all the time.'

'I know. And it means so much. Sometimes it's the only thing that gets me through the day. When things get rough, I close my eyes and think of you and Sonya. I tell myself I'm doing it for you and it makes me feel better.'

'You are our hero. I want everyone to know how proud I am of you.'

'If you want to live, if you want my parents to live, don't tell a living soul.'

'I won't.' Irina shivered, thinking of Katerina and her insinuating whisper. She pulled her scarf tighter around herself, trying to get warm. But it was impossible. Where was the mild Ukrainian winter? In January 1943, the wind was unprecedentedly harsh and the temperatures plummeted to minus twenty. The only warmth was coming from his hand in hers and his loving gaze.

'What are we going to call our new baby?' He pressed her to himself and hid his face in the scarf covering her hair. 'How about Alexander? Don't you think it's a fitting name for a warrior? Like Alexander the Great.'

Looking up into his face, her heart breaking with love, she replied, 'I was thinking, Tanya.'

'Tanya?' He laughed as if he couldn't believe what he was hearing. 'What a strange name for a boy.'

'What makes you think we are having a boy?'

'We already have a beautiful baby girl. This time I know it will be a boy. Our son. But I don't really mind. I'll be happy with either.' Ignoring the passers-by, he kneeled in front of her, opened her coat and kissed her stomach through three layers of clothing. 'You are amazing, you know that? You think you are proud of me? You have no idea how I feel about you! Building life inside you, carrying our baby, protecting him from the world. I've only been this happy once before, when we found out you were pregnant with Sonya.'

'It wasn't war then. Everything was different.'

'Yes, it was. But the war is not forever. It will be over soon—'

'Will it? It feels like it will never be over. I suppose I'm lucky. Other women have husbands at the front. They haven't seen or heard from them in over a year. They don't know if they are dead or alive.' Irina saw them at work every day. Lonely women with no means to support themselves, persecuted by the Nazis for having a husband fighting on the Eastern Front.

'Mark my words, Kiev will be free before the end of the year. The Red Army is advancing. Once the Nazis are out, these women's husbands will come back.'

'Not all of them will come back,' whispered Irina.

'No. But I will come back to you. We'll be happy, we'll finally be able to live our life, together.'

Occasionally he glanced at the road that remained empty – thank God. Silently Irina prayed the truck would be delayed, so she would have another minute with him, and another. Maybe it wouldn't show up at all and her husband would stay home with her. She couldn't bear to say goodbye and watch him walk away from her again. Every time he left, she wondered if it was going to be the last time she saw him. What if this was all they had? What if he stepped on that truck and never came back, like so many other men across the Soviet Union?

She blinked rapidly, chasing her tears away. *I'm not going to cry over him as if he's already gone*, she thought.

But when she saw the truck turning the corner and making its way towards them, she could no longer help it. The tears ran down her face, even though her skin was raw from the wind, even though he was squeezing her tight and telling her he would see her soon. 'Not soon enough,' she kept repeating, her voice barely a whisper. 'Not soon enough.' He kissed her one more time, a lingering kiss of longing and regret, and before she knew it, before she could ask him not to go, he was in the passenger seat, waving goodbye. She watched silently as the truck carried her husband to war, towards bullets and explosions and death, while she remained in the middle of the street, helpless and alone.

Irina stood under a streetlight for a few moments, pulling his scarf tight over her head and kissing the material that had touched his neck, then turned around and walked slowly back. She didn't want to go home. What she wanted more than anything was to take Sonya and jump on that truck with Maxim, come what may. She was ready to follow him to hell and back if it meant they could be together.

When she returned, Kirill and Zina were arguing over a golden necklace, while Sonya was crawling in circles on the carpet, pulling books off the shelves. 'You gave me this necklace on the day Maxim was born. The only way you are taking it away from me is if I'm dead,' grumbled Zina.

'We need to eat, woman. Be reasonable. We can't eat a necklace.'

'Just listen to yourself. You'd sell your soul for a piece of bread. And your family too. Where is my wedding ring? I took it off because it was too small. Now it's gone. Please don't tell me you gave that away too. Is nothing in this house sacred anymore?'

Irina picked up her little girl and sat in a chair, hugging her close, searching for comfort in her warmth. She felt so empty inside, so sad and lonely, even though she was surrounded by people. She wished her mother was alive. Everything would have been different if only her mother was alive. Missing her mother was like a dull ache inside her chest that never went away. Mama could always tell when Irina was upset or worried or frightened. She had a sense for such things and knew just the right thing to say to make her feel better. What would Mama say if she could see her now? Irina closed her eyes and felt for her mother's soul out there, trying to imagine her beloved face. Grit your teeth and wait, she would say. Better times will come, if only you wait long enough. Every cloud hides sunshine behind it.

But Irina's only sunshine had left in a military truck and all she could do was wait and pray that one day he would come back to her.

'You should have been more careful,' she heard. It took her a few moments to realise Zina was talking to her.

'Careful?'

'It's a bad time to have a child. We barely have food for one. I think you should get rid of it.'

Horrified, Irina said nothing.

'Zina!' exclaimed Kirill. 'What are you saying?' It was the first time Irina heard her kind and gentle father-in-law raise his voice to his wife.

'I'm only thinking of her. Trying to spare her the heartbreak. You know what happened to a friend of mine? Her daughter had a baby a few weeks ago. Then the Nazis marched in and dragged her away, put her on the train to Germany. Without her mother's milk the little girl died. There was nothing they could do. They tried to give her cow's milk but it made her vomit.'

Irina put her hands over her ears, not wanting to hear Zina's cruel words. She wanted to scream.

'This is not the time to have another baby,' concluded Zina. 'When the war is over, by all means, have as many as you want. But not now.'

Irina stood up with her daughter in her arms. 'I don't think it's up to you,' she said as calmly as she could. Then she walked out, her head held high.

In the kitchen, she placed Sonya in her highchair, giving her a piece of roasted beetroot to chew on and her favourite doll to play with. When the girl was happily mumbling to herself, Irina put her head in her hands and cried. This baby was supposed to be a secret for her and Maxim to share, one beacon of light in the darkness of war. Her pregnancy was the hope she desperately needed to survive. It was God's way of telling her that life went on, despite everything. She tried to imagine Maxim's face as he held her in his arms and told her how happy he was. That nothing bad could happen to them now. But all she could hear was Zina's heartbreaking words.

Irina didn't want to admit it to herself, but Zina's voice sounded just like the one inside her head. At work she heard hundreds of terrifying stories. She saw women driven to despair by their impossible choices. More than anyone she knew the risks. By speaking of her fears out loud, by giving them a voice of their own, Zina had made them real, and suddenly the hope and the joy were gone and only the dread remained. That was what Irina was crying about at the kitchen table, surrounded by dirty dishes, while her daughter was giggling in her highchair. Not Zina's hurtful words but her hope melting away.

What was she thinking, having a wartime baby? Zina was right. She of all people should have known better. While their country was torn apart by Hitler, there was no chance of a normal life for her and Maxim, no matter how much they lied to themselves and pretended otherwise.

She put her arms around her stomach and whispered words of love to her unborn baby. Maxim's unborn baby. What Zina suggested was unthinkable. How could she look Irina in the eye and say such heartless words? How could she think such heartless words and not be ashamed?

The door opened and Irina saw Kirill. Self-consciously she wiped her tears away but it was no use. After crying for so long, she knew her face was as red as the beetroot Sonya was chewing on. Kirill closed the door and sat next to her, taking her hand in his and squeezing it with affection. 'That was a terrible thing for Zina to say. I'm sorry you had to hear that.'

Irina sniffled and nodded. She couldn't speak. Instead of calming her, his kindness made her cry harder.

'Forgive her. She doesn't know what she's saying.'

'How can she be so cruel?'

'I'm not trying to make excuses for her, but she's just worried about everyone. She loves everyone so much.'

'Not me.'

'Yes, you. Of course, you.'

'She never accepted me. Never thought I was good enough, as a wife to her son, as a mother to her granddaughter. All I ever get is criticism.'

'She just wants everything to be perfect. In her heart, she loves you. And that's what matters.'

'I don't believe that.'

'You know I've been with Zina since we were at school. Childhood sweethearts, we were. We met what feels like a hundred years ago at a school dance. When I first saw her, she was screaming at the top of her voice at two teenage boys. I can still see her face, twisted and red from anger. They were bullying her next-door neighbour, a tiny boy with glasses. She said if she ever saw them near him again, she would pull their legs off one by one and feed them to them for breakfast. Those were her exact words.'

'I can imagine.' Through her tears Irina smiled.

'The boys were bigger than her, but I've never seen anyone run so fast. I think that was the moment I fell in love with her. She was fearless, standing up for what she believed in, protecting someone close to her, even though she was outnumbered and weak. Believe it when I say this, Zina has a loving heart. Unfortunately, it comes with a sharp tongue. She truly cares about you and Sonya. And she would do anything for you. How many people can you say that about these days?'

Irina shrugged. Hardly any, she thought to herself. 'Then why does she say such hurtful things?'

'We always hurt the ones we love the most. She doesn't want anything bad to happen to you. She sees doom and gloom everywhere. Don't listen to her. God will protect you and the baby. Everything will be all right. You'll see.'

He stood up and walked around the table, collecting the plates. Irina jumped to her feet to help him. 'Don't worry,' he said. 'Why don't you play with Sonya? Just look at those chubby cheeks and that perfect smile. She'll cheer you up in no time.'

'Thank you,' whispered Irina, her hands shaking. 'Thank you for being so kind.'

Silently she watched Kirill as he rinsed the dishes in a bucket of water and dried them with a cloth. She could imagine Maxim looking just like this when he was older – his hair grey, his shoulders stooped a little but still tall and strong and larger than life. How lucky Zina and Kirill were to have what they had, a lifetime together, long years of joy and sadness, of children and grandchildren, of occasional disagreements and ever-lasting love. What Irina wouldn't give to have all that with her husband.

Chapter 5

Lisa had barely slept, her empty stomach aching and rumbling through the night. Her first thought when she got out of bed was, breakfast! But Masha had other ideas – she had to check on Anton. Not to appear selfish, Lisa trudged to the hospital with her friend leaning on her arm. The snow had finally stopped and for the first time she could see clearly. Now, she could make out the meadow, the white-capped trees like wedding cake toppers shimmering in the sun, the barely visible dugouts like burrows of giant animals. The wind had quietened down and not a branch moved in the air. So peaceful it was and so serene, it was as if the outside world did not exist. Here in the tranquil woods, Lisa could almost forget that only a dozen kilometres away there were fighting, death and devastation. It was as if there was no war, no Kiev occupied by the enemy, no Soviet Union bathing in a river of blood spilled by Hitler, only unblemished snow as far as the eye could see.

Inside the hospital dugout, they found Anna asleep in a chair and Anton awake and squinting at a book under a small kerosene lamp.

'You'll ruin your eyesight,' said Masha matter-of-factly as she examined his leg. 'What are you reading?'

He lifted the book. It was *Gallic Wars* by Caesar. 'I'm no warrior,' he said. 'I'm not even that brave and this, being a partisan, hasn't been easy for me. So I read about other wars to remind myself others have done it before me.'

'Does it help?'

'Sometimes.'

Not looking up from the dressing she was changing, Masha said, 'You stopped a train headed for Germany. You freed hundreds of people. Thousands more won't be taken away from their families because the rail tracks have been destroyed – by you. You are not just brave. I think you're a hero.'

'Stop that,' said Anna, opening her eyes and sitting up. 'Find another partisan to flirt with. This one's taken.' She smiled and glanced at Anton with affection.

When Anna heard that the girls were thinking of staying at the battalion, she suggested they should go to see Azamat immediately. 'Before you change your minds. Or before he leaves for the day.' Beaming, she added, 'It will be great to have two girls my age here. You can't imagine how lonely I've been.'

'What about Anton?' asked Lisa.

'What about him? It's not like I can talk to him about anything important, like clothes or make-up.' Anna laughed at her own joke, self-consciously straightening her trousers that were a few sizes too big, held together by a rope and sporting holes around the knees.

'Will you come with us to speak to your papa?' Lisa asked, suddenly nervous.

'Sorry, girls. You're on your own. I couldn't leave him.' Anna pointed at Anton, who was ear-deep in his book and didn't notice. 'I'm afraid the minute I leave, something bad will happen to him. And I couldn't bear it if anything happened to him. I'll just stay here and endure another five hours of discussion about Caesar, God help me.'

The two girls walked across the meadow towards a small

dugout known as the headquarters. According to Anna, this was the heart of the battalion, where all the important strategic decisions were made. Lisa could hear her heart pounding. She could swear Masha could hear it too, because she kept asking if Lisa was all right. Yes, Lisa would nod, I'm fine. But it was a lie. The truth was, she was afraid for her life. She was afraid the partisans would realise she wasn't good enough to be here and put her on the first truck back to the city. And at the same time, she was afraid they would let her stay here, at the heart of the battle for Kiev.

When they approached the headquarters, Lisa hesitated, hiding behind her friend. 'Come on, scaredy-cat,' said Masha, pulling on her sleeve. 'If you can't face Azamat, how will you fight the Germans?'

'Who said anything about fighting the Germans?'

'You want to be a partisan, don't you?'

If Lisa could turn around and run, she would have. But there was nowhere to run.

Azamat was at his desk, leaning over a map of the area and marking something with a red pencil. He was a general planning his next campaign and here was Lisa, interrupting his important work with her silly request. She took a few shallow breaths, lost for words. Masha was braver. She had every reason to be brave, thought Lisa. She was a nurse. The partisans needed her. Before Azamat had a chance to look up from his map, Masha blurted out, 'Sorry to bother you. We were wondering if it was all right if we . . . We would like to stay here, at the battalion.'

He studied them for a moment with a kind smile on his face. 'Why don't you sit down?'

The girls perched on a long wooden bench across the desk from Azamat. Lisa avoided looking at him, in case he could read the fear in her eyes.

'How old are you, girls? You both look like you should be at school.'

'I'm nineteen,' said Lisa, fighting an impulse to raise her hand before she spoke, like she was at school.

'And I'm twenty-one and married. My husband is fighting. I want to do something too.'

'A partisan battalion is a tough place for young women. For anyone, really,' Azamat said. 'Are you sure this is what you want? It won't be easy.'

'You think living in occupied Kiev was easy? Or riding on that train? I'm a nurse,' said Masha. 'I want to make a difference. From what I've seen, you could do with my help.'

'And from what I've heard, you've already helped. Anton was lucky to have you here. But I want you to think carefully about your decision. You've only been here one day . . .'

'Two,' corrected Masha.

'Two. I'm sure you've noticed that we have no running water, no comforts, no protection from the elements. We are exposed to extreme weather and the enemy, who are desperate to kill us off. And when I say desperate, what I mean is, they will stop at nothing.'

'It doesn't bother us,' said Masha. Lisa remained silent. Everything Azamat was saying bothered her a great deal but she wasn't about to admit it.

'It will. Sooner or later it bothers all of us and it's only natural.' He took off his glasses and wiped them on his handkerchief, finally replacing them on the tip of his nose. 'At the start of the war, we had three times as many people here. Many wanted to hide in the woods, stay out of the enemy's way and wait out the war. They didn't last in the battalion. Soon they realised we don't stay hidden for long. Our job is to make the Germans' lives as difficult as possible. We go out looking for trouble. We take up weapons and fight. That's what drives us, that's our purpose.'

'I have a purpose too – I want to help people,' said Masha.

'What about you?' Azamat turned to Lisa. 'Why do you want to stay here?'

With the attention now on her, Lisa froze. She wanted this kind man to be impressed with her, just like he was impressed with Masha. She wanted him to praise her, just like he had praised

Masha. She racked her brain for something smart to say but all she could think of was, 'I want to help too. I will learn how to shoot. I will go out with the partisans. I can be brave, I know I can. Please, let me stay. I have nowhere else to go. I'm good at sewing too. I sew all my own clothes. And you could do with some new ones.' She pointed at his uniform that was falling apart and hoped Masha wouldn't expose her lie, having seen her struggling with a needle as if she had never held one in her hand before. But Masha remained quiet, smiling at her friend.

'That would be useful indeed, if only we had any fabric. But we don't. Our shoes are falling apart too. We have a cobbler at the battalion but nothing to make the shoes from. But we could always use some help around here. Can you cook?'

'Of course,' said Lisa, who had never cooked and didn't know how.

'Come with me,' said Azamat, putting his map in a metal safe and locking it. Obediently Lisa and Masha followed him in silence as he walked outside and across the meadow, shouting out greetings and waving to the other partisans.

The cafeteria dugout was warm from the bodies crowding the tiny space and from the clay stove burning in the kitchen. 'I have a helper for you,' said Azamat to Yulya, who had an apron around her large hips and a knife in her hands. He pushed the reluctant Lisa forward. Something sticky and unpleasant was bubbling in a large pot. The smell was suffocating and Lisa felt like the walls were closing in on her. Once again, she wanted to turn around and run. She loosened her scarf and opened her coat.

'I don't need any help,' grumbled Yulya, shaking the flour off her hands.

'And yet every mealtime you complain you don't have enough hands to do everything. Well, here I am, bringing you an extra pair.'

Yulya looked Lisa up and down. She seemed doubtful, as if she could see straight through her and knew she had never set foot in a kitchen before, other than to eat. 'Can she even cook?'

Lisa frowned. This woman was talking about her as if she wasn't in the room. 'I bet I can cook better than you.'

'We'll see about that. I don't have a spare apron. But here is a knife and there are some potatoes that need peeling.'

'You want me to start now?'

'You have anything better to do?'

'I would like to have breakfast first,' mumbled Lisa, wondering what she had gotten herself into. It was all right for Masha. She was doing what she had always wanted to, while Lisa was stuck with a mountain of potatoes.

'She would like to have breakfast,' mimicked Yulya. 'What would you like? Buttermilk pancakes with some strawberry jam perhaps, or a ham and cheese omelette?' Lisa perked up but then saw the sarcastic expression on the woman's face and realised Yulya was making fun of her. 'I'm afraid you missed breakfast. The porridge is gone. Before you can eat, you have to make your food.'

'Come on, Yulya, don't be so hard on the girls. Find them something to eat. You know what Napoleon said. An army marches on its stomach,' said Azamat, winking at Lisa. 'I'll leave you to it. Welcome to the partisan battalion, girls.'

He waved goodbye and walked away, lifting his body through the small opening with difficulty. Lisa wanted to run after him and ask him not to go. She didn't want to be left alone with grouchy Yulya, who watched her through narrowed eyes and made her nervous. She regretted saying she knew how to cook.

Yulya found two small boiled carrots and the girls chewed them in silence. When the cook was out of earshot, Masha said, 'She seems nice.'

'Delightful,' replied Lisa grimly.

'It could have been worse. We could be in Germany right now.'

'Easy for you to say. You don't have to answer to a cranky witch who looks like she wants to put you in a pot and eat you.'

'Yes, but did you hear what happened to the nurse before me?

She was carrying a wounded partisan from under the enemy fire and got hit. The partisan survived. She didn't.'

The girls were silent for a while, staring into their plates. 'Is that what we signed up for? To come under enemy fire? Is that expected of us?' whispered Lisa, shuddering. 'Maybe we should do what Anna suggested and ask Maxim to teach us how to shoot.'

'My job is to save lives. Not end them. I could never shoot anyone.'

'Not even the Nazis?'

'The Nazis are people just like everybody else.'

Lisa thought of her grandmother as she lay dying in their kitchen after a German officer shot her. She thought of her father, lost in a Nazi prison camp, and of her fiancé, hanged for a crime he didn't commit. She thought of her friend Olga and thousands of other Jewish people, walking to their deaths through the streets of Kiev. 'No, they are not. They are monsters.'

'Perhaps. But I couldn't kill one. I have a job to do and I want to get on with that job. God will protect me. I don't need to know how to shoot.'

Secretly, Lisa was relieved her friend had said no to lessons with Maxim. She could see herself alone in the woods with him, just the two of them, his hand on hers as he steadied her rifle, his face close to her face, and felt a shiver of excitement just thinking about it.

Masha pushed her plate away and got up to her feet. 'I'd better run. Anton is waiting for me.'

'I have to get on too. A bag of potatoes is waiting for me.' Lisa said it with a smile, although inside she felt like crying. But then she thought, *The partisans have saved me from a certain death in Germany. The least I can do is peel some potatoes.*

Instantly, she felt better.

*

In the meadow skirted by century-old oaks, with a hundred pairs of eyes on her, Lisa took off her kerchief and her hat and, in a trembling voice, swore to protect the people and the motherland, to stay faithful and true, to be brave and relentless in her fight against the oppressors, to be vigilant and guard the battalion against spies and traitors, to carry out her tasks to the best of her ability and to be not afraid of death. As she repeated the oath after Azamat, who stood in front of her, thin and frail but with his head held high, she wondered how one could not be afraid of death. The people in front of her risked their lives every day but had they never been afraid? And if they were afraid, did that make them any less brave?

Masha hadn't hesitated when she took the oath earlier. She had made it look so easy. And why not? She didn't have anything to prove. Everyone in the battalion already knew she was a hero.

As Lisa said the words, trying not to think too much about what they truly meant, the image of a young nurse sprang to her mind, selflessly dragging a man twice her size away from the battlefield, inching her way to safety only to get hit herself. Suddenly she found she couldn't continue and stood mutely with her mouth open. This wasn't a Young Pioneer camp, where Soviet boys and girls marched to the sound of military bands, learnt how to put up tents and build fire. This was a partisan battalion during the most brutal war the Soviet Union had ever known. It wasn't pretend; it wasn't make-believe. It was life and death.

She looked up, about to tell Azamat she couldn't go through with it. It didn't bother her that the whole battalion would know she was a coward. She was still so young. There was so much she hadn't done. She had never even travelled outside of Kiev. She had never been married or had a child. She had never told her sister how sorry she was. What if she never saw her again?

But then she noticed Maxim in the crowd, smiling encouragingly at her. When their eyes met, he nodded with approval. *You can do it*, he seemed to say from across the clearing, and suddenly there was no one else around but the two of them. Maxim believed in her. More than anything, she wanted to prove him right. She might not care what the others thought but she cared what he thought. She took a deep breath, shut her eyes and finished the oath.

Azamat shook the girls' hands and said, 'With great joy we welcome our new sisters into our family. I can see that your hearts are true and you are going to be great assets to the battalion. Our fight is just. God is on our side!'

Hats flew up in the air and the battalion cheered. Despite her misgivings, a warmth spread through Lisa and for the first time in a long time she felt like she belonged, like she was no longer alone.

In the afternoon, Lisa's excitement melted away a little when she had to go back to the cafeteria and peel more old vegetables, stir the stew on the hot stove and scrub the tables and the floor. Somehow the knife was too blunt to cut potatoes but sharp enough to slice Lisa's finger until it bled, while the heat from the stove made her head hurt. And Yulya never stopped complaining. Nothing was good enough for her. The stew was too watery, the potatoes too hard, the kitchen counter too dirty.

Grumbling to herself, her finger throbbing, Lisa picked up a bucket and stepped outside to fetch some snow to wash more potatoes. As she bent down, a sharp, cracking noise startled her. She thought she saw movement in the woods behind the cafeteria dugout. Placing her bucket down, she walked a dozen steps to take a better look. Under an evergreen pine tree, bare-chested and red in the face, Maxim was chopping wood. As she watched him raise his arms and bring the axe down on a piece of kindling, Lisa felt short of breath and a little giddy. She couldn't take her eyes off his back and his bare shoulders.

'Aren't you cold?' she asked, shivering and pulling her coat tighter around herself. 'I'm cold just looking at you.'

He put his axe down and turned around. 'I will be if I stop moving. The work keeps me warm.'

His stomach was flat, his arms huge. He looked very strong. Blushing, she glanced away, at the trees above his head, at the blue skies and the pale sun. He watched her expectantly and she desperately searched for something witty to say, a joke or a clever comment. But all she came up with was: 'Anna told me you are good at shooting.'

He looked like he was struggling not to laugh, like she had just said the most amusing thing. 'I suppose I am good at shooting.'

'She mentioned you teach people sometimes.'

'I do teach people sometimes.'

Lisa reddened. 'I was wondering . . .'

'Do you want me to teach you how to shoot?'

She nodded. 'That would be wonderful. If it's not too much trouble, of course. I would really appreciate it.'

'Of course, it's no trouble. How are you settling in?'

'We used to go on a lot of camping trips when I was a child. It feels a bit like that, but colder.'

'You surprised me, you know. I never expected you to stay here and work so hard. Breakfast was delicious.'

'It was delicious because I didn't cook it. Yulya refused to let me anywhere near the stove this morning. She changed her mind at lunch but I think she regrets it. I'm mostly on potato-cutting duty.'

'Well, the potatoes were cut especially nicely yesterday. I remember thinking Yulya could never have done such a splendid job.'

She tried to keep a smile from her face. 'Thank you. I'm glad you liked them. I better get back or Yulya will be looking for me.'

'Be ready for our lesson after lunch on Saturday.'

He winked and turned his back to her, raising the axe in the air and letting it fall with ease. Lisa didn't just walk back to the kitchen, she flew, the heavy bucket of snow the only thing slowing her down.

Chapter 6

It was still early when Irina finished her work for the day. The sun was shining and the sky was clear, but for a few black dots moving fast over Kiev – the German patrol aircrafts. As she walked, the city seemed to be holding its breath, as if waiting for something. Other than the din of the plane engines in the far distance, there were no other noises, no cars driving past, no loud groups of soldiers. The few Soviet citizens who hurried through the streets were quiet and fearful, aware that the city no longer belonged to them.

Kirill usually took Sonya to the neighbours' apartment to play with their children in the early afternoon. Irina didn't want to return to an empty house or, worse, be alone with her mother-in-law. After Zina's hurtful comment, Irina met every word from her with silence. She cooked dinner as quickly as she could and fed Sonya in her bedroom, then waited for Zina to go to bed before she had something to eat herself. When Irina did run into Zina in the kitchen, the older woman made no attempt at reconciliation.

Not only were the German-occupied streets hostile, her home had become hostile too.

Instead of heading back to Kazanskaya Street, she walked to Tamara's building on Kirilovskaya. Her friend's tiny two-bedroom apartment was Irina's refuge, the only place where she could relax and be herself. Today, like most days, it was untidy, with clothes and books strewn over the floor. Tamara looked slightly untidy herself, having just returned from a nearby village, where she had traded her winter coat for a kilo of potatoes. Her hair was wild, her mascara smudged. Still, she was beautiful, in a vulnerable sort of way. Now that her passport was stamped with a fake marriage and she was safe – for the time being – from mobilisation to Germany, Tamara smiled more often and laughed louder. Only a trace of fear was left in her eyes. But that was hardly unusual. Everyone Irina met had fear in their eyes.

Irina and Tamara were sitting at the dining table, two steaming cups of tea in front of them, just like so many times before the war. The difference was now there were no biscuits or cake or blinis to go with the tea. There was no carefree laughter or happy smiles, either.

'I can't believe she'd say that,' exclaimed Tamara after Irina told her how Zina stormed into her room and shouted at her for breastfeeding Sonya. She wanted to tell her friend about the other thing Zina had said – the unspeakable, heartbreaking thing about her pregnancy. But saying it out loud meant thinking about it again and Irina couldn't bear it. 'It's none of her business how long you breastfeed your child for.'

'I know.'

'It's your decision as a mother.'

'I know.'

'Does she have no respect for personal space? Ignore her. I always said she was a witch. She looks like one, with that mop of grey hair. She sounds like one. And she acts like one too.'

'When I hear her voice, my hands start to shake and I feel physically ill. Even when she says something completely innocent, like "pass the salt, please".'

'I can't say I blame you.'

Irina rubbed her hands in a futile attempt to warm up. The apartment was freezing. 'And then I feel so guilty. She's Maxim's mother. My mother-in-law. How can I hate her so much?'

'It's not your fault. You've been as patient as a saint. If I were you, I would have told her exactly what I thought of her a long time ago.'

'How can I? I live in her house. If it wasn't for her, I would have nowhere to go.'

'Come and stay with me. You know you're always welcome.'

'Thank you, my dear. I would love to stay here with you but what would Maxim say?' She sighed, thinking how wonderful it would have been not to have to deal with Zina day in and day out. 'I keep thinking maybe it's my fault somehow. Maybe it's me who's doing something wrong. She brought up such a wonderful son. She can't possibly be all bad.'

'I think he's wonderful despite her, not because of her.'

Irina suspected Tamara was right. 'I don't know how much longer I can take it. She crosses all my boundaries. When Sonya was a newborn baby . . .' Irina shuddered at the memory. 'It was such a difficult period. She was crying all the time, wouldn't feed, wouldn't sleep anywhere other than in my arms. I was going out of my mind. And instead of help and support, all I got from Zina was put-downs, arguments and criticism. No one has ever made me feel the way she does. Sometimes I think the only way I can be happy is if she's no longer in my life.'

'You can't live like that. It's not healthy for you or Sonya. Life's too short, now more than ever.'

'I feel so guilty for having these thoughts. It's a vicious circle of hatred and guilt. It seems so petty, with the war and the real suffering all around. But it hurts so much. I feel like there's a war zone inside our house. Ever since Maxim and I got married . . .' She shook her head, unable to continue.

'Have you told Maxim how you feel?'

'He'll never understand. He adores his mother.' Her hatred for Zina was the only secret Irina had ever kept from Maxim.

He was her soulmate and her one true love. They shared everything. But not this. She didn't want to force him to take sides, though wasn't sure if that was because she didn't want to hurt his feelings – or because she didn't know whose side he would choose. 'Anyway, let's not talk about her anymore. Tell me about your young man. I want to know everything. How did you two meet?'

Tamara's eyes lit up and she took a sip of her weak tea. 'My best friend introduced us.'

'But I am your best friend.'

'Exactly.'

Heavy footsteps resounded in the communal corridor outside and Irina felt her body tense. She expected a series of loud knocks on the door, followed by German voices telling them to open up. Irina's arms went around her belly protectively. But Tamara didn't seem concerned. As she was rummaging in the cupboard for something sweet for their tea, some honey perhaps or a square of sugar forgotten on a shelf somewhere, a key turned in the lock. 'Speaking of the devil,' she said. 'That's him.'

'Who?' Irina caught a glimpse of her pale face in the mirror. Her hands were shaking.

Tamara continued excitedly, 'I can't wait to introduce him to you. Of course, you already know each other. But . . .' her voice dropped to a whisper '. . . as my fiancé. He asked me to marry him last night.'

Irina took a few deep breaths and told herself to calm down. She really had to get her nerves in check. When she looked up, she saw Dmitry standing in the doorway. 'What are you two whispering about with such secrecy?' he asked, grinning.

'Secrecy?' Irina cried, relieved beyond belief and a little taken aback. Dmitry was the last person she had expected to see. 'Look who's talking. All this time you two were seeing each other and I had no idea!' She tried to make her voice sound stern but failed. Nothing could please her more than seeing her best friend, who was like a sister to her, with a man like Dmitry. Someone she could trust with all her heart. Someone who would take care of her.

'I was just about to tell Irina how we became a couple,' said Tamara. 'Why don't you join us? I'll pour you some tea.'

Dmitry hung his coat in the corridor and sat at the table next to Tamara, his chair almost touching hers. They linked hands under the table and Tamara rested her head on his shoulder. Dmitry's face was glowing. 'We got together by almost getting arrested, that's how. We were giving out some leaflets at the station. You know, telling the population that the Nazis are lying and the Red Army is advancing—'

Tamara interrupted. 'Let me tell the story. I do it so much better. I hid the leaflets in the basket I was carrying, under some old clothes. Suddenly, a Nazi officer approached and demanded to search the basket. He was two metres tall and had the ugliest face I've ever seen. I said to him, you want it? Here it is. And put the basket over his head, pushing him as hard as I could.'

'You should have seen her. She was magnificent,' said Dmitry, his affectionate gaze on Tamara.

'I can imagine,' said Irina, her chest swelling with pride. She had known Tamara since kindergarten and her friend never ceased to amaze her.

Tamara continued, talking quickly as if in a hurry to get the words out. 'And then we ran as fast as we could. The Nazi tried to give chase, once he freed himself from the basket and the garments. But it was crowded and soon he lost sight of us. We hid in the cellar of an abandoned house and didn't come out until the next morning. It was the scariest night of my life. Also, the happiest.' Tamara put her hand out, showing Irina her ring. 'And last night Dima took me back to that house. He made it look so nice, with ribbons and candles. And he asked me to marry him. As soon as I saw the ring, I said yes. How could I not? It had once belonged to his grandmother.'

'Are you marrying the ring or the man?' asked Irina, laughing. Their happiness was contagious.

'She said yes before I even stopped talking. I could have been saying, "Will you cook and clean for me for the rest of your life?"'

'Wasn't that exactly what you were saying?' Their eyes locked and for a moment they were quiet, as if forgetting Irina was in the room with them. 'You and I are going to be related!' exclaimed Tamara, jumping up and down and hugging Irina. 'Like real sisters. Married to cousins.'

Irina remembered what falling in love was like only too well. For her it had felt like diving off a tall building, not knowing if you would make it to the ground alive, and yet, being unable to think of anything but him and feeling nothing but happiness. Seeing them so excited, with their arms around each other, smiles wide on their faces, Irina longed to tell them about the baby. She almost opened her mouth and did so, but then she thought of Zina's cruel words and dread like poison spread through her.

What if her mother-in-law was right and the war was not a good time to have a baby? What if something went wrong? She couldn't bring herself to tell them.

February 1943

Chapter 7

Although the rest of the battalion woke at six, Lisa's day started at five. The partisans had to eat before they left on their daily missions, and someone had to prepare breakfast and set the tables. To Lisa's dismay, that someone was her. *That's only fair*, she would tell herself as she lay exhausted on her straw bed in the mornings, unable to force herself to get up and face her chores. Everyone else risked their lives to fight the Nazis, even Anna. Masha helped the partisans and nursed them back to health. It was up to Yulya and Lisa to make sure the others were fed. She was grateful to be in the woods and not on the dreaded train of death headed to Germany or, worse, in a factory on the outskirts of Berlin somewhere without food or water or sleep, numb with utter exhaustion. Despite the monotony of her daily tasks, despite the fact she had spent her whole life trying to avoid housework of any kind, for the first time Lisa felt like she was doing something worthwhile. These people had saved her. Slowly, one peeled potato after another, she was paying them back.

Every morning, she dragged herself out of bed, bleary-eyed and unhappy, set the tables and cooked porridge that was nothing but gruel and melted snow. After the cooking was done, she brought food to the partisans and carried the empty plates to the kitchen, washed the dishes in snow as best she could, scraping until her hands felt raw, cooked stew for lunch and potatoes for dinner, and then spent the rest of her day mending uniforms until her back was aching.

Three times a day, Maxim came to the cafeteria and she served him his food. He always had a smile on his face and a few cheerful words for everyone. Every time she saw him, she forgot all about her exhaustion and laughed shyly at his jokes, while inside she was melting at the sight of him, his dark hair, his height and his white teeth. Was it her imagination or did everyone in the cafeteria fall quiet as soon as he walked in? He drew all eyes like a magnet.

Late at night, Lisa would collapse into her bed, barely able to say goodnight to Masha and Anna, who looked as tired as she felt. In the past, she often had trouble sleeping as she worried about one thing or another, a boy she liked or an argument with her sister or a school assignment. Not anymore. Despite the uncomfortable straw and the cold, every night she would fall into a deep sleep the minute her head hit the bed and wouldn't open her eyes until Yulya's voice, the most unpleasant alarm clock, would wake her at five to start another excruciating day.

On Saturday morning, Lisa didn't drag her feet but jumped out of bed, wanting to sing at the top of her lungs. Today was the day she was seeing Maxim for her shooting lesson and she no longer cared about the backbreaking work or the cold or how tired she was. All she wanted was a moment to herself, so she could stay in bed, hide under the covers and whisper his name to herself: *Maxim*.

Seven more hours to go! How was she going to get through them?

Not very well, apparently. At one point Yulya ran into the kitchen, her eyes bulging, both hands waving, and shouted at Lisa, 'What do you think you're doing? The porridge is burning!'

Lisa was busy constructing an imaginary conversation with Maxim. In her mind, she was incredibly witty and he was laughing at her every joke, while his adoring gaze never left her face. Yulya's voice cruelly interrupted her reverie and she snapped to attention, but it was too late. The smoke filled the room and the precious oats were stuck to the bottom of the pot, a rancid smell emanating from them. Yulya shook her head but didn't say another word. When she stormed off, she looked angry enough to hit somebody.

Understandably, the men were as upset as Yulya. They grumbled and complained but still devoured every burnt bite before dispersing on their missions. Still, Maxim didn't seem to mind. He winked and said, 'Was there a fire in the kitchen today?' It was all Lisa could do to smile in reply and look straight at him as if nothing was happening. Her hands were trembling so much, she almost dropped his empty plate on the floor as she made a hasty retreat.

When the partisans left, Lisa cleaned up and washed the plates, then cut the potatoes for lunch. 'What time is it?' she asked Yulya.

'Two minutes since the last time you asked. What is wrong with you today? You're not yourself.'

Lisa was stirring chicken soup when Masha walked in and sat at a table next to her, silent and wide-eyed.

'What is it, Masha? Why do you look so sad? Is it Anton? Is he not getting better?'

'Oh no, he's much better. I'm pleased with his recovery. He'll be back to normal in no time.'

'I'm glad to hear that. Anna must be so happy.'

'She won't stop thanking me. Even gave me her fur hat to wear.'

'She gave you her favourite hat? That's very kind of her.'

'I suppose.'

'What is it, then?' Lisa joined her friend at the table, making sure to move the pot of soup off the stove first. One incident with burnt porridge was enough for the day.

'It's this weather. I wish it would snow again,' said Masha. 'It was uncomfortable but at least it wasn't so cold. The snow tempers everything.'

'I know what you mean.' Lisa was freezing in her bed at night and on her walk to the cafeteria in the morning. As she cooked, she felt warmer, but it didn't last because Yulya had forbidden to keep the stove going for a second longer than was necessary. 'But what do you have to worry about? You are the only one at the battalion with a fine fur hat.'

'It's not me I'm worried about. It's the men. They keep coming back from sentry duty with frostbite. I don't have enough beds for everyone. I don't have anything to treat them with.'

'Winter is almost over. Once spring is here, this problem will go away. I for one cannot wait!'

'By then it will be too late. How can I do my job if we have no medical supplies, only bandages? The limbs are getting infected and I feel so helpless.'

Lisa put her arm around her friend and was about to say something soothing when Yulya walked into the room, dragging a sack of flour behind her. 'Look at you, gossiping idly when a hundred people are coming for lunch in . . .' she looked at her watch '. . . ten minutes! You two should be ashamed of yourselves.'

'I'm just finishing my break,' said Lisa, not stirring from her chair.

'And I don't work here.' Masha jumped to her feet, almost knocking her chair down. 'I better get back to my actual job. I have patients waiting.'

When she was gone, Yulya turned to Lisa with her arms on her hips. She opened her mouth to say something but Lisa interrupted. 'How do you expect me to feed a hundred men with thirty potatoes and one hundred grams of chicken?'

'It won't be the first time. Save the potato peel. We can fry it for dinner,' said Yulya.

'We have no oil left. I can't make meals out of nothing. And every mealtime the men come up to me asking for more. What am I supposed to tell them? You can't have more, you have to go and risk your life on an empty stomach?'

Yulya's shoulders stooped. Suddenly, she looked old, her hair thin and grey, her face drawn. 'Tonight we might have more. Danilo took a few partisans to the villages on the west bank of the Dnieper to look for food. The villagers help us, although God knows they don't have much to give either. My husband is in charge of the food operations. We raid German households, take their cattle. But it's getting more and more difficult. And with so many mouths to feed, it's not enough.'

Lisa still found it hard to believe that the round and sharp-tongued Yulya was married to monosyllabic Danilo, sharing a small dugout with him at the outskirts of the little settlement. Yulya had told her she'd followed her husband to the partisan battalion because she couldn't bear to be apart from him. That, too, was hard to believe. Lisa had never seen the two of them exchange as much as a word or a look. Then again, other than his outburst at the assembly on her first day here, she had never seen Danilo exchange a word with anyone. He seemed to communicate in grunts and gestures.

Yulya added, 'No more breaks in the morning or afternoon. You can have an hour for lunch. And no arguments. By helping these men fight the enemy, you are helping our country.'

When Yulya wasn't looking, Lisa mimicked her, rolling her eyes. No breaks during the day – as if she wasn't working hard enough. But she couldn't be upset for long. Only one more hour to go!

For lunch Lisa had a small bowl of soup – warm water with half a potato floating in it. She sat with Masha, who was silent like Danilo, and stared into her bowl, hoping more soup would miraculously appear. Even after every morsel was gone, she was still hungry. How was she supposed to get through her day, to cook and clean and sew when all she could think about was food? How did the others do it? They sat in ambuscades in the freezing cold for hours, shot their rifles, mined bridges, cut telephone cables and never complained. Azamat – and Napoleon – were wrong when they said the army marched on its stomach, because this army had nothing in theirs. Exhausted, undernourished and ready to fall, on and on they marched regardless.

After they finished eating, Masha begged Lisa to come with her to the headquarters to talk to Azamat. Lisa happily agreed. She had half an hour before her shooting lesson and needed to get away from the monotony of the cafeteria and Yulya's grim face.

They found Azamat pacing the little room inside the headquarters, his hands behind his back. When he saw them, he stopped and smiled.

'I need to talk to you,' said Masha, getting straight to the point in her usual manner. 'We have too many men with frostbite. The hospital is full.'

'Tell me about it. It's the same in every battalion. I have no one to send out there to fight the enemy. It seems the weather is fighting their battles for them.' He shook his head sadly.

'All we have is warm water and bandages. I can't save their limbs with those. I need animal fat. Goose, duck, anything really.'

'I'll talk to Danilo. He might be able to help.'

'Thank you. But we need to do more. Prevention is important.'

'How do we prevent frostbite? While these extreme temperatures last, there's really not much we can do.'

Masha stood up straight, like a soldier at attention. 'There are some things we can do. Shorten the amount of time men spend on sentry duty. An hour maximum, then swap. Tell them to line their boots with grass. Teach them to bind their feet with cloth.'

Lisa watched her friend with awe. How brave she was, standing up to Azamat, telling him how to run his partisan battalion. Even more astonishing, he didn't get offended or tell her to mind her own business. All he did was nod and say quietly, 'Those are excellent suggestions. I will talk to the men.'

As the girls were saying goodbye outside the cafeteria, Lisa said, 'I'm impressed! You went in there like a general.'

'What choice do I have? The men's lives depend on me.'

After Masha went back to work, Lisa snuck into their dugout

and sat on her bed. She took a few deep breaths to calm down, wishing she had a mirror to see what she looked like, wishing it was summer and she could dress up in a pretty dress for him. How she longed for some make-up to make herself more striking, some mascara to draw attention to her eyes, the colour of deep sea, some lipstick to make her lips fuller. All she could do was rub her face extra hard with snow, brush her teeth extra vigorously with baking soda and straighten her hair with the tips of her fingers before she adjusted her drab coat, her old hat and kerchief, and trudged through the snow towards the meeting point.

Maxim was already there, four rifles in his hands. Lisa wondered why they needed so many but quickly forgot about it because he was looking at her and saying, 'You are nice and early. Ready to learn?'

Lisa wanted to say she'd been ready for days, that she'd been counting the hours. But all she did was nod eagerly in reply.

'We still have five minutes. Let's wait for the others.'

'What others?' she asked, her heart falling.

'Here they are.'

When she looked up, she saw two young men walking towards them.

'Thank you for being punctual. There's nothing worse than waiting in this cold,' said Maxim, smiling at Lisa, who couldn't meet his gaze. So much for being alone in the woods with him. 'Lisa, meet Alex and Sergei. They've been with us for a few months now.'

The men shook Lisa's hand. She barely nodded.

'Here are your rifles. I thought we'd start with the Soviet-issue Nagant. Nice and easy.'

As if in a trance, she followed the three men to the secluded spot where the lesson would take place. The rifle was heavy and made it difficult for her to walk through the snow. Bear ran in front of them, barking excitedly, scaring the birds away. Like dark clouds they fled from the nearby trees. Lisa fell behind a few paces, watching Alex and Sergei with loathing, as if they were solely responsible for the disappointment she was feeling.

Smiley and light-hearted, Alex said, 'This will be great. I can't wait to learn how to shoot.'

The heavy-set Sergei, who looked as gloomy as Lisa felt, replied, 'What's the point? If our army couldn't stop the Nazis, what can a group of people hiding in the woods do? We have no food, no equipment. We are just cannon fodder for the Germans. In the end, they'll kill us all.'

'If that's how you feel, what are you doing here?' asked Maxim. Lisa could tell he didn't approve of Sergei, even though he tried not to show it.

'I have nowhere else to go. They killed my entire family.'

Alex said, 'How can you say there's no point? Before they kill us all, we have to make them pay for what they are doing to us. We have to resist. We can't take this lying down.'

'Will it bring my family back?'

Alex continued, ignoring Sergei. 'My parents had a German officer staying with them last year. Whenever he had to travel somewhere, he would always ask whether there were partisans on the road. One day I said to him, here you are, going to the front, an old soldier, why are you afraid of the partisans? And you know what he said? He said, at the front, if you get wounded or taken prisoner, chances are you'll live. But when facing partisans, in both instances you are dead. That's why I joined. I wanted the Nazis to be afraid of me.'

'That's exactly what we want. We want them to be afraid. And you know why?' said Maxim. When he spoke, Lisa paid attention. He had a presence about him, an assurance she had never seen before in any other man. As if he knew his own heart, knew exactly who he was and was proud of it.

'Why?' asked Alex. Both young men looked at Maxim with awe. Lisa saw him through their eyes. An experienced partisan, one of the best snipers in the Soviet Union, responsible for killing hundreds of German officers. Her heart swelled with pride, as if his achievements had something to do with her.

'Because if they are afraid of us, they will continue sending units against us.'

'And that's a good thing?' asked Lisa, shivering.

'Of course. The more the better. A unit on a mission against us means one fewer unit for the Red Army to deal with. And that's what we are here for. To help our army fight for our motherland.'

They came to a clearing surrounded by snow-capped birch trees. The sun was shining through the branches, giving them a magical halo, like angels sent to these woods to watch over them, and all at once Lisa felt like she was a million miles away, in a fairy-tale land somewhere. If it wasn't for the rifle dragging her down, if it wasn't for the men talking about killing other human beings as if it was nothing out of the ordinary, she would have forgotten all about the war.

They formed a circle around Maxim. As he spoke, Lisa studied his face. How handsome he was, how his eyes lit up with passion. Feeling a little light-headed, she placed the butt of her rifle in the snow and leant on it.

'As partisans, our mission is to make the Nazis' lives unbearable, by whatever means possible. It's our job to make them regret they ever came here. Don't let them relax for a moment. Damage them physically and emotionally. Our goal is to appear suddenly and disappear before they know what's hit them. Stealth and care, not brute force. We can't afford to get caught alive.'

Lisa didn't want to think about the implications of getting caught alive.

'Soon you will learn that every operation is different,' continued Maxim. 'No two are alike. You can't take longer than one second to judge the situation and make a decision. One second is everything to a partisan. Being careful doesn't make you a coward, it makes you smart. And being smart means you will achieve much more for your country than if you get yourself caught. Do any of you play chess?'

Sergei raised his hand and said, 'I was a national champion two years in a row.'

'Very well. Then you will know that chess players think two steps ahead.'

'More than two, you have to—'

'That's right,' interrupted Maxim. 'And that's what we have to do here. In a chess competition, not thinking ahead will cost you a medal. Here, it will cost you your life. The stakes are higher. It's better to be prepared, to take your time and think. The partisan is like a fisherman. We throw our lines out and wait. We don't rush. Patience is key. As partisans, we have an important job to do. You know what they call us? The third front. Like Alex here said, the Nazis are afraid of us. Let's show them they have every reason to be.'

'Is it true that you have shot thousands of Nazi officers?' asked Sergei, who no longer looked gloomy.

'It's not true.'

'I heard there's an award out on your head.'

'I hope not,' said Maxim.

'What is it like to shoot someone? To take someone's life?' asked Alex. Lisa could swear he was dying to shoot somebody.

'What do you think it's like?'

'I don't know. I've never done it.'

'It's different for everyone.'

'What was it like for you?' asked Lisa quietly.

'It wasn't easy. And doesn't get easier. But we do what we have to, even when it's hard, because we have no other choice.' Maxim coughed as if to hide his embarrassment and said, 'Let's get to work, shall we? In the battalion, we have three types of rifle: Soviet, Polish and Japanese. We also have guns, machine guns and mines. Unlike food, we have plenty of ammunition. But we still have to be careful. We don't want to waste a single bullet because once we run out, that's it. You heard Azamat. We don't shoot unless we are certain of our target. We take aim carefully and remain calm.'

Lisa wasn't sure she could do that. Remaining calm had never been her strong suit, especially under pressure. As she learnt how to stand, how to hold her rifle correctly, how to reload and take aim, her gaze searched out Maxim. His eyes twinkled when he talked about shooting. He held his weapon gently, with care, like it was something he loved dearly.

After Maxim had talked them through each step, he set them up with targets – a branch or a mark on a tree's bark. Lisa was surprised they would be shooting with ammunition so soon, and a little bit nervous, but she understood the partisans didn't have time to waste.

'Press, don't pull the trigger. But not before you are focused on the target,' Maxim said to Lisa, coming from behind and standing so close, her face would touch his tunic if she turned around. She tried hard to concentrate on what she was doing and failed because she could feel his breath in her hair. Her hands trembled and she missed her target time and time again. But she persevered and, every now and then, she hit it and Maxim cheered. Her heart swelled with pride at his praise and each time it spurred her on to try harder.

By the end of the lesson, her arms and shoulders were aching, but it was all worth it. Maxim told her she was his best pupil of the day.

Chapter 8

As Irina made her way to work, careful not to slip on the ice, all she could think of was her husband at the partisan battalion. It had been nine days since they had said goodbye. Nine days of not hearing, of not knowing if he was all right. If anything happened to him, would someone knock on their door to give them the bad news? And how long would it take? Would the family go through their day, have their meals, clean their plates, read their books, go to work, go to the village for food, and not even know their husband, son and father was no longer with them?

That was what Irina was afraid of as she navigated the treacherous ice on Kirilovskaya Street. That her world had shattered and she didn't know.

On the corner of Priorskaya and Makovskaya, in broad daylight, a group of Nazi officers surrounded a Soviet family. Irina watched in horror as the butts of the German machine guns came down hard first on a man's head and then a woman's. Three little girls, ranging in ages from three to six, screamed in fear.

A small crowd gathered. The mother looked up to them from the ground, small rivulets of blood running down her face, her hands pressed together as if in prayer.

'It's the Litovins,' said an old woman to Irina's right. 'They owned a bakery before the war.'

'They were feeding the partisans. The poor family, they're doomed,' said another woman.

Irina shook with fear. Today it was a family who supplied food to the partisans. Tomorrow it could be Maxim himself.

The Nazis forced the parents to their feet and took them and the children away. Even after they had disappeared around the corner, Irina could hear the girls' crying. Then gunshots sounded. When all was quiet again, she shuddered as if waking from a nightmare and continued on her way, her heart breaking.

'One day,' she whispered to herself. One day the tide would turn and the Red Army would be back. And then the Nazis would pay, for every life they had taken and for every square metre of the Russian land they had burnt.

When Irina looked up from the muddy snow, she noticed a tall smiling man walking towards her out of the corner of her eye. *He looks like Maxim*, she thought and glanced away. But then the man waved and started running in her direction. It *was* Maxim!

'Irina,' he cried, lifting her off the ground like she was a porcelain doll, fragile and precious.

'Maxim!' she whispered. 'I didn't expect to see you here. Oh, Maxim!' And then she couldn't say another word, so relieved was she to see him.

They stood quietly for a moment, lost in each other. Finally, he took her hand and led her to a small church around the corner. Irina was surprised she had never noticed it before. While the buildings on either side had been destroyed by fire, the blue-and-white church remained intact, as if God Himself was protecting it. It was damp inside and completely empty. The Bolsheviks had turned the church into a science museum, but she could still see the outline of the cross on the wall. It made her feel strangely comforted, as if someone was looking out for her.

'I was just thinking of you,' she said, touching his face. 'And here you are.'

'I had to see you. I had to make sure you're all right. Azamat is picking up supplies from Kiev today. I begged him to take me on his truck.'

'Please thank him for me,' she said, her hand on his cheek.

His face felt rough, unshaven. His eyes were warm. 'How are you feeling?'

'Nauseous all the time. Tired. But otherwise well.' She couldn't stop smiling. Maxim was here. It was a miracle. 'Let me run to work quickly. I'll tell them I'm sick. We can spend the day together. We'll go and see Sonya. She keeps asking for her daddy.' She trembled with excitement. When was the last time they had spent a day together? She couldn't remember.

'I wish I could, but I have to go soon.' He laid his coat down and they sat on the floor, her head on his shoulder.

'How long do you have?'

He glanced at his watch. 'Ten minutes. I can't make Azamat wait or he might not take me with him next time.'

'Oh no.' A moment ago, she would have given anything just to lay her eyes on him. Ten minutes together was an unexpected gift. But at the thought of saying goodbye so soon, her heart ached.

Maxim looked inside his rucksack. 'I brought some eggs. A bag of oats. Last time, you hardly had any left. Also a loaf of white bread and a sausage.'

'I can't remember the last time I had sausage. Where did you get it? Let me guess. The Germans?' When he nodded, she said, 'What a generous nation.' She unwrapped the sausage, bringing it to her face and smelling it. Feeling slightly queasy, she wrapped it back up. 'I'll take it home for Sonya.'

'Have some bread. And here is some garlic. When did you last have garlic?'

'Thank you. I've been craving garlic.' Gratefully she took a chunk of bread. 'You can't imagine how hungry we've been. All I think about is food. And you.'

'It must be the pregnancy.'

She nodded, thinking, *He doesn't realise how little food we've been getting.* 'What about you? Do you have enough food?' He looked thinner than the last time she had seen him, his face gaunt, more angular. There was dark stubble on his cheeks.

'Sometimes. Not always.' Seeing her worried eyes on him, he added, 'We are doing all right. There are a hundred people in our battalion. That's a lot of mouths to feed.'

'Why don't you have some sausage? You look like you need it.' She handed it to him but he pushed it away.

'No, I don't. I'm not the one eating for two. We don't have much time. Tell me everything. How have you been?'

She told him about her work and all the funny things Sonya was saying. How she ran to her every evening. How she couldn't stop asking about her papa. She told him about Dmitry and Tamara getting married.

'Dmitry and Tamara together!' he exclaimed, visibly surprised, amused, delighted. 'Those two are like chalk and cheese. The complete opposite. My cousin is a bookworm. If he could spend his life locked in a library, he'd be happy. And your friend is a social butterfly.'

'Opposites attract. Just look at us.'

'What do you mean? We are as similar as two people can be.'

'I like painting and all the finer things in life. You like guns.'

A shadow passed over Maxim's face. 'I don't like guns. After this war is over, I hope never to see a gun again. Anyway, maybe it's exactly what Dmitry needs. Maybe she'll be good for him.'

'I've never seen the two of them so happy.'

She asked him how he spent his days away from them, even though she was afraid of what his answer might be. She didn't want to know about the danger. What she wanted was to hold him tight and never let him go again.

'We are counting the days till summer. None of us can remember what it's like to be dry and warm. Oh, and we have some new recruits. Two girls.'

'Girls? Are they pretty?' Irina smiled to show she was only joking.

'I don't know, I haven't noticed. They are awfully young. Too young to be in the woods.'

'How are they coping?'

'Not too bad. One of them is a nurse. The other one . . . I don't think she has anywhere to go. She's eager to help, to learn how to shoot, so I've been teaching her. She looks so sad sometimes, I wonder if she's all right.'

Irina wanted to say that maybe she and Sonya could come and stay with him too. If two young girls could do it, why not them? But she didn't say it. There was little point, especially now she was pregnant. Maxim would never agree to it. 'I'm so scared, Maxim. For you, for Sonya, for the baby.'

'Don't be scared. I'm not going anywhere. And I will look after you. When the war is over, we will get a little house of our own. In one of the villages by the river, perhaps. I know how much you love the water. I'll get a job as an engineer. You will teach at a village school. We will be together.'

'A house by the river sounds wonderful. Just you and me and our little ones. After the war is over, I don't think I want to stay in Kiev anymore. Maybe we could leave. Go someplace else. Somewhere by the Black Sea. I've never seen the sea, have you?'

'I have seen it once, in Crimea as a child.'

'What was it like?'

'It was cold and green and endless. But I was small. Everything seemed big to me. I remember seeing a jellyfish and a big crab.'

'I heard that it almost never snows in Yalta. And when it does, the snow melts before it hits the ground. Wouldn't it be wonderful, to live between the mountains and the sea and to never see snow again?'

He smiled, but then said, 'I don't think I could ever leave Kiev. My life is here. My parents are here.'

She didn't reply. What was she thinking? Of course he would never leave his parents, even if it was to start a new life with her.

When Maxim walked Irina to her office on Priorskaya Street, she refused to say goodbye to him. 'Maybe if I don't say it, you won't have to go.' He held her close and showered her with kisses, finally letting go of her at the bottom of the steps leading to the front door of the building that housed the registry office. She ran up the steps in a few big strides and turned around. He was still there, looking up with a smile on his face. 'Don't run,' he shouted. 'The stairs are slippery.' Then he kissed his gloved hand and waved. Raising her own hand, she waved back, her heart hurting.

Once she was inside, she rushed up the first flight of stairs and peered out the window. Maxim was gone. The street below was empty.

*

At home, Irina found Zina with Dmitry in the kitchen, while Sonya was in her chair chewing a corner of her book. As a picture of farm animals disappeared in her mouth, the little girl looked cheekily at her mother and cried, 'Mama!' Irina took the book from Sonya, extracted the half-chewed page from her mouth and kissed her silky dark head, glaring at her mother-in-law for allowing the child to munch on paper. But Zina wasn't looking at her. 'Here, have a piece of bread,' she was saying to her nephew. 'I wish I had more to give you.'

'What is in this bread? It tastes like sawdust.' Dmitry poked the bread with his finger and wrinkled his nose.

'It's made from millet hulls,' said Irina. At the bread factory, two types of bread were being produced. Golden-crusted and delicious, for the Germans. Grey, heavy and impossible to eat, for the Soviets. Each of them received two hundred grams of the awful bread a week. As a worker, Irina received slightly more. 'They don't want to waste their precious wheat on us.'

At the sound of Irina's voice, Zina pursed her lips and turned sharply away. Irina wanted to tell her she had met Maxim. But seeing the expression on Zina's face, she couldn't bring herself to say anything. She would tell Kirill later.

The wall of silence in the house weighed heavily on her. Once Zina had realised her daughter-in-law wasn't talking to her, she had stopped talking to Irina also. At the sight of the women so openly at war, Kirill became sadder and quieter every day, until he too barely said a word. Only Sonya's laughter could still be heard in the house, as she chased the cat around the living room or played dollies with the clothes pegs Irina brought in from the garden.

'Don't worry, Zina Andreevna. I'm not hungry,' said Dmitry, pushing his plate away. 'Tomorrow I will get some food from the village. What would you like?'

'How about some milk and butter, and some flour, so I can make blinis?' Zina laughed at her own joke.

'I can't promise you that, but I might be able to get some potato peel and maybe even a few whole potatoes.'

After Zina left to see a friend, Irina sat down at the table wearily, cradling Sonya in her lap and ruffling her hair. Her heart soared at the thought of Maxim and the time they had spent alone together at the little church.

'Did something happen between you and Zina? All week you've barely said a word to each other,' said Dmitry.

'I'm just tired, that's all. My days are too long.' Irina stretched her legs out. Her feet and back were aching. The tiredness and the queasiness were supposed to get better in the second trimester. Only one more month to go. She couldn't wait to feel her baby's first kick, to experience the tiny hiccups inside her tummy, to finally meet him for the first time when he was born. Maxim was convinced they were having a boy and now Irina thought of the baby as a boy too. Not that she minded. She would be just as happy with another little girl. Smiling, she placed her hand on her tummy and tried to imagine her baby curled up safe and sound inside. 'Why aren't you with Tamara?' she asked Dmitry. 'She said she was making you dinner when I saw her in the street earlier. Potato pancakes, better than the German bread, even without salt or eggs or sour cream.'

'Potato pancakes, my favourite,' he said wistfully but didn't make a move to get up from his chair.

'Then why are you still here? Did you two have a fight?' Irina almost laughed out loud at the impossibility of it. She couldn't imagine Tamara having a fight with anyone but especially not with Dmitry, the kindest man she'd ever known.

Dmitry shrugged, his face twisting.

'What happened?' Irina prodded.

'Tamara lied to me. She said she'll marry me and all this time . . .' Dmitry reached into his pocket and pulled out a passport. Opening it, he glanced inside as if hoping that whatever had upset him wasn't there anymore. 'I was going to the registrar to find out about getting married, so I took her passport. Look what I found. She's already married.' He threw the passport on the table with disdain.

He looked so sad, Irina wanted to hug him. Picking up the passport, she glanced inside. 'Is that all? You are upset because her passport is stamped?' She pointed at the stamp stating that Tamara Semenova was married to a man called Ivan Sidorov. She couldn't help it: she laughed.

Dmitry looked taken aback and more than a little hurt. 'You think it's funny? Who is this Ivan, anyway? She's never mentioned him before.'

'That's because he doesn't exist. He's a figment of my imagination.'

'*Your* imagination? I don't understand.'

Irina pointed at the stamp. 'That's my signature. I placed the stamp here a month ago, to keep Tamara from going to Germany.'

'So it's not real?' Dmitry's eyebrows shot up in disbelief. 'She's not actually married?'

'Of course she's not married. How do you think single women have been avoiding mobilisation to Germany?'

'Thank God.' Dmitry jumped up to his feet and gathered Irina in a hug, practically dancing with her on the spot. 'I can't even tell you how happy that makes me. I don't know what I'd do without her. I feel like I've been looking for something my whole life and didn't even know it. And suddenly, here it is. You know what I mean?'

'I know exactly what you mean,' said Irina, thinking of Maxim's arms around her as he told her he would always take care of her. That he wasn't going anywhere.

'But how will we get married now? Her passport is already stamped.'

'Let me see.' It was fortunate that she had affixed the stamp in the middle of the passport. Undoing the staples holding the document together, she took the page with the stamp out. 'Here you go. Tamara is free once again to make an honest man out of you. Now go! Don't let those potato pancakes go cold.'

Chapter 9

One freezing day in the middle of February, when the snow came down hard but brought little relief from the cold, a miracle happened. The partisans raided a German household and brought a whole chicken to the settlement. Danilo reverently carried the bird into the kitchen and handed it to the ecstatic Yulya, who was bouncing on the balls of her feet in excitement. Two hours later, the chicken had browned in the oven and smelt delicious, sitting proudly in the middle of the table. When the time had come to serve it, Lisa, who had been eyeing it with longing, picked up a knife. The ache in her stomach was unbearable. It was the same ache she had been living with ever since the first Nazi soldiers set foot on the streets of Kiev, but it didn't mean it was getting any easier. It wasn't something one could get used to. As she eyed the delicious roasted meat, the likes of which she hadn't seen in over a year, all she wanted was to take a few morsels for herself, not much, just a small slice of the white breast and a pinch of the crispy golden skin. Her mouth watered just thinking about it. But she could hear the hungry voices outside. She could imagine the partisans' hungry faces. These men and women, while feeling just as hungry, went out to fight and protected Lisa from the Nazis. They needed the food more than she did. She couldn't take even the smallest bite.

When Yulya saw Lisa eyeing the chicken, she cried, 'Step away from the table. I will carve the bird myself.'

Lisa trembled with indignation. Did Yulya think she was going to steal some? Reluctantly she passed the knife to the older woman, throwing one last regretful glance at the bird. She wondered if Yulya would take a slice for herself. The woman looked so starved and exhausted, she could definitely do with some meat. But no, Lisa watched her carefully as she divided the chicken. Not even a gram disappeared into her mouth. When she was done carving the meat, Yulya told Lisa to fetch some plates and carried the bird to the large cafeteria table behind which two dozen partisans were already queuing. Clearly, she didn't trust Lisa even with all those eyes on her because she served the meat herself, placing a tiny bit on each plate next to a couple of old carrots and potatoes.

The partisans were loud like children on New Year's Eve waiting to open their presents. As Lisa walked through the hall, collecting empty plates, all she heard was, 'Comrade Smirnova, can I have some more?' She couldn't bring herself to tell them that the tiny bit of meat was all they were going to get.

At a small table in the corner, Alex and Sergei were sitting close together, smoking. As Lisa approached to collect their plates, she overheard Sergei saying, 'Women in the partisan battalion! How absurd! And now they think they can learn how to shoot, wasting everybody's time.'

Lisa's mouth slid open in shock as she slowed down and stopped behind them. All this coming from a man who couldn't even shoot straight. The nerve! She felt the tips of her ears burning.

'Leave them alone. What have they done to you?' asked a broad-faced man called Arthur, tucking into his vegetables with delight, having already finished his chicken. 'Look at this delicious lunch they've prepared for us. Without them, who'd feed us?'

'You call this lunch? An old potato and a tiny bit of chicken. It was so small, I couldn't even taste it. But you're right, their place *is* in the kitchen. And that's where they should stay. Instead, they think they can be soldiers like us.'

'I agree,' said Alex, nodding. 'Life in the battalion would be easier without them. When they are around, you have to watch your language, you have to wash.'

'When was the last time you bothered to wash?' exclaimed Arthur, mockingly covering his nose and shuffling away from Alex on the wooden bench.

'With women around, we don't have the freedom to be men. Even here. Even at war.'

'Shut up. It's good to have them here. They inspire us. If a woman is fighting, we men have no choice but to do our best,' said Arthur.

'What do girls know about fighting? Ninnies, all of them.'

Seething, Lisa collected their bowls and stormed back to the kitchen. Making sure Yulya wasn't around to see what she was doing, she reached under the bench where the vegetables were kept. Some carrots at the bottom of the pile were so old, they had turned to putrid liquid before they could be used. Yulya had been nagging Lisa to clean the mess up for days. Now Lisa was glad she hadn't got around to it yet. Picking up a spoon, she scraped off some of the rotten gooey mass, mixing it with rice pudding in the two bowls meant for Alex and Sergei.

Hesitating only a moment, her hands trembling slightly, she served the bowls with a straight face, not looking at the two men and not responding to their teasing comments. This would teach them, she thought with satisfaction. Maybe next time they would think twice before making disrespectful comments about women, who risked their lives and worked as hard as the men, who were just as brave and just as determined, if not more so.

And if the two men got sick and she could have Maxim all to herself during their next shooting lesson, even better.

*

At lunchtime the next day, as she waited for the lesson to start, Lisa looked nervously around, hoping Sergei and Alex wouldn't appear and ruin everything. But there was no sign of them and the closer it got to twelve o'clock, the more confident she became that her plan had worked.

She couldn't see Maxim but behind the pine trees she spotted Bear, running towards her with a stick in his mouth. His tail was wagging and he danced around her as if inviting her to play. 'Here, Bear, here,' she called him. He bounced like a ball, finally approaching her for a stroke and placing the stick in her hand. Having observed him with his master, Lisa knew Bear was a gentle giant who wouldn't hurt a fly – unless someone he loved was threatened – and she was no longer afraid of him. Gently scratching him behind his ear, she picked up the stick and threw it as hard as she could. Bear ran after it, almost overtaking the stick and jumping up to catch it mid-air. 'Good boy,' she cried, clapping her hands.

When Bear ran back to her, she put her arms around his thick neck, repeating what a good boy he was. Her hat fell off her head and her long auburn hair covered her face. She barely noticed, giggling and tickling the dog.

When she looked up, she saw Maxim staring at her from across the clearing. His expression reminded her of the way her older brother Stanislav would look at her sometimes when she did or said something endearing. There was amusement on his face, and tenderness. She blushed.

'I'm sorry I'm late,' said Maxim, smiling.

'No problem at all. Bear kept me company.'

'You two looked like you were having a great time. Are you ready for our lesson?' There were only two rifles in his hands.

'What about the others?' When she said it, her voice didn't tremble and she didn't lower her gaze.

'They both seem to have a mild case of upset stomachs. They won't be joining us today.'

'I hope it's not my cooking? I told you I'm a lousy cook.' She felt a sense of triumph, only slightly tinged by guilt. All was fair in love and war. And this was both.

'That's impossible. The chicken, all five grams of it, was the best I've ever had.'

Lisa smiled happily and didn't tell him Yulya had refused to let her anywhere near the bird. As they walked, she watched Bear, who never strayed more than a few metres away. 'Bear is the best. It feels like he can read your mind sometimes.'

'Sometimes he can. I love dogs. Always had dogs growing up. The dog is the only creature that loves you more than it loves itself.'

'That's what my grandmother always said. When I was two, she bought us a puppy, saying every child needed a dog to grow up with.' As she thought of her grandmother's kind smile and soft voice, of the way her warm hand felt as she took little Lisa to the playground, of the pain on her face when she lay in their kitchen in Kiev, dying, Lisa felt close to tears. Not wanting Maxim to notice, she turned away from him, towards the forest and a flock of birds spooked by the exuberant Bear.

'My first dog was older than me,' said Maxim. 'I always felt like he was looking down on me. Like he was smarter than me. I remember taking him to dog school with my papa and training him to do tricks. He could fetch anything – keys, newspapers, glasses. Papa was happy he didn't have to get out of his chair to get his daily news. Mishka was the smartest dog in all of Kiev.'

'My dog's name was Mishka too!' cried Lisa, stunned by the coincidence. 'He wasn't smart like your dog though. Once he put his head in an empty tin of tuna and ran around the house, knocking into walls because he couldn't see where he was going.'

Maxim laughed so hard, it warmed her heart. She couldn't help it: she laughed too. It felt like it was just the two of them in the woods, with not another living soul for miles. Her neck was killing her after the gruelling hours in the kitchen and she walked slowly, her rifle behind her back, her shoulders slumped. Once or twice she slowed down and placed the rifle on the ground to rest.

'Are you all right with that? Do you want me to carry it?' asked Maxim.

'I'm fine,' she said, wincing as she picked up the rifle.

'Here, let me help you.' He carried two rifles like they were matchsticks. Lisa wished she could be strong like him. More than that, she wished she could place her hands on his arms and shoulders and feel the muscles with her fingertips.

'Why aren't you in the Red Army?' As soon as she said it, she wished she hadn't. What if he thought she was criticising him? 'Not that you aren't doing enough.'

'I did join the Red Army when the war started. But then they retreated east and I stayed. Abandoning Kiev to the enemy seemed wrong. I've known Azamat since I was a child. When I heard he was recruiting people for the partisan battalion, I decided to join.'

'Did they look for you, in the army?'

'By that point, the army was in such confusion, I doubt that they did. I suppose I'm a deserter in a way. But I feel I can do more good here, on the soil where I was born. This is my home. I could never leave.'

'I remember waking up one day and learning that the Red Army had left Kiev. I don't think I've ever been so scared in my life. It felt like they had forsaken us, running for their lives. Like no one was fighting for us anymore.'

'I didn't run. I'm still here, fighting.'

'Had I known it back then, I'd have felt much safer.' When Lisa thought of those terrible weeks after the first bombs had fallen on Kiev and Molotov's voice had come on the radio, announcing the country was at war with the most formidable enemy the world had ever known, all she remembered was her stomach dropping in dread, and a desperate hope that Stalin and the Red Army would protect them from the hated Nazis at any cost. But little by little this hope had dwindled and only the relentless, never-ending fear remained.

Lisa and Maxim arrived at their clearing, and once again she was stunned by the beauty around her. Not a branch swayed in the wind, not a leaf. The azure of the skies and the white of the snow were overwhelming. Being alone with him was overwhelming. This wonderful feeling was worth two upset stomachs. 'The woods are beautiful, don't you think?' she asked.

'Very. Sometimes I look at it all and my breath catches. Then I remember it's no longer ours, that it belongs to the Nazis, and it breaks my heart.'

'Where did you learn how to shoot?'

'I followed my cousin Dmitry to a competitive shooting school when we were kids. He soon got bored and stopped. But I became obsessed.'

'And very good at it.'

'I suppose. I started competing and showing good results. First in Kiev, then in all of Ukraine. When I started working as an engineer, designing bridges and roads, I didn't have much time and stopped practising for a while. Then the war started and it took on a whole new meaning. It was no longer a hobby. It was something that could make a real difference.'

'I never had an interest like that. At school, I flitted from one thing to another. Chess, sewing, dancing. But I was never serious about any of them.'

'That's because you haven't found your passion yet.'

She nodded but looked at him and thought, perhaps I have. Perhaps in these woods I have found my passion.

Maxim was a good teacher, patient and kind. And Lisa was a good pupil, eager and attentive, hanging on his every word. This time around, she did much better. She reloaded her rifle in half the time and hit twice as many targets. When they were walking back, Maxim told her she was a natural. 'Better than Sergei and Alex?' she wondered aloud.

'Much better.'

A small part of her wished they were there to hear it.

Outside the cafeteria, he handed the rifle back to her. 'Why don't you keep it, now that you know what to do with it?'

Trembling, Lisa took the rifle, amazed at herself. Before the war, she would never have dreamt of handling a dangerous weapon. Her father had guns when she was growing up, but he kept them safely locked away, forbidding anyone from touching them. She still remembered his horror stories of accidents and shooting lessons gone wrong. Although not the most obedient child, she never approached the gun cabinet, her fear keeping her away. And here she was, with a rifle of her own!

She watched him walk away, a little light-headed, as if instead of learning how to shoot they had been drinking cheap wine and playing a guitar in the woods. When Maxim was finally out of sight, she went back to the kitchen and sleepwalked through the rest of her day, thinking of him.

That night, she took the rifle to bed with her, telling the girls it made her feel safe. But the truth was, it was the first present Maxim had ever given her and she was never going to part with it. It meant more to her than all the jewellery and pretty dresses in the world. If she could, she would wear it around her finger like a wedding ring, so it would always be with her.

Chapter 10

The little apartment on Kazanskaya Street was always filled with visitors, even more so since the war had started. Irina never understood how her disagreeable mother-in-law could have so many friends. From Podol to Leonovka, there were farmers who owed her a favour and seamstresses who couldn't say no to her. Zina was a retired administrator who missed her job terribly, and so she had made it her business to collect food and clothes for the partisans. Once a month a grouchy woman named Yulya arrived with empty bags and Zina ushered her into the kitchen, where the two of them drank endless cups of tea and gossiped in hushed voices for an hour or so. Irina thought Zina and Yulya had a lot in common. Neither of them seemed to have a kind word to say about anyone.

Today, nothing but a bag of wilted carrots waited for Yulya in a wooden crate under the table. When Zina's back was turned, Irina took half a carrot for Sonya, who loved them. Then she cooked some oats and melted snow in a kettle for their tea. With the little girl balanced on her knee, a spoon in one hand and a bowl of porridge in the other, she listened to Zina and Yulya as they talked about the war.

'I have hardly anything to give to you today. I'm so sorry, my dear. Even the farmers don't have much left,' said Zina, looking embarrassed, as if the hunger in Kiev was her fault.

'I don't know how much longer we can last. How can we do our job when all we think about is food?'

'That's exactly what the Nazis want. To starve us until we admit defeat.'

'At this rate they might soon succeed. We still have some supplies hidden away in the woods for a rainy day. Other units aren't so lucky. The Nazis have raided their hiding places. The state of those people.' Yulya shook her large grey head. 'They can barely walk, let alone fight.'

'Don't worry, winter's almost over. Once the summer is here, it will be easier.'

'If we survive until summer,' grumbled Yulya.

'I do have some new uniforms for you today.'

Yulya perked up. 'That will cheer the men right up. After a year and a half in the woods, we are wearing rags. How we got through the fiercest months, I will never know. And what a freezing winter it's been.'

Zina nodded. 'Unheard of. It's as if nature itself is resisting the Germans.'

'Nonsense. Have you seen how well they are dressed? It's us who are suffering the most, sleeping in the snow, starved and frozen. You know how many men lost their fingers to frostbite? Fortunately, we have a new nurse who soon put a stop to that. A bright girl, Masha. What would we do without her?'

Irina remembered Maxim mentioning the nurse the last time she saw him. The thought of their brief meeting in the church warmed her heart. Sonya finished her porridge and Irina lifted her in her arms, to wipe her face and give her some lukewarm water from the kettle. She was looking forward to snuggling in bed with her little one. After a long day at work, confronted with horrors of war until she felt like screaming, she could barely keep her eyes open.

While Zina was in the living room fetching the uniforms, Yulya smiled at Sonya and poked her tongue out. The little girl giggled.

'What a lovely child. And she looks just like her father,' Yulya said.

'Thank you.' Irina smiled politely, wondering how quickly she could slip away without offending their guest.

'Does he come to see you often?'

'Not as often as I'd like.'

'I'd be careful if I were you. There's a young little thing who recently joined us, crazy about your husband. Watches him like a bear watches honey.'

As she looked at the woman's insinuating face for clues, Irina forgot all about sleep. 'What are you talking about?'

'They've been spending a lot of time together. He's teaching her to shoot, or so they say.' Yulya lowered her voice. 'Personally, I think they are up to something. Every couple of days they go off into the woods together, just the two of them. Afterwards she comes back with the biggest smile on her face, like a cat that got all the butter.'

Irina shook her head in confusion. 'Who goes off into the woods together?' Was this woman saying Maxim was having an affair? All of a sudden, Irina found it difficult to breathe.

'Maxim and a girl called Lisa.'

Irina's heart thudded painfully inside her chest but she forced her fists to unclench, forced her face into a carefree smile. 'I have nothing to worry about. I trust Maxim.'

'I wouldn't trust any man, especially around someone like Lisa. Selfish and lazy and too pretty for her own good, with her red hair and green eyes. And that's all men care about. A pretty face.'

Fighting tears, Irina excused herself, and on shaking legs carried Sonya to the bedroom. As she rocked her little girl to sleep, all she could think of was the young and attractive rival Yulya had described. Ever since Maxim had left for the partisan battalion, she worried about so many things. She worried about the enemy bullets, the evil tongues and the ill-wishing neighbours who would be more than happy to betray a partisan to the Nazis for a piece of bread. She worried about the hunger and the cold. But it had never occurred to her to worry about another woman.

As she lay awake in the dark, she thought of her husband and a beautiful red-haired girl, alone in the woods together. In her overactive imagination, she saw arms that weren't hers around her husband's back, lips that weren't hers on his lips, a body that wasn't hers intertwined with his. She saw her husband kissing another woman, whispering sweet nothings in her ear in that hoarse voice Irina loved so much. She saw his beloved eyes admiring another woman and felt physically ill.

This is wrong, she told herself. She shouldn't doubt Maxim because of a careless word from someone who loved to gossip and stir up trouble. Why should she believe Yulya, who knew nothing about their relationship, over her husband, the man she shared her life with? Irina chased the horrible images away, trying to think of the look on his face as he held her in his arms, his voice as he told her he loved her and only her. She tried to fill her head with images of the two of them together, of the day they met, the day they got married, so young and in love, of the day Sonya was born, turning Irina's life upside down and filling her heart with happiness. Why would Maxim throw it all away?

But the happy images faded quickly and the annoying little voice inside her head remained: if her own father, whom she had loved and trusted unconditionally, could leave them for someone else, turning his back on their little family for a pretty stranger, why not Maxim, too?

Irina's father had been the love of her life. Not that she saw much of him when she was a child. He was a talented young architect who designed buildings all over the Soviet Union. On the rare occasions when he did come home, he filled their tiny apartment with joy and laughter. Every day around him was a celebration and his bags were always filled with presents. Dolls in bright dresses from Moldova, sweets from Kazakhstan, oil paints and brushes from Moscow.

When she had found him downstairs one day with his bags packed, she didn't think twice about it. 'Daddy, what will you bring me this time?' He hadn't replied but hugged her close, telling her to look after her mother. A week later she had found out he had met another woman and had no intention of ever coming back. Irina didn't understand. Did the love they shared mean nothing to him? Did his daughter mean nothing to him? She'd longed to ask her father these questions for most of her adult life but never got a chance because she had never seen him again. He died from a heart attack a year later.

The young Irina didn't know how to live without her father. She didn't know how to fill the void in her heart where her father had once been. And neither did her mother. This void consumed her, until she withdrew inside herself, her vacant eyes staring through Irina and not seeing past her grief. Within a few weeks her mother seemed to disappear altogether. And then two months later her body was found in a nearby lake and Irina's world collapsed.

She had lived with heartbreak since she was twelve years old, until she met Maxim and he mended her heart. But after she fell in love with him, her insecurities got worse, not better. Day after day, night after sleepless night they whispered to her in grating, unpleasant voices until she could no longer bear it. Did he really love her? Why did he choose her over so many other, more attractive women? And the scariest thought of all: what if he met someone else, someone younger, prettier and smarter? Little by little, the voices in her head threatened to rob her of her happiness with the man she loved. But gradually, as she saw his eyes light up with love for her, she believed in herself a little bit more. She believed in him.

And now here was Yulya giving Irina's insecurities a name: Lisa.

The next day, a Sunday, Irina was home alone with her daughter. The two of them sat side by side by the window, hoping to catch a few rays of late winter sunshine. Downstairs, the German soldiers were going through their exercises. In February 1943, they were no longer the young blond warriors in shiny green helmets who had marched through the streets of Kiev at the start of the occupation. Most of them were bald and middle-aged, some of them wounded. It seemed Hitler was fast running out of men to throw in the meat grinder of the Eastern Front.

Shouting and the sound of marching feet scared Sonya, who clung to her mother and whined softly. Irina covered Sonya's face with kisses, tickling her and throwing her up in the air until tears turned into giggles. Giggling herself, Irina wrapped her little one in her arms. She tried to put Yulya's revelations of the previous day out of her mind. Sunday mornings were her precious time with her daughter. She couldn't let anything ruin it, not the marching feet outside, nor the old woman with her insinuations.

A knock outside sent a familiar shiver of dread through Irina. When she opened the door, she was overjoyed to see her friend Tamara outside.

They huddled around the kitchen table. Sonya was balanced on her favourite Auntie Tata's lap, while Irina filled her friend in on the details of Yulya's visit and what she had said about her husband.

'Maxim? Never!' exclaimed Tamara. 'That's one thing you don't have to worry about. That man adores you.'

'You think?'

'I know! The two of you are my dream couple. I always wanted to find someone who would love me as much as Maxim loves you.'

'And now you have. How is Dmitry?'

'He still wants to marry me, after three months together.' Tamara said it as if she couldn't believe it. 'But honestly, you and Maxim have a fairy-tale romance. Why would he throw that away?'

'He's a man, isn't he? Besides, we hardly see each other.'

'You know what they say. Absence makes the heart grow fonder.'

'What if he wants more? What if he likes this girl? What do I do? Do I confront him?'

Tamara placed her hand on Irina's and shook her head. 'There is nothing to confront him about. He's not doing anything wrong.'

'Do I say anything?'

'Of course not. You don't want him to think you are doubting him.'

But I am *doubting him,* Irina wanted to say. *I am doubting my loving, wonderful husband who has never given me a reason not to trust him.* She felt like the most despicable human being for allowing her past to affect her present. But she couldn't help it. 'If I don't ask, I won't know the truth. And even if I ask, he might not tell me.'

'You already know the truth. You know what the two of you have together.'

'Yulya said this Lisa was too pretty for her own good. She said no man could resist someone like her.'

'Why are you listening to this stupid Yulya? What does she know? Maxim loves you. He married you. He wants to spend his life with you. You have nothing to worry about.'

More than anything Irina wanted to believe her friend. If only she could ignore the little voice inside her head whispering that she wasn't good enough.

March 1943

Chapter 11

Lisa lived every day in fear. Sometimes rumours reached her about a partisan from another battalion who had been caught and tortured by the Nazis. She would grit her teeth and turn away, pretending she hadn't heard, because she didn't want to know. Sometimes she wished she could stay inside her dugout all day to avoid the horror stories, but it was impossible. Masha tended to the wounded and told Lisa all about it. Anna went to Kiev, witnessing unspeakable atrocities by the Nazis, and told Lisa all about it. At breakfast, lunch and dinner, the conversation often centred around the deaths, the tortures and the executions, as if the only way the partisans could deal with their fears was by talking through them.

And all Lisa could think of was: who was next? She was afraid for her family, whom she thought about all the time, despite everything. For her older brother, standing up to the Nazis on the Eastern Front. For her younger brother, too cheeky and honest for his own good, and her sister, who was quick to give her heart away and never listened to reason. For her father, the strongest man she knew, lost and broken by war. For Maxim, who left the settlement every morning to fight the greatest evil the world had ever known, fight at any price, even that of his life, and for

Masha, who was her closest friend, even though they had met only weeks ago and didn't have much in common. But most of all, she was afraid for herself.

Since Lisa had joined the battalion in January, the partisans had completed over a hundred missions. While she cooked and cleaned and sewed, complaining bitterly about the cold and the hunger, they left the woods to detonate, mine and destroy. Three villages had been freed from the Nazi clutches. Hundreds of German soldiers had been killed, and a dozen high-ranking officers. But the partisans had suffered losses too. In the first week of March alone, when the sun shone spring-bright and the snow thawed into small rivulets that ran cheerfully among the trees, three men were shot by the Nazis as they tried to defend the city hall in the village of Belichi. Two more died from their wounds at the hospital under Masha's caring supervision, following an ambuscade gone wrong. These were the men Lisa had seen in the settlement almost every day but had never spoken to, the men who had eaten her food and waved a friendly greeting as she collected their empty plates.

The sense of loss she experienced at the deaths of these almost-strangers took even her by surprise. She felt numb and hollow inside, as if she had lost a friend or a loved one. She never asked Masha how she was coping. She didn't need to. Her friend's grim face and red-rimmed eyes with dark circles underneath spoke for themselves.

Now that Anton had left the hospital and resumed his daily partisan activities, going on life-threatening missions with a crutch and a bandage, Anna returned to the dugout and spent her evenings sewing and chatting with the girls under the light of a kerosene lamp. Tonight, however, she looked like she would rather be anywhere else but here because Masha and Lisa were quizzing her about Anton and teasing her mercilessly.

'I've known him my whole life. As long as I remember, he was always there. We were childhood sweethearts,' she finally admitted.

'That's what I call true love,' said Masha, patiently stitching a patch over someone's sleeve.

'Anton says when the war is over we'll get married. We'll get a little house in Buki, which is where we grew up, and have children of our own. Doesn't it sound wonderful? To live somewhere quietly and not have to worry about the enemy bullets or the hunger or anything. I feel a little dizzy every time I think about him. Like I drank a bottle of wine on an empty stomach or something.'

'Have you ever drunk a bottle of wine on an empty stomach?' asked Lisa. When she thought about Maxim, she felt a little bit like that too. She was dying to share her feelings for him with her two friends. She felt she might burst if she had to keep them to herself a moment longer. But she knew the timing wasn't right. Sooner or later, everyone would know. She was certain of it.

'I've never even tried wine.'

'I've never met anyone who's never tried wine. Even my brother Nikolai had some on New Year's and he's a baby.'

'Before the war I was so protected. Mama and Papa never let me go anywhere by myself. All I did was study and practise my piano for hours. All I knew was musical scores and books.'

'What about Anton? Did your parents know about him?'

'They found out eventually but didn't approve. They thought we were too young to be seeing each other. I had to sneak away in the evenings to meet him. One day Papa caught me. I would have felt better if he shouted and punished me but he just looked at me with disappointment. I've never been so ashamed in my life.'

'Did you stop seeing Anton?'

'Of course not. But there were no more lies after that. I would tell Mama and Papa I was going to see him. And they would wait for me in the dining room. No matter what time I returned, they would still be up.' She sighed sadly and looked down into her hands. 'At first, we were waiting till we were older to get married. Now we are waiting for the war to end. Don't you feel like your whole life is on hold?'

'This is our life too. And we must make the most of it. We must find a way to live,' said Masha.

'How do we do that? I feel so miserable all the time. Cold, hungry, afraid. What kind of life is this?' demanded Lisa.

'It's not great. But it might be all we have.'

*

When it was time for their next shooting lesson, Lisa waited for Maxim eagerly, like a schoolgirl on her first date. Her red hair was blowing in the wind, free and wild with no kerchief or an ugly hat to hide it from the world. This morning she had begged Anna to let her borrow her jacket and it hugged her figure fetchingly. The snow was finally melting, running in cheerful rivulets among the trees. The mild weather and the promise of summer in the air filled Lisa's heart with joy. Despite the dirt in her hair that she could never fully get rid of, and the ache of hunger in her stomach, despite the Nazis only a few kilometres away and the rumours of destruction and death that filled her with horror, on this beautiful day Lisa felt reborn, like the forest and the trees and the flowers were reborn in the first flush of spring.

Her eyes were searching for Maxim but it wasn't him she saw walking towards their meeting place outside the cafeteria. It was Alex. Lisa's stomach dropped in disappointment. There had been no more lessons since Maxim had given her the rifle. He was hardly ever at the battalion, and what little time he had he spent at the headquarters, buried in maps with Azamat. This once, she was hoping to be alone with him again.

Alex waved to Lisa and smiled. She didn't smile back. He said hello. She mumbled something in return.

'You look nice today. Going somewhere special? A cinema perhaps, or for an ice cream with friends?' Alex laughed at his own joke while Lisa glared at him. 'How about after this lesson is over, you and I take a walk in the woods, just the two of us?

It's a lovely day for it. The first day we've had this year that isn't brutally cold. Let's make the most of it.' He looked Lisa up and down, unashamedly appraising her slim body. It was as if he was seeing her for the first time.

Aghast, Lisa opened her mouth to say something sharp in reply. Fortunately, at that moment Maxim stepped out of the headquarters and she forgot all about Alex. She wondered if Maxim noticed her the way Alex did. Did his eyes linger on her? He was cheerful and friendly and shook both their hands. As they set off towards the clearing, Alex walked two steps ahead and seemed to pay no attention to the conversation, which was just as well because Lisa was flirting shamelessly with Maxim. She wanted to believe he was flirting back because his smile was wide on his face when he spoke to her and his eyes sparkled. But he had the same smile and the same sparkle for Masha and for Alex and for Sergei too. If only she could ask him how he felt about her.

'Maxim, such a good Russian name. And yet, you don't look Russian at all.'

'My father is Mongolian.'

'Like Genghis Khan?'

He chuckled and nodded, visibly amused. 'Like Genghis Khan.'

'That explains it. In your veins runs the blood of one of the greatest warriors who has ever lived. No wonder the Nazis are afraid of you. That's what I'm going to call you from now on. The great Mongolian warrior.'

'You, on the other hand, couldn't look more Russian. Who do you get your red hair from?'

'My grandmother.' She blushed and brushed a strand of hair away from her eyes.

'Your green eyes?'

'My grandmother too. When she was young, she was quite the beauty. My grandfather had to fight every man in town for her hand.'

'You must miss your family so much. What do your parents do?'

'Papa was a captain in the militia. He was arrested and taken to a prison camp by the Nazis. We don't know where he is now or if he's all right.'

'I'm sorry to hear that.'

She shrugged, terrified she would cry in front of him. Was it because she missed her father or because it had been a while since she had talked about her family? 'Mama is a piano teacher.'

'They must be beside themselves with worry, knowing you are with the partisans.'

'They have no idea I'm here. I haven't spoken to them in months.'

'What happened?'

Even though it was the last thing she wanted to talk about, she had to say something because Maxim was watching her with a genuine interest that warmed her heart. 'I did something terrible and they will never forgive me.'

'Terrible? Why do I find it so hard to believe?'

'My sister and I had a disagreement and my whole family turned against me. They never tried to understand, never even listened to my side of the story . . .'

Suddenly she really was crying, and Maxim had his hand around her shoulders, comforting her. 'They are your family,' he said. 'And there's nothing more important in the world than family. Whatever differences you've had in the past don't matter anymore. Especially now that it's war.' She leant into him and inhaled, trying to catch his scent. More than anything she wanted to lift her face and kiss him. 'My family means the world to me,' he continued. 'My parents, my wi—'

'Hey, boss,' said Alex, turning around. 'Do you have any tobacco? I'm all out.'

'Sorry. I don't smoke.' Maxim moved away from Lisa.

'Who should I ask? I'm desperate.'

'For all the gold in the world you won't find tobacco at the battalion right now. The men are ready to sell their souls for a few grams.'

'That's too bad. I can fight on an empty stomach but I can't live without my smokes. I'd rather chop my hands off.'

'Can't hold that rifle without your hands, soldier,' said Maxim, winking at Lisa, who was still wiping her tears but whose heart was soaring with hope. She didn't care if Alex knew how she felt about Maxim. She didn't care if the whole battalion knew. She wanted to climb to the top of the highest pine tree and shout his name for the whole world to hear.

*

It was late and the work in the kitchen was done. Sore and exhausted, her back and neck aching, her eyes red from the smoke, Lisa fell into a chair, relishing a rare moment of stillness. Since she had joined the partisan battalion, she hardly ever got a chance to be still. She was always moving, her feet trudging, her hands scrubbing, peeling, cutting or stirring. No wonder she always felt faint and out of breath.

The cafeteria filled with people, mostly men, but she could see a few women here and there, laughing and chatting. The partisans were carefree like only those who risked their lives and made it safely through the day could be carefree. Lisa tried to look relaxed, waving to Masha, motioning for her to join her, pouring some of her tea into another cup and offering it to her, while her gaze searched the room for Maxim. He wasn't difficult to spot. In a room full of people, he was a head taller than everybody else, his shoulders broader, his hair darker, his laughter louder. The others were nothing but greyscale figures on an old and faded black-and-white photograph, while he was vivid and bright. Lisa couldn't possibly continue staring at him or Masha was bound to notice. Reluctantly she turned away but every now and then she glanced in his direction and her heart melted at the sight of him.

As his friends nudged him on, Maxim picked up a guitar and everyone fell silent. Now all eyes were on him and Lisa didn't have to hide anymore; she could watch him openly. He touched the chords gently, lovingly, and when he sang, his voice was deep and sensual, unlike any Lisa had ever heard before.

I loved you, and I probably still do,
And for a while the feeling may remain . . .
But let my love no longer trouble you,
I do not wish to cause you any pain.

As he sang the popular war tune, Lisa felt tears fill her eyes. It was as if Maxim serenaded her and her alone. She no longer felt like an outsider. She knew that she was right where she needed to be, that for better or worse this partisan battalion was where she belonged. Her fingers found the rifle she kept under the table. She touched the cold metal of the barrel and smiled. His present was like a special link between them, a secret the two of them shared.

'What are you grinning about?' asked Masha, her eyes focusing on her friend.

'I'm not grinning,' replied Lisa, still smiling but making a conscious effort to avoid glancing in Maxim's direction.

'You are lit up like a kerosene lamp. What is going on?'

'Nothing. Just remembered something.'

'What? Come on, tell me. I could do with some cheering up.'

Lisa was thinking of a suitable lie to tell her friend when the woods shook with an explosion. Startled, she dropped her cup and it rolled under the table, the tea spilling over her trousers. 'What was that?' she cried. Before anyone had a chance to reply, another explosion burst overhead.

'It's only the Germans,' said Yulya, who was sitting next to Danilo at a nearby table. 'Don't worry, it's nowhere near us. It just sounds close because it's so loud.'

'*Only* the Germans?' repeated Lisa, dumbstruck and shaking. It wasn't like she hadn't been through bombings before. Kiev had been bombed for three months before the Nazis entered the city. With the amount of shelling it had endured, it was surprising any of it was left standing. But here in the woods, she thought she was safe, from bombings at least. The whole point of being here was that the Germans didn't know where they were. The explosion felt intrusive, threatening the order of things.

'We are at war – or did you forget?' said Yulya.

How Lisa wished she could forget. And in these woods, hidden from the world, sometimes it was an easy thing to do. Except, wounded partisans kept coming back from their missions and Masha was run off her feet in her makeshift hospital. Except, the hunger never went away. Except, Maxim left every morning and Lisa watched the road all day long, praying he would come back safely. 'Why are they firing? Who are they firing at?'

'They are firing at the woods because they know that's where we are hiding. They don't know our exact location or they would be here in an instant. And you know what they say. When a dog can't bite, it barks.'

'That's one dog whose bite is as bad as its bark.'

'Only if they find us.'

Lisa wondered whether it was a question of when, not if. How deep were the woods around Kiev? Deep enough to hide a large group of people indefinitely? Even a broken clock was right twice a day. What if the Nazis stumbled upon them?

The other partisans didn't seem concerned. When the shelling quietened down, the laughter and the cheerful voices resumed. Maxim strummed his guitar. Someone else started singing, as if what had happened was nothing out of the ordinary. And perhaps for them it wasn't. Perhaps if they worried about every bullet and every bomb, they would never leave their dugouts, and so they had become desensitised to it. They must have been cut from a different cloth because, even if Lisa lived in the woods for a hundred years, even if she spent a thousand years under the German fire, she would still be afraid.

She wished the man who was singing would stop. One, he was extremely bad at it. Her ears were hurting as much from his singing as from the sudden explosions. And two, she wanted to hear Maxim's breath-taking voice again. But when the man fell quiet, she heard shouting outside. Two gunshots followed.

Grabbing their weapons, everyone rushed towards the exit. When Lisa stepped out, she saw a group of partisans led by Azamat, surrounding a man with his hands bound behind his back. He was short and square, dressed in a German uniform, with the face of a pig – pink, round, with tiny eyes and a large snout of a nose. Alex and Sergei were holding him up by his shoulders. Danilo was waving a torch over the man's head, as if determined to set him on fire.

'If you try to run one more time, I will shoot,' said Azamat. 'And this time I will be aiming for you, not the trees behind you.'

The man cowered away from him. If two pairs of hands weren't gripping him tight, he would have slumped to the ground.

'German?' demanded Maxim, approaching the little group.

'Ukrainian,' replied Azamat.

'A policeman!' exclaimed Danilo. 'Tie him to a tree and kill him.'

'No, please. I'll do anything. I know things. I know the Nazis' movements. Please, comrades. I'll tell you everything,' pleaded the man, abruptly springing to life.

'We are no comrades to you,' barked Danilo.

Azamat gave the traitor a push and he fell into a puddle of melting snow, looking up at them with his pig eyes and pressing his bound hands to his chest. 'Comrades, I swear, I can be useful to you. I will wash away the shame of what I've done by helping you fight the enemy. Please, allow me to join you.'

'Nothing will wash away the shame of what you've done,' someone shouted.

'Please, believe me! I'm prepared to give my life for the motherland.'

'You don't know the meaning of the word. First chance you get, you'll be running off to the Germans.' Maxim spat on the ground in anger and turned away from the traitor, as if merely looking at his face offended him.

'I swear I won't. Please, can I have some water? I'm dying of thirst. And something to eat.'

'If we had anything to eat, we wouldn't waste it on a traitor like you,' said Danilo.

'I might have joined the Nazis but I've never killed anyone. I'm not a killer. Please, don't hurt me. I've never harmed a living soul.'

'You were captured with a machine gun in your hands, ready to fire at us. And you would, given half a chance.' Turning to Alex and Sergei, Danilo added, 'I told you what to do. Tie him to a tree and shoot him.'

The two men steered the traitor towards a tree, looking as pale and shaken as he did. The prisoner resisted, shouting, 'I've worked for the Germans for a long time. They trust me. I can help you.'

Azamat hesitated. 'If what he says is true,' he said to Danilo softly, 'he could be very useful to us.'

'And you trust him?'

'He would do anything to save his skin.'

They brought the man into the cafeteria and gave him a raw potato. Gratefully, he grasped it, shoving it into his mouth like he hadn't seen food in months. He didn't stop talking the whole time. 'My name is Matvei. You must think I'm a terrible person for turning my back on my people but I'm not. Weak, yes, a coward, yes. I was afraid, you see. You don't joke around with the Germans. I'm young, I have a family. I don't want to die.'

'Why didn't you join the partisans?' asked Maxim.

'I'm not cut out for combat. I'm not brave.'

Pointing at Lisa and Masha, Azamat said, 'Look, traitor, our girls are eager to go out and fight. They learn how to shoot, they are not afraid to join us. And you . . .' He shook his head in disgust.

'I will help you. You'll see. Please, don't kill me,' repeated the man.

As Lisa lay awake that night, all she could think of was the man's face with his tiny eyes and square mouth pleading for his life. Matvei was a Soviet man, just like everyone at the battalion. And yet, he was not like the rest of them. Shivering in her underground bed, waiting for much-needed sleep to come, Lisa had never felt so helpless. What was the point in what the partisans were doing if the people they were trying to protect, people like Matvei, chose to turn their backs on their country and betray them?

Chapter 12

At work that morning, as she listened to a husband whose wife was killed in front of him for selling some eggs outside their front door, Irina felt a sharp pain in her abdomen, as if a dozen needles were piercing her insides. On shaking legs, she staggered to the bathroom. When she got there, she leant on the wall and tried to catch her breath. Looking down at her white skirt, she saw blood. The loud German voices outside and the distant humming of aeroplanes subsided. All she could hear was the ringing in her ears. Was she losing the baby? 'Please God, no,' she whispered, sliding to the floor.

*

She didn't remember how she had left work or made it to Tamara's house but there she was, in her friend's bed, curled up under a threadbare blanket, howling in agony, still bleeding. Tamara nursed her like a child, rocked her head in her lap, spoon-fed her soup and wiped her tears away. At first Irina couldn't speak, mutely staring into space with vacant eyes. Tired and spent, she felt numb inside, and only her heart was a pulsing ball of pain inside her chest.

Tamara sent Dmitry to Zina to tell her what had happened and to ask her to look after Sonya. Hours later, when Irina could speak again, in a hoarse, alien voice she said, 'I wanted this baby so much. It was to be our salvation. A sign from God that He hasn't forgotten us.' She thought she had run out of tears but they came to her now and she cried silently.

'Sh-sh-sh,' whispered Tamara, stroking her hair.

'It's all my fault.'

'Don't be silly. How is it your fault? These things happen.'

'I was supposed to keep this baby safe. And I didn't. How will I tell Maxim?'

'Maxim would never blame you for something like this. Besides, how do you know you've lost the baby? Some bleeding is normal during pregnancy. Maybe you should see a doctor.'

'Some bleeding, yes. But not like this.' How could she explain to her well-meaning friend that she felt hollow inside? She knew in her heart that her baby was gone. 'I feel like there's darkness all around me. Like there's no point in anything anymore.'

'Don't say that. You still have Sonya and she needs you.'

The thought of her daughter filled her with warmth and the iceberg of grief inside her melted a little. She had to see her, to hold her in her arms, so she could feel like she was still alive, like there was hope. But the thought of facing her mother-in-law made her groan out loud. 'I can't go back there. Not after what Zina told me. A few weeks ago she said . . .' Irina struggled to get the words out. 'She said I should get rid of the pregnancy. That it's not the right time to have a baby.' Her teeth chattered.

Tamara widened her eyes and stared at Irina. 'What kind of person says something like that?'

'She wished my baby harm and now . . .' Irina couldn't continue. 'I don't think I could ever look at her again.'

Tamara's arms tightened around Irina. 'You are not going back there. I'm going to get Sonya and the two of you can stay here for as long as you want.'

Irina had no energy to argue or even to think of Maxim's reaction when he came home one day and found his wife and daughter gone. She wished she could close her eyes and sleep for a thousand years. She longed for forgetfulness, for oblivion. For the first time in her life, she understood her mother's actions. Sometimes, simply to go on required more strength than one possessed. What a relief it would be, what a perfect way out, if she could just drift away and not feel and not think.

But she couldn't do it to her daughter. She knew only too well how Sonya would feel if her mother deserted her.

*

Irina's life was divided into a series of *before* and *after*. She had been so happy once – *before* she lost her mother, *before* the Nazis arrived in Kiev, scorching the very earth they walked upon, *before* Maxim left for the partisan battalion, *before* she lost her baby. She had been happy and didn't even know it. How ironic it was that she only realised how lucky she had been when something terrible happened.

It took everything she had not to stumble under the enormous weight of her loss as she walked to work with Sonya in her arms and sat at her desk all day with her little one balanced in her lap, talking to people, consoling and trying to help. It was easy to lose herself in someone else's heartache. And there were so many heartaches. She saw people who had lost their loved ones, people who had no means of supporting themselves, who were desperate for a piece of bread to give to their children and those who'd had those children taken away from them. Everyone had a story to tell and each filled Irina with dread, making her own ghosts retreat a little in the face of so much suffering.

But the ghosts never retreated far enough. For a week, at her friend's house, Irina would wake up and for a few blissful moments not know where she was or what had happened. And

147

then, sitting up in her makeshift bed on Tamara's living-room floor, she would remember, and her shoulders would cave and her eyes would dim. Moving slowly as if in a fog, she would kiss her daughter good morning, give her some oats and a little bit of water, read and play with her, the whole time waiting for the oppressive weight to lift, so that she could breathe easier.

Sometimes Dmitry came to visit in the evenings. He didn't ask any questions, not even why she wasn't staying with Zina and Kirill anymore. Irina suspected that Tamara had told him. Could she blame her? If the situation was reversed, she would have told Maxim everything. Irina was grateful to Dmitry for not prying and not looking at her with pity. All he and Tamara talked about was their upcoming wedding. They seemed incapable of keeping their hands off each other. When they sat in the kitchen next to Irina, their cups of tea going cold in front of them, their hands, knees and shoulders touched. But even the sight of the happy couple didn't penetrate the wall of grief Irina had built around herself. Only Sonya's smile could do that. The little girl, who seemed to have grown up so much in the last few weeks, showered her mother with kisses and put her chubby arms around her, as if she could sense her need for affection.

Every day on the way home, Irina stopped at the little church where she had seen Maxim last. She sat in the spot where she had sat then, closed her eyes and prayed. Frantically she prayed for a ray of light in the sea of darkness. She imagined Maxim's arms around her and felt a little less alone.

Day and night, she could hear the distant drone of German aircraft, hovering over Kiev without a reprieve. How she hated them! What were they doing in her city, above Tamara's house, watching over them as they lived and grieved and tried to forge a normal life? There was no escape from the ominous shapes moving through the bright Ukrainian sky, just like there was no escape from the dark thoughts whirring inside her head.

One evening, when Dmitry and Tamara had gone out and

it was just Irina and Sonya at home, painting on some old newspapers, there was a knock on the door. Irina's hair was messy. Her hands had red oil paint on them, like blood streaks from her fingers to her elbows. Out of breath, thinking it was her friend coming home early, she opened the door to a grim Maxim standing outside. For a moment when she saw him – tall, unsmiling and imposing – she forgot how to breathe.

'What are you doing here?' he asked before he even stepped over the threshold. 'I came home and you weren't there. Mama told me they hadn't seen you in a week. They are beside themselves. I didn't know what to think.' She didn't trust her voice, so she motioned him in. 'What happened?' he asked quietly, stepping inside.

She couldn't take the intensity of his eyes on her. Looking away, she started crying. He dropped his bag on the floor and pulled her to him, while Sonya bounced through the bedroom door, shouting 'Daddy'.

Maxim let go of Irina and picked up Sonya, throwing her up in the air, covering her face with kisses. Then he turned back to Irina. 'Ira, you are scaring me. Is everything all right with the baby?'

'I'm so sorry,' she whispered, unable to say anymore.

His face darkened, as if a light had gone out. 'Please, don't cry,' he said, holding her close, tears in his eyes. 'We'll have another. We'll have a dozen. As many as you want. You'll see.'

It should have been comforting but wasn't. Because Irina would never have *this* baby. She didn't know how to explain it to him, so she didn't say anything, nor could she meet his gaze. He led her to the kitchen and made a strong cup of tea for her. In his rucksack he found a radish and some bread. She didn't touch the food but gave a large chunk of bread to Sonya.

A few moments passed. 'When did it happen?' he asked.

'A week ago, at work.' She shuddered at the memory of herself on the floor of that bathroom, feeling life seeping out of her.

'You poor girl. I'm sorry I wasn't with you. I feel so bad. You were here all by yourself. Why didn't you stay home, so Mama could look after you?'

A tremor ran through Irina at the thought of Zina. 'I just needed some time to myself. To think, to be alone.'

'Why would you want to be alone at a time like this?' He took her hand in his and brought it to his lips, kissing her fingertips. 'My parents are frantic with worry. They don't understand why you just left. Mama is especially upset. I told her you didn't mean to offend her.'

'Offend her? I'm sure she understands perfectly well why I had to go,' exclaimed Irina, a wave of sudden anger making her hands tremble. Zina, whose every word was hurtful and unkind, was offended because Irina no longer wanted to be the target for her cruelty. She took a deep breath. Who cared what Zina thought anyway? It didn't matter. Nothing mattered anymore.

Visibly taken aback by the tone of her voice, Maxim let go of her hand. 'What do you mean?'

'She's cruel to me all the time. Nothing I do is ever good enough for her. She told me I should get rid of the baby. And now he's gone.'

'You misunderstood. The last thing Mama would have wanted was to hurt you. She was so happy when we told her about the baby.'

'You see her through rose-coloured glasses, always have. As far as you are concerned, she can do no wrong. She's made my life hell since the day we met. You have to be blind not to see it. Well, I can't do it anymore. I can't stay in the same house as her.'

'I don't know what's gotten into you. Mama's done nothing but support you. She insisted you live with us . . .'

'So that she has someone to pick on.'

He turned away from her, lowered his voice. 'No, Ira. So that you have a place to stay. You've lost both your parents. Why can't you get along with mine? I know you are hurting. What happened is terrible. But don't take it out on us.'

'Us! Exactly! It's always you and her against me. You always take her side.' Irina was shouting. She was horrified at herself, at the overwhelming anger towards the man she loved more than life itself. But she couldn't help herself. All the pain and heartache of the past week was bursting out and she was powerless to stop it.

'*Against* you? No one is against you. Mama took you in. Gave you a roof over your head. Treated you like a daughter. And this is how you repay her.'

'I can't believe you are raising your voice. When I need your love and support the most, when I feel like my heart is breaking, you are turning away from me because of her.'

'Not because of her. Because of you. Listen to yourself. So much poison inside you. Where did it all come from?'

She couldn't believe they were fighting. In all their years together, she had never spoken to Maxim like this. 'Why don't you ask your mother? You can't even imagine what she puts me through every day. And you left me alone with her.' She covered her face with her hands and sobbed.

'Please, don't cry. You'll scare Sonya. I've never seen you like this before. I don't understand what's happening. My parents love you. I love you. Why are you so upset?'

'Yes, you love me and God knows how many others.'

He looked hurt and confused. Her heart aching, she looked away from him. 'You're a man. And men are not to be trusted around a pretty face.'

'I live in the woods with the partisans. What pretty faces are you talking about?'

She opened her mouth and almost said Lisa's name out loud but the disappointment on his face stopped her. He looked like he couldn't believe she would say such a thing at a time like this. She didn't want to hurt him with her suspicions. They were both already hurt enough.

'Get your things together; we are going home,' he said.

She wanted to tell him that she didn't want to go back, but

knew there was little point. He wasn't going to stay here with her, and she didn't want to waste any more of the time they had together arguing.

While she wrote a short note for Tamara; Maxim threw some clothes in a small bag. In silence they walked outside. Irina was carrying Sonya, who had fallen asleep in her arms. Maxim walked so fast down the road, she couldn't keep up. At first she tried to match his speed, then she slowed down and stopped. When he noticed that she had fallen behind, he came back for her but still didn't say a word.

A quiet and dark house greeted them. Maxim's parents were asleep, thank God. She wouldn't have to deal with Zina until tomorrow.

After settling Sonya, Irina got straight into the bed she shared with Maxim and her daughter, and waited for him to join her. When he finally came in an hour later, she held her breath, waiting for his arms around her. Whenever they'd had an argument in the past, they made sure they never went to bed upset. Maxim was not the one to hold a grudge forever or punish her with his silence. And she couldn't stay angry with him for long.

He got into bed quietly and turned to the wall. Irina shivered, unable to sleep, unable to bear the space between them. She wondered if he felt sad and lonely like her, if he was waiting for her to touch him and tell him how sorry she was. In the dark she felt for him in their bed and placed her hand on his arm. He didn't stir. Was he pretending to sleep, so he wouldn't have to talk to her?

They had mere moments together, snatches of time the war allotted them. Was this how they chose to spend them, silent and turned away from each other? Tomorrow he would leave and it would be weeks before she saw him again. What if today was all they had? What if he walked out the door and never came back and the last words he'd heard from her had been angry and unkind?

It was all Zina's fault they were fighting. Everything bad in

Irina's life happened because of Zina. Black hatred spread like mould inside her until there was no other feeling left, until she could think of nothing else. Again and again she went over Zina's words in her head. The words that hurt like daggers, that stayed with her and continued to cut long after they had been uttered. Irina had a collection of the most hurtful incidents put away safely in her mind to be recalled at will, anytime she wanted to feel sorry for herself.

Sometimes she heard voices in her head that sounded just like Zina. *You are useless. Maxim deserves better. No wonder your father left you.* Irina wished she could ignore the voices, but they knew just what to say and how to say it to make her believe. Every time she heard them, she hated Zina a little bit more, for making her doubt herself, for poisoning her with self-loathing.

She didn't want life to be ruled by her demons. They robbed her of happiness with her husband, of the joy of motherhood, sucked all the light out until there was nothing but darkness. She didn't want to hate anyone but she especially didn't want to hate Zina, her husband's mother, her daughter's grandmother. Surely even Zina had redeeming qualities? Irina tried to look at Zina the way a stranger might look at her – objectively. What would someone who didn't know her see when they met her for the first time? She was a good mother – loving, loyal, indulgent, unselfish and a little obsessive. Maybe that was the problem. Zina hated sharing her son with another woman. She couldn't accept the fact Maxim had a family of his own, that his allegiance was to someone else, that she no longer came first.

Still, what happened was between Zina and Irina. She shouldn't have said anything to Maxim. He didn't deserve it. Zina was his mother. Nothing could change that. What if the situation was reversed? What if Irina's mother was still alive and Maxim said something bad about her? Irina would be devastated. She'd feel torn between her mother and the man she loved. Is that how he felt now? Like he had to make a choice?

In the yellow light of the moon outside, she could see him clearly, lying on his back, his eyes closed. She didn't care if he recoiled from her. She needed him. And she knew he needed her. Careful not to wake their daughter, she crawled over to him and cradled his head, kissing his forehead. By the way his breathing changed, she knew he was awake. 'I'm sorry,' she whispered. 'I'm so sorry.'

His arms went around her and he pulled her to him. 'I'm sorry too. Please, don't cry.' His lips were on her wet cheeks, on her trembling lips.

'I didn't mean anything I said.'

'I know. You are just hurting. We all are. It's all too much for one person to bear.'

'I shouldn't have said all those terrible things.'

'It's forgotten. I'm always here for you; you know that, don't you? Even when I'm far away. I never stop thinking of you and Sonya.'

'And I never stop thinking of you. I know Zina is your mother and you love her. I don't want you to have to choose between us. I'll do my best to get along with her. I'll try harder, I promise.'

'Mama can be harsh sometimes but she means well. I'll have a word with her. It will be all right.' He fell quiet for a moment, as if gathering his thoughts. 'About the other thing. I'm not like your father. You are the only one for me. I don't want anyone else. You do know that, don't you?'

'I know. It's so difficult here without you, day after day. And the baby . . .'

'We'll have another baby. As soon as the war is over, we'll have another baby.'

'It feels like it will never be over. Kharkov is in German hands again. I heard at work today.' Kharkov was a beautiful green city five hundred kilometres from Kiev, where Irina's mother had lived when she was younger. Having spent many summers visiting her maternal grandparents in Kharkov, Irina had many wonderful childhood memories of the place and loved it dearly. She rejoiced when the Soviets had retaken it from the Nazis only weeks previously. Unfortunately, they didn't hold it for long.

'It will be over sooner than you think.'

Irina tried to imagine life after the war and couldn't. The vision eluded her like an early-morning dream. 'But what if . . .' She hesitated.

'What?' He prodded her in the dark.

'What if we don't make it?' Every day she saw death on the streets of Kiev. To survive another day, let alone months or years, however long it took for the war to end, would require a miracle.

'We'll make it. God has a plan for those who are good and who believe in Him. He will protect us.'

Irina wanted to tell him that her mother had been a good person too. She had believed in God and loved everyone around her. She had been kind and helped those in need, whether it was a neighbour's child who needed clothing or a stray cat that was cold and starving. If God couldn't give Irina's mother the strength to live after her husband had left, how could he protect Irina and Maxim in war?

*

Before he left the next morning, Maxim embraced Irina and said, 'I don't believe in many things in life. But I believe in you. And that's what I'm fighting for. To give you and Sonya a better future.'

Her heart aching, she watched him walk away from her again. She had never felt more ashamed. Maxim believed in her and yet, she couldn't find it in her heart to believe in him. She'd allowed insensitive words from a gossipy old woman to sow distrust in her heart. *Never again*, she promised to herself. *I know what we have. I will never doubt him again.*

All too soon, the truck arrived. Maxim hugged her goodbye, and then leapt inside. 'Take care of yourself and Sonya.' She heard his voice, muted by the noise of the engine, barely audible, as if he was already slipping away from her. The truck started moving and Irina wanted to shout, to wave her hands, to beg it to stop, so she could have another minute, another moment in time with her husband. But all too soon the truck was gone, disappearing around the corner, while she remained motionless on the spot, looking at the road, at the buildings destroyed by fire, at a group of grim-faced Soviets ambling past.

At home she sat at the kitchen table and didn't move, while Sonya played with building blocks by her feet. The front door opened and footsteps resounded in the corridor but Irina didn't look up. Only when she heard Zina's voice did she turn around.

'Maxim told me what happened. I just wanted to say how sorry I am.'

What a hypocrite, thought Irina. Zina had wanted this baby gone. She had made it clear from the start. And now she'd got her wish. She must be overjoyed.

But Zina didn't look overjoyed. She looked old and weary. There was none of the usual angry gleam in her eyes and no condescending smirk on her face. Irina could swear the woman had been crying. She couldn't remember the last time she had seen her strong and authoritative mother-in-law cry. It frightened her a little.

'I was able to get some sour cream in the village,' said Zina, placing her hand on Irina's. Another anomaly. In all the years Irina had lived here, her mother-in-law had never reached out and touched her. Zina added, 'It's not much but enough for you and Sonya for dinner tonight.'

Suddenly and inexplicably, the formidable foe Irina had come to fear and loathe so much had turned into a frail old woman, harmless and distressed. 'Why don't you have some?' asked Irina. Zina looked like she needed some sour cream herself, so thin had she become in the recent months.

'Absolutely not. I won't hear of it. You are a nursing mother. You need it.'

Irina couldn't take the expression on Zina's face. There was pity and heartbreak and something else, too, something Irina had never seen before. It almost looked like compassion. Quietly, affectionately, Zina said, 'My mother, God rest her soul, had half a dozen miscarriages. It didn't stop her from having five children. Don't despair. You are still so young. Plenty of time to have another baby.'

The knot of tension Irina had carried inside her for the last few weeks melted a little. 'Why don't we share the sour cream?'

'All right,' said Zina, producing the sour cream from a basket and scooping up a tiny bit on a teaspoon, just enough to place on the tip of her tongue. 'That's it. The rest is for you and Sonya. I insist.'

'Thank you,' whispered Irina. This unexpected act of kindness from someone who had never shown her any in the past affected her so much, she was afraid she would break down in front of the older woman. For the first time in her life, she felt something resembling warmth towards Zina. The feeling was so new and unfamiliar, she sat in silence for a moment, contemplating it.

'Earlier this morning I saw you lifting Sonya by her arms and swinging her in the air. You shouldn't do that again. She's still so little, her joints are fragile. You can really hurt her, you know,' said Zina, placing the dirty spoon in the sink.

And just like that, the warmth was gone. But the hope remained that, one day, the two of them could learn to tolerate one another, if only for Maxim's sake.

April 1943

Chapter 13

Shivering under the rain, Lisa waited for the morning assembly to begin. She didn't attend the assembly every day but today she had two reasons to be there. One, she needed a break from the kitchen. Yulya was in a particularly foul mood that morning. Lisa saw Danilo run for his life after a brief encounter with his wife, and decided to follow his lead.

But the second and main reason Lisa stood with the rest of the partisans in the rain was because she was hoping to catch a glimpse of Maxim. He'd been away on an important mission and she hadn't seen him for a few days. She needed to lay her eyes on him to make sure he was safe.

Next to her was Masha, who in the last few weeks had lost so much weight, she no longer reminded Lisa of a round, blonde, rosy-cheeked bun. She was waving her arms and talking a little too loudly for the public place. 'Leo was brought in yesterday, with a gunshot wound. All I can do is change his bandage. I have nothing for the pain, nothing to control the infection. He keeps crying for something to take the pain away. I wish I had some vodka to give him but even that is gone.' She pulled Lisa by the sleeve of her drab jacket. 'Are you listening to me? You seem a million miles away. What are you looking at?' She followed Lisa's gaze. Maxim was walking towards the clearing.

'I'm listening,' said Lisa, regretfully tearing her gaze away from Maxim. 'There isn't any vodka at the battalion. Probably a good thing too. We don't want the partisans getting drunk and making mistakes. Many men here had a problem with alcohol. Not anymore. This place cured them.' Masha was still staring at her without saying a word. 'What? Why are you looking at me like this? Maxim told me.'

'Well, if Maxim told you . . .' replied Masha slowly. Both girls watched Maxim for a moment as he stopped in front of the partisans and exchanged a few words with Azamat. 'He's quite handsome, isn't he?'

'I don't know. I haven't noticed.' The lie slipped off Lisa's tongue effortlessly. She didn't even blush.

'Of course you haven't.'

Through the streaks of rain Masha's face looked mischievous and teasing. Did she suspect something? Did everyone suspect? Were people talking? Lisa didn't have much time to contemplate how she felt about the battalion gossiping about her because the partisans fell quiet. Maxim was speaking. 'The Nazis are bringing more troops into Kiev today. Thanks to Matvei, we know where and we know when.' All eyes turned towards the traitor, who no longer wore the German uniform but a Red Army one, though he was still followed by two partisans at all times. Maxim continued, 'Our goal is to stop them. We have identified ten locations perfect for an ambuscade. We will need all hands on deck for today's mission.'

Lisa felt a panic rise inside her, the likes of which she had never experienced before. This was what she had been preparing for all along when she was learning to shoot in the woods alone with Maxim. The rifle he had given her all those months ago was not a toy or a sentimental token of his affection. It had a purpose. It had meaning. Was she ready? Was she brave enough? Suddenly she wished she had stayed in the kitchen where she belonged, even if it meant enduring Yulya's grumbling.

To Lisa's horror, Masha raised her hand and declared she wanted to join the partisans. 'I'm sure my patients can spare me for a few hours.'

'Are you out of your mind? Why are you volunteering for this?' hissed Lisa, pinching her elbow as hard as she could.

'I feel like I should be doing more. I want to make a difference.'

'You're already doing so much. Without you the wounded would have no chance. You want to go out and shoot the Germans? I thought you said you could never kill anyone. You don't even know how to shoot.'

'Not shoot the Germans, but help our people if they get wounded. By the time they bring them here, it's too late. I should be out there with them, tending to them right away. The nurse before me went into battle with them, carried them from under the enemy fire, bandaged them on the snow.'

'Yes, and where did it get her?'

'I can't sit here, doing nothing.'

'You can hardly call what you do *nothing*. If you go with them, you could get yourself killed.'

'This is not the time to think about myself.'

'What's gotten into you? I don't understand you at all.'

Masha leant closer to Lisa and whispered in her ear, 'No, I don't understand *you*. Why are you even learning how to shoot? Is it just so you can spend time with him?'

Before Lisa had a chance to reply, Masha stormed back towards their dugout.

As Lisa ambled after her friend, she looked at the beauty around her. The grass glistened in the rain, emerald green and abundant. The trees reached for the sky that was a particularly brilliant blue that morning. Would she ever see it again? The raindrops landed on her face, running under her clothes and sending shivers through her skin. Would she ever feel it again? If she picked up her rifle and followed the others to war, would she make it back alive?

*

Because Matvei had indicated ten locations where the Nazi troops would pass, Maxim divided the partisans into ten groups. Normally, Lisa would be overjoyed to find herself in the same group with him. But, as she sleepwalked after the men on unsteady legs, she had to hold her breath and squeeze her fists tight to stop the tears from coming. No one could see her cry. It would be mortifying, she thought as she wiped her damp cheeks with the back of her hand and tried hard not to fall down, her rifle dragging behind her like an unwelcome reminder that death was waiting for them at their destination. It felt like she was walking to her own execution. When she looked up, she saw Maxim marching ahead, grim, silent and determined. He didn't hesitate, didn't lose his footing, as if they were on a pleasure excursion and not a mission that could cost them their lives.

While they were in the forest, the men spoke in soft voices.

'We should be careful. The Germans patrol this area at all times.'

'We need to be fast. In and out, or we're in trouble.'

'Are you sure you know where you're going, boss?' asked Alex. How did he always manage to position himself so close to Lisa? She was getting tired of his never-ending invitations for a walk in the woods together. Why couldn't Maxim ask her instead?

'I don't, but he does.' Maxim nodded at Bear, who was running in front of them and sniffing the ground.

'After all this time in the woods, I still can't find my way around,' said Alex. 'I feel like I'm in the ocean. Everything looks the same and no matter how hard I try I can't see the land. It would be different in the open fields where you can stand up and see everything.'

'Yes, and everyone can see *you*. Including the enemy.'

Soon, Lisa stopped listening to them, the terrible thoughts inside her head becoming louder. She imagined German machine guns pointing at her and Maxim, bullets flying, the trees around them burning. Was it her fear talking? Or was it a premonition? The ground under her feet was wet and slippery. She concentrated on walking, on putting one foot in front of the other carefully and methodically, but the horrifying images didn't go away.

After an hour of walking, Maxim consulted his map and announced they were there. He told everyone to find a partner and climb one of the many tall trees overlooking the road. Lisa was glad she was close to him instead of at the tail of the procession. She pushed Alex out of the way and said to Maxim, 'Can you be my partner? It's my first time. I feel a little nervous. It would be good to have my teacher next to me.'

'Of course,' he replied. 'And don't worry. It's not my first time but I'm nervous too. Everybody gets nervous.'

When Lisa looked around, the clearing was already deserted, as if a large group of partisans hadn't been there only moments ago. Even though she knew her comrades were hidden in the nearby trees, she couldn't spot them, nor could she hear their voices. It was as if she and Maxim were alone in the woods once again. Cheeks burning and hands shaking, she followed Maxim to a tall pine tree and climbed after him. To make it easier for her, he carried both their rifles, leaving Lisa with her tiny rucksack. 'Thank you,' she said when she was perched next to him. 'What do we do now?' The evergreen branches hid them completely, while the road was in full view in front of them. Maxim was so close, if she reached out, she could touch his leg. She tried to keep her hands steady on her rifle instead.

'Now we wait. I told you, that's ninety per cent of what we do. And sometimes it's the hardest part.'

After half an hour of staring at the empty road, Lisa's eyes watered from the wind and her back became stiff. She could feel sharp needles in her legs, a sure sign a cramp was coming. She moved her feet slightly and winced. Nothing could possibly be as bad as this – waiting for the lightning to strike. The anticipation of something horrible made her wish it would come sooner. The palms of her hands felt clammy and her throat was dry. 'Do you ever get scared?' she asked to break the silence.

'Of course. I'm only human.' He took a swig from his Thermos. 'Want some tea?'

At first she shook her head but then the thought of sharing a drink with him filled her with such warmth, she said, 'Yes, please.' Taking the Thermos from him, she sipped the tea slowly. 'I don't believe you. You seem unbelievably brave.'

'Brave people get scared too. It's how you deal with that fear that matters. Whether you turn around and run, or whether you keep going.'

'How do you do it? How do you keep going, knowing the next bullet could kill you?' Reluctantly she gave the Thermos back. The tea was warming her from the inside. She was no longer shivering in her wet clothes.

'I like to imagine all the others before me who had to face something like this. Other warriors, fighting other wars. Sometimes . . .' He hesitated as if he was too embarrassed to tell her. 'Sometimes, I pretend I'm one of them. I imagine I am Napoleon, Caesar or Alexander on one of their many campaigns.' He shrugged. 'It helps when things get tough.'

She laughed, and for a moment forgot all about her fears. 'You're lucky I am your tree companion today. I can tell you everything you ever wanted to know about Napoleon.'

'Why is that?'

'My grandfather is a history professor, specialising in Napoleonic history. He's obsessed with the man. Napoleon was all he ever talked about. It was inspiring, really, seeing how passionate he was about his work. My grandfather, I mean. Not Napoleon.' She felt herself blush and stopped talking.

'Prove it. Tell me something I don't know. I'm fascinated with Napoleon's marshals. Those men were legends. Do you know anything about them?'

'Let's see. There was Joachim Murat, married to Napoleon's sister. Napoleon made him king. Murat was his best friend and right-hand man but unfortunately, he betrayed him and turned his back on him. He was hungry for power and was executed by his former subjects.'

'Go on.'

'Then there was Michel Ney. His nickname was "the bravest of the brave".'

'The bravest of the brave. I like the sound of that.'

'I thought you might. He changed sides a couple of times but in the end was loyal to Napoleon. He was executed by the royalists. Then there was Alexandre Berthier, Napoleon's Chief of Staff, who mysteriously fell to his death out of a window. Some people believe the royalists killed him to stop him from joining Napoleon at Waterloo.'

'Is it all gloom and doom? How about something with a happy ending?'

'There was Jean Soult, who amassed a huge fortune and died at his castle at the age of eighty-two.'

'See, I didn't know any of it. Tell me more. I don't care if it's real or made-up.'

'With the lives these people lived, there's no need to make anything up. The reality is so much more fascinating than fiction could ever be. My grandfather calls them giants. And he's right.'

Lisa thought of something interesting to tell Maxim. Would he appreciate the story of Napoleon and Josephine: the romance, the betrayal and the ultimate forgiveness but no happily ever after? Or the miracle of the 18th of Brumaire? And what about the adventure of the first Italian campaign and the heartbreak of the withdrawal from Moscow? Or the unprecedented and astonishing return from Elba that had all of Europe stunned into disbelief? As they waited for the Nazi convoy in the quietened woods, with the birds chirping peacefully as if there was no war, Lisa told Maxim of marshals and generals, of wars and campaigns, of heroes and traitors. Little by little, she brought to life men long dead but not forgotten, and weaved unbelievable stories so he would find her interesting, so he would like her more.

Finally, her efforts were rewarded when he said, 'I enjoy talking to you. It sure makes the time pass quicker.' She wished she could see his face but it was obscured by the branches between them. She could swear he was smiling. She looked at herself through his eyes and liked what she saw. She was witty, funny and smart. To have a man like Maxim, an experienced partisan, respected by everyone he knew, hang on her every word made her feel important. She didn't want their conversation to end.

As she was about to tell him she enjoyed talking to him too, she felt the branches tremble. A second later, Maxim spoke and his voice sounded different, more tense. The banter of only moments ago was gone. 'This is it. Get ready.'

Lisa's heart sank all the way to her feet. 'I don't see anything,' she muttered. And then she noticed movement in the far distance. A few dark specks appeared on the road and soon turned into cars. She wanted to delay them, wanted to pause time, so that she could prolong this special moment between the two of them. But there was no delaying the inevitable. When they approached, she saw that the convoy consisted of a black Mercedes and a dozen trucks.

Lisa reached for her rifle – reached for her rifle in readiness to shoot a human being. She couldn't believe it. Was this real or was it a terrible nightmare from which she would soon awaken?

She heard his voice. 'Just like I taught you. Sight your target and calmly press the trigger. There is no time for emotion.'

Lisa watched the enemy procession through her binoculars. At the back of the first truck was a group of Nazi officers, talking excitedly, pointing at the woods in front of them. Their faces were animated and alive, their arms moving. Lisa took aim at one of them, a tall broad-shouldered man with a moustache and a cigarette, and waited for Maxim's signal. 'Now,' he shouted, and as the sound of gunshots blasted around her, she pressed the trigger. Even though her hands were trembling, the officer fell like a broken doll, limbs flailing. His face was no longer animated or alive. He remained motionless on the floor of the truck, while the Germans raised the alarm and reached for their weapons.

'That's my girl,' said Maxim. Lisa breathed heavily, the rifle limp in her hands, refusing to believe what had just happened. She had killed a man. One moment there was life, the next it was gone, extinguished like a candle, and she was responsible.

In her stupefied state she could feel the leaves moving around her. At first she thought it was the breeze but then she realised it was bullets and squeezed her eyes shut in fear. They were so close, she could feel them swarm around her like angry bees. This was it; she knew it. The next bullet was going to hit her. 'Get down,' shouted Maxim, his voice muted by the artillery. She bent down as low as she could to the branch.

The vehicles came to a halt. The Mercedes rolled off the road, hitting a tree trunk. One of the trucks had a flat tyre. The soldiers opened random fire at the woods but couldn't see where the partisans were hiding. Soon they were all cut down by the return fire from the trees. In a few minutes it was over.

'That's it. All clear. We can get back now,' said Maxim, pressing her hand.

Dazed, Lisa climbed down to the ground.

*

The trip back to the settlement was a joyous affair. It was nothing like their quiet journey in the morning. The men were talking, singing and slapping each other on the backs. Before they set out, Maxim gathered everyone together. 'I am happy to report that not only have we achieved our objective, but we have also done so with zero losses, while the enemy was completely wiped out. We were able to do this because of our diligence and detailed planning. Well done, my brave brothers and sister. I am proud of every one of you.'

Lisa felt like Maxim was talking directly to her. Her first mission was a success. Why did it feel like something tremendous and terrible had happened to her, something she would never recover from? Her heart overflowing with feeling, she watched Maxim as they walked. His face was covered in grime and there were circles under his eyes but he carried himself tall and proud, and when he noticed her looking at him, he smiled. A knowing smile, as if they shared a secret. As if between them was a special knowledge, a bond forged in battle. They had one common goal, one true desire – to see their motherland and Kiev free. And that goal brought them closer.

But as they followed Bear back to the settlement, accompanied by triumphant war songs and the playful clang of Alex's balalaika, Lisa couldn't get the German officer's face out of her mind.

*

The other groups had similar success. Triumphantly they had achieved their mission with zero losses and the battalion was celebrating. Maxim's guitar hummed late into the night, while Lisa sat alone at the nearby table, her adoring eyes on him.

Alex, whose eyes were on Lisa, sidled up to her, opened his bag and tipped the contents onto the table. 'Look what I found in the Germans' rucksacks. Jewellery, silver cutlery, even paintings. Would you like a brooch? A pair of golden earrings?'

'What were you doing, going through their things?' asked Lisa with barely disguised contempt.

'Someone had to. They stole all this from our people. While the officers rob our museums and art galleries, remove truckloads of wine, fruit, leather, wool and cattle, the soldiers take people's personal belongings.'

'And of course, being the righteous person that you are, you will return all these items to their rightful owners.' Glaring at him with disdain, she picked up her cup of tea and moved to another table. Dumbfounded, Alex watched her for a moment, then proceeded to collect his loot and put it back in his bag, muttering under his breath.

The next morning, Yulya greeted her with a smile on her face. And here was Lisa, thinking the woman was incapable of smiling. The porridge was already on the stove and even the potatoes had been peeled. Stirring with one hand and wiping the table with another, Yulya said, 'I hear there's a new sniper in our midst. Congratulations! I was wrong about you. You are not just a pretty face who can't cook.'

'Thank you,' muttered Lisa, not meeting Yulya's gaze.

'Just my luck. I'll have to find a new assistant.'

'What do you mean?'

'I trained you, only for you to leave the kitchen and join the partisans.' But she didn't sound displeased.

'Who said anything about leaving the kitchen?' Lisa took the rag from Yulya, turning away from her to the tables that needed cleaning. Her head was heavy after a sleepless night. Her eyes felt raw, as if there was sand in them. For the first time since she had arrived, she didn't think with horror about the day ahead. To her surprise, she was looking forward to losing herself in the work. The stove that pumped heat and burnt her face, the blunt knife that cut her fingers, the mountain of plates that needed to be loaded with food and carried to the waiting partisans no longer filled her with dread. There was no death inside the kitchen, no lifeless eyes staring through her, no lifeless mouths open in silent screams.

As the morning wore on, Lisa wasn't sure if it was her imagination, or if the other partisans were treating her differently. It was as if she was no longer invisible. Even Danilo grunted a short greeting when she walked into the cafeteria, carrying a samovar with boiling water. Everyone seemed to know she had shot an officer and they treated her like a hero, when she felt like the most despicable human being that had ever lived. There was something unfair about this war that made taking someone's life not only acceptable but commendable.

She was on her knees scrubbing the floor when Masha walked into the kitchen. Lisa found herself staring at her friend's shoes.

'All hail the hero!' exclaimed Masha. Lisa didn't look up from the bucket of murky water. She was contemplating getting up and going outside to change it but the effort required was too much. Masha nudged her and added, 'I'm so proud of you. Everyone here is talking about you. How brave you were, how cool under pressure.'

'Cool? I killed someone, Masha. Do you understand what that means?'

'He was one of them. You told me so yourself, remember?'

'And you told me it didn't make them any less human.'

'No one invited them here. We are merely defending ourselves . . .'

'Masha, I'm sorry. I can't talk right now. I have a million things to do. I'll see you later.' To her horror, Lisa felt tears streaming down her face.

'Are you all right? I've never seen you this upset. I thought you would be happy. I came to congratulate you.'

'I'm fine. I don't want to talk about it.'

Lisa rose to her feet and walked away, without a glance at the dirty rag, the bucket of water or Masha, who was watching her with shock.

She suspected that, for as long as she lived, she wouldn't forget the German officer's stare after she had shot him. He would haunt her forever, no matter where she was. It had taken a fraction of a second. One moment, he was alive, laughing, thinking, hoping for something. The next, he was gone. Life was fragile, in times of war especially so, and Lisa wanted desperately to see her family again, to make sure they were safe, to put her arms around them and hear their voices. None of the disagreements they had had in the past seemed to matter anymore.

Lisa didn't want to be alone because the ghosts inside her head scared her. But if she heard one more word of congratulations, she would scream. What she needed was to keep busy. Earlier she had noticed they were running low on oats and potatoes. On the way out of the cafeteria, she grabbed a bag and a large key hidden behind a loose wooden board. She was going to walk to the storage place where they kept their food supplies and get some more. The walk would do her good. The brisk spring air would clear her head; the sun on her skin would remind her that she was still alive, that she was breathing and feeling, even though she had taken someone's life, even though she had become a murderess.

'Need help?'

The voice made her jump. She looked up from the footpath to see Matvei blocking her way. 'I'm fine,' she said. 'Just going to get some food from the cellar.'

'Why don't I come with you? Then you won't have to carry it all by yourself.'

'They let you walk around the battalion by yourself?' wondered Lisa aloud.

'People trust me now. They are grateful for what I've done.'

Lisa shrugged and said she didn't need any help. He followed her anyway. She opened her mouth to ask him to leave her alone but didn't know how to say it without appearing rude. She had no energy for a confrontation, so she walked next to him in silence, while he never stopped talking. 'In my heart I've always been loyal to my country. But we all do what we have to do to survive.'

'No one else here has turned their back on their own people.'

He glanced at her thoughtfully and cleared his throat. 'Do you have any children?'

She shook her head, walking deliberately fast, the empty bag swinging in her hand.

'I have three,' he continued. 'The love we feel for our children is stronger than anything we will ever experience. It's primal, instinctive. It will make you do anything, endure anything. If I joined the partisans, my family would pay for it, like so many others. Do you know what they did to the families of partisans in my village? They burnt them alive, in front of everyone, to make an example out of them. And then they burnt their houses.

But because I helped the Germans, my children can live. They have food. They are safe. For that I would sacrifice everything I have, even my soul.'

'And you did. You sacrificed your soul, sold it to the devil.'

'Perhaps. But I don't believe in all that. You know what I believe in? Providing for your children. Staying alive for your family.'

'By whatever means possible?'

'Absolutely.'

'Tell me, how do you sleep at night, knowing what you've done?' Lisa had killed an enemy officer and couldn't stop thinking about it. But Matvei betrayed his own people. How did he look at himself in the mirror and not flinch?

'You think what I've done is treason. But the Germans think the opposite. They view what *you* do as treason. It's a matter of perspective, you see. And while there is a Nazi regime in Ukraine, what they believe is all that matters. Who do you think will have a longer, happier life? Me, who sold my soul to the devil? Or anyone else here, who opposes the established order?'

When they returned, Lisa thanked him for helping her carry the bags and disappeared quickly into the kitchen. She was glad to finally be alone with her thoughts, but a niggling feeling remained. After everything Matvei had said, she knew they couldn't trust him. She had to warn Maxim.

*

Lisa found him at the headquarters, bent over maps and documents, a red marker pen in his hand. Bear was curled up under the table and didn't raise his head when Lisa came in, only his tail twitching in acknowledgement.

'What are you doing?' she asked, perching on the bench across from him.

'Like Marshal Ney, I am planning our next campaign.' Maxim smiled and his eyes twinkled. 'What can I do for you?'

Just seeing his face made her heart lighter. How did he do it? He didn't even have to say a word and already she felt better. 'I wanted to talk to you about Matvei.'

'What about him?'

'I know it's thanks to him that yesterday's operation was such a success. Everyone is treating him like one of us. But can we really trust him? You know what they say. Once a snake, always a snake.'

'I don't trust him, not a bit. At the same time, I know he'll do anything to save his skin. He betrayed his people to the Nazis, and he'll betray the Nazis to us. His knowledge of their operations is useful for us right now.'

Having spoken to Matvei, having seen the determination on his face and not a trace of remorse, having heard his justification for what he'd done, Lisa knew Maxim was right. 'We have to be careful. He'll betray us again just as easily.'

'Don't worry. His every step is being watched.' He stood up, walked around the desk and sat next to her. If she reached out, she could touch his face. More than anything in the world she wanted to touch his breath-taking face. His unblinking eyes were on her. 'Have I told you how proud I am of you? I have taught you well.'

She couldn't even smile in reply. 'Do you remember your first time?'

'The first time I killed someone? Like it was yesterday. I couldn't sleep for a week afterwards.'

'So it's not just me?'

'Trouble sleeping?'

'Every time I close my eyes, I see his face. I can't help but wonder if he had a wife and children. If his parents are waiting for him. What kind of a man he was.' Lisa was so afraid she would burst into tears, she closed her eyes and counted to ten.

'Just because it's war, we don't stop being human. And neither do they. They are people, just like us. Following orders, just like us. What you are feeling is completely normal.'

'Everyone is talking about me like I'm some kind of a hero this morning. But I don't feel like one. I took someone's life. Because of me, he'll never come home. His family will never see him again. His children will grow up without a father. I feel like . . .' she searched for the right word '. . . a monster.'

'If you're a monster, what does that make me? You can't think like that or you will drive yourself crazy. For better or worse, we are soldiers. This is what we do. It wasn't our choice to have our country invaded. All we are doing is standing up to defend it. And he was a soldier too. He knew what he was in for. He was prepared to take lives and he did. And he was prepared to die for his beliefs.'

'Are you saying he deserved this?'

'No one deserves this. But it is what it is. Don't think of his family. Think of yours. Think of what this war is doing to those close to you. All because the Germans chose to come here.'

'But what if he didn't want to come here? You said so yourself. They are just following orders.'

'They chose a madman as their leader. And now the whole world is paying for it. It's only fair that they should pay for it too. Yes, you pulled the trigger but his death is not your fault. It's not on your hands. And you need to remember that. Because next time it won't be any easier and you need to be prepared.'

Lisa wanted to tell him there wasn't going to be a next time. She couldn't go through this again. 'I can't stop thinking about the expression on his face just before . . . He seemed so animated, so alive. And in a second, he was gone.'

'I've never told anyone this, so don't go repeating it and ruining my reputation. But the first time I killed a German soldier, I broke down. I cried like I've never cried in my life. You get used to it and that's the scary part. The horrible, unnatural part.' He was silent for a moment, as if lost in the past. 'You have to believe we are doing the right thing. That it's for the greater good. We are fighting to rid our country of this evil, whatever it takes.' He stared into his hands and when he finally looked up, his eyes were dark with sadness. 'My best friend was executed because he was Jewish.'

'One of my friends, too.'

'One night, his whole family was taken away. Their house was burnt and all who tried to stand up for them were arrested, myself included. I managed to get away. Others weren't so lucky. Next time don't think about them as human beings, because no human being is capable of such atrocities. You killed one of them. You did the world a favour.'

'What if he wasn't like that?'

'But what if he was?'

Lisa no longer felt like crying. She was no longer afraid because she knew she could tell this man anything, could share the inner-most secrets of her heart and he would understand. That night she slept soundly and when she closed her eyes, it wasn't the German soldier's face she saw. It was Maxim's.

May 1943

Chapter 14

It was a beautiful spring day that reminded Irina of carefree times when the world was at peace. Everywhere she looked, she saw new life emerging from a long sleep. At lunch, she walked through Berezovyi Gai Park, which was filled with lilacs and narcissus. She passed pear, cherry and apple trees blossoming in the gardens, their heady scent making her heart beat faster with hope. It was as if nature had forgotten there was a war on and was celebrating a new beginning with all the exuberance and delight it was capable of.

Irina wished she could forget too, if only for a moment. If she closed her eyes, she could see herself on the bank of the Dnieper, jumping in the water stark naked while Maxim watched her with longing. The beginning of them as a couple, when they had nothing to fear and everything to hope for. She could see herself as a little girl, building a sandcastle, while her mother and father frolicked in the water as if they didn't have a care in the world. But then she would open her eyes to the burnt-down buildings and the bomb craters. She would open her eyes to the self-satisfied German faces and the desperation in the eyes of the Soviets walking past. Feeling desperate herself, she would cling to her memories of that other, happier life. The sky was a clear blue then too, just like today. And the nightingales were chirping, just like today. But unlike today, there had been no enemy aircraft overhead and no grey uniforms on the streets of Kiev.

Irina's job today was to make house calls on the streets under her supervision, looking for young people who were hiding from mobilisation to Germany. She hated this part of her work. Every family had its own story, its own heartbreak. Fathers killed at the front or lost in prison camps, grandparents shot at Babi Yar, the ravine of horror where the Nazis systematically massacred tens of thousands of Kievans. And hunger, unabating, debilitating, with no end in sight. How could she add to these people's heartache and take their children away from them, even if her job depended on it?

I am not the right person for this job, she repeated to herself as she walked wearily down the street.

The little wooden hut she visited first was nothing but bare walls. Even the furniture was gone. She stood uncomfortably, unsure what to do with herself or where to turn. There was no sofa, not even a chair to sit on.

'We gave our dining table away yesterday. Received half a dozen eggs for it and a jar of milk. Had a real omelette for dinner, the likes of which we haven't had since before the war,' said the lady of the house, a pale round-faced woman called Sima. Irina suspected she was no older than forty-five but she looked like an old woman, frail and broken. 'I'm sorry we have no food to offer you. There's nothing left.'

Irina glanced at the empty room. 'Don't apologise. I'm not here to eat.' What she was here for was to collect two children and take them to a warehouse in Podol, where they would go through a medical exam and be sent straight to a German factory. In her folder she had a list of twenty people, their names, ages and addresses, as well as their next of kin and how to contact them.

When Sima heard the purpose of Irina's visit, she started to cry and wouldn't stop. 'My eldest daughter just came back from

Germany last week. I didn't even recognise her. Her hair was completely grey and she's only twenty-three.'

Like me, Irina thought and shuddered.

'And now they want my two youngest? When is enough going to be enough? They came here and they bled us dry and when we couldn't take it, they bled us some more.' The woman dabbed her eyes with a handkerchief. 'Please, don't take them away. Do they have to go today? I couldn't bear it. Please . . . What's your name?'

'Irina.'

'You look so young. Do you have children?'

'I do, yes.'

'Then you can imagine what it's like to see your son or daughter taken away from you. To not know if you'll ever see them again. If anything happened to them, I don't know what I'd do. Please . . .' Sima took Irina's hand and squeezed it. Irina felt an ache in her heart that wouldn't go away.

'I won't take them away. In fact, I can help you. If your boys don't mind digging trenches, I can get them an exemption from Germany.'

'Thank you so much,' cried the woman, smudging tears and dirt over her face. 'You have a kind heart. God bless you and protect you.'

'I would rather die than help the Nazi pigs defend Kiev from our soldiers,' said the youngest of the two boys, who was reading an algebra textbook on the floor nearby. From her records Irina knew he was sixteen but he looked about ten, so thin and under-nourished he was.

'Me too,' said his eighteen-year-old brother, glaring at Irina as if she was responsible for every Nazi atrocity in Kiev.

'You will do what the nice lady tells you to do and you will thank her,' said their mother, her hands on her hips.

'They'd have to shoot me before I do anything for them,' said the younger boy.

'The trenches are not going to help them,' said Irina quietly. 'Believe me, they won't stop our soldiers.'

'You really think so?' asked the younger boy, looking at her uncertainly.

'Of course. And once the Red Army gets here, you'll be able to join them. You can help fight the Nazis. You won't be able to do that if you are in Germany.'

The boys appeared to mull it over for a moment. Finally, they exchanged a look and nodded. In their eyes there was joy, at being taken seriously, at being seen as soldiers by this tall, grown-up woman with a notebook. To thank Irina, the mother gave her a book of poems by the Ukrainian poet Taras Shevchenko and an embroidered picture she had made herself. She walked Irina out, all the way thanking her and shaking her hand.

At lunch, Irina found a quiet place in the park and sat on the new grass. Opening the book in a random place, she read the lines written by the great poet:

If only I could see
my fields and steppes again.
Won't the good Lord let me,
in my old age,
be free?
I'd go to Ukraine,
I'd go back home.

And all she could think of was, how much longer? How much longer would the people of the Soviet Union have to suffer?

On the way home from work, she was turning the corner to Kazanskaya Street when she bumped straight into Tamara, who grabbed her hand and pulled her into a quiet alley. Her friend's eyes were wide and her whole body, it seemed, was shaking. At the sight of her, Irina felt a panic rise inside her. She wanted to ask what was wrong but couldn't get the words out.

'You can't go home right now,' said Tamara, blocking her way.

'I have to go home. I have to get Sonya. Why? What happened?'

'Don't worry, Sonya is with Dmitry.'

'Are you going to tell me what's wrong?'

But Tamara didn't reply, leading her in the direction of her house. Irina had never seen her friend so agitated. When they were safely inside, Tamara poured herself a glass of water, as if trying to delay the inevitable. Finally, she said, 'The Gestapo are at your house. They are questioning your parents-in-law.'

That dreaded word, *Gestapo*, sent a shiver through Irina. There was only one thing they could possibly want from Zina and Kirill. Having a son in the partisan battalion was enough to get them both killed. Having a son like Maxim, someone the Nazis were desperate to get hold of, meant they would be tortured and beaten until they gave him up. But if Irina knew her parents-in-law at all, they would die before they gave him up. At the thought of what was ahead of them, she felt unsteady on her feet and had to lean on the wall for support. 'How do you know this?'

'Dmitry told me.'

As if on cue, Dmitry appeared in the doorway. 'I just got Sonya to sleep. She kept asking for her mama.'

'Is she all right?' asked Irina, rushing to the bedroom. Only when she saw her daughter, sleeping peacefully on Tamara's bed, tucked under a warm blanket, could she breathe freely again. 'Tell me what happened,' she said when she returned to the kitchen.

Dmitry glanced away from her and out the open window at a group of German soldiers laughing outside. 'I was taking Sonya for a walk when I saw the four Gestapo officers pushing their way in. Poor Zina. Poor Kirill. All I wanted was to help them. But what could I possibly do?' His hands trembled.

Pressing his hand gently, Irina said, 'There was nothing you could do. Thank you for taking care of Sonya for me.' What if her daughter had been with her grandparents when the Gestapo arrived? Her heart ached at the thought.

'It will be all right,' said Tamara. 'They haven't done anything wrong. They don't know where to find Maxim. Once the Germans realise that, they will let them go. But in the meantime, it's not safe for you and Sonya to return home. You can stay with me for as long as you want. If anyone asks who you are, I'll tell them you are my cousin from Kharkov.'

'What about Maxim? We must get in touch with him. He'll know what to do. He'll know how to help them.' Even as she said it, a blind terror paralysed her. Yes, her husband would do anything to help his parents, of that she was certain. But what if he did so at risk to his own life?

'I'll see what I can do,' said Dmitry.

Irina couldn't close her eyes at all that night. With dread in her heart she watched the moving shadows on the wall, from the trees trembling in the wind, and the cars passing by, engines roaring, and wondered if she would ever see her parents-in-law again. How long would it take for the person who had denounced her parents-in-law to notice her one day as she stepped out of Tamara's building? How long before they heard the sound of boots marching through the front yard and up the communal staircase, and a heavy fist knocking on the door? How long before the Gestapo came for her and Sonya?

Irina thought of all the nights she had spent unable to sleep, resenting Zina. How she had wished her mother-in-law was gone from her life for good. How ironic, now that she finally got her wish, that she would give anything to hear Zina's voice again.

Because of the work she did, Irina knew better than anyone that once the Nazis got hold of someone, they never let them go. Trembling, she held her daughter's little hand through the night and wondered where her parents-in-law were. Had they been threatened, tortured, beaten? It didn't bear thinking about. Her heart ached for Kirill, who treated her like a daughter and never had a cross word to say to her, or anyone. And it ached for Zina, who in the last few weeks had been a changed woman. Gone were the demands, the snide comments, the soul-destroying criticisms. Irina had hoped it was a new start for the two of them. Maybe they could learn to live together after all. She had never told Zina she thought of her as family. And now she never would.

As soon as the morning dawned, colouring the sky red, Irina was out of bed and dressed.

'Where are you going?' asked Tamara, who was brushing her hair in the bathroom.

'Please, look after Sonya for me. I won't be long.'

'You can't go back home. It's not safe.'

But Irina was already out the door. When she reached the building where she had lived with her husband and parents-in-law, she slowed down and glanced in the window of their apartment on the ground floor, trying to catch a glimpse of what was inside. The shutters were drawn and everything was quiet. Nothing betrayed the fact that only a day ago something terrible had happened here.

Irina's heart thudded with pain at the sight of the porch that held so many happy memories. This was where Maxim had lifted her in his arms and carried her over the threshold on the day they were married. This was where he had told her he loved her for the first time and where Sonya had taken her first step. Irina wondered if she would ever come back here again. And if she did, would her home be filled with voices, like it had always been? Or would silence greet her?

Dmitry had told her in no uncertain terms not to go inside their apartment. It wasn't safe. But she had to see with her own two eyes that the apartment was empty and her parents-in-law were gone. She had a feeling she would open the door, step into the familiar corridor and hear Zina's voice and the sound of Kirill's guitar. But all was quiet inside the little apartment. Their boots were by the door and their winter coats were hanging on their hooks, as if waiting for them. Nothing was out of place. Slowly Irina walked to the living room. Kirill's newspaper was folded on his favourite armchair, Zina's glasses were forgotten on the table. It was as if her parents-in-law had stepped out for a minute and any moment would come back.

Gritting her teeth and trying not to cry, Irina locked the door behind her and walked up the stairs, knocking on Katerina's door. She thought she could hear something, a pitiful sound like a cat meowing. When she pushed the door, it gave way easily. 'Hello?' cried Irina. The crying stopped. Slowly she made her way down a dark corridor into the kitchen, where she saw the neighbour sitting at the table with her head in her hands.

At the sight of her, Irina trembled with anger. She could still see the smirk on Katerina's face when she had come to her office and made her threatening remarks all those months ago, demanding to know if Maxim was still in the partisan battalion and every German officer's worst nightmare. 'It was you, wasn't it? You told the Nazis about my husband.' Irina's voice was breaking. She swayed and grabbed the table to steady herself. 'Because of you, the Gestapo took my parents-in-law.'

Katerina looked through Irina like she wasn't in the room. She was grey and unkempt and looked like she hadn't washed or brushed her hair in days.

'What did they give you in return? Money? Food? What did you sell us out for? God can see everything, you know, and you will pay for this. One of these days you will pay.'

Finally, with a great effort Katerina's eyes focused on Irina. 'What did you say about your parents-in-law? The Gestapo took them?'

'Don't pretend you know nothing about it. It's all your doing. You came to my office and told me you knew about Maxim. Now, suddenly, the Gestapo take his parents. Don't tell me it's a coincidence.'

'I haven't said a word to anyone. I haven't left the house this week.'

Something caught Irina's attention. A desperate quality to Katerina's voice, the heartbreak in her eyes. She looked like a shadow of her former self. Her eyes were red from tears, her movements slow. 'Is everything all right?'

Katerina took in a sharp breath, as if gathering her strength. It took her a few moments to reply. 'My daughter is gone. A bomb exploded as she was leaving the factory in Berlin.'

Her legs becoming weak, Irina sat on a chair. 'How do you know this?'

'Her friend returned from Germany yesterday. They sent her back because she was too sick to work. She saw it happen.'

'I'm so sorry,' whispered Irina.

'I sent her to Germany because I thought she would be safe there. Now I wish she'd stayed here, where I could keep an eye on her. What happened is my fault.'

'It's not your fault. You did what you thought was right. You did your best to help your child.' Irina placed her hand on the neighbour's shoulder but Katerina didn't seem to notice.

As Irina staggered out of her old building and ambled towards Tamara's little house, where her daughter was waiting for her, all she could think of was: if it wasn't Katerina, then who? Who was this invisible enemy who wished them harm?

Chapter 15

As the weeks went by and the snow melted away, their food supplies seemed to melt away with it. The portions Lisa served to the partisans became smaller and smaller. All she heard three times a day, during breakfast, lunch and dinner, was: *Please, Comrade Smirnova, can I have another plateful? Not much, just a little bit to tide me over. I've been so hungry.* Another mealtime, another *Please-Comrade-Smirnova* from another hungry mouth, another pleading pair of eyes. Lisa would smile and shake her head, explaining politely that she didn't have more, that if she let them have another plateful, someone else in the battalion would have to go without. Every mealtime, her heart broke a little bit more at the sight of these starving men, who risked their lives to protect her from the Nazis. But at the same time, it took all her willpower not to help herself to some of their food. Sometimes, Yulya's cold stare was the only thing that stopped her. The emptiness in her stomach and the dull ache of hunger never went away, not even after she would devour her butter-less oats for breakfast, her watery stew for lunch and her stale bread for dinner. Her clothes were hanging off her and she could barely remember what it felt like to be full, to not want more, to not think about food. When she awoke in the morning, just before she fell asleep at night and every moment in between she would imagine her grandmother's blinis, her mother's borscht and her sister's cabbage pies.

But every morning and sometimes in the afternoons, she would look up from the dirty plates and see Maxim. And when she would catch a glimpse of his tall silhouette across the cafeteria, her heart would skip with joy and she would forget about everything. She would forget about her fears and her hunger, about the dwindling provisions and her aching back. In the evening, after the work was done, she would lie on her back with her legs dangling off her little bed and think of him and everything he had ever said to her. She would think of the difference between the Soviet and the Japanese rifles, of how to make every shot count and how to hide your tracks in the woods, of the Red Army's position and what a great support the partisans were to them. She would feel proud of herself for being here, for doing her bit because he had once told her he was proud of her. She would think of the way his forehead creased in concentration as he watched her take aim all those months ago when he was teaching her how to shoot, of the way his lips curled upwards when he smiled.

Lisa wanted to tell everyone about her feelings for him because if she didn't share it with another human being soon, she might suffocate. She longed to tell her sister, remembered they were no longer speaking and felt sad. She longed to tell Masha but something stopped her. What if she confided in her friend and Maxim rejected her? Though it seemed impossible to Lisa, for how could he not want to be with her, when she felt *this* for him?

But one evening, Masha came to the dugout late at night, perched on Lisa's bed, where she was busy thinking of Maxim with her hand pressed to her heart, and said, 'I saw the two of you together.'

Lisa sat up in bed and looked around. She hoped Anna wouldn't walk in and hear this conversation because she had a big mouth and loved to gossip. 'What are you talking about?'

'You and Maxim. You were in the cafeteria, sitting close together. You were so absorbed in him, you didn't even see me.'

'We were just talking. He was telling me about yesterday's ambuscade. They liberated three more villages this week.'

'When were you going to tell me?'

'Tell you what? There's nothing to tell.' Lisa, who wished with all her heart there was something to tell, looked Masha in the eye and smiled.

'It's the expression on your face when you are with him. You look so happy.'

'There's nothing going on between us.' *Yet*, she wanted to add but didn't.

'But you wish there was, don't you?'

'Why are you saying it like it's a bad thing? Like I'm doing something wrong? We are both free and can do as we please.'

'You might be free, Lisa. But Maxim isn't. He's married. He has a wife and a daughter in Kiev – or didn't you know?'

While Masha spoke, Lisa was thinking of walking through the woods with Maxim. She was remembering what it felt like when his hand brushed hers accidentally just before they said goodbye the day before. Then Masha's words cut through her reverie, dragging her back to reality. One moment, she was planning her future with Maxim. The next, she was hearing words like *married* and *wife*, random words that couldn't possibly have anything to do with him. She was grateful for the darkness inside the dugout. She didn't want Masha to see her face. All she managed in reply was a hoarse and disbelieving, 'How do you know?'

'Anna told me.'

'I don't think it's true. Anna is a terrible gossip. When she has nothing to say, she makes things up.' Lisa clasped her fists and shook her head. Her vision became blurry.

'I'm sorry to be the one to tell you, but it's better if you know sooner rather than later. Before you get in too deep.'

Lisa didn't want to admit to Masha that she was already in too deep. She was in big trouble because she couldn't take a breath without him in her thoughts. That night, as she lay flat on her stomach and stared into space, she felt angry and betrayed, as if he had cheated her or lied to her, as if the mere fact that she had feelings for him meant he owed her something. Because she could never hate him, she hated his wife, the faceless woman who only a few hours ago she didn't even know existed.

Everything she had ever read told her this wasn't going to end well. Anna Karenina fell in love with a man who was not her husband and threw herself in front of a moving train, begging God to forgive her. La Mole fell in love with the beautiful Queen Margot, married to the Protestant prince, and was tortured to death in a dark dungeon. Scarlett O'Hara fell in love with someone else's husband and lost everything. But Lisa wasn't Scarlett and Maxim wasn't Ashley. She knew he had feelings for her too. A girl could always tell. If he still cared about his wife, he wouldn't smile at Lisa with *that* expression on his face. Maybe in fiction married lovers were doomed forever. But real life wasn't fiction. Lisa and Maxim were going to write their own story.

Lisa wished she could speak to Maxim openly and ask him . . . Ask him what? How dare he fall in love with someone else all those years ago? Didn't he know Lisa was about to come into his life? How dare he promise himself to someone else when she couldn't see herself without him?

'I'm sure their relationship is practically over,' she said to Masha the next morning as the girls were getting ready for work. Lisa's head felt heavy after a sleepless night. She brushed her teeth listlessly, not looking at her friend. 'He never talks about her. Not once has he mentioned her to me. If he loved her, he would have said something. When we love somebody, we think about them all the time.'

'Just because he didn't say anything, doesn't mean he doesn't think about her. He doesn't share his every thought with you, does he? Remember what Anna told us? He's a very private person. Never talks about his personal business.'

'We spoke about our families and he didn't say a word. They've probably been married for a while now and he's tired of her.'

'That's just wishful thinking on your part. You know nothing about them. But what you do know is that he's married. It's a fact and you can't change it, no matter how much you might want to.'

'Maybe he doesn't want to be married anymore.'

'They have a child together. If you try to come between them, you'll be breaking up a family. That's selfish, Lisa.'

'Everyone is selfish. When it comes to love, everyone is out for themselves. And just because he's married, doesn't mean he's happy. How many happily married people do you know?'

'My husband and I.'

'That's because you are newlyweds.'

'I'm not trying to upset you. I just don't want you to get hurt. Even if you manage to attract him, you'll never keep him. Married men don't leave their wives.'

'We'll see about that.'

Wide-eyed, Masha watched Lisa as if she had never seen her before. 'Even if he does leave her for you, why would you want a man who can get tired of someone after a few years? How could you ever trust him?'

'I'm not just someone. Why would I feel this way about him if it wasn't meant to be?'

'People often fall for someone they are not meant to be with. Otherwise there wouldn't be so many songs and books about unrequited love. You can't build your happiness on someone else's heartbreak.'

'Don't you understand? If I don't do anything, it will be my heart that's broken.'

Masha put her jacket on and turned towards the exit. Not looking at Lisa, she said, 'You are my friend, but I can't support you in this. It's a sin. What if someone did this to me? If my husband left me for someone else, I don't know what I'd do. It breaks my heart to know you would do this to another woman over a silly crush.'

'It's not a crush. It's once in a lifetime. I can think of nothing else, I can't sleep, I can't eat. I feel like I'm burning inside. If only you knew what I feel. And I am going to fight for him, Masha, I swear.' But her friend could no longer hear her. She had stormed out of the dugout without a backwards glance.

Chapter 16

Two days after Zina and Kirill had disappeared, Irina was playing with her daughter in the garden behind Tamara's house, a tiny square of paved land where nothing grew but tufts of grass peeking between the concrete slabs. Undeterred by the unforgiving terrain and determined to have something green to look at, Tamara had filled the space with potted plants, arranging them in a straight line like soldiers on parade. But like most of Tamara's passions, this one was short-lived, and the tulips and geraniums had quickly been forgotten. All that was left of them were some dry twigs desperately begging for water.

Sonya was jumping up and down and trying to push the pots to the ground. Irina was glad Tamara was out looking for food and couldn't see it. She would have been horrified at such treatment of her once precious possessions.

'Grandpa! Want Grandpa! Horsey!' cried Sonya.

Irina's breath caught. Her little girl was missing her grandparents. She didn't understand why they were gone, and neither did Irina. They had done nothing wrong. Their only crime was having a son who hadn't given up. And why should he? The Nazis had marched into Kiev, razing the city to the ground, enslaving, murdering and starving its people. Who could blame Maxim for standing up for what he believed in? Who could blame his parents for bringing up their son to be a man they could be proud of?

She wondered where her husband was. Despite Dmitry's best efforts, they hadn't been able to get in touch with him. He still didn't know his beloved parents were gone. The thought of having to tell him filled Irina with trepidation. Would he blame himself? Would he feel responsible for what had happened?

'Horsey, horsey,' repeated Sonya, pulling her mother by the sleeve. The little girl's dark hair was longer than it had ever been. Her dark eyes twinkled at Irina with mischief.

Irina shuddered as if woken from a bad dream. Crouching next to Sonya, she put her arms around her and said, 'Would you like Mama to be horsey today?'

'No, no, Grandpa!'

'Grandpa went away for a little while. He'll be back soon.' Tears in her eyes, Irina forced her face into a happy smile for her daughter's sake. 'And while we wait for him, Mama will be horsey.'

'Mama horsey, Mama horsey.' The girl continued to jump, her excitement unabated.

Irina lifted her daughter gently and placed her on her shoulders, with both her chubby legs dangling, the way Kirill would do, then she started prancing around the garden, doing her best to imitate a horse. After five minutes of this, she was out of breath and exhausted. Her back was killing her. No wonder Kirill looked like he was about to fall down every time she saw him.

Up and down they bounced, Sonya squealing in excitement, when one of Tamara's potted plants tripped Irina up, and the two of them went crashing to the ground. Irina groaned out loud from a sharp pain in her foot but soon forgot all about it because her daughter was crying. Ignoring her throbbing ankle, she lunged for Sonya and picked her up. The little girl continued to cry, her face scrunched up like a prune. Her arm was bleeding where a broken flowerpot had cut her, and her left knee was grazed.

As fast as she could, Irina carried the distraught child inside the house, placing her squirming, kicking body on the couch and examining her. Then she rushed to the kitchen, where she fetched some water and a cloth. What she needed was some iodine and a bandage. She remembered seeing a medical kit in Tamara's bedroom one day when her friend had cut her finger while peeling potatoes for dinner. Irina lifted Sonya in her arms, not wanting to leave the crying girl alone while she was searching for bandages, and ran across the hall to the bedroom, where she placed her daughter on the bed and rummaged through the drawers of her friend's wardrobe.

She spotted the familiar medical kit under a messy pile of clothes. When she picked it up, she noticed a thick stack of money underneath. She was in such a rush to help Sonya, her brain didn't register what it was she was seeing, only that it looked out of place, like it didn't belong in the drawer, didn't belong in the house at all. She put it to the back of her mind and rushed to Sonya.

The little girl was screaming hysterically, her legs and arms flailing. Irina quickly dabbed some iodine on the cut, provoking a new outburst of inconsolable crying from Sonya and making Irina feel terrible for inflicting more pain on her daughter. Then she applied a bandage and picked the girl up carefully, rocking her like a newborn baby, kissing her wet face, singing a soothing rhyme, while her own tears rolled down her cheeks into Sonya's hair. She felt like the worst mother in the world. How could she have been so careless? Because of her, her little girl was hurt.

At first Sonya was whimpering like a frightened puppy. Then her breathing slowed down and she fell asleep. Irina stayed with her for a little while, whispering over and over how much she loved her. 'Everything will be all right,' she repeated. 'You and I are going to be just fine. Everything will be all right.' Who was she trying to convince, herself or her daughter?

After half an hour of rocking and singing, she placed the sleeping girl on the bed. Gathering the bandages, she shoved them back into the medical kit and carried it to the wardrobe, remembering the sense of unease she had experienced when she was going through her friend's drawer. Holding her breath as if afraid of what she was about to find, she moved Tamara's clothes to one side.

Under the clothes were Nazi Reichsmarks.

Stunned, hardly believing her eyes, Irina reached for the rolls of notes. She had never seen so much money in one place in her life. Her heart plummeted in a sudden premonition. Why would Tamara keep German money hidden in her apartment? She was about to count the money when she heard the key turning in the front door. Placing the Reichsmarks in her pocket, she walked out of the room to meet Tamara.

Her friend breathed in with a smile on her face. 'Wait till you see what I've found for dinner.' She lifted her string bag and Irina saw half a dozen eggs and some carrots. She wondered if Tamara had paid for them using money from her drawer. Involuntarily she took a step back. Tamara didn't seem to notice. 'It's warm like summer outside. I hope it's still nice next week.' She paused, as if waiting for Irina to ask what was so special about next week. When Irina didn't say anything, she continued, 'Dmitry wants to go to the registry office next Tuesday. Finally, we are doing it. I'm going to be a married woman. Can you believe it?'

'I can believe it,' said Irina, her hand on the money in her pocket.

'You are so pale, like you've seen a ghost. Is everything all right?' Tamara came close to Irina and drew her into a hug. It took all of Irina's willpower not to pull away.

'Sonya had a bad fall in the garden.'

'Oh no! The poor little mite, how is she?'

'Better now. I just got her to sleep.'

'Sleep is the best medicine.' Tamara paused, watching Irina. 'We need some tea. Everything is better after a cup of tea. Can I make you some?' Irina shook her head but Tamara pulled out two cups anyway and filled the kettle. 'I can't wait to marry Dmitry.

If only I had something nice to wear. I can't possibly marry him in the same old dress I've been wearing everywhere. But I don't have the money to buy anything else. And even if I did, no one sells or makes anything anymore.'

'Money? What about this?' Irina took the banknotes from her pocket and threw them on the table. She didn't say anything but watched her friend's face carefully, for clues, for an explanation.

'Where did you get that?' exclaimed Tamara. Her smile vanished.

'I was going to ask you the same question.'

'What are you doing, going through my things?'

Suddenly, Irina knew. It wasn't finding the money that had alerted her that something wasn't right. It wasn't even the improbability of Reichsmarks appearing in her friend's drawer as if out of nowhere, the Reichsmarks that were clearly a payment for something she had done, something that benefited the Germans and therefore could only be a betrayal of her own people. No, it was the expression of guilt on Tamara's face. 'It wasn't Katerina, was it? It was you,' Irina said quietly, hardly believing herself and yet realising it was the only plausible explanation. Her insides froze in horror. How could this be?

'What are you talking about? Who is Katerina?'

'You were the one who betrayed us to the Gestapo.'

Irina was hoping Tamara would deny it. Then she could believe her, apologise for doubting her and explain it away by the stress she'd been under lately. They could laugh about the misunderstanding and go on as before. But Tamara didn't deny it. She lowered her head as if in shame and looked away. Her voice didn't waver when she said, 'I didn't betray you. I betrayed Maxim's parents.'

'They are my family. How could you, Tamara? We've been friends since kindergarten. You are like a sister to me.'

'I didn't mean to do it. I'm so sorry. I didn't mean to do it!' Tamara slid into a chair and placed her elbows on the table, wringing her hands. All the while, she repeated the words like a prayer. *I didn't mean to do it.*

Irina put her hands over her ears as if to shield herself from her friend's excuses. 'You betrayed them for a handful of Reichsmarks.'

'It's not about the money. I wasn't even going to keep it.'

'But you did keep it.'

'It wasn't about the money.' Not raising her eyes, Tamara rubbed mascara over her face with clenched fists. 'Zina wasn't even nice to you. I couldn't stand the way she treated you.'

'She's still my husband's mother.'

'They came for me again, Ira. The Nazis. They no longer cared about some stupid stamp in my passport. As of last week, they started taking married women to Germany and even those with small children. I was told to pack my things and report to the station within two days.'

'What does that have to do with my parents-in-law?'

'Don't you understand? I had a choice. It was either give them information or a certain death in Germany.'

'Yes, you did have a choice. You chose your life over the lives of two innocent people.'

'Remember Tonya from school? She left for Germany three weeks ago. I just found out from a mutual friend that she died. She was the strongest, healthiest girl I know and she died from overwork and malnutrition. I couldn't face it.'

'Why didn't you come to me? I helped you once, I would have thought of something.'

'I didn't have the time. The Nazis were after me. I had to think fast.'

'So you opened your mouth and condemned my parents-in-law to a certain death?'

'I'm sorry. I feel so terrible. Now that I think about it, I can't believe I could do such a thing.'

'Nor can I.'

'I was so afraid, Ira. You can't even imagine! What was I supposed to do? What would you have done in my place?'

Irina didn't know what she would do if she was at risk of

being taken to Germany, of leaving everything and everyone she loved behind, leaving her daughter behind. But she knew what she wouldn't do. She would never throw two innocent people off a cliff to save her own skin. She watched Tamara's shaking mouth and tear-stained face, her trembling hands and quivering shoulders. *Who are you?* she wanted to say to her friend. *I don't even know who you are.* But there was little point.

'I hope you can forgive me one day. I didn't do it to hurt you. I would never do anything to hurt you and Sonya.'

'You didn't think this would hurt me? Just imagine what it will do to Maxim, to our future together. It will change everything.' Irina couldn't stop herself from shaking.

'I'm sorry. I didn't think.'

'No, you didn't.' Irina narrowed her disappointed eyes on her friend. 'Poor Dmitry. What will he do when he finds out?'

Tamara clasped her hands together, tears in her eyes. 'He can never find out. Please, promise me you won't tell him. It will break his heart.'

'I won't tell him. You will.'

'We are friends. How can you do this to me?'

The disbelief on Tamara's face almost made Irina laugh out loud. It was the same disbelief she had felt when she discovered the money in her friend's bedroom. 'I could ask you the same question.'

'Why would you want to hurt Dmitry?'

'I'm not the one hurting him. You are. I don't want him to make the biggest mistake of his life. He has no idea who you really are. *I* had no idea who you are and I've known you my whole life.'

Irina couldn't look at her friend anymore. She couldn't take the pain and distress on Tamara's face because she didn't want to feel sorry for her. She wanted to hate her for what she'd done. Turning around, she walked back to the bedroom, where Sonya was still sleeping, the cut on her arm dark brown from the antiseptic. How could her best friend, someone she'd known for as long as she could remember, do something so despicable? Despite the years they had spent side by side, Irina realised Tamara was a complete stranger to her. The person Irina thought she knew couldn't have done this. The friend she had loved like a sister couldn't have gone to the Gestapo, knowing the price for her actions would be the death of two innocent people.

Irina thought of all the times she had complained to Tamara about her mother-in-law, of the long hours talking late into the night, sharing confidences and heartbreaks. How many times had she told her friend how much she hated Zina? Was what had happened Irina's fault? If she hadn't confided in her friend, would Zina and Kirill be safe now? Irina's guilt weighed heavily on her as she lay in bed holding her daughter and praying for a miracle.

*

For once, Irina was grateful for her work. She needed something, anything, to take her mind off what had happened. Today her task was to check that the driveways had been swept clean, as per the Nazi order. With Sonya in her arms, she knocked on the door of the first house and a woman opened it, small, underfed and exhausted. Irina could hear children's voices coming from inside the living room. It sounded like the woman had an army in there. 'Sweep the driveway?' exclaimed the woman. 'I would do it, if only I had a minute to myself. They will set the house on fire or kill each other if I leave them alone.' She sighed wearily. 'Why don't you come in? My name is Valya.'

The army turned out to be four boys, ranging in ages from a toddler to a ten-year-old. Feeling guilty for harassing this poor woman about something as ridiculous as sweeping the driveway, Irina followed Valya to the living room and stood uncomfortably, looking at the bare walls and the poorly dressed children rolling around the floor. There was no furniture, no couch to sit on, no table or chairs.

Valya sighed. She looked close to tears. 'We've exchanged every-thing we had for food. How are we going to live now?'

'And your husband?'

'Killed at the front in 1941. His first real battle, poor man. My youngest can't walk. He was born with weak hips. It takes all I have to put food in his mouth.'

Irina looked at the woman, at the thin faces of the children, and her heart ached. 'Don't worry, I can help you. Where is your broom?'

While Valya was busy breaking up a fistfight between the two older children, Irina placed Sonya in a swing in the front yard and swept the driveway clean. Afterwards, she washed her hands under a pipe, adjusted her hat and called out to Valya, who had one boy by the scruff of his neck like a puppy and another by his arm. 'All done. Now you don't have to worry about a fine.'

'I don't know how to thank you. If only every inspector was like you.'

'Don't worry. From now on it's just me on your street. If you need anything, don't hesitate to ask.' Irina wished she had some food to give to Valya for her little boys but she had barely enough to feed her own daughter. The familiar feeling of helpless-ness washed over her and she blinked away the tears of shame because, no matter how hard she tried to help, she could only do so much. She cursed the Nazis as she said goodbye to the woman who looked like she was about to fall over from hunger and exhaustion.

'God bless you. Who are you? You are not like the rest of them,' said Valya as Irina was walking through the gate with Sonya.

'My name is Irina. I was a schoolteacher before the war.' The words resounded heavily in her heart. It felt like a lifetime ago. A lifetime of misery and fear.

The last house under her jurisdiction was bigger than the rest, with a porch and two large oak trees framing it like a painting. There was a swing between the trees, on which a fat ginger cat was sleeping. The woman who answered the door was plump like the cat and just as ginger. The house was unbearably hot. A wood-burning stove was lit in the kitchen. On the table Irina could see a plateful of pies, a large chunk of butter, eggs, milk, a few slices of cheese and a loaf of bread, golden and delicious. Irina was so hungry, she almost collapsed at the smell of food. She stood for a few moments, unable to take her eyes off the table.

'Are you here to check the driveway? I'm so busy in the kitchen, I forgot all about it. I will do it right away.' The woman didn't invite Irina to sit, nor did she offer anything to eat or introduce herself.

Irina thought she had walked into a parallel reality. Who had butter, milk and cheese in such abundance? It didn't seem like the woman cared about rationing her food, like everybody else in Kiev, in Ukraine, in all of the Soviet Union. It was as if there was plenty more where it all had come from. Only when Irina checked her records did she understand. The woman was what was known as Volksdeutsch – Russian of German descent. People like her enjoyed special privileges under the Nazis, especially if they were sympathetic to the new regime. Often sympathetic meant denouncing their friends and neighbours to the Gestapo and sending them to a certain death for as little as walking out into their garden to get a bucket of snow after curfew.

'Is there anything else?' asked the woman rudely. 'Because if there isn't, I have to take the pies out before the meat gets too dry.'

Irina opened her notebook. 'The driveway should have been done yesterday. I'm afraid I'll have to issue a fine.'

It felt strangely satisfying to stamp and sign the fine notice and hand it to the woman, who shrugged as if it didn't concern her.

When Irina and Sonya returned that evening, Tamara was sitting at the dining table, her eyes red. 'I feel so bad, Ira. I don't know what I was thinking. How could I do that to them?'

'You are asking me?' Sonya was wriggling in her arms. Irina let her go and leant to kiss her daughter on the head. She didn't look at Tamara.

'I didn't think it through. I didn't think they might kill them.'

'What did you think the Gestapo did to families of partisans? Invite them for tea and feed them blinis?'

'I thought they would question them and let them go.'

'You're a liar. You knew exactly what you were doing.'

'I promise, I didn't think.' Tamara shook her head and her hair fell over her face in a wall of entangled curls, shielding her from Irina.

'You *did* think. But only of yourself.'

'How can I live with myself after what I've done?'

Irina didn't feel like comforting her friend. She wanted to tell her she would find a way. Selfish people always did.

'Please, don't tell Dmitry. He's my life. I can't imagine living without him.'

'He has the right to know who you truly are.'

'I thought you were my friend.'

'How can I be your friend? Tomorrow, when you feel hungry or threatened again, you'll sell me to the Nazis for a piece of bread. You'll sell my husband and my daughter. And Dmitry, too. You are a user, Tamara, cruel and self-absorbed. I could never trust you again. And neither should Dmitry. I regret the day I met you. I wish we were never friends.' As soon as she said those words, Irina wanted to take them back, but it was too late. Tamara stared at her in silence. She looked like she had been slapped.

Irina locked herself in the room with her daughter and spent the next couple of hours packing what few belongings they had. After everything that had happened, she couldn't stay here for a moment longer. Once everything was packed, she sat on the bed next to her sleeping daughter and thought about her options. She couldn't return to the apartment she had shared with her parents-in-law. Once she was seen there, how long would it take the Nazis to take her and her daughter into custody and use them as leverage against Maxim? Her other friends were long gone – some lucky enough to evacuate before the Nazis arrived, others taken by the

Nazis, because they were Jewish, because they had a father or a son fighting in the Red Army, because they had concealed prohibited weapons or distributed anti-Nazi propaganda.

If it was just her, she would sleep on the street rather than stay in Tamara's apartment. But she had to think of her daughter. Sonya's safety was all that mattered. Until they heard from Maxim, Irina had nowhere to go.

The little girl woke up and instantly started crying. 'Are you hungry, darling?' whispered Irina, thinking longingly of the eggs and carrots in Tamara's string bag. But she would never take Tamara's food. In the kitchen she had some boiled potatoes left over from the day before. She picked up Sonya and left the room. The apartment was quiet. There was no sign of Tamara in the kitchen. Peering into Tamara's bedroom, Irina saw that the doors of her wardrobe were open, revealing empty shelves. Tamara had taken all her clothes and the blood money she had received from the Gestapo for betraying Irina's parents-in-law.

She was gone.

*

Two days after Tamara had left, on a summer-warm morning with the breeze wafting in through the open shutters and bringing with it the scent of narcissus and angry German voices, a key turned in the door, making Irina spill the porridge she was carrying. Throwing a regretful glance at what was their last cup of oats, she turned around and saw Dmitry in the doorway, flustered, unshaven and out of breath. She felt close to tears at the sight of him. He still had no idea what Tamara had done or that she was gone. Irina didn't want to be the one to tell him. She didn't want to be the one to break his heart.

'I was able to send word to Maxim. I didn't tell him about his parents, just that we need to see him urgently,' he said once they'd sat down opposite each other at the dining table. Irina had a cup of steaming hot tea in front of her. Dmitry had a glass of cold water. 'He'll be here in a few days.'

In a few days! The cup in her hand trembled with anticipation, with sadness. A part of her was desperate to see her husband. He had an incredible ability to make her heart a little lighter just by being around. One glimpse at his beautiful face and her troubles disappeared. If only she didn't have to be the one to tell him about his parents. The last thing she wanted was to cause him pain. 'I can't stop thinking about Zina and Kirill. Where do you think they have taken them?'

Dmitry looked inside his hands, as if searching for answers. 'I wish I knew. They could be anywhere right now.'

'I wonder if they are still alive.'

'The Nazis will keep them alive for as long as they are useful to them. They don't have Maxim yet. So yes, his parents are probably alive.'

But for how long? Irina wanted to ask but couldn't. She was trying hard not to cry. 'Zina was a force of nature,' she said, remembering Kirill's story about her mother-in-law standing up to two boys who were harassing her neighbour. 'She couldn't stand injustice of any kind.' And then she thought, *Why am I talking about her in past tense, as if she is already dead?* Shuddering, she continued, 'And Kirill is the kindest man I've ever met. I miss him so much. I wish I had a chance to tell him that he's been like a father to me.'

'You don't need to tell him. In his heart he already knows.'

'Tamara always had a soft spot for him. She always said he had a heart of gold.' But it didn't stop her from going to the Gestapo and sentencing him to a certain death. Irina looked away from Dmitry, to the blotches of spilled porridge on the floor, to the curtains twitching in the wind.

'Where *is* Tamara? I was able to find a dressmaker who could adjust one of her old dresses to make it look like a wedding dress. She'll be so pleased.'

There was no joy or excitement in Dmitry's voice. He sounded tired, as if he was done with it all. Irina understood. There was no place for joy in their lives, even with a wedding to plan. And now there wasn't going to be a wedding. How did she tell him that? When she had first found out about Tamara's betrayal, Irina was convinced Dmitry deserved to know the truth. But now, as she was facing him, she wasn't so sure anymore. 'Tamara is not here,' she said as quietly as she could.

'She didn't have to go out today. We have enough food for dinner tonight. And here, I brought some potatoes . . .' He noticed the expression on Irina's face and stopped.

'She left, Dima.'

'What do you mean, left? Where did she go?'

'She has a cousin in Podol somewhere. I assume she's staying with him. I don't know exactly. She didn't say.'

'But why would she go away now, when we are about to get married?' He laughed in grim disbelief, before his face crumpled in confusion. 'Is it me? Did I do something?'

'Of course not.'

'I thought she was happy. Did something happen? Did she say anything? Is there someone else?'

'Not as far as I know.'

'Well, do you know where this cousin lives? I will go and find her, bring her back. At the very least we can talk. Whatever it is, we can work it out. It's the wedding, isn't it? She's getting cold feet. It's a huge step and I know it happened quickly. But I thought she wanted it as much as I did, or I wouldn't have asked her to marry me.'

'I don't know where her cousin lives. I'm sorry.'

Dmitry's shoulders stooped and, when Irina next looked up at his face, he looked older by years. He disappeared behind a newspaper but Irina knew he wasn't reading. The newspaper didn't move, the pages didn't turn. The house felt so quiet without Tamara's laughter. The silence felt heavy and uncomfortable, like a premonition of something terrible to come. Irina wished for voices, for Kirill's soft singing, for the murmur of Maxim's guitar, even for Zina's never-ending complaints. Anything to take her mind off the thoughts inside her head.

As she was scraping the breakfast plates clean and rinsing them with water she had brought from the pump, she heard the sound of planes. A distant din at first, gradually it grew closer, until it was no longer quiet in the little apartment.

It was not unusual to hear aeroplanes in occupied Kiev. The German observers were in the sky day and night, never letting Irina forget that she was living in a city at war. But now she heard something else, something she hadn't heard in over a year and a half: a familiar whistling sound. It was followed by a loud explosion, deafening her momentarily and making her cry out in terror. The plate she was holding flew to the floor, shattering into a hundred tiny pieces and adding to the racket. As if through a thick layer of cotton wool, she heard her daughter's petrified shrieking. Placing both arms around her, Irina pressed her close to her heart, shielding her from danger.

'The Germans are bombing us? But why?' Irina exclaimed when all was quiet again.

'I don't think it's the Germans, Ira. Why would they bomb the city that already belongs to them?' said Dmitry, glancing out the window at the fires blazing in the distance.

'Are you saying . . .'

'I think it's the Red Army.'

The Red Army! Irina's heart trembled with joy, until another explosion shook their building, lighting up the sky and making her and Sonya cry out in panic.

'Don't be scared,' said Dmitry. 'They'll be targeting strategic objects. Factories, rail stations, bridges, not civilian buildings. Their aim is to push the Germans out.'

'I'm not scared,' Irina murmured. It was a lie. A mother was always scared, if not for herself, then for her little one. But she didn't want Dmitry to see that. 'Let them come. The sooner the better.' What was a little shelling if it meant the hated Nazis would soon be gone from Kiev for good?

More Soviet planes could be heard, releasing bomb after bomb after bomb. The explosions seemed closer, as if seeking them out. Irina cradled her crying daughter, whispering soothing words in her ear.

Dmitry pulled her by the arm, pointing in the direction of the front door. 'It's best if we take cover. Just in case.'

Irina thought it was an excellent idea. When the three of them were huddled under the communal staircase with a dozen people from nearby apartments, hoping for more bombs and at the same time deathly afraid of them, Dmitry said, 'It was her, wasn't it?'

'What?' Irina could barely hear him over the explosions. In the dark under the stairs she couldn't see his face.

'It was Tamara who betrayed Zina and Kirill.' It didn't sound like a question. It sounded as if he already knew.

'What makes you say that?'

'It's the only possible explanation. She's always asking about Maxim, wanting to know everything. Where he is, what the partisans' plans are. And the food!'

'The food?'

'When the rest of us are starving, she always has bread or cheese or meat. I could never understand it, until now.'

Irina lowered her head. She felt the deepest shame, as if it was her and not Tamara who had been exchanging information for food and money.

'You are not denying it,' said Dmitry.

'I'm not confirming it, either.'

'You don't need to. I already know.'

'The partisans would kill her if they knew.'

'No one must ever know.' Although his voice was trembling slightly, Dmitry sounded calm. Irina's heart was breaking for him.

'You really do love her, don't you?' She put her hand on his shoulder, wanting nothing more than to take his pain away. If only it was possible. 'And she loved you too. I've never seen her eyes sparkle like that for anyone.'

'If she loved me, how could she do this? Zina and Kirill were my only family.'

'I guess she didn't think. Or rather, she thought about herself first. Maybe she didn't realise the danger she was putting them in.' Irina couldn't believe she was defending Tamara after everything she'd done. She fell quiet.

'I'm glad this happened now and not after we were married,' he said bitterly.

They stayed hidden for over an hour. Eventually the Soviet planes were gone, leaving behind something the people of Kiev hadn't known in a very long time – hope. That night, as she lay awake and listened to the silence, Irina thought of Tamara and Dmitry's happy faces as they talked about their wedding. She thought of Dmitry's heartbreak and despair. As much as she wanted to hate Tamara, she couldn't. Yes, her friend had been weak. And yes, she had betrayed them in the worst way possible. But that was what war and despair did to people. They made them commit acts that were out of character, acts they didn't even know they were capable of.

In the dark, she thought of the planes that had come to liberate her city. She imagined Red Army soldiers on the streets of Kiev, red Soviet flags on every building and not a swastika, not a grey uniform in sight. She imagined walking outside with her head held high and feeling at home in the place where she grew up. Would that day ever come? And would Zina and Kirill be there to see it?

Would any of them?

*

The next morning, Dmitry insisted Irina and Sonya move out of the apartment. 'Tamara betrayed you once,' he said. 'She could do it again.' He took them to a small empty house in Podol, a few

212

tram stops away from Tamara's apartment back when the trams were still running, where Irina spent the next few days taking her daughter to work with her, nursing her on a small folding bed in the tiny bedroom, cooking their meals on a camp stove that only worked sporadically, and waiting for Maxim.

It was Sunday, Irina's only day off, and she was grateful she could stay home with her little one. She always felt fearful walking on the streets swarming with German soldiers, but having her child with her turned this fear into a blind panic.

All morning she glanced out the window, hoping to see Maxim walking down the road. When it was lunchtime, with still no sign of him, she took Sonya for a nap and fell asleep with her, lulled by her quiet breathing. When she opened her eyes, she saw Maxim sitting next to her, watching the two of them with a smile. Irina's heart skipped and she crawled across the bed, careful not to wake her daughter, whispering his name and putting her arms around him.

'Ira, I'm so happy to see you! You have no idea.'

How long had it been? It felt like an eternity since she had last laid her eyes on him. If only they could stay like this forever. But all too soon he pulled away from her.

'Dmitry told me to come straight here. Did something happen? Why aren't you home? Did you have another argument with Mama?'

Even though she'd rehearsed what she was going to say to him, despite miserable days and sleepless nights thinking about this moment, she didn't know how to tell him. She must have looked terrible because his face lost all its colour.

'What happened?' he whispered.

'Let's go into the kitchen. I don't want to wake Sonya. Let me make you something to eat. You must be starving. I have some carrots. I can cook them for you . . .'

She made a move in the direction of the kitchen but he grabbed her hand. 'Ira, stop. Look at me.' She looked at him and, unable to take the expression on his face, burst into tears. 'Now you are scaring me. Will you tell me what's going on? Where are Mama and Papa?'

A German aeroplane was humming in the distance. A car horn sounded. Somewhere, a woman was screaming hysterically. Irina didn't hear any of it. All she could see was his anguished face in front of her. It was as if he already knew. 'They are gone, Maxim. The Gestapo . . .'

Maxim clenched his fists so hard, his knuckles cracked. 'They came for them?'

She nodded. 'About ten days ago. We haven't heard from them since.'

'You are right. We shouldn't have this conversation here. Let's go in the kitchen,' he said gloomily, throwing a quick glance at his sleeping daughter.

Her knees were trembling so much, she tripped over and almost fell. Maxim didn't offer to help. He didn't seem to notice but sank into a chair in the kitchen and stared into space silently, his face blank.

'It's all my fault,' he said, his voice breaking. When he looked up, there was such agony in his eyes, Irina gasped. 'They took them because of me. It's exactly what I was afraid of. Ever since I became a partisan . . . But no one knew about us here. We kept it a secret from everyone. Who told the Gestapo on us?'

It took her a moment to reply. 'Some people knew. Zina had many friends. It could have been anyone.' She couldn't tell him about Tamara, she realised. Because she wanted to protect her friend? Or because she wanted to protect herself? If Maxim knew Tamara was responsible for this, he might blame Irina. She held him and kissed his tears away, whispering soothing words, telling him everything was going to be all right. If only she could believe it herself.

When she placed a plate of boiled vegetables in front of him, he pushed it away and stood up. 'I have to go.'

'Where are you going?' she asked, trying to fight a dark cloud of foreboding.

'Home.'

She exhaled sharply, her hand on her mouth. It was exactly what she'd been afraid of. 'You can't go there. It's not safe. The house is probably being watched. Remember, they are looking for you. This is exactly what they are hoping for. That one day you will show up, searching for your parents.'

'Exactly. It's me they want. Once they have me, they will let them go.'

'Are you out of your mind? You are just going to walk in there and . . .' She couldn't continue. The words got stuck in her throat.

'They are my parents, Irina. I can't just sit back and do nothing. If I don't help them, they will die.'

'Help them by handing yourself in?'

'What choice do I have?'

'Don't you understand? If the Gestapo have you, they'll have no use for your parents. They won't let them go. They will kill them. And then they will torture and kill you.' She shuddered at the thought. 'Sonya can't live without her father.' *I can't live without my husband*, she wanted to add.

'What do you suggest? That I do nothing?'

That was exactly what she wanted to suggest. The Gestapo had Maxim's parents. As terrible as that was, nothing they did could change that. Maxim risking his life to fix the unfixable wasn't going to save them, but it would condemn him. Although she knew it was impossible, she wanted him to accept what had happened and go on with his life. She wanted him to let his parents go, so that he could live, so that she would have a husband and Sonya would have a father. Did that make her a terrible person? Was she selfish for wanting him to do nothing to save his parents' lives? She couldn't say any of it to him. She knew there was only one thing that was keeping Maxim from breaking down right there in the kitchen and that was a hope that he could still do something for them.

Taking his hand, she said, 'As long as they are useful to them, they will keep your parents alive. And that will gain us some time. Don't do anything in a hurry. Sleep on it. Think about it. Talk to the others. Azamat, Danilo. They might have some ideas.'

He sat back down. 'You might be right. We need to plan this carefully. Too much is at stake. But I'm not giving up. I couldn't live with myself if I did nothing.'

'I know.'

'They are my parents.'

'I know.' She couldn't stop herself from shaking, couldn't stop her hands from fidgeting, picking up cups and wiping invisible crumbs off the table. How could she keep him safe when he would give anything to save his parents, even his life?

'Pack your things. We have to go.'

'Where are we going?'

'It's not safe for you in Kiev. It would kill me if I lost you and Sonya. I couldn't bear if anything happened to you too. Then I would have nothing to live for.' Her heart beat faster with hope. Was he finally going to allow her to join him at the partisan battalion? But when she asked, he said, 'It's too dangerous. You can stay with Azamat's wife. She lives in the village of Buki. No one will find you there.'

Disappointment must have been written on her face because he drew her into a hug and told her everything was going to be all right. *All right how?* she wanted to ask. The last thing she wanted was to stay with a stranger when her husband needed her help and support. When he needed her to stop him from doing something reckless.

June 1943

Chapter 17

Lisa's dinner break was long over but she lingered in the cafeteria, trying to muster enough energy to go back to the stuffy kitchen and clean up. Every day they received less food, but she was still expected to report for work, to stir, chop and scrub until she could barely stand. It didn't help that she hardly saw Maxim anymore. Whenever she did catch a glimpse of him, he looked like a different man. There was no more laughter, no more guitar, no pleasant chatter with friends. His stubble had grown into a beard and hid half his face. There were circles under his eyes and his shoulders were stooped as if weighed down by a thousand worries.

A few times she'd approached him and asked how he was, if he wanted more food or something to drink. He barely grunted in reply. Gone was the easy-going, cheerful Maxim she had fallen in love with. In his place was a grim and monosyllabic individual who never looked up from his newspaper or maps. In the first week of June, Maxim turned into Danilo's twin: quiet, distant and brooding.

There was no sign of Yulya's chastising face and Lisa remained in her chair, absent-mindedly listening to Masha, who was reading a letter. 'And then he says, never a moment goes by when he doesn't think of me. He can't wait to hold me in his arms and it won't be long before he's here, on the outskirts of Kiev. Lisa, I'm going to see my husband soon! Can you imagine? After two years, we'll be together again.'

'I'm so pleased for you, Masha,' said Lisa, forcing a smile. The Ukrainian summer was finally here, the sun strong on her bare skin. In a different life, she would have liked nothing better than to run to the river and take a dive, splashing in the warm water without a care in the world. But these days, all she saw was the inside of the kitchen dugout, the hot stove, the dirty floor and the dwindling pile of potatoes. The Nazi officer she had shot still haunted her and she hadn't been on another mission with the partisans since. All she did was cook and sleep.

Masha covered the letter with kisses, folded it carefully and pressed it to her heart. 'It's the first letter I ever got from him.'

'How did you get this one?' There had been no correspondence and no news of any kind from the territories free from Hitler's clutches since the occupation started.

'The Red Army are not far from Kiev! And Oleg is one of them. Apparently, some partisans have been in contact with them. That's how he sent me this letter. You know what that means? Soon this war will be over, and all this will be behind us. My mama will come back. We can finally live a normal life, and maybe Oleg and I can have a baby. That's all I want. To start a family.'

'You are so lucky. You have so much to look forward to.' Lisa wanted to cry. Everything she wanted with Maxim, he already had with someone else, and there was nothing she could do about it.

'One day you'll be happy too. When the war is over, you'll meet someone.'

'I have met someone.'

'Someone else, I mean. Maybe the fact Maxim is married is a sign that he's not the one for you. You are still so young. You'll forget him soon enough.'

'Maxim is the only one for me. And I will never forget him.'

'He's not, darling. And you will.' Masha stroked Lisa's hair.

'I thought I was in love before, with a boy called Alexei. But it was nothing like this. Now I realise I was in love with the idea of love, of having someone propose to me and saying yes, of planning a wedding. I was too young then. Only now do I understand what love is all about.'

'But you are not even together. This feeling, it's all in your head. Love is only real when it's mutual.'

But Lisa wasn't listening to her. 'Why does he have to be married? I feel like my whole life is crashing down around me.'

'Not your whole life, silly. Just the life you imagined for yourself. A few months ago you didn't even know him.'

'Well, I'm not giving up. I'm going to fight for him.'

'What can you possibly hope for?'

'Maybe his wife doesn't love him. Maybe she'll meet someone else.' Lisa said it uncertainly, like she knew it was impossible. Who wouldn't love Maxim? And who in their right mind would even glance at another man when married to someone like him?

'You say it like you want her to leave him. What if he loves her? If you care for him, how could you wish it on him?'

Lisa turned away from Masha and saw Yulya walking towards them down the narrow path between the tables. Her face was twisted – in anger? Lisa nodded at her empty plate and said, 'I was just about to get back to work.'

But Yulya didn't seem to hear. Lisa had never seen the cook this agitated. Her eyes were wide and her chin wobbled. She opened her mouth to say something but her words were lost in the sound of an explosion. The ground under Lisa's feet and the walls around her shook. Masha screamed, grabbing the edge of the table. White-faced, Lisa stood as if rooted to the spot and looked questioningly at Yulya.

'What's happening?' cried Masha, the letter she was holding lovingly a moment ago forgotten on the floor.

Machine guns resounded in response to her question. This time the din of artillery didn't seem distant, roaring at the outskirts of the forest. This time it felt like the enemy was right here, outside the cafeteria, closing in on them.

'We need to go,' Yulya shouted, her eyes round with fear. 'Find a safe place before it's too late.'

'Too late for what? What is going on?' asked Masha. But Yulya didn't reply, shepherding the two girls away from the table and towards the exit. When they were halfway there, Lisa wrestled her hand out of Yulya's grip and ran across the cafeteria to a little table in the corner where she usually cut vegetables. She reached under the table and felt for her loaded rifle with her hands, finally taking it out. Trembling, she joined the two women, who seemed petrified as they watched the mayhem outside. It was as if someone had disturbed a large ant hill. The partisans jumped out of their dugouts, scattering in different directions, weapons in hand. Soon they were climbing trees and hiding behind rocks, all under the accompaniment of gunfire that seemed to get closer and closer.

The Nazis were no longer the dog that barked because it couldn't bite. They knew exactly what they were doing. And they were here, a few hundred metres away from the little settlement. Lisa wondered where Maxim was and whether he was safe. She wondered what was going to happen to them. Despite Yulya pulling on her arm, she couldn't walk out into the open space, where bullets whizzed past like angry bees. As hard as she tried, she couldn't force her feet to take her to safety. Yulya yanked her forward and shouted, 'We need to go. Soon they will be here.' Lisa could barely hear her over the roar of the artillery.

Dragged by Yulya, who was a lot stronger than she looked, Lisa moved forward. Like a robot, she put one foot in front of another without thinking, without feeling. The machine guns deafened her as she clung to the damp soil and grabbed the foliage with her bleeding fingers that she had cut with a knife that morning. Like a lizard she crawled across the clearing that over the last few months had become her home but was now scorched earth. Bullets cut the grass and hit the ground around her like a torrential rain. *This is it*, she thought, a silent groan trapped in her throat. *The next bullet is going to find me. I will remain here, forever in these woods, and no one will know what happened to me. I will never see my family again.* Unable to crawl any further, she put her hands over her ears and screamed. She screamed with all her might but could still hear Yulya's voice, could still feel her hands shaking her with vigour. 'Follow me or I will leave you here. We need to get to those trees, or we're lost!'

Lisa looked up into Yulya's face. It was completely white but her eyes were burning with determination as she pulled the two girls behind her.

Yulya found a giant oak tree, old and knobbly and large enough to shelter a garrison, let alone three terrified women. Under the shower of German bullets they climbed as high as they could, hiding in the leaves. Lisa clung to the tree as if her life depended on it. Finding refuge in the branches, she peered out but couldn't see anything beyond smoke. Something exploded overhead and she felt her hands shaking. If she wasn't sitting firmly astride a branch, she would have fallen out.

The partisans had dispersed and the settlement seemed deserted, but for half a dozen bodies left on the ground. When she saw them, Lisa stifled a cry and wanted to climb down and run to them, peer into every face to make sure it wasn't Maxim or Anna. At the bottom of the hill, behind the canopy of smoke, she could just make out grey shadows, their rifles and machine guns pointing at the settlement. Men in hated Nazi uniforms were not the only ones moving swiftly towards the partisan battalion. There were others too, wearing civilian clothes, waving and gesticulating. With horror Lisa realised they were Ukrainians who had turned their backs on their people and were helping the Nazis. Shaken, she watched the little figures surrounding them like locusts, the guns in their hands spitting out death.

Out of the trees and from behind the rocks, the partisan rifles barked in response.

Lisa leant closer to her branch, embracing it like a lover, like it was the only thing standing between her and death. This was her greatest fear realised. Since the moment she had arrived at the partisan battalion, she'd been afraid of the day the Germans would find her hiding place in the woods. Now that this day had come, she felt like she was living her worst nightmare. She should have returned to Kiev and made amends with her family. With luck, the Nazis would have left her alone. But the woods had seemed so peaceful, so serene. So safe. And look at her now, besieged, under attack and trapped in what had turned into hell on earth within minutes.

'The cursed Nazis!' shouted Yulya, who was hiding in the branches above. 'Soon the day will come when they will pay for everything.'

'How did they find us?' asked Masha, her voice barely audible.

'Someone betrayed us. And I have a good idea who that someone was.'

Lisa thought of Matvei's pig-like face as he told her he would do anything to survive this war. She had been right not to trust him. She searched for him in the swarms below, but the enemy was still far off and the visibility was low. She didn't see him.

The bombs landed closer and closer, making the earth tremble. With every explosion Lisa squeezed her eyes shut and thought, *This is it, this is how I'm going to die.* She wished she knew a prayer. With every burst of machine-gun fire, she repeated, 'Please help us, God. Please help us!' Could God hear her? She could hardly hear her own thoughts. Another bomb, another 'Help us, God.' It was comforting, as if now that she had said the words, her safety was in someone else's hands. And a good thing too – she couldn't trust herself to save her own life. She could barely trust herself to hold on to the tree branch without falling out, so afraid was she of what was happening around her.

'You have your rifle! Do something! Shoot at them! What are you waiting for?' shouted Yulya.

It took Lisa a few moments to realise the older woman was talking to her. She had forgotten all about her rifle that was uselessly dangling behind her back. Shuddering as if awoken from a deep sleep, she pulled it closer, thinking, *What's the point? Could it make a difference?* Despite the incessant fire from the partisans, the enemy kept coming and there was no end to them. Even though she held a weapon in her hands and knew exactly how to use it, Lisa had never felt so helpless.

The rifle felt heavy in her sweaty palms. It almost slipped and fell to the ground but she grabbed it just in time, holding it tighter and bringing it into position, just like Maxim had taught her. As she was about to shoot – pressing not pulling the trigger – an ear-splitting noise was heard and she felt the tree under her feet shift and keel to one side. 'We've been hit,' she heard through the ringing in her ears. Was it Masha or Yulya? It was impossible to tell. The desperate screaming – was it them or was it her? Dropping the rifle to the ground, Lisa held on for dear life. As if in slow motion, the tree toppled over, a heavy branch hitting Lisa in the face. A sharp pain pierced her wrist.

For a few moments, everything went dark. When Lisa opened her eyes again, she was on the ground, her arm trapped under a thick branch. Her vision was blurry and her temples ached. As if through a fog she noticed flames. Yulya and Masha, where were they? She lifted her head but all she could see was the fire devouring what was left of the oak tree that had served as their shelter.

Lisa called out their names but couldn't hear beyond the whistling of bullets. Pulling with all her might, twisting and turning and screaming in frustration, she tried to free her arm but couldn't. Her eyes stung from the smoke and her tears blinded her.

The flames licked the branches like grotesque orange tongues. As each terrifying moment trickled by, the fire was gaining momentum, reaching for her, breathing hot death in her face, cracking and whistling and whispering. How long would it take before it was upon her? Another minute, a few seconds?

A part of the tree collapsed, hitting Lisa hard on the head, and she could no longer hear the terrifying cacophony of war, nor see the flames that were inching their way closer.

Everything was gone. Even the pain was gone.

Chapter 18

In the village of Buki, two hundred kilometres west of Kiev on the left bank of Rastaviz River, with the sun bright in her eyes and the scent of apple trees in full bloom in her nostrils, Irina was weeding the garden. Not that Azamat's wife Agnessa had much growing there, just some carrots and beets and a couple of bushes of undernourished tomatoes. Before the war, she had chickens and goats and even a cow, but on the second day of the occupation two German soldiers had marched in and taken them. On the third day of occupation, they arrested Agnessa's old father for being a Communist. Almost two years later, Agnessa couldn't talk about it without tears in her eyes. Irina couldn't hear about it without tears in hers either, thinking of her parents-in-law, lost in a Nazi prison camp, perhaps forever.

Agnessa had told Irina proudly that the vegetables in the garden would last them all winter if they were careful. Looking at the tiny patch, Irina was doubtful. But she wasn't about to pass up the opportunity for some physical work in the fresh air. Ignoring her aching knees, she trimmed and pruned and pulled at the pesky weeds that kept reappearing, no matter how hard she had battled with them the week before. There was something about being close to the soil that made her whole body relax and her chest feel lighter. This land was here long before the Nazis had invaded. And it would be here long after they were gone. It was a reassuring thought that filled her heart with hope.

In June 1943, she had every reason to be hopeful. Even the German-controlled, Nazi-propaganda-filled *Ukrainian Word* printed only good news these days. The Nazi party had been dissolved in Italy. 'The enemy', meaning the Red Army, was gaining ground. No one seemed to know where exactly they were but what Irina did know was that the Nazis were dedicating significant resources to digging trenches and fortifying Kiev. That, more than anything, spoke to her about the Soviets' imminent arrival. And here, under the blue skies with not an aircraft in sight this morning, hidden away from the world behind the tall tomato bushes, she could sense the end of the war the way swallows sensed the approach of spring.

As she continued with her task, whistling a popular tune under her breath, Sonya crawled through the grass, then stood up and toddled towards her mother. 'Mama, a man!' she crooned, pointing in the direction of the fence. 'Mama, man!'

Irina looked up from the carrots she was tending and squinted in the sun. A tall young man, almost a boy, was staggering through their garden, as if he was drunk or hurt. When he approached, Irina saw blood on his face and tunic. He was wearing the same tattered Red Army uniform as Maxim. Although this man with his blond hair and slim build looked nothing like her husband, Irina paled and her heart pounded with dread.

The young man widened his eyes as if trying to tell her something, then swayed and tilted sideways. Irina leapt to his side but it was too late. By the time she got to him, he had collapsed on the grass. She called out but he didn't respond. His eyes were closed.

She tugged at his arm, trying to shift him, but he was too heavy. There was no way she could move him on her own.

Scooping Sonya up into her arms, she ran towards the house. 'Agnessa! Are you there? There's a wounded partisan in our garden,' she shouted through the door.

'Hush, child,' exclaimed Agnessa, placing her knitting on the table and her finger to her mouth. 'Not so loud. You never know who might be listening.'

Irina muttered an apology and together they rushed to the garden. Irina saw Agnessa's face go white at the sight of the man. She ran through the carrots, crushing them with her feet, and took his hand. 'Anton! Can you hear me?'

'You know this boy?' asked Irina.

'It's my daughter Anna's sweetheart. He joined the battalion only eight months ago.' She stroked Anton's cheek, whispering, 'Can you hear me?'

Irina crouched by the older woman. 'He's still breathing,' she said.

'Wheezing. Is he going to be all right?' Agnessa's hands shook as she held Anton's head in her lap.

'He's covered in blood. Let's get him inside and clean him. Then we can call a doctor. You know a doctor, don't you?'

They lifted the young partisan and carried him into the house, placing him on a small folding bed on the porch. Agnessa unbuttoned his tunic. 'He's been shot,' she whispered, pointing at a gun wound in his left shoulder. 'He lost his parents nine months ago. Poor boy hasn't been the same since. My daughter and he are inseparable. What if something has happened to her? I couldn't bear it.' It took Agnessa a minute to compose herself and wipe the tears from her face. Together they cleaned Anton's face and chest, careful not to touch the raw flesh torn by the bullet. Anton groaned but didn't open his eyes. Agnessa cried, 'The doctor. We need the doctor.'

'I'll fetch him. Stay with Anton. Just tell me where to go and look after Sonya for me.'

Irina didn't have to go far. The village was small and consisted of a dozen houses, a boarded-up and padlocked library and a shop that in the distant pre-war past sold white bread, fresh out of the oven and delicious. Now it was a collection point for sheets and blankets for the wounded Germans. Once a week, a small window opened and a grim Ukrainian man with an eye patch and a broken arm divided the unpalatable German-issue bread among the dwindling village population. Irina walked past the shop and turned the corner to the doctor's house.

When she returned, accompanied by an old man who walked with a limp but seemed eager to help, Anton hadn't regained consciousness and Agnessa had worked herself into a frenzy, crying by his side as if he was already dead. She looked like she could do with the doctor's attention herself. 'He said he didn't want to live without his parents. When the Nazis shot them, he said he wished he was there, so he could die with them. And now this! It's as if God has heard him.'

'Trust me, God had nothing to do with this,' said the doctor. 'Why don't you let me take a look at him?'

To Agnessa's tearful relief, the doctor pronounced that Anton's wound wasn't life-threatening. He removed the bullet, cleaned and bandaged the shoulder.

Before he left, the doctor said, 'Anton needs complete rest. If he develops a fever, send for me at once. I'll come back tomorrow to check on him.'

That evening, Irina settled Sonya to bed and had just closed her eyes herself, when she thought she heard noises. Someone was walking outside. Under the bedroom door she could see flashes of a kerosene lamp. She stepped out into the corridor to find Agnessa standing there. In her white nightie, with her face pale and her grey hair loose around her shoulders, she looked like a ghost. 'I thought I heard a groan,' she said wistfully. 'Here it is again.'

The two women ran to Anton's side. His eyes were open. Unfocused and confused, he was looking around the room as if not quite sure where he was. 'Agnessa Mikhailovna,' he whispered. 'Is it you?'

'Anton, dear! Don't talk. The doctor said you are going to recover but you need to rest.'

He didn't seem to hear. Fear was in his eyes. 'I came straight here. I didn't know where else to go.'

'You did the right thing. You know this is your home. You are safe here.'

'Nowhere is safe. Not for us. I was lucky to get away.'

Irina wanted to ask what happened but her voice failed her. The familiar dark foreboding gripped her and she could do nothing but stare at Anton, who tried to sit up in bed and groaned in pain, falling back on the pillow. 'We were surprised by the Nazis. I've never seen so many of them in one place. Our battalion is completely wiped out.' Irina heard him but refused to understand. Her legs gave out and she sank into a chair. If the battalion had been wiped out, where was her husband and the father of her child? Where was Maxim?

In her mind, she could see him at the house in Podol a few weeks ago, collapsed over the kitchen table, devastated by the news of his parents. She could see him safe in her arms in the small church in Priorka, whispering that he would always be with her, that he would never leave her. And she believed him. To this day, she believed him because the alternative, a life without him, was too terrible to contemplate. And here was Anton, bringing her worst fears to life with his words.

As if from a great distance, she heard Agnessa's broken voice. 'Wiped out? What about the others? What about Anna? Azamat?'

'I don't know,' whispered Anton. 'It was hell on earth. I don't know if anyone else survived.'

*

How did she make it through the night without crumbling? Maxim and Irina were supposed to grow old together. They were supposed to live a long married life together, waking up in each other's arms, cooking meals, arguing, making up, taking their daughter to kindergarten and school. Having more children. Having grandchildren. What had happened to their dream?

Letting go of the sleeping Sonya's hand, Irina slid to the cold floor and remained there with her head on the floorboards, sobbing quietly. She tried to imagine Maxim's face, alive with laughter, and couldn't. She tried to feel him out there and couldn't. It was as if he was truly gone. With everything she had, she clung to one remaining sliver of hope, despite the dread and the horror inside her. Because she couldn't imagine her life without her one shining light, she hoped for a miracle. Her husband, the love of her life, couldn't have left her. It was impossible. She had already lost so many people she loved. She couldn't lose him too.

As hard as she tried, she couldn't get Anton's words out of her mind. He had told the two women the Nazis appeared without warning, surprising the battalion as they were relaxing after a long day. One minute there were songs and laughter and jokes. Someone was strumming a guitar. The next, the woods exploded in gunshots and screams of agony. Before the partisans even realised what was happening, a dozen of them had been cut down. All Anton could think of was finding Anna. He didn't know where she was or whether she was safe. Instead of taking cover, he crawled under the torrent of bullets through the grass that wasn't tall enough to hide him, crawled from one dead body to another, glancing into the lifeless faces of his friends and shouting in anguish, his voice lost in another explosion, another burst of machine-gun fire. And then a sharp pain in his shoulder.

For a long time, he lay face down on the damp ground. When he came to, the partisans, what was left of them, had hidden away in nearby rocks and trees and were firing at the Nazis who never stopped coming. There was no end to the dark shadows running towards the settlement. Relying on his one good hand, Anton made it to a large tree and hid inside a hollow. He didn't know how long he spent there. It could have been a whole day or a couple of hours. When he finally emerged, it was quiet in the woods, as if the horrifying attack had been nothing but his imagination. For a moment he doubted himself, wondering if it had all been a bad dream. But then he saw the bodies scattered around the meadow. Gritting his teeth, he checked every one of them, looking for signs of life, looking for Anna. He couldn't find her.

Dawn came, surprising Irina on the floor, trembling and stiff. But even as the sun filled the room, she couldn't move. Maybe if she stayed in one spot long enough, refusing to accept the unacceptable, it would all go away. If only she could ignore her fears, they would vanish like an early-morning dream. She wanted to hide from the ugly world forever. But her little girl needed feeding, cleaning and changing. The water had to be boiled and the porridge cooked. Finally, Irina forced herself to get up, kiss her daughter's peaceful face and make her way into the kitchen, where she did her chores without giving it a thought, walking around slowly, as if every little movement brought pain.

Anton was asleep on the porch, his body shuddering every now and again, as if in his dreams he was reliving his ordeal. Agnessa was already in the kitchen, washing the floor. The table, the cupboards, even the windows sparkled. Irina wondered if she'd been up all night, cleaning. Everyone dealt with grief differently, she realised. While she wanted to crawl into a hole and disappear, Agnessa couldn't sit still without breaking down. The two of them embraced in silence and then the older woman whispered, 'Courage! We don't know anything for certain yet.'

The word *yet* filled Irina with terror. With her fist in her mouth to stop herself from screaming, she leant on the kitchen table and watched the porridge as it burnt on the stove. She couldn't believe it; she was angry with Maxim, for leaving her, for giving his life to the greater good and abandoning his family. What were they going to do without him? Would her daughter even remember him when she was older? It broke Irina's heart that Sonya might grow up not knowing her father. There was a knock on the door and Dmitry came in. Irina rushed to his side. Although Dmitry wasn't part of Maxim's partisan battalion, he worked closely with the partisans and often spent time at the battalion. She was relieved to see him alive and well. 'Thank God! I was so worried about you. Do you know anything?'

'The battalion was attacked at dawn the day before yesterday. It seems the Nazis knew the exact location and went all out.'

'What does that mean? What happened to the partisans? How bad are the losses?' Irina looked into his pale face, hoping for good news. But he had no news. His voice was hoarse, as if he hadn't slept the night before either.

'That's what we are trying to establish.'

He put his arms around her, and she sobbed into his shoulder. 'I don't know how I am going to live without him. I don't want to live without him.'

'Don't cry. You'll scare Sonya. You have to pull yourself together, for her.'

'I don't want to lose him. I can't lose him.'

'Let's not panic until we know for sure.'

Dmitry told Irina and Agnessa he had sent people to villages close to the partisan battalion to see if anyone had seen or heard anything. 'I'll go there myself and try to find out what happened.'

'Eat something first,' said Irina. 'We have some soup.'

But just like Irina, Dmitry couldn't look at food. After he left, the two women huddled together around Anton's bed. They couldn't read, sew or knit. They could barely talk. Agnessa had an old black-and-white photograph in her lap, of a young couple holding a newborn baby wrapped up in a woolly shawl. 'When Anna was a child, all she wanted was to be a musketeer or a pirate. No fairy princesses for her. I remember staying up all night, making her a musketeer costume for a ball at school. I still have it in the attic somewhere. She looked dashing in it. She was always a warrior, my Anna. So when Azamat went into the woods, she wanted to go, too. I forbade it, of course, but she refused to listen to a word I had to say.' Tears fell in her lap as she spoke and the faces in the photograph became blurry, as if they were about to disappear altogether.

Irina couldn't bear the woman's anguish as she cried for her daughter and husband. Holding her own daughter close, as if to protect her from evil, she patted Agnessa's hand. In silence they waited for news. Irina's heart stopped at every noise and every shadow outside. What if it was Dmitry, coming to confirm their worst fears?

Dmitry returned in the evening, his face grim. He looked almost as if he didn't want to tell them what he knew. Irina braced herself, clenching her fists, grinding her teeth together.

'It's not good, I'm afraid. There's no one left at the battalion. No one alive, anyway,' he said. Irina forced herself to focus on his face but couldn't see much through her tears. All she could hear was the tick-tock of the clock on the wall and the noise inside her head.

Agnessa prompted, 'Tell us what you found out, young man.' She was trying to be so brave but her lips trembled from the effort.

He sank into a chair, as if broken by the weight of what he had witnessed. 'Whatever happened out there, it must have been brutal. There are dead bodies everywhere, both our men and the enemy. We counted forty dead partisans. That's almost half of the battalion.'

Irina tried to stop her hands from shaking. 'And Maxim?'

'We didn't find him or Anna or Azamat. The settlement seems abandoned. If there were survivors, they must have moved on somewhere. Where, I don't know.'

'There are other partisan battalions around,' said Agnessa. 'Maybe they went there.'

'It is possible. Unfortunately, we don't know their exact locations. We are searching the villages and the nearby woods.'

The women sat as if in a trance, while Dmitry had some dinner, fed Sonya and spoke to Anton. Not touching her food, Irina stared at the flowers on Agnessa's faded wallpaper until they blurred into one. The walls swayed in front of her as if she was drunk.

Irina watched the silver hand of the clock on the wall as it showed one o'clock, two o'clock, three in the morning. Another minute of agonising uncertainty, another sleepless and miserable hour. Irina's heart thudded in the dark.

So many times in the past she had had nightmares about something like this happening, a horrifying dream in which Maxim would be falling into an abyss while she was trying to save him, to reach out a hand to him only for him to slip through her fingers and vanish. She would wake up shaking and afraid and then breathe out in relief because it was only a dream. As she sat on the floor and stared at the clock, her heart aching, Irina prayed she would wake up.

At five in the morning, Dmitry and Agnessa finally succumbed to exhaustion and fell asleep in the living room, leaning on the table. Anton slept on his folding bed on the porch. Sonya was curled up under a warm blanket in her mother's bed.

Irina was the only one who was still awake when she heard someone knocking. Wearily she got up and walked on shaking legs to the door, dreading bad news.

In the doorway, blocking the rising sun, stood Maxim.

Irina couldn't help it, her hand flew to her mouth and she cried out. At first, she thought she was imagining him. He was an illusion, nothing more. She had longed to see him so much, her subconscious was giving her what she wanted. Mutely she watched him. Maxim looked like a shadow of the man she knew and loved. His face was white and thinner than she remembered. His stubble was growing into a beard. His eyes were dim. He stared at her for a second with a forlorn expression on his face, as if he, too, had thought he might never see her again.

With the rising sun behind him, it looked like he was on fire. In silence she reached for him. He didn't disappear under her touch but took her hand in his and brought it to his lips, kissing the tips of her fingers. She whispered his name. He gathered her in his arms and pressed her to him, and they stood close together, not moving, not talking, barely breathing.

'You are alive!' she cried finally, tears streaming down her face. 'I was going out of my mind. I thought I'd lost you. I was so afraid.'

'Ira, please, don't cry. I'm fine.' His lips were on her face and he was kissing her tears away.

She led him to the kitchen, closing the door behind them. She didn't want to wake the others. They needed rest and Irina needed some time alone with her husband. She couldn't believe she was seeing him again. 'Anton is here. He told us the Nazis attacked the battalion, said it was like hell on earth.'

'It was hell on earth. But it's over now.' He seemed reluctant to talk about it. Could she blame him? Patiently she waited, sitting next to him at the table and clinging to his arm. After a moment of silence, he continued, 'Someone betrayed us. It was a well-planned operation and the Nazis went all out. They knew exactly where to find us and didn't spare the forces or the ammunition. It was a massacre.'

'How bad are . . .' she stammered '. . . the losses?'

'Bad. Those of us who survived gathered at the battalion near Emilchino.'

'I can't believe someone would do this. Betray you like this.'

'I can't believe it either.' He shook his head with sadness.

'Do you know who it was?'

'We have some suspicions.'

'Someone from the battalion?' From the expression on his face, she suspected it might be. He shrugged and didn't reply. She put her arms around him, squeezing softly, trying to make him smile. 'I can't believe I'm seeing you again. It's a miracle! I don't know how I lived these past twenty-four hours. I was imagining all sorts of things . . .'

'You won't get rid of me that easily.'

'What about Azamat and Anna? Are they . . .'

'They are at Emilchino battalion. They are safe.'

'Thank God! I better wake Agnessa. I can't wait to give her the good news.' Irina jumped to her feet and rushed out of the kitchen. In the doorway she paused and turned around. 'No more separations, Maxim. I'm coming with you, no matter where you go. And if you try to stop me, I will divorce you.'

'On what grounds? Trying to keep you safe?'

'Keeping me away from you.'

'Imagine what would have happened if I had listened to you and you and Sonya were with me when the Nazis attacked. I can't bear thinking about it.'

'If I was there, we would be together and I wouldn't live for a whole day and night, thinking I was never going to see you again. I mean it. No more separations.'

'You can't imagine what it's like out there. When I'm facing the Germans, I can't be worrying about you too.'

'You can't imagine what it's like *here*. Not knowing if you are dead or alive. Not knowing where you are. For once, think about how it feels for me.'

'That's all I ever think about.'

'Then let us come with you. Because being away from you is unbearable. I know it's dangerous. But it's dangerous everywhere.' *Look at what happened to your parents*, she wanted to add. 'At least we'll be together.' She could see by his face he was torn about it. She pressed his hand and added, 'Having us there will be good for you. You won't be coming back to an empty dugout. At the end of every day, we will be waiting for you. Imagine what it would be like to come home and see me and Sonya there. It will make all the difference in the world.'

His face brightened. 'You might be right. Now more than ever I need you by my side.'

There was something in his eyes, a fleeting fear that was soon gone. But Irina was too happy to dwell on it. 'Thank God,' she whispered. 'By your side is where we belong.'

'What about Sonya? It's too dangerous in the woods for a small child. Is there anyone you trust who could look after her for us?'

Irina looked up, horrified. 'You want to leave Sonya behind?'

'Until it's safe to have her with us.'

'No.' Irina shook her head adamantly. 'No!' she repeated, louder. 'I won't be separated from my daughter. Anywhere I go, she comes with me.'

'Think about it logically. Our settlement was attacked. Many people died. It could happen again.'

'And what if something bad happens to her here and I'm not there to protect her?' What he was saying was impossible. How could he even suggest it? 'Besides, she's still breastfed. She can't do without her mama.' *I can't do without my baby*, she thought. Maxim must have seen it in her face because he didn't argue anymore but walked over to her and drew her to him, kissing her deeply. As they stood in the dark kitchen with their foreheads pressed close, for the first time in as long as she could remember, she had hope. Because finally they would be together.

Chapter 19

In a crowded hospital room built of wood and straw, Lisa listlessly chewed on a piece of bread, staring into space. Every time she closed her eyes, she saw the woods burning and their settlement crumbling under enemy onslaught. After their tree had caught fire, she woke up to find herself in someone's arms, being carried to safety. All she could see was pine trees, evergreen, tall and peaceful. Peaceful! There were no flames rushing for her through the branches, no bombs raining from the sky, no machine guns roaring in deathly fury, as if the whole nightmare scenario had been nothing but a bad dream. Except that her wrist was throbbing, providing a grim reminder that it had been real. Her head had felt heavy and painful, as if filled with broken glass. Her ears were ringing. She had groaned and closed her eyes.

Whoever was carrying her had placed her gently on the grass. 'Lisa, are you awake? Can you hear me?'

She thought she recognised the voice. Opening her eyes, she found herself looking into Maxim's face. She couldn't help it: she smiled with relief at seeing him so close. Somewhere nearby, Bear barked. 'What happened to me?' she murmured.

'A burning tree fell on you. You are lucky to be alive.'

He sat on the ground next to her, watching her with kindness. She lowered her gaze. 'My wrist . . . It hurts so much. And my head feels sore.' She pressed on her temples with her one good hand, feeling groggy and disorientated, like she had woken up with the worst hangover of her life. She didn't know where she was or where they were headed.

'You probably have a concussion. Don't worry. I'm taking you to another battalion. They have doctors and nurses who will take a look at you. You are going to be just fine.' Bear appeared by her side, carrying a stick. His tail was wagging, like he was pleased to see an old friend.

'Wait. Masha and Yulya were with me. Are they safe?'

It took him a while to answer. When he did, his voice was so low, she could barely hear him. 'Yulya didn't make it. I'm sorry.'

'Oh no.' Lisa thought of Yulya as she dragged two petrified girls to find shelter through a swarm of enemy bullets. She thought of her with her apron on, commanding the little kitchen like a general commanded his army. 'I don't believe it. Yulya was the strongest woman I know. If she didn't make it, what chance do any of us have?'

'Yulya was a wonderful person. Under her grumpy exterior was a heart of gold.'

'She saved my life. If it wasn't for her, I would have never made it to safety.' Lisa stifled a sob. 'And Masha?'

'Azamat and Danilo have Masha. They went ahead to the Emilchino battalion. We'll see them when we get there.'

'Is she all right?' She tried to read the expression on his face but it was impossible. He made his face unreadable. What was he hiding from her?

'She's badly burnt.' When Lisa cried, he took her hand and pressed it. 'We have to have faith. She's still alive. That's good news.'

'I suppose.' She was quiet for a moment. 'What about Anna?'

'Anna is safe. She's with her father.'

'Thank God,' Lisa whispered. 'I was trapped under that tree.

I couldn't move. The tree was burning.' She could still see the flames licking the branches around her. She trembled.

'I got to you just in time.'

'You saved me,' she whispered. 'Why did you do that?'

'What do you mean?'

'You risked your life to save mine. Why?'

It felt like the whole world had retreated, as if it no longer existed. It was just the two of them in the deserted forest and nothing else mattered. His face was close to hers and his eyes softened. Any moment now he would lean in and his lips would touch hers. Lisa closed her eyes and held her breath in anticipation of their first kiss. She had been imagining it for so long and here it was, the moment she'd been dreaming of as she lay shivering in her cold bed made of straw. She could feel his breath on her face, could almost taste his lips.

But he didn't kiss her. All he said was, 'Anyone would have done the same in my place. We were completely surrounded by the Germans. You and I were lucky to get away. Not everyone had made it out alive.'

'How many . . .' She hesitated. 'How many didn't?'

'Many. We won't know the exact number until later.' He was no longer looking at her. Lisa held her head low and cried. In the last five months, the partisans had become her family. The little battalion had been her home and now it was gone without a trace. Everything seemed so hopeless, like there was no light left in the world. 'We need to keep moving,' said Maxim. 'Are you hungry? They will have some food for you at the other battalion.'

She shook her head. For the first time since the war had started, the thought of food made her feel sick. She wanted to close her eyes and fall into a deep sleep, so she wouldn't have to think of the inferno that had devoured the clearing where a hundred people had lived and breathed and hoped. But most of all, she wanted to feel his arms around her again. Nothing and no one could comfort her the way he did.

'I'll carry you on my back, all right? Can you hold on?'

'It's too hard for you, with all your things and a rifle. I can walk.'

She tried to get up and immediately fell back down.

'Come on,' he said, hoisting her on his back. She held on to his neck, wrapping her legs around him. In his hands he carried his rifle and his rucksack. With Bear running ahead, they moved in silence through the woods. She listened to his breathing and almost drifted off, letting go of him for a moment and sliding down. He caught her just in time and helped her up again.

Leaning her head on his shoulder and hoping he wouldn't notice, she inhaled his scent. Suddenly she no longer felt afraid. As long as she stayed like this, with her arms and legs around him like a bear cub climbing a tree, she was going to be safe. He would protect her from the cold and the hunger and from the enemy bullets. He would protect her from doubt, heartbreak and sadness. Now that he had risked his life to save her, she belonged to him irrevocably.

Even though her wrist was killing her and her vision was blurry, Lisa didn't want the journey to end. 'Are we lost?' she asked. It felt like they'd been walking in circles for hours. All she could see was trees. There was no end to them and they all looked the same.

'Don't worry. I grew up playing in these woods. Besides, I have a map. We won't get lost.'

She wanted to tell him she wasn't worried, that nothing would please her more than getting lost in the woods with him. But all too soon, the trees parted and they came to a wide open space. On the outskirts of a large meadow, partially hidden by trees and bushes, she could see huts made of straw and wood. 'Where are we?' she asked weakly. She wanted to close her eyes and sleep for a thousand years. More than anything she longed to forget.

'Remember I told you there were other partisan battalions scattered around these woods? This is one of them. They have good facilities here. A hospital with real nurses and even a doctor. They will look after you.'

As they neared the huts, Lisa spotted Azamat and Danilo, their faces grim and muddy. She saw wounded partisans on stretchers and new faces leaning over them, helping them up, offering them water, towels and something to eat. Those who could move did so as if in slow motion, shell-shocked and uncertain. Lisa recognised Alex and Sergei and her heart filled with a joy that surprised her. She had never thought she would be happy to see those two. But here they were, like old friends she thought she had lost forever, and it was as if a small part of her previous life was back. She couldn't see Masha anywhere.

Maxim carried her to a large hut that turned out to be a hospital, placed her on the bed and said goodbye, leaving her in the capable hands of a nurse called Alya. Lisa wanted desperately to ask him to stay. But she knew he was needed elsewhere.

Alya never stopped shaking her head as she examined Lisa's wrist, talking in a deep voice that seemed to belong to someone else, someone bigger and stockier and more substantial than the five-foot-four girl with braids. Just like Masha, she seemed kind and caring and genuinely in love with her job. 'You poor people. My heart breaks for all of you and what you had to go through.'

Lisa felt so tired. She barely had the energy to speak. 'My friend was brought here a while ago. Her name is Masha,' she said quietly, watching Alya's face for clues.

'The blonde girl with severe burns?'

'Yes, that's her.' Severe? Lisa wanted to ask what Alya meant but was too afraid. What if she told her Masha wasn't going to make it? 'When can I see her?'

'She's still unconscious. When she wakes up, I'll let you know.'

'Is she going to get better?'

Just like Maxim, Alya hesitated before answering. 'Only time will tell, dear. Can you move your wrist for me?'

Wincing, Lisa moved her wrist. 'It hurts.'

'The good news is, I don't think it's fractured. If it was, you wouldn't be able to move it at all. It looks like a bad sprain. You need to rest it for me. You think you can do that?'

Lisa nodded while Alya bandaged her wrist. 'What about my headache? My head feels so heavy. I'm all dizzy and confused.'

'You said a branch fell on you? It's probably a concussion. Were you unconscious for any period of time? We will keep you in hospital for a couple of days. Limit exposure to bright lights and loud sounds. Your body needs time to heal. No strenuous activity.'

'We better tell the Nazis not to attack until I make a full recovery.'

Alya laughed, but then added, 'You also need to avoid unnecessary movements of your head and neck.'

'Great! It gives me an excuse to lie in bed and do nothing.'

'Drink plenty of water.'

'Do you have anything stronger?'

'If you have any difficulty talking, severe headaches, increased heart rate or double vision, let me know right away. You are one lucky girl. You'll be back to normal in no time.'

Thanks to Maxim, Lisa thought. *I'm lucky because of him. If it wasn't for him, I wouldn't be here at all.* The thought that she could have died filled her with horror, but the memory of Maxim carrying her to safety made her feel warm inside, and a little less lonely.

On beds all around her were other wounded partisans, some sleeping, others moaning in pain, but some were laughing or playing cards. Somewhere, a fight broke out over the only real pillow in the whole battalion. She heard a nurse telling the two men off. 'This is a hospital. We don't injure people here, we heal them. Shame on you. You do this again and I will take the pillow away.' She spoke to grown men like they were children and they quietened down, apologising profusely.

In the morning Lisa was still exhausted, having spent the night wide awake, her wrist aching, her heart aching, thinking about all those people who had died so senselessly, so unexpectedly. One minute they were enjoying a rest, the next running for their lives, while swarms of grey uniforms closed in on them. Before she had her breakfast, she asked Alya to take her to Masha. As she sat in a small wooden chair by her friend's bed, the palm of her hand pressed to her chest, Lisa tried not to show the shock she felt at the sight of her. Masha's face and most of her body had been bandaged. If it wasn't for the blonde hair, she wouldn't have recognised her. For a moment she thought it was some mistake and it wasn't Masha in front of her at all but some other woman mangled by war. For a long time she sat by her friend's side and held her hand, telling her how happy she was that she had met her on the train of death that fateful day in January, how lucky everyone at the battalion was to have her as their nurse, how everyone was waiting for her to get better, that she would get better soon, before she even knew it. If only she could believe her own words. But how did one recover from something like that? Not an inch on Masha's skin was intact.

'Will she recover?' she asked the nurse, a plump girl with a permanent frown on her face, as she returned to her own bed.

'If she does, it will be a miracle. Her injuries are very severe.'

Lisa crept back to her bed, lay face down on her damp blanket and didn't get up until lunchtime.

The only thing that took her mind off Masha was Maxim. He had stood in front of enemy bullets and pulled her unconscious body from under a burning tree. He'd risked his life so that she would live. If this wasn't proof of his feelings for her, she didn't know what was. After having been in the woods with him, after looking into his eyes and seeing the affection there, Lisa no longer had any doubt. It wasn't just her imagination. He felt for her.

All day she waited impatiently for him to come and see her. She drove Alya crazy, asking her what time it was. Finally, the nurse had become so annoyed with Lisa, she gave her a watch. Eagerly Lisa stared at the little hands as they moved around the dial, wondering where Maxim was. She remembered him saying something about going back to the original settlement to take care of the bodies. The thought made her tremble with despair.

He is probably back by now, she thought when it was four in the afternoon. *He is having his dinner,* she thought at six. Soon it was seven and then eight and still there was no sign of him. When the night fell, she knew he was unlikely to visit but she didn't fall asleep until the little watch showed three in the morning.

She woke up at nine, feeling groggy and exhausted.

'Maxim came to see you. But you were asleep, so he left,' said Alya.

Lisa cursed herself. Why couldn't she have stayed awake a little longer?

Lisa spent the day sitting in silence next to Masha in her little chair, watching her friend's face for any signs of life. In the afternoon, she asked Alya for a comb and some make-up. 'Make-up! I don't even remember what that is. Next you'll be asking me for a cigarette!' Alya laughed like Lisa was crazy but she did bring her a comb. Lisa washed in the common tub as best as she could with one hand, her wrist still bandaged and raw. She scrubbed her face and hair with soap, and then combed her hair. She didn't touch her food.

When Maxim finally appeared in the evening, looking tired and unshaven, Lisa's heart soared. He had that effect on her, an ability to make her forget all her fears just by being there. 'Look what I have for you,' he said, watching her with a smile.

In his hands Lisa saw a hunk of cheese. She felt her stomach rumbling. Unwrapping the cheese, grinning at him, she shoved it in her mouth and mumbled a thank you.

'You are welcome. I was worried about you.'

She felt a warmth spread through her. He had been worried about her. As she lay here thinking of him, he was thinking of her too. And he'd brought her a present. It meant so much. 'Don't worry. Alya says I'll be good as new in no time.'

It was dinnertime and those patients who could walk were

in the hospital cafeteria in the hut next door. Only Masha in the far corner and a man with a broken leg and perforated lung remained in the room, sound asleep two beds down. On the small table next to her, a fat candle was burning, making Maxim's eyes dance in the flickering light. 'I'm glad to hear that. We need you back.' Did he mean the partisan battalion needed her? Or that he needed her? 'The losses are greater than we thought,' he was saying. 'Forty people are dead. Almost half of us.' His voice broke.

'I can't get my head around it,' she whispered. 'How could Matvei do this? Betray us in such a way?'

'We don't know for sure if it was him.'

'Of course it was him. Who else could it be?'

He looked at the ground and shrugged. 'How is Masha?'

'Not so great. Still unconscious.' Lisa was too sad to continue.

'Come here,' he said, hugging her. She sobbed, the long hours of fear and frustration, of hope and heartbreak and despair spilling out as she buried her face in his chest. She felt light-headed from sadness, from his body so close to hers, and suddenly she knew exactly what she had to do. Maxim needed to know how she felt about him. And she needed to know if he felt the same way. She couldn't go on another day, not knowing. Taking a deep breath, she reached for his hand, brought it to her lips and kissed it. Their eyes met. She could hardly take the intensity of his gaze but didn't look away. Her lips parted. She waited and waited and when nothing happened, she leant forward and kissed him. He didn't return her kiss but took his hand from her and moved slightly away. 'Lisa, what are you doing?'

He didn't sound angry or upset. Just sad and extremely tired. But it wasn't what she wanted to hear. Shocked and embarrassed, she looked at the straw of her bed, at the rocks and soil of the floor, at the man two beds down groaning in pain in his sleep. 'I just wanted you to know how I feel about you,' she muttered.

He hesitated for a moment. 'You're a wonderful girl. You'll

make some man very happy one day. But I'm married. I have a wife and daughter whom I love dearly.'

'I thought you had feelings for me too. Was I wrong?'

'We are friends, that's all. I love my family.'

After months of dreaming of him, of imagining this exact moment, she couldn't believe her ears. 'You must feel what I feel. This thing between us. I didn't imagine it, did I?'

'I care for you very much, as a friend, as a younger sister, but that's all. My wife and daughter are everything to me. Especially at a time like this.'

Mortified, Lisa bit her lip, trying to draw blood, to obliterate the pain in her heart with another, more tolerable pain. She refused to look at his solemn face or think of his heartbreaking words until after he was gone. She didn't want to cry in front of him.

He added, 'Had I known you had feelings for me, I would have told you this earlier. I would have made my position clear. I'm sorry I didn't.'

'Perhaps you did. I just didn't want to see it.' And even now, as she lay on her hospital bed, helpless in front of him, she didn't want to see it. She expected him to turn around and say he was only joking. That it was her he wanted after all. Her cheeks were burning and she knew her face must have looked bright red.

'No hard feelings?' he asked, avoiding looking at her.

Forcing a smile, she nodded. 'No hard feelings.'

No hard feelings, even though her heart was breaking.

She turned to the wall, unable to watch him as he walked away. Exhausted, she cried quietly, wishing she could erase the last ten minutes from her memory and at the same time wanting to run after him and beg him to change his mind. But she didn't move. She knew he wouldn't change his mind. He had made his feelings clear.

Chapter 20

Outside the hospital, life went on as before for the surviving partisans. They woke up, put on their tattered uniforms and cooked their breakfast. Then they picked up their rifles and rode their horses and trucks into the scorching woods to fight evil and seek their revenge. When they returned, they had their dinner, melancholically strummed their guitars, smoked, sipped their tea and wished they had something stronger to numb their pain, to give them one cheerful moment, even if it was just an illusion. They slept, restless and afraid, only to do the same thing all over again the next day, and the next.

But inside the hospital, time stood still. Having given the watch back to the nurse, Lisa didn't know if it was morning or noon or night. There were no windows and the sunlight didn't penetrate the heavy wooden structure. The only indication of the time of day was the nurses' voices as they told Lisa to have her breakfast, lunch or dinner. It was as if the outside world did not exist. And if she followed the nurses' directions and took her medicine, if she woke up in the morning and did as she was told until it was time to go to bed, she could lose herself in her daily routine and pretend that her heart wasn't breaking.

Two days after they had arrived at the Emilchino battalion,

Anna came to see Lisa at the hospital. 'I'm sorry I haven't been to visit you before. I had to go back home. Mama is beside herself.'

'It's fine, don't worry about it,' said Lisa, who was pleased to see a friendly face. After what had happened between them, Maxim hadn't been to see her again. Masha was mostly sleeping. All Lisa did was stare into space and think of Maxim and think of the men and women she had spent the last few months with, forever gone. She had never felt more alone. 'I'm glad you're here. It's nice to see you.'

'I can't stay long. I came to say goodbye.'

'Where are you going?'

'Home. I want to stay but Mama won't hear of it. My partisan days are over.' Anna looked sad enough to cry. 'But that's all right. Anton is there too. I get to spend more time with him while he's recovering.'

'I wish I could go home,' said Lisa, meaning it. She was done with this place. After the attack, everything seemed so hopeless and bleak. She couldn't face Maxim. The partisans from her battalion moved around like ghosts, grim and despondent. She would never see Yulya again. And Masha was dying.

Anna rubbed her eyes and attempted to smile. 'We are the lucky ones. Our rope broke that day when our settlement was attacked.'

'What do you mean?'

'It's an expression my papa always uses. Once upon a time, under the Tzars, if a man was condemned to die by hanging and the rope broke, his life was spared.'

'So?'

'So, four days ago, our rope broke. We are lucky to be alive.'

'But so many others aren't,' said Lisa, who didn't feel lucky at all. Too much was broken inside her, too much was hurting.

'How is Masha? I went to see her this morning but she was sleeping,' said Anna.

'That's all she seems able to do these days.' Masha hadn't regained consciousness yet. Her fever wasn't going down. Under her customary smile, Alya was pale with worry whenever she checked on Masha.

'When she wakes up, give her my love. Tell her she can keep the hat I lent her. It's the best thing I've ever owned but I want her to have it.'

'She'll be pleased.'

Anna got up and hugged Lisa. 'Stay in touch. And good luck!' she said, placing a crumbled piece of paper in Lisa's hand. 'Here is my address. When all this is over, promise you'll come to see me.'

'I promise. Thank you for everything.'

After Anna left, Lisa couldn't sleep, so she spent the night by Masha's side, reading from an old tome of Lermontov's poems under the twinkling light of the kerosene lamp.

No, I'm not Byron, it's my role to be an undiscovered wonder,
Like him, a persecuted wand'rer, but furnished with a Russian soul.

I started sooner, sooner ending, my mind will never reach so high.
Within my soul, beyond the mending, my shattered aspirations lie.

Her hands shaking, she repeated the lines in which the tragic poet had predicted his own death and thought, how did he know? How did he know he wouldn't live to see thirty? Did he feel apathetic and afraid, unsure of his own destiny and place in the world, like a raft adrift in the ocean? Did he feel just like her?

In silence she watched as Alya changed Masha's bandages. Her friend's beautiful face was a mess of raw burns. Every time she saw it, Lisa's chest hurt.

'Please, wake up,' she whispered to Masha after Alya was gone. 'I need you now more than ever.'

She thought she heard something from Masha's bed, a rustle of sheets, a small groan.

'Masha, can you hear me?' She squeezed her friend's hand gently.

Masha opened her eyes and looked at Lisa. 'What's going on?' she whispered. 'Why are you trying to pull my arm off?'

'You slept for three days straight.'

'I don't feel so good,' Masha said, her voice breaking, as if every word required a superhuman effort from her. She slowly touched her face and winced. 'I feel like my whole body is on fire. And my face . . . Why does it hurt so much?'

'You have a lot of healing to do. It will take time. But before you know it, you'll get better and this will be nothing but a terrible memory.'

'Can you tell me what I look like? Please.' Her friend's voice trembled.

'You look beautiful, just like always.' Lisa wanted to shower her friend with kisses but didn't want to cause her any more pain. She kissed the tips of her fingers. At the sound of Masha's voice, Alya came over, chatting to her cheerfully. She examined Masha and brought her some water and a piece of bread.

Masha took a sip of water but didn't touch the food. 'I don't think I can chew it. My face is in too much pain.'

'Here, I'll help you.' Lisa broke the bread into tiny pieces and fed it to her friend. Masha gulped it down but choked, coughing it all up. Lisa passed her a glass of water.

'What is happening to me?' she muttered when she could speak again. 'Am I going to die?'

'Of course you are not going to die,' cried Lisa, horrified. 'You are going to be just fine. You'll make it, you'll see.'

'Yulya didn't make it.' The girls were silent for a moment. Then Masha said, 'Danilo pulled me out of that tree, you know. And then he found Yulya and she was already gone. If it wasn't for me, he would have got to her earlier and she might have lived. Because of me, Yulya is dead.'

'Not because of you. What happened is not your fault.'

'I bet Danilo disagrees. I bet he blames me.'

'No one blames you, darling.'

'What about you? You were in that tree when it collapsed. How did you survive?'

Lisa hesitated before saying, 'Maxim helped me. He carried me to safety. If it wasn't for him, I wouldn't be here.'

Masha's eyes dimmed. She blinked and looked straight at Lisa. 'I don't judge you, you know. For Maxim. I understand. We can't help who we fall in love with. And I know what it's like to love. It's not something you can fight, not even when everything is against you.'

'Thank you,' whispered Lisa. She couldn't tell her friend that she'd kissed Maxim and he'd rejected her. She couldn't even think about it without cringing. To put it into words was impossible. 'You're like a sister to me. I wish my actual sister was more like you.'

'You never talk about her.'

'There's not much to say.'

'It's war, Lisa. You have to forgive your family. Who knows how much time we have left.'

Something in Masha's voice caught Lisa's attention. She sounded so resigned. 'Don't be silly. You have your whole life ahead of you. You are going to get better and then your husband will come back . . .'

'I don't want him to see me like this.'

'Nonsense. He won't care about a few burns on your face.'

'Not just my face, Lisa. Look at me.'

'You are beautiful and he loves you. You'll start a family, just like you always wanted. Your mother will come back to Kiev.'

'Why do I feel so tired? Like my body is giving out. Like it's refusing to go on.' Masha was breathing heavily, her eyes wide in her bandaged face.

'You just need some rest. Sleep is the best medicine.'

'Didn't you just complain I slept for three days straight?' Masha tried to smile and winced. 'Write to my husband and tell him I love him. And write to my mother.' Masha's eyes closed. Her voices sounded so weak, Lisa had to make an effort to hear it. 'Tell her not to wait for me anymore.'

In the little chair by her friend's side, grasping her hand

desperately, Lisa drifted in and out of sleep, praying for Masha all the while. In the morning, Masha's fingers in Lisa's hand were cold. She was gone.

*

The next few days were a blur. Lisa left the hospital, moved in with the battalion's two nurses, Alya and Luba, and was given some tasks around the camp – cleaning, doing laundry, mending uniforms. She waded through her days as if in a fog, and in the evenings she fell into bed, exhausted. For once in her life, she was thankful for the exhaustion. It left her with little energy to think.

Three days after Masha died, Maxim came to see her as she was sewing outside her hut. 'How are you holding up?' he asked.

'Not great,' she replied and burst into tears. Seeing the perplexed expression on his face, she realised he must think she was crying because of him. She wiped her face and added, 'Masha . . .'

'How is she?'

'She died.'

'I'm so sorry. I just got back. I had no idea.' He was quiet for a moment. 'I didn't know her that well, but she was a wonderful person – selfless, caring and kind. The men adored her.'

'She had become like a sister to me. Everyone who knew her adored her. Whoever was responsible for this . . . I want them to pay. Was it Matvei?' When he shrugged, she added, 'It was, wasn't it? I told you he was not to be trusted. Are you looking for him?' She shook with indignation at the thought of the man's greasy face and his tiny eyes.

'Whoever did this has to live with it for the rest of his life. Even if we never catch him, that's punishment enough.' Maxim looked away from her. He seemed uncomfortable and ill at ease. 'About the other day,' he said finally. 'I hope you are not too upset. It was never my intention to hurt your feelings.'

'I'm fine. And you didn't.' The fact that he had brought it up meant so much to her.

'My wife and daughter are coming to the battalion. I wanted you to hear it from me.'

Lisa took a sharp breath. 'Thank you for letting me know,' she said, forcing her voice to sound steady, while inside she felt like dying.

August 1943

Chapter 21

Lisa stood knee-deep in the river, wringing someone's dirty shirt with all her might, trying as hard as she could to scrub off the dark stains. At her feet was a basket of blood-soaked, sweat-soaked garments and as she rubbed the material on the ridged surface of the washboard, the throbbing in her wrist reminding her of her ordeal, she couldn't help but feel that she no longer belonged here. She thought of her job in the kitchen with longing and daydreamed of Yulya's cranky voice greeting her every morning, of the hot stove burning her fingers, of a pile of potato peels in the sink. How she had hated that job, and yet, now that she no longer had it, she felt lost.

The whole battalion had come to say goodbye to Masha on the last day of June. Every person there had wept, Lisa most of all. After a month had passed, she was still weeping.

Like ugly black spiders, the Nazi patrol aircrafts crawled through the sky, reminding Lisa that the peaceful murmur of the river and the unblemished green canopy of the leaves were nothing but an illusion, temporary and misleading; that at any moment the forest could erupt with gunfire and death. Putrid smoke rose from behind the trees and sometimes, on a windy day like today, she could smell fire. The Nazis were burning the bodies of tens of thousands of people executed at Babi Yar. As she inhaled the smell of human flesh, she wanted to scream in pain, to wail like a wounded animal because what was happening to their people and their country was something out of her worst nightmare, something she couldn't have even imagined when she was growing up, happy and protected by her family. And yet, here it was, the terrifying reality.

But occasionally, like a harbinger of better things to come, a Soviet plane would appear over their settlement. Moments later it would be gone, leaving something behind that was permanent and precious – hope.

This morning Lisa was wearing a dress Anna had given her before she left. The dress was emerald green, like the trees around her, like the colour of her eyes. It barely covered her knees and when it got wet, like now in the river, it clung to her like a second skin. With the sun playing in her hair and the thin fabric hugging every curve of her body, Lisa knew she looked a vision. If only Maxim could see her.

At the thought of Maxim, her hands started to shake. She let go of the shirt she was holding and cried. She cried for her friend Masha, whom she missed desperately. She cried for Maxim, who saved her life but couldn't be with her because he belonged to someone else. She cried for all the people the war had taken from her: family and friends and those she barely knew but mourned nonetheless. She could allow herself a good cry here by the river, with not a soul around. Afterwards, she would go back to the settlement with her head held high, as if nothing had happened. And no one would be able to tell what was in her heart.

Later that morning, having cooked a couple of tiny potatoes on top of the burning coals someone had left for her, Lisa sat under a large oak tree on top of a hill and placed her plate in her lap. It was her favourite spot because from here she could observe the hustle and bustle of the settlement without being seen. She had never felt at home here like she had at the other battalion. Because Masha and Anna were no longer with her? Because her hopes for Maxim had been dashed? Or because she was disillusioned and tired of it all? She didn't know exactly why, but she felt like an outsider.

The battalion was an anthill of activity this morning but she barely noticed any of it. Her gaze was firmly on Maxim's hut. She didn't mean to spy on him but sometimes she couldn't help it. Something happened to her when she saw him. For a few minutes the sun seemed to shine a little brighter.

A few times he had noticed her and waved but never approached her. This morning she was going to talk to him and she had a perfect excuse. She would tell him she was ready to join him and the other partisans on their missions. She had never forgotten the sense of camaraderie, of a common goal, the connection the two of them had shared in the past. She missed that. She missed their friendship.

It was crowded under Lisa's tree this morning. It seemed other partisans had discovered her secluded spot and were enjoying their breakfast under the canopy of heavy branches. An old man she had never met before was playing a guitar, while a couple of young people were nodding in time to music and humming a tune. Another man was reading a newspaper and shaking his head in disapproval. 'What nonsense they write. One minute the Red Army has been destroyed, the next, it forces the Nazis to give up important cities and cede territory. It sounds like Orel was liberated.'

The music fell quiet. All eyes were on the man with the newspaper. 'The Red Army must be close,' said the man with the guitar. 'They are no longer taking people to Germany. They force them to dig trenches instead. The cursed Nazis are scared for their lives.'

Lisa perked up. People were no longer being forced to Germany for work. That was good news indeed. And how far was Orel from Kiev?

The man with the guitar continued, 'You won't believe what I saw yesterday. Trucks of paintings and furniture. Hundreds of cars and motorbikes, filled with valuables, leaving Kiev.'

'The Nazis are evacuating?' asked the man with the newspaper.

'It seems that way.'

Her heart in her throat at the thought of the Nazis leaving the Ukrainian capital, Lisa almost forgot all about Maxim. She thought of the feeling of dread, uncertainty and helplessness as she watched the hated grey uniforms march through the streets of her city for the first time. That day, she had been devastated at the loss of Kiev. And yet, she couldn't have even begun to imagine what was to come. Nothing could have prepared her for the deaths of her loved ones and the life of fear she had led since. If only she could be there now to see the monsters leave.

If the Nazis were evacuating, did that mean the Red Army was coming to Kiev? She was about to ask the man with the newspaper about it because he seemed to know everything, when she saw Maxim emerging from his hut. She rose to her feet and waved, trying to attract his attention. He waved back and she started walking in his direction when a young woman emerged from the hut, holding a child. She was wearing a light blouse and a pair of men's trousers. Her arms were bare, her dark hair long and loose around her face, her eyes big and innocent. She looked fresh and young, like she didn't belong in these war-torn woods. The little girl was all long curls and toothy smile, her face turned to her father.

Lisa froze, wishing she was invisible. She wondered if she could go back to eating her breakfast but it was too late – she was only a few paces away, Maxim was watching her expectantly and so was his wife. She hesitated. 'Maxim . . .' She wanted to tell him she was ready to join him and the other partisans, that she wanted to do her bit for the motherland because she wanted him to be proud of her again. But his wife's hand was in his, and when she looked at him, there was such unrestrained joy in her eyes, the words got stuck in Lisa's throat. Was it Lisa's imagination or did the woman watch her suspiciously, as if she knew her? Suddenly it all seemed so pointless. She coughed to hide her confusion and said, 'I heard the Nazis are leaving. Is it true? Is it safe to return to the city?'

'Some units are withdrawing. But the majority are still in Kiev. The front is moving closer every day but it's going to take months.'

'Still, it's good news, isn't it?'

'It's the best news we've had in two years.'

With a heavy heart Lisa watched Maxim and his little family join a group of partisans at the bottom of the hill. They laughed and joked, played with their daughter and shared their food. Every once in a while, their eyes would meet and they would smile at each other with such familiarity, such affection, Lisa couldn't take it. She had to turn away, to the man with his newspaper, to the grey smoke that rose from Babi Yar and filled her soul with terror.

*

Everything filled Irina with joy that afternoon – the sun, the clear blue skies with not an aeroplane in sight and the birds chirping overhead, but most importantly, finally being with Maxim after a year and a half of separation. To fall asleep in his arms, to wake up in his arms, to see him play with his daughter, to be able to talk to him not once every few weeks but every day – no words could describe what it meant to her. She had to wait a couple of weeks until he took care of some business he refused to discuss with her but now they were finally together and Irina couldn't be happier. She had dreamt of this for so long and now that it was real, she still had to pinch herself every now and then to make sure she was awake. She knew Maxim felt the same. His eyes lit up at the sight of his wife and daughter when he returned to the battalion every evening. Before he had left that morning, he hugged her and told her that having them there made this place feel like home.

The hut she shared with Maxim and Sonya was small, with barely space for a bed and a table, but it was all theirs, the first place they could call their own. Irina was determined to make it cosy and clean. While her daughter was asleep on top of a small woolly blanket, Irina swept the floors, ran outside, borrowed some baking soda and a towel from a cranky old woman called Ramona and tried her best to scrub the dirt off every surface. There was only so much she could do in a dwelling made of soil and branches but after an hour of hard work the place looked more cheerful, even though it still smelt damp. Irina opened the wooden door and sat outside on the grass with her sewing. What happiness it was to wait for her husband, while cleaning his house, looking after his daughter, making his meals and mending his shirts. At last, they could be a real family.

There was something magical about the stream of water swishing softly through the rocks nearby, the leaves whispering in the breeze and the sun reflecting in the river. Her breath caught and she paused to take it all in, absorb the beauty through her skin, forgetting for a moment that they were living in a country at war.

It was already dark when Maxim returned. In silence he hugged her. His face seemed troubled. Fully clothed and still in his shoes, he perched on the bed and sat for a while without a word, while Irina chatted quietly, telling him all about her day. Outside, Bear was barking and someone's guitar cried late into the night.

Without acknowledging what she had said, he muttered, 'It's all my fault. Everything that happened is my fault.'

At the note of desperation in his voice, she crawled across the bed to him and took his hand. 'What are you talking about? What is your fault?'

He startled as if she had woken him from a dream. She could see him clearly in the light of a candle burning on the table. His face looked distorted, his eyes dark. He didn't say a word, only stared into the near-darkness.

'You are still blaming yourself for your parents, aren't you? It wasn't your fault,' said Irina.

'Of course it was. The Nazis are not interested in my elderly parents. They are using them to get to me. I've never felt more helpless in my life.'

'Once they realise they don't know where you are, they'll let them go.'

'Do you really believe that?'

'Yes, I do,' she lied.

'They are my parents, Irina. I have to help them.'

'What can we do, Maxim? Is there anything we can do?'

His shoulders caved in and he didn't reply. She held him in silence, the joy of the day dissipating, a sudden dread making her heart ache in its place.

October 1943

Chapter 22

Partly to impress Maxim and partly to take her mind off missing Masha and her family, Lisa went out with Danilo's group of partisans to mine a bridge on the Kiev–Korostenj train line. A week later, she went out again, to cut telephone cables near Spartak Station. Both were quiet, stealthy and well-planned operations that were put into practice quickly and without a hitch, leaving her with a sense of accomplishment she hadn't experienced in all the months she'd spent in the kitchen.

In the second week of October, the rain came down hard and looked like it was never going away. The summer was well and truly over. Just like before, Lisa could never get dry or warm. Her clothes, her bed, her hair were damp. There was mould growing inside her boots. As she shivered through the night under a woolly kerchief that wasn't large enough to cover her legs, she wondered how much longer she would have to live like this. Like everyone in Kiev and the Soviet Union, she held her breath in anticipation and waited for the news of the Red Army. Every now and then, she would hear distant bombing and know the tide was turning. This barely perceptible change was apparent in the expression on everyone's faces – the smiles were wider, the eyes twinkled with hope. The change was in the red star she sometimes glimpsed on a plane's fuselage. It was in the desperate words she read in the Nazi-controlled newspaper.

We will never be defeated. The German spirit is indestructible. We will never weaken or allow the Bolsheviks near our borders, screamed Hitler from the pages of the *Ukrainian Word*, while the Red Army was closing in on Kiev.

Lisa was gawking at a dozen Soviet planes in the sky, fighting the urge to jump up and down and wave her hands, when a group of partisans appeared, dragging a large man behind them, his legs and hands bound. He was dressed like a peasant and when they came closer, she recognised Matvei's puffy face. He looked thinner than she remembered, half-hidden behind a matted beard. But the tiny pig eyes were unmistakable. When Lisa looked at him, something inside her shifted. She thought of Masha's kind face, of her voice trembling with joy as she read her husband's letter. She thought of the way her eyes lit up as she dreamt of a better future once the war was over. The better future that would never come, because of the man cowering in front of Lisa. Shaking with anger, she stared at him without a word. She wanted to hurt him, to make him pay for what he'd done to her friend and so many others. She wanted to put her hands around his neck and squeeze.

The men pushed Matvei so hard, he flew to the ground and landed in a puddle of water. 'Please, don't kill me,' he pleaded, his face twisted in fear. Lisa couldn't blame him for being afraid. To his left was Azamat, his eyes dark like black clouds. To his right was Danilo, red in the face and breathing heavily, like a bull about to charge. And all around him the others were gathering, like Mongolian hordes intent on revenge. The men were coming closer to look in the eyes of the traitor responsible for their friends' deaths. If their thunderous faces couldn't instil terror into Matvei, nothing could.

Danilo said, 'There's a name for what you've done. Treason. Punishment for treason is death.' In Danilo's face, Lisa saw the reflection of everything she was feeling. Disdain, anger, hatred. And heartbreak. Lisa had lost her best friend but Danilo had lost his wife. She felt such overwhelming pity for him, she wanted to cry.

'I didn't do anything,' murmured Matvei, backing away from Danilo on his haunches and crawling backwards. But he didn't have anywhere to go. The ranks were closing around him.

'We've heard that before,' said Azamat.

Matvei tripped over a branch and fell in the mud. No one made a move to help him up.

'Our battalion was attacked because of you. Forty people are dead,' said Danilo.

'It wasn't me. I swear, it wasn't me. I didn't breathe a word to anyone.'

'You would sell your own mother to the Nazis if it meant a better life for you.'

'If it was me, why would I still be in Kiev? Why wouldn't I hide? I might not be trustworthy but I'm not stupid.'

'You *were* hiding, snake. Or we would have found you sooner.' Danilo spat on the ground and turned away, as if he couldn't bear looking at the man.

That evening, the partisans were celebrating. They sat in a big circle in the hall, guitars in their laps, while outside the rain beat down on the settlement, steady like a drum. Lisa sat next to the two young nurses she was sharing a hut with, Luba and Alya, who laughed and joked and sang popular songs with the men. Her eyes were on Maxim, who was surrounded by friends, Sonya in his lap, his wife by his side. The two of them didn't touch, nor did they hold hands, but there was such intimacy in the way they looked at one another and the way Irina leant in his direction when she spoke, Lisa felt sick to her stomach with sadness.

*

The day Irina's life changed forever started out just like any ordinary day. There was no warning, no indication that something terrible was about to happen. It was barely dawn and Sonya was crying. Irina woke with a start, for a moment not knowing where she was. She reached out her hand, searching for Maxim in the dark but his side of the straw bed was empty. She remembered he was on sentry duty that night and got up to comfort her daughter.

After five minutes of rocking and singing, all Irina wanted was to go back to bed. Having only slept sporadically, she felt heavy-headed and confused. But Sonya had other ideas. The little girl was wriggling in her arms, eager to start her day. Irina fed her some bread, then wrapped another piece of bread in a kerchief, picked up Sonya and walked across the settlement and through the forest to find Maxim. As she put one foot in front of another carefully, afraid to trip over on a slippery rock or a branch and hurt her little girl, she could smell the smoke. Once again, just like at the start of the war, Kiev was burning. The fires blazed across Darniza, Slobodka, Truhanov Island and the villages on the left bank of the Dnieper, inching their way to the city. It was light as day in the woods before dawn. She was afraid of the fires, even though she knew they meant the Red Army was close, battling for Kiev. The echo of distant battles reached her sometimes in the quiet of the night.

Even though it was early, there was movement in the woods. The partisans were waking up and crawling out of their dwellings, stretching and yawning like bears in spring. Among them was a group of newcomers, men and women who had arrived from the forbidden zone, established by the Nazis for the protection of Kiev. A few days previously, notices had appeared around central Kiev, telling residents to vacate their houses. Anyone caught inside the forbidden zone would be shot. What the notices didn't say was that the city was mobilising for the imminent threat of the Red Army. The Soviets' excitement was short-lived and quickly gave way to fear. Before the Red Army reached Kiev, would the Nazis destroy it? In their death throes, would they kill everyone who was left in the city?

Irina couldn't wait to take her family back home. Every day, she was afraid for Maxim who went out in his truck to fight the Germans. She was afraid for Sonya, who wasn't getting enough food. Although it was peaceful and quiet at the battalion, the undercurrent of anxiety never went away. The Nazis had found their settlement before. What would stop them from finding it again?

As Irina walked in the direction of the prison hut her husband was guarding that morning, Ramona sidled up to her. 'Sonya looks so cute today! I swear she gets cuter every day. Just look at that curly hair!' The old woman looked uncharacteristically chipper that morning. Her usually grim face was stretched into a smile. 'Wait till I tell you my news. In fact, it's best if I show you.' As if by magic a leaflet appeared in her hand. 'These were dropped from a plane over Syrez last night.'

'So what? We get Nazi leaflets all the time. I just ignore them. It's all propaganda, not a word of truth to them.'

'This is not a Nazi leaflet, my dear. Take a look.'

Irina unfolded the piece of paper. 'Citizens of Kiev,' she read in the light of the fires in the distance, made even fiercer by the rising sun. 'Your army is at the gates. Continue to resist the oppressors and wait for us. The end to the occupation is near.' She looked up from the leaflet, tears in her eyes. 'I don't understand. Is this . . .'

'From the Red Army! Rumours are, they are on the right bank of the Dnieper. The Nazis left Kanev and Tripolye.'

'How far is Kanev?'

'Not far. Our army could be here tomorrow. We could be freed at any moment.'

'Ramona, that's fantastic!' cried Irina, embracing the old woman and feeling like dancing on the spot. 'Can I keep this?'

'Of course. We have dozens of them.'

Irina folded the precious paper reverently and hid it in her pocket. If no one was around, she would have kissed it. Hugging

Sonya close, she no longer walked through the forest, she flew. Having been on sentry duty all night, Maxim probably hadn't heard about the leaflets. She couldn't wait to tell him. All they ever wanted was for the war to end and their married life to start. And now it was no longer a distant dream.

When she reached the sentry post, Irina heard Azamat and Danilo talking in agitated voices. Bear was barking and sniffing the ground. Maxim was standing with his head held low. Behind him was the prison hut with its door open.

'You must have fallen asleep and let him slip away,' said Danilo, not taking his accusing eyes off Irina's husband.

'I didn't close my eyes all night.'

'How could he have escaped unassisted? I tied his hands myself yesterday evening,' said Azamat.

'Then someone must have helped him,' said Danilo. 'And I will not rest till I know who this someone was.'

'What happened?' asked Irina, stepping forward, her heart skipping a beat at the sight of their solemn faces.

Maxim looked at her grimly without a word. It was Azamat who said, 'Matvei is gone. Alex brought him his breakfast this morning but he wasn't there.'

'Disappeared like a thief in the night on your husband's watch,' said Danilo.

'Are you implying Maxim had something to do with it?' asked Irina. She had never liked Danilo. The man was rude and unpleasant.

'All I'm saying is, he was guarding the prisoner and now he's gone.' He threw a look of contempt at Maxim, who remained silent. Why wasn't he speaking up for himself?

'Come on, Danilo,' said Azamat. 'It's Maxim we are talking about. He's beyond suspicion. There must be a logical explanation.'

'What explanation?' barked Danilo. But Azamat had no answers. And by the look on his face, neither did Maxim.

*

274

Her rifle by her side – she wasn't taking any chances – Lisa sat by the river, her feet dangling close to the water. She loved coming here, to ward off the ghosts that haunted her, making sleep impossible, to be alone and think about the day ahead. She heard a noise. A branch breaking, a shuffling of feet on leaves. Was it her imagination playing tricks on her? Or was someone here?

There was a glimmer of light on the horizon, from the fires and the moon, just bright enough for her to make out a large silhouette moving in her direction. Whoever it was stopped frequently, turning around and looking behind him, as if to make sure no one was following.

She shivered at the thought of being alone with this unknown man. Figuring her best defence was offence, she grabbed her rifle and shouted, 'Stay where you are! Or I shoot.'

The man, whoever it was, froze on the spot, his hands out in front of him as if signalling to her to stay calm. Enough light fell on his face for her to recognise the dirty blond hair and the large clown nose. 'Matvei!' she exclaimed and lowered her weapon. Taking advantage of her surprise, he stepped away from her and turned around as if to run.

'Freeze! Raise your hands!' She took aim once more and he paused. 'What are you doing here?'

'They let me go. I'm walking back home.'

'I don't believe you. After what you've done, they would shoot you first before they let you go.'

'Maybe they realised I'm not the man they are looking for. Maybe they found the person responsible.'

'What are you talking about? You are the person responsible.' The rifle in her hands trembled.

'What makes you so sure?'

'Because you told me once you would do anything to survive, to make your life and your children's lives easier.'

'And because of that, you think I gave up the partisans' location to the Nazis?'

But Lisa wasn't listening. She was shaking with anger. 'Remember Masha? You must have seen her around. A beautiful girl with blonde hair and a kind smile. A nurse, saving lives, doing her bit to help others. She died. Remember Yulya, our cook? She died, too. And so many others, all because of you. And this is why I don't believe that they would let you go. How did you really get away?'

'I was lucky, I suppose.'

She wanted to point out that he was here, in front of her, on the wrong side of her rifle. How lucky was that, really? 'Turn around and start walking. I'm taking you back to the battalion. One sudden movement and I shoot. And believe me, I know how to use this thing better than you think.'

'You are making a mistake. It wasn't me.'

'Masha was my friend, you bastard. One of the best friends I've ever had. Now move.'

In silence she walked behind Matvei towards the settlement. If only Maxim could see her now. He would be so proud of her. He had taught her well. And thanks to everything he had taught her, she had caught the traitor responsible for so many partisans' deaths and was bringing him back, so he could pay for what he'd done.

When they arrived, the sun was just beginning to rise. The battalion was aflutter, with Danilo shouting commands, his eyes bulging with barely concealed anger. They were organising a search party, getting the dogs ready, the rifles and the horses. Into this commotion Lisa walked in, weapon in hand, with the man they were all looking for. Danilo stopped talking and watched her with amazement. Azamat gave an order to two partisans to seize Matvei and take him away.

Wearily, Lisa lowered her rifle. And then she saw Maxim. He didn't look proud or happy for her. He looked like he had seen a ghost, like he was afraid for his life.

*

Maxim was walking so fast, Irina had to run to keep up with him. Running was difficult with a wriggling two-year-old in her arms and she fell a few steps behind, watching his silhouette and the burning flames in the distance. Uncharacteristically, Maxim didn't offer to help, nor did he slow down to make it easier for her. He didn't seem to notice she was there at all. She increased her pace, finally catching up with him. 'Wait till I show you the leaflet Ramona gave me. It's from the Red Army! Can you believe it?'

He didn't seem to hear her. If he did, he didn't say a word.

'Soon we can go back home. Your parents might come back. Our army will be liberating the prison camps, right?'

Still nothing.

'Well, that worked out well,' continued Irina. 'Lisa is quite the hero. You taught her well.' She glanced at Maxim, who seemed lost in thought. Something in his appearance caught her eye and she slowed down again, her breath coming out in heavy puffs. His skin looked grey, like he was about to be sick. His eyes looked dark, as if he hadn't slept in days. 'You look tired. What happened out there? Did you fall asleep?' She pulled him by his sleeve.

He startled and blinked, as if surprised to find her next to him. 'I didn't fall asleep.'

'How did Matvei get away? Someone must have helped him, but how did they get past you?'

They were only a few metres away from their hut. Maxim stopped and turned to her. For a few seconds, they stood in silence, appraising each other. He waited for a group of partisans to walk past before he said, 'I let Matvei go, Ira.'

'Never mind, he's back now and you won't get in trouble, thanks to Lisa,' Irina began, and then stopped. 'What did you just say?'

'I let Matvei go.'

'You let him go? But why?'

'Because he didn't do it. He's not the one responsible for the Nazi attack.'

'How do you know he didn't do it?'

'I just know, all right?'

'So you released him?'

'I wasn't about to let an innocent man die for something he didn't do.'

She watched his face for clues, trying to understand. But he wasn't making it easy for her. His face was unreadable. 'You've been guarding him every third night. Why did it take you two weeks to let him go?'

'I was hoping they would see sense. But they were going to shoot him in the morning. And I couldn't let that happen.'

They walked a few steps to their hut. Once inside, Maxim sat at their little table, his head low. Unable to look at the dark expression on her husband's face, Irina watched their daughter as she crawled around the room like a wound-up toy, lively and fast. Then she approached Maxim, put her arms around him, kissed his forehead and said, 'Let me make you something to eat. You must be starving, out there all night.'

'I need to go. I need to talk to Azamat.'

'You've been up all night. You must be exhausted. Have a rest and then go out.'

'Then it might be too late.'

He left without a further explanation. When the door closed behind him, a distant explosion shook the woods. Sonya's face crumpled and tears filled her eyes. Irina rocked her, whispering that after lunch she would take her outside to look for bunny rabbits. Even the promise of her favourite pastime didn't calm the little girl. She was inconsolable. And only when the shelling fell quiet did she fall quiet too.

Irina barely noticed the sound of war. She was becoming accustomed to it. But she couldn't ignore the dull ache inside her chest, like a premonition of bad things to come. She read to her daughter and played finger puppets with her. She found a piece of stale bread for her lunch but didn't touch the food herself. When Maxim didn't return after three hours, she picked up Sonya and went looking for him.

A large group of partisans was gathered in the clearing among the birch trees. Azamat was talking. 'I know some of you have been thinking of joining the Red Army and fighting the enemy as Red Army soldiers. Now that they are so close, the thought is tempting. To wear a uniform, to do our bit. But I'd like to remind each and every one of you that you are already doing that. The minute you joined our ranks, you became soldiers. Our orders are clear. Our duty is to stay in the rear and push the Nazis out. This is how we can help the Red Army. Only when the enemy leaves Kiev for good can we join the Red Army.'

Danilo appeared, followed by Matvei, who seemed to walk freely among the partisans, with his hands unbound and no one watching him. Irina breathed out in relief. Maxim's plan had worked. He must have managed to convince everyone Matvei was innocent. She didn't know why her husband thought that was true, but she trusted his judgement. No doubt Maxim would be pleased. She couldn't wait to see him.

Danilo whispered something in Azamat's ear and Irina saw the older man's mouth open in surprise. All at once he looked as grim and shell-shocked as Danilo, who stood in front of him with an expectant look about him, as if waiting for Azamat to make a decision. But Azamat wasn't making a decision. He seemed lost for words.

Danilo turned to the other partisans. 'Something important has come up. We will continue this meeting tomorrow. I apologise for the interruption.'

Azamat and Danilo walked away, while Matvei was left unsupervised in the meadow. Irina picked up Sonya and went home to wait for Maxim. For the rest of the afternoon, she busied herself with cleaning and playing with her daughter. As the sun traversed the sky and disappeared behind the tallest trees, Irina scrubbed and polished and crawled on her knees and elbows, pretending to be horsey for her little girl.

Soon it was night time and the eerie light of the distant fires played on the walls and made Irina shiver with unexplained dread. All the chores had been done, their dwelling was sparkling clean and Sonya was asleep. Irina sat outside, her sewing untouched in her lap, a kerosene lamp beside her, and stared into the night.

There was no sign of Maxim.

*

As the months passed, Lisa went to a lot of trouble to avoid Alex, who refused to take no for an answer. She even started having her meals inside her hut and coming to work late, when most partisans had left for the day. But despite her best efforts, Alex always managed to find her. He hovered over her in the kitchen, followed her around like a love-sick puppy while she did her chores, offering his help only occasionally, and even asked if he could come inside her hut one day, so they could have some time alone together.

And now, as she leant on a tree with a book in her lap, he sat down next to her, saying, 'I don't think we are safe here. Everyone is behaving like the threat doesn't exist. But the Nazis come here all the time, to collect wood for their hospitals. It's only a matter of time before they stumble upon us.'

'I don't think they are behaving like the threat doesn't exist. I think they know it exists and are ready for it.'

'Like they were ready for it back in June? I'm telling you, we need to go deeper into the woods.'

'You mean, hide?' she asked with as much disdain as she could muster, even though Alex was only saying aloud what she had often been thinking to herself. The Nazis finding them again was one of her greatest fears. Although five months had passed since the attack, she still had nightmares about it.

'It's not hiding, it's survival. With the Red Army so close, it's only smart.'

'The Nazis are more scared of us than we are of them,' said a voice behind them. 'Did you see the signs they put up on the roads around Buki?'

Lisa thought she recognised the voice. Turning around, she saw Matvei standing behind her smiling his sickening smile at her and Alex.

'The signs that read: *Careful, strong partisan presence*. They avoid these roads because they are afraid.'

Why was Matvei talking to them like he was one of them? And even more perplexing, what was he doing, walking around the settlement unsupervised? Didn't she just single-handedly bring him back under the muzzle of her rifle after he had tried to escape? She was about to ask these questions when out of the corner of her eye she saw a group of partisans walking slowly across the clearing. She recognised Danilo and Azamat, and in front of them walked a man with his shoulders stooped and his head held low. The sun was setting behind him, tinting the tops of the trees bright orange. Her eyes must have been playing tricks on her because she could swear the man was Maxim, and that there were handcuffs around his wrists.

Lisa rose to her feet to see better but the small group had disappeared behind the trees. Were they taking him to the prison hut that was until recently occupied by Matvei? 'What is happening?' she asked no one in particular, unsure what to do. A part of her wanted to run after them and find out everything she could. But she remained rooted to the spot by the sheer impossibility of the scenario she had just witnessed.

'I believe they found the person responsible for the Nazi attack on the partisan battalions.'

'What are you talking about, Matvei?' asked Alex. 'Maxim is not that person.'

Lisa remained mute.

'It appears that he is indeed that person.' Matvei seemed to be enjoying himself tremendously. His eyes twinkled in triumph at Lisa. 'He is also the one who let me go.'

'Maxim let you go? Why would he do that?' asked Lisa, finding her voice.

'All I know is, they have arrested him for treason and I am now a free man.'

Lisa turned away from Matvei in shock. She felt like Alice in Wonderland, falling down a rabbit hole and finding herself in a world where nothing made sense. Black was white and white was black. There must have been some mistake. The man who had taught her how to shoot, whose blind loyalty and commitment had inspired so many others, who had dedicated his life to fighting the Nazis and whom she had grown to love and respect simply could not do what Matvei was accusing him of.

*

Irina walked as if through a mist, moving her feet on the sandy soil with difficulty. The thunder overhead was deafening. The ear-shattering sound was amplified by the explosions roaring over Kiev and together they sang a ghastly duet, making the earth tremble. The rain was lashing her face and her boots filled with water, yet she didn't notice any of it.

Earlier that day, Azamat had come to her hut and told her that her husband had been arrested for treason, punishable by death. Something about supplying the Nazis with classified information. She had stopped listening after the word *death*. Everything went dim, as if someone had turned the daylight off. And now she felt like she was wading through darkness, lost and unable to find her way.

There had been a misunderstanding. Of that she was sure. She repeated it over and over to Azamat, who nodded in agreement, his face grey, looking like he had aged ten years overnight.

'We'll get to the bottom of what happened,' he had said to her. 'Don't worry.'

The makeshift prison was nothing but a hut made of straw and clay. A gust of wind could blow it away. Maybe they could escape together, go back to Kiev and hide until the end of the war. Misunderstanding or not, its consequences could be dire.

'Make this meeting count, Comrade,' came a voice from under the nearby tree. On the ground, his back resting against a tree trunk and a rifle between his legs, sat Danilo, sneering at her.

'What?' she asked, shuddering. 'What did you say?'

'Make this meeting count. It could be your last.'

She didn't reply, not because she didn't want to but because she couldn't force the words out through her dry throat. On shaking legs, she walked past the man and into the tiny structure.

A candle was living out its last moments on the floor. In the light of the feeble flame Irina saw Maxim and her heart hurt. His hands were handcuffed, his legs bound. He lay on top of a pile of dirty straw. His eyes were open but he didn't seem to see her.

'Oh my God, Maxim! Look at you. How can they treat you like this?' She was whispering in case the horrible man outside could hear her, her arms around her husband, her lips on his grimy face.

He stirred and sat up straight. 'It's fine, Irina. I'm fine.'

'There's a sentry outside. They are guarding you like a common criminal. Like you've done something wrong.'

'I *have* done something wrong.'

'The man outside . . . Danilo . . .' She spat the name out like it was a curse. 'He told me to make this meeting count. That it could be our last. Why would he say that?'

'What do you think they are going to do to me?'

'What can they possibly do to you? You haven't done anything wrong.'

Maxim was silent for a long time. Irina could see in his face that he didn't want to talk about it. She couldn't blame him. She didn't want to talk about it, either. All she wanted was to free him from the ropes and the cuffs and whisk him to safety, take him somewhere where they could live their happily ever after without fear.

He looked calm and detached, as if he was a thousand miles away and not in a tiny hut lying on dirty straw. She shook him slightly. 'I don't know why they think it was you. Why don't you tell them they've made a mistake?'

'Because they haven't made a mistake.'

'What do you mean? Why would you of all people give the partisans up to the Nazis? It's preposterous. They must be out of their minds to even suggest it.'

'They told me they would let my parents go.'

'They can't possibly believe . . .' She stopped. 'What?'

In a broken voice he said, 'After my parents were taken, I lost my mind. I forgot all about caution and went to Kiev to find them. I asked questions, approached the wrong people. Someone must have betrayed me to the Nazis. One day they stopped me on the street and ordered me to follow them.'

'Oh no.' Irina shuddered. A realisation chilled her. She was to blame for this too. Because of her best friend, Maxim's parents had been taken by the Nazis. And now here they were, in a hut with an armed guard outside, Maxim handcuffed and guilty of an unspeakable crime. For a moment she was lost for words.

'It happened just before you and Sonya came to the battalion,' he whispered.

*

The round interrogation table was covered with papers. The officer sitting across from Maxim, clean-shaven, blue-eyed and wide-faced, never took his eyes off him. The light coming through the window bounced off the swastika on his armband. The man was small and fidgety. Maxim imagined putting his hands around his neck and pressing hard. Even though one of his hands was handcuffed to the radiator behind him, he could easily reach the Nazi pig with his other and kill him right here, right now.

Kill him and then what? Behind the half-open door, the corridors were teeming with German soldiers. He would never make it out of here alive. And if he did anything reckless, his parents would pay with their lives, or worse.

He could hear heavy boots resounding down the long corridor. The door flew open and his parents appeared, flanked by two German soldiers and a Ukrainian policeman. Maxim couldn't help it, he gasped at the sight of them. They looked older by years, stooped, grey, their faces gaunt and bruised. Had the Nazis been torturing them? Maxim's hands trembled and his teeth chattered.

'Mama, Papa,' he whispered as they rushed to him. With his one free arm around their withered bodies, he cried like he hadn't cried since he was a child.

'Maxim, darling, Maxim, my love, my dear little boy,' repeated his mother. 'I can't believe I'm seeing you again. I can't believe I lived long enough to see your beautiful face.'

His father placed his hand on Maxim's shoulder. His eyes narrowed, as if he too couldn't believe he was seeing him again. 'What are you doing here, son? How did they find you?'

'I came here to help you. Don't worry about anything. I will sort it all out.'

'Don't trust a word they say. You can't help us. We are beyond help,' said his father, while his mother cried, wrapping her arms around Maxim's head. 'You should have stayed away. Forget about us. Why did you walk straight into their trap? It breaks my heart to see you here.'

'Forget about you? Never.'

'The only thing that got us through the day was knowing they would never find you,' said the old man grimly.

In the corner, the policeman whispered something to the officer. 'That's enough,' the officer barked, waving his hand in an imperious gesture. 'Take them away.'

Helplessly Maxim watched as the two soldiers dragged his parents away. 'Don't tell them anything,' shouted his father through the doorway. 'Don't let the bastards win. It's not worth it.'

The butt of a German rifle came down hard on his elderly father's head. Maxim rose to his feet and cried out but his voice was lost in an ear-splitting shriek. It was his mother, hands flailing, eyes wild. She screamed and screamed until the soldiers dragged her away.

Frantic, Maxim yanked his handcuffed arm away from the wall with all his might, wrenching the radiator out of its socket. He was like a rampant bull, furious and crazed, raging against his fate, against his parents' fates. Then something heavy came down on his head and he tasted blood.

As he drifted in and out of consciousness, Maxim knew – no matter what it took, he was going to kill the flat-faced worm sitting in front of him with a sarcastic smirk on his face.

*

With gritted teeth and clenched fists, Maxim said, 'But I didn't kill him. Instead, they tortured me. Day after day they did everything they could to break me. And still I refused to tell them anything. Only when they brought my parents back and threatened to shoot them right in front of me, while waving a map in my face, I must have pointed at the location. I can barely remember, I was delirious with pain, hunger and lack of sleep.' He dropped his head in his hands and his shoulders heaved.

'I'm so sorry! Do you hear me, Maxim? I'm so sorry!' murmured Irina, clasping him to her chest, her tears falling on his face. 'It wasn't your fault. Anyone would have crumbled under such pressure.'

'For a split second, I was lost. And I will never forgive myself. I was coming back to talk to Azamat, to tell him our location has been compromised, that we had to move the battalion. But I was too late. The Germans were faster.'

'The Nazis let you go?'

He nodded. 'I was supposed to obtain more information for them. The locations of all the other battalions around Ukraine. They were so certain they had me exactly where they wanted me, they let me go.'

'Wait, but how did Azamat and Danilo know it was you?'

Irina could swear she could hear Danilo's breathing outside, heavy and threatening. She shivered. Seconds trickled by before Maxim replied, 'I told them. I would have told them sooner but the thought of you and Sonya stopped me. But I couldn't let them shoot Matvei for something he didn't do. And I couldn't live with myself after what happened. It was killing me. Those people were my friends. Because of me they are dead. I deserve the worst punishment there is.'

Irina sobbed, her face in his shoulder. 'Why haven't you told me? You were going through all this by yourself. Why didn't you say anything?'

'I didn't want to burden you.'

Burden her? Was he serious? 'We are in it together. For better or worse.'

'I was afraid you would turn away from me. And I couldn't bear it if you did that.'

'I would never turn away from you. You and Sonya are my family. Nothing could ever change that. We'll get through this together. They are not going to kill you. They will banish you, send you away.' She clasped his hand, her eyes burning.

'I'm a traitor, Irina. And I'm ready for what's to come.'

'But I'm not ready. I can't live the rest of my life without my husband. Sonya can't live the rest of her life without her father. Can't you see what you've done to us?'

'I'm sorry.' There were tears in Maxim's eyes.

They sat in silence, not touching, not looking at each other. 'I don't believe they'll go through with it. The partisans are not murderers,' Irina said.

'But I am.'

'They are our friends. You've lived with these people for over a year. You've known many of them your whole life.'

'That only makes what I've done so much worse.'

'No,' she whispered. 'No, no. What can we do? There must be something we can do.'

'There's nothing we can do but accept the inevitable.'

She remained with him in his little bed made of straw, crying and begging for a solution, for a way out. She knew she had to go back to her hut where a neighbour was watching Sonya but she couldn't tear herself away from him. What if Danilo was right and this was the last time she was ever going to see him? The night with him was filled with heartbreak but it was a million times preferable to the agony of being in their empty bed without him. While she could still touch him, she had hope.

*

Soft voices reached Lisa from inside the prison hut where Maxim was held captive. She could barely hear them as she stood outside, uncertain what to do, whether she should wait or walk inside.

'Please tell me it's not true. Tell me there's been some mistake.' She recognised Azamat's voice.

'I wish I could tell you that, but I can't.' It was Maxim, sounding croaky, like he was recovering from a bad cold.

'We'll fight it together. We'll prove you're innocent. They'll see they've got the wrong man.'

'They haven't got the wrong man.'

'You are like a son to me, Maxim. I've known you since you were a boy. We've been through hell and back together. I know what you are capable of. And what you are incapable of. Why are you lying? Who are you trying to protect? To betray us to the enemy, to lead them here . . . That's impossible.'

'It is true, nonetheless.'

Lisa shifted from foot to foot, her face flushed. Did Maxim just admit that the accusations were true? Did he just admit to delivering the partisans to the Nazis, condemning them to death? Just like Azamat, she refused to believe it. In a barely audible whisper, Maxim added, 'They had my parents.'

'Ah.'

'If I didn't do what they wanted, they would have killed them.'

Lisa's hand flew to her mouth as she listened to Maxim's story. The cursed Nazis, it was all their doing and one day they would pay. Not only did they rob and kill and burn their country to the ground, but they put honest men before impossible choices. The blood of forty partisans was on their hands. But it was also on Maxim's hands and she couldn't comprehend it.

When Azamat spoke, he sounded sad and extremely weary. 'I know you didn't mean to give in to them, but you were bargaining with the devil, son.'

'I know. And I'm sorry, for everything. Every night I close my eyes and all I can see is the faces of the people who died because of me. If only I could turn back time.'

'Loyalty can be a virtue, or it can be quite the opposite. In your case, your devotion to your parents blinded you. I doubt the Nazis will let them go. They will demand more and more until there is nothing left. And look at you now. There is almost nothing left. Are your parents free? Unfortunately, your immense sacrifice was all for nothing. I want to save you, Maxim, and I'll try my best. But they are crying for your blood, Danilo especially.'

'I understand. And I don't expect you to. Even I know I'm beyond saving.'

Azamat walked out with his head hung low. He shuffled past Lisa without seeing her. She stood at the entrance, watching Maxim as he lay there with his eyes closed. She thought he had fallen asleep and was about to turn around and walk away when he opened his eyes and saw her. 'Hey there,' he said.

'I heard your conversation with Azamat.'

'Are you disappointed in me? Because of me, your best friend is dead. Other people too.'

'I'm not disappointed in you.' She wanted to tell him she was disappointed in the war that had an ability to break anyone, even the best of people.

'You should be. I'm disappointed in myself.'

He closed his eyes and suddenly looked so tired, she knew he wanted to be alone. 'I just wanted you to know I understand,' she said before she walked out of the prison hut.

Outside, shivering in the rain, she thought of the man lying on the dirty straw, with his skin grey and eyes dull, and her heart ached. Yes, because of his mistake, many people had died. But had she been faced with the same impossible choice, could she honestly say that she would have acted differently? Maxim was the strongest man she knew, the most dependable and loyal. If he could be broken, what hope did the rest of them have? How many others would have crumbled sooner?

With tears in her eyes, she thought of Sonya, giggling and calling for her daddy, running to him as fast as she could, wrapping her chubby arms around his legs. She thought of Irina's adoring eyes on her husband as he played his guitar and smiled affectionately at his wife. His family needed him. Only a few short months ago Lisa would have given anything to take Maxim away from his wife. But having seen the three of them with one another, having witnessed the love they shared and the heartbreak they were facing, she knew she would do anything in her power to keep them together.

November 1943

Chapter 23

Irina lived the next few days as if in a daze. If anyone had asked her what she'd done, she wouldn't be able to say. And yet, outwardly, her life continued as before. She got up in the morning and rocked her daughter. She bathed Sonya in the little baby bath Maxim had found for her in a village somewhere and cooked their meagre breakfast. Outwardly, she was functioning, but inside she was dying. Although she looked after her daughter, she didn't look after herself. She didn't wash or brush her hair or eat. She barely slept. Every afternoon she walked unsteadily to the prison hut where Maxim lay on his straw bed with his hands and feet bound, awaiting his fate.

And then the unthinkable happened. At an assembly one morning Danilo announced Maxim was condemned to die. Irina never attended the assembly but she was walking past with a bucket of water and when she heard it, she stumbled and fell, the water spilling on the ground. She pressed her head to the damp soil and wailed like a wounded animal, like a fox caught in a trap. But no one paid her any attention. Her voice was lost in a chorus of other voices.

'He's innocent,' someone cried. 'You are sending an innocent man to his death.'

'Maxim is the best partisan this country's ever known. Go on, shoot him. What a nice present for the Nazis,' said someone else.

'Are you out of your mind? Are you going to allow this, Azamat?'

These people Irina didn't even know were standing up for her husband. No one believed Maxim was guilty. But Irina barely heard them. Leaving the bucket on the ground, she stumbled through the meadow, not looking where she was going. She could no longer cook or bathe or feed. She could no longer look after her daughter. Thank God for Ramona, who helped her, because all Irina could do was lie in bed and stare in front of her with unseeing eyes.

And that was where Lisa found her later that afternoon. 'No more moping around. You need to come with me,' she said, taking her hand as if they were friends.

Irina didn't move from her bed. Even opening her eyes required a tremendous effort. 'Come with you where?'

'To see Azamat. He's the only one who can help us.'

'Us?'

'I don't know about you but I'm not sitting here and doing nothing. Maxim has made a mistake. I know him well and he's better than this. He saved my life twice. Once, when I was on the train headed to Germany. And again, when our settlement was attacked. I owe him.'

Lisa helped Irina get dressed and together they walked outside. The pale October sun blinded Irina and she leant on Lisa's shoulder. She felt like she herself was condemned to die, like she was seeing the world for the last time. Was it her imagination or were the partisans watching her with pity? Azamat was not at the headquarters but Danilo was. Irina backed away at the sight of him. There was no point talking to Danilo about mercy. He was not a merciful man. But Lisa was having none of it. She pulled Irina inside and the two of them stood in front of Danilo, mute and accusing.

'If you are here to plead for him, save your breath. He's been tried and condemned to death.'

'Tried by what authority?' demanded Lisa.

'By the council of war.'

'In other words, by you and a few of your cronies. What about a court hearing? What about justice?'

Irina could feel Lisa's hand tremble in hers. From fear or from anger, she wasn't sure. But Danilo didn't seem to care. He carried his own anger like a weapon in his hand. 'And those who died because of him? What about justice for them?'

'So that's how it is? An eye for an eye?' asked Irina, turning away so she couldn't see the bloodthirsty expression on Danilo's face.

'Is there any other way?'

'We are not barbarians. We are not Nazis.'

'Tell that to those who died at the hands of your husband.'

'We have a small child. Have mercy on her, if not on him. She's innocent in all this and she needs her father.' She shivered, adding in a small voice, 'Please.'

'Your husband should have thought about his daughter when he gave up our location to the enemy. The people who died, they had families too. Children, parents, husbands and wives.' Danilo's face clouded over. Irina knew he was thinking of Yulya, burnt to death because of Maxim.

'Don't you think there have been enough deaths?' exclaimed Lisa.

'Not nearly enough, when it comes to traitors.'

'Maxim is no traitor. He made a mistake.'

'He condemned all of us when he disclosed our hiding place. He's responsible for the deaths of almost half of our people.'

'The Nazis are responsible for their deaths. Not him. They tortured him until he couldn't take it anymore.'

'He was weak and selfish.'

'Don't talk about him in the past tense, as if he's already dead,' cried Irina. To her horror, she started to cry. She didn't want

Danilo to see her tears. She wanted him to think she was strong, like Lisa. She wanted him to know she would stop at nothing to save her husband.

'He might as well be dead. And in a few days, he will be.'

'This is a partisan battalion. Not a racecourse for your personal ambition. Let's go, Irina. We'll come back when Azamat is here.'

'Don't waste your time, girls. Azamat agrees with me. The decision has been made.'

At the door, Lisa turned to Danilo and said, 'If you were in Maxim's position, can you honestly say you wouldn't have done the same? If they had a gun to your loved ones' heads, what would you do? And what wouldn't you do?'

Before Danilo had a chance to reply, the two women were gone.

*

Irina was nestled into Maxim's shoulder, trembling from head to toe. He held her gently, as if afraid these were their last moments together. When she was without him, her insides froze with unspeakable horror and she moved through her day as if in a stupor. And only when she was with him did she feel alive. He had an incredible ability to make her heart lighter just by being close, the way he did when she was in Kiev, dreading every Nazi patrol, afraid for her daughter's life, doing her best to avoid her mother-in-law with her sharp tongue. When he whispered how much he loved her, there was an intensity to his voice that broke her heart. She wanted to absorb him through her skin, to keep him with her forever. To keep him safe. There was a raging panic inside her, a suffocating anger – at him, at herself and at the people who were trying to hurt them. And there was pity too, for him and those who had died because of him.

'We are not giving up,' she said. 'We'll talk to Azamat. He can stop them from doing this.'

His finger was circling the palm of her hand. Slow reassuring movements that were meant to soothe her but didn't. 'Who is we?'

'Lisa is helping me. She's been really supportive. It seems she's the only one who understands what I'm going through. The only one who cares.'

'There is no use. They will never let me go.'

'You made a mistake. You don't deserve to die for that mistake.'

'An unforgivable mistake that cost many lives. Of course I deserve to die. Whatever happens, I'm ready for it. I am not afraid.'

'But *I* am afraid because I can't lose you.' They were both silent for a long time. Nothing could be heard but the din of heavy rain outside. Irina tried not to think about what was coming but couldn't help it. She couldn't imagine it. Here he was, by her side, kissing the palm of her hand. And yet, he was slipping away from her and there was nothing she could do about it. 'Can't you see?' she whispered. 'I can't live without you.'

'You are going to have to learn,' he said grimly, his arms tightening around her.

'Never,' she whispered. 'Never. I can accept anything – prison, labour camp, exile, as long as you live. As long as I know that you are out there somewhere, that one day you will come back to me.'

'Labour camp? I would rather die.'

'Sonya and I will follow you. We will wait for you.'

'You want to take our two-year-old daughter and follow me to a Gulag in Siberia or Kolyma, to inhumane conditions, to wait for what?'

'To see you again. For the end of your sentence.' The thought made her sit up in excitement. It was a glimmer of hope in their hopeless universe.

'You will be waiting for twenty years. And when I'm released, I won't be the same man anymore. I will be broken, no good for you. Besides, what makes you think I would even survive the labour camp? Not many people do. You'd just be replacing a quick and merciful death with a slow and painful one. Believe me, I prefer it this way.'

'How can you say that?'

'You haven't thought this through. If I live, you will be the wife of a traitor. Do you know what that means? When you least expect it, they will come for you. They will knock on your door and take you away to one of those labour camps you talk so longingly about.'

'It doesn't matter, as long as one day we can be together.'

'They will take Sonya away from you. Our daughter will grow up without knowing her parents. This way is better. Partisan justice is swift and, with luck, once it's done, the authorities will not hear about it. When I'm gone, you and Sonya will be safe.'

'Is that why you wanted us close to you? Because you knew this was coming? Is that why you finally let us join you here at the battalion?'

'I wanted you close so I could spend what little time I had left with you. I wanted you close so I could protect you.'

'So there is no way out for us? Either way, we are doomed.'

'I am doomed. But not you. I die so that the two of you can live.'

She held his strong body in her arms and cried. Inconsolably she cried for all their happy moments together. The day he had introduced her to his parents and Kirill said she was the most beautiful girl he'd ever seen. When Zina had glared at him, he added, 'Besides my wife, of course.' And Maxim beamed, looking at Irina like she was everything he had ever wanted. The day they had brought their daughter home. They locked themselves in their room, and no matter how many times Zina knocked on the door, they pretended they didn't hear, so it could be just the three of them for those precious first few days as a new family.

The morning after their wedding, when they packed a little suitcase and told Maxim's parents they were going to their dacha, so they could be alone together. 'When will you be back?' Zina had demanded, her mop of grey hair bouncing with indignation.

'In a few days,' replied Maxim. They had stayed there for three weeks. They were the happiest three weeks of Irina's life.

She cried for the happy moments because they would never come again. Had she known she was living through the best time of her life, she would have savoured every second a little bit more. She would have laughed louder, held him tighter, kissed him harder, made love to him longer. But she hadn't known. She had thought they would have a lifetime of happy moments together, that they would grow old together and die surrounded by children and grandchildren. And now this life was being snatched away from them and Irina couldn't bear it.

With a creak and a sigh, the candle burnt to nothing. All hope was gone and soon only the darkness remained. Still they clung to each other under the cannonade of distant battles like their lives depended on it.

Chapter 24

Lisa saw Maxim everywhere. Not yet dead, he was haunting her like a ghost. Here he was, leaning over her, teaching her how to take aim and press the trigger. And here he was again, by the trees, chopping wood, his body glistening in the frosty air as her adoring eyes worshipped him. And here the two of them were, her hurting body in his arms as he carried her to safety at risk to his life.

All around her, life continued as before. The partisans woke up, went about their daily tasks, departed on their missions, returned, sang and played their guitars. They gathered in circles – without him – and spoke about things other than him, as if he was already gone. How could that be? How could the world go on as if nothing had happened when Maxim was shackled a hundred metres away, awaiting death?

As she made her slow way towards her hut with two boiled potatoes on a plate, rain running down her face like tears, she saw Danilo sitting on the grass with his back to a tree, staring into space. He looked thinner, less imposing. Was he always this grey and Lisa had never noticed? She was about to walk past when, to her surprise, he waved and motioned for her to join him. 'Why don't you sit with me? Just for a moment?'

She sat next him, not saying a word. And for a while, neither did he. Finally, rubbing his eyes as if he was waking up from a dream, he said, 'Do you believe in God? Do you ever go to church?'

Astonished, Lisa watched Danilo. Until this day, he had never said a word to her unless she spoke to him first. And now he was asking her if she believed in God. 'I grew up in the Soviet Union. Of course I don't go to church.' She didn't answer his first question. She didn't know what she believed in anymore.

'That's true, there's no place for religion in the Soviet Union. And yet, God is everywhere. Take this sunset, for example. Isn't it the most beautiful thing you've ever seen?'

'I suppose.'

'There is so much beauty around us, even at a time like this. Especially at a time like this. So close to our own deaths, that's when we appreciate life, don't you think?'

Lisa didn't reply, her eyes on the sunset. She thought about Maxim, close to death at the hands of the man sitting next to her.

Danilo's fingers fiddled with his cigarette but he didn't light it. When he spoke, his voice was barely audible. 'I know Yulya could be grumpy at times, but she was the kindest woman I've ever met. She loved kids so much. We had three of our own and five foster children. For her sixtieth birthday, just before the war, they all came to our house to celebrate, with spouses and children of their own. It was pandemonium but I've never seen her so happy.' Danilo's head dropped to his chest. 'She believed in forgiveness. She wouldn't have wanted this. And I can't do it. I can't go through with it.'

Lisa's heart thudded with hope. Was it possible? Was he talking about Maxim?

'I was so angry at him at first. We all were,' he added. 'But as time passed, so did my anger. Nothing can bring Yulya back. And I can't destroy one of God's creations in cold blood. It's not my place to do so. There will come a day when everyone will face the higher judgement. Not the judgement of our peers but that of God. And when I stand before Him, I don't want a comrade's death on my conscience, no matter what he did. Who am I to decide if he lives or dies? He, too, will one day face the judgement. Let it be on his conscience.'

'Do you mean it? You will let him go?' Lisa was crying with relief. She didn't want Danilo to see it but, fortunately, he wasn't looking at her.

'I wish I could. The others have lost too many loved ones and are demanding justice.'

Lisa's heart fell. 'What can we do?'

'Leave it to me. I will think of something.'

As she ran to tell Irina what had happened, she thought how wrong she'd been about Danilo. He was nothing like she had imagined. She was convinced it was Yulya, helping her from above, influencing her husband. For the first time in days, her heart filled with hope.

*

They had two days left together. In two days' time, Maxim was going to be shot at dawn. When Irina had first heard the order, she was surprised she could continue breathing. It felt like something had exploded inside her. She was prepared for it, was expecting it and yet, she couldn't take it.

She had been spending all her time with Maxim, bringing Sonya to see him, trying to make the most of what little time they had left. 'I love you. And I always will. Don't you ever forget that,' Maxim said to her while she was cradling his head and crying softly, her tears falling in his hair.

Instead of soothing her, his words broke her heart. Why did it feel like he was saying goodbye?

'Do you remember the first time you saw me?' he asked.

'At a friend's birthday party. How could I forget? All the girls were vying for your attention and you didn't even notice me. I had to pluck up my courage and ask you for a dance.'

'You're wrong. I did notice you. It might be the first time you saw me. But it wasn't the first time I saw you.'

'What do you mean? That's when we met, wasn't it?'

'The first time I saw you was three weeks before that day. You were standing by the river, in bright sunshine, a paintbrush and palette in your hands, a canvas in front of you. The painting you were working on was perfection. The river you had painted looked better than the Dnieper itself. But I barely glanced at it. All I could see was you, your dark hair around your face, your eyes burning with passion, the most beautiful smile on your lips. For a moment I forgot where I was going.'

'I had no idea.'

'And the only reason I didn't ask you to dance was because I never thought someone like you would like someone like me.'

'So if I didn't ask you, you would have let me leave without talking to me?' She pinched him lightly and kissed the tip of his nose.

'No way. Then and there I knew this was the girl I was going to marry. You were not going anywhere.'

At the thought of the two of them young and in love, before the war, before the fear, before *everything*, she burst into tears, wrapping herself in his body, so comforting and warm. So alive.

'Don't cry,' he whispered. 'Look what we've been given. Most people never experience love like this. We are so lucky.'

'You're right. I *am* lucky,' she whispered. 'So lucky to have met you.'

He was about to say something else, perhaps how sorry he was or perhaps how he was always going to be with her, no matter what, when there was a knock on the door and the sentry asked Irina to leave. Even partisan prisons had visiting hours that didn't extend past midnight. Reluctantly she had to tear herself away from him, and when her arms were no longer holding him, it was like a piece of her heart had died. She felt empty and bereft. Tomorrow was their last day together. The day after tomorrow she couldn't bear thinking about.

Back home, Irina closed her eyes, snuggling closer to her sleeping daughter, seeking comfort. But there was no comfort. Her heart was in turmoil. She felt a familiar nausea at the back of her throat, a metallic taste in her mouth. Was it just nerves? Or was it more than that? She tried to remember when her last period was and couldn't. Could it be true? As she was about to lose her husband, had God heard her prayers about another baby?

She heard a noise. When she opened her eyes, she saw Lisa perched on the edge of her bed.

'I have a plan,' said Lisa. 'I can help you get Maxim out of here.'

Irina sat up. 'How?'

'Danilo is helping us. He came up with the perfect idea.' Lisa's eyes sparkled.

'Danilo? He's the one who wants Maxim dead.'

'Not anymore. He told me he doesn't want his death on his conscience. Apparently, he's quite religious. Who would have thought?'

'And you believe him?'

'Why else would he be offering to help us? Just listen to this.' Lisa practically danced on the spot. 'Alex is standing guard at the prison hut tonight. As we all know, he's partial to drink. I have a bottle of vodka under my pillow right now and a pack of sleeping pills we can add to it. All we need to do is give it to him. He'll be asleep soon after. We can get Maxim out. Then the three of you can escape.'

Irina's heart was in her throat. She could barely speak. 'Are you sure we can trust Danilo?'

'What choice do we have?' Lisa appeared thoughtful, then added, 'He thought of everything. He really seems to want to help us. He told me there will be a truck waiting for us. If only there was someone we trust who could drive it.'

'I can drive. I learnt before the war. My papa loved cars. He left me and my mother when I was young. I thought maybe, if I learn to do what he does, I'll feel closer to him and then I'll understand why he left.'

'And did you?'

'No. For a long time I thought it was because of me. Maybe I wasn't good enough for him.'

'Did he leave your mother for another woman?' When Irina nodded, Lisa continued, 'My friend Olga's father left when she was ten. One moment he was there, the next he was gone. After he left, she just . . .' She searched for the right word. 'Disappeared. Not physically but emotionally. She was still going to school and coming over to play but she just seemed absent. For years, she wasn't herself.' She fell quiet for a moment. 'Your father knew how his actions would affect you. And he didn't care. He didn't leave because of you. He left because of *himself*. I don't know him but maybe he's the one who wasn't good enough.'

Irina looked at Lisa's flushed face and said, 'You would do this for us? You'd be risking your freedom, possibly your life. If we're caught . . .'

'Maxim risked his life to save me. Now it's my turn. No matter what, he doesn't deserve to die. Like he once said to me, he will live with what he's done for the rest of his life. That's punishment enough.'

'You have feelings for him, don't you? Sometimes I see you looking at him.'

Lisa looked away, as if she couldn't face Irina as she admitted having feelings for her husband. 'He's been my dream for a long time. And that's what he'll stay. A dream.'

Irina nodded. 'I understand. Thank you for helping us.'

'It's the least I can do.'

'If we manage to get away, where will we go? We have no one to turn to.' Once, they had family in Kiev. She had her best friend. But the war had taken everything. Well, she would be damned if she let it take her husband too. She would fight tooth and nail for her happy ending.

Lisa was quiet for a moment, as if making her mind up about

305

something. Finally, she said, 'I will take you home to my family. The occupation is almost over. The Red Army is coming to Kiev.'

'That might not be a good thing for me and Maxim. After what he did, I mean.' Irina shivered.

'I know someone who could help. His name is Yuri. He can get new documents for you and Maxim. You can leave Kiev, start a new life somewhere where no one knows who you are. But let's get you out first. We'll worry about the rest later.'

'How can I ever thank you?' whispered Irina.

'No thanks necessary. I want him to be happy. If it's not with me, so be it.'

Irina hugged the woman who was in love with her husband, the woman who once wanted nothing more than to take him away from her, and whispered, 'God bless you. We will never forget what you've done for us.'

And in the far distance, the earth shook with explosions as the battle for Kiev was underway.

*

Beyond the dark woods, smoke rose from the city of Kiev, bleeding and burning once more. As Lisa coughed, gasping for air, she wondered where the Red Army was. Explosion after terrifying explosion reassured her the Soviet soldiers were nearby, coming to liberate them from Hitler's clutches. She didn't sleep for a moment that night. Was it the sound of war or knowing what was in store for them the following day, when she was to help Maxim and his family escape?

As she trembled from fear in her cold bed, she thought about her family. She thought of her sister's face as she screamed that she hated Lisa and would kill her with her own two hands if she ever saw her again. She thought of her mother as she turned her back to her and told her to leave. Of months of heartbreak and loneliness and having no one to talk to. Could she forgive them? Could they forgive her? It was war. There had been too many losses. Maybe it was time to leave their differences behind and move forward.

Besides, they were her family. Maxim had told her family was the most important thing in the world. And he was right.

She had once felt like she had no purpose in the partisan battalion, like she didn't belong there. Time and time again she had wondered why she ended up there against all odds. But now she knew – helping Maxim and his family had been her purpose all along. Irina and Sonya needed their husband and father. And Lisa would save him for them.

The next day, while Irina and Maxim were together inside the prison hut under the eager rifles of the sentries, Lisa sleepwalked through her day, lost in thought. When she went over the details of that night's operation, her hands shook and her throat went dry. She held no illusions. What they were about to do was treason and punishable by death. If they were caught, there would be four of them, including Danilo, in that prison hut awaiting execution. But for the first time in her life, she didn't hesitate. She owed Maxim and she wasn't going to stop until she repaid that debt.

As soon as the sun went down on the little settlement in the woods, Irina and Lisa walked to the spot where the truck was waiting for them. Irina carried Sonya. Lisa carried two small trunks, walking gingerly on the carpet of dry leaves, brown and sad. Despite her woolly coat that was two sizes too large, Lisa couldn't stop shivering. In her pocket was the precious bottle of vodka with sleeping pills crushed into it. When Lisa saw the truck parked in the spot designated by Danilo, she raised her eyes to the darkened skies and mouthed a prayer of gratitude to God and to the grouchy man she had underestimated so much.

When Lisa was a little girl, she often played cops and robbers with her brothers and sister and her friend Olga. She felt a little bit like that now – excited, scared and eager for the game to begin. The only difference was that the stakes were higher. But she couldn't allow herself to dwell on it – if she did, she would fail. And she could not afford to fail. Three other lives depended on her.

Outside the prison hut, Alex was sitting leaning against a tree trunk, a rolled-up shirt under his head. In front of him was a deck of cards. One by one he picked the cards up and arranged them in front of him in an order he alone could understand.

Irina stayed behind, hiding in the bushes with Sonya, while Lisa approached. 'What are you playing? Can I join you?' she asked in her most seductive voice.

He looked around as if expecting her to be talking to someone else. But since there was no one else around, he waved for her to sit down, eyeing her suspiciously. 'I'm playing solitaire. I don't need a partner for that.'

'I knew you were here all by yourself and thought you could do with some company. Nights on sentry duty can be so dull.' Lisa smiled flirtatiously. She was a good actress. She could do this.

'I don't buy that. You never even bothered to talk to me before. What's changed? Could it be that you want something from me? Could it be that your sweetheart is inside?'

Lisa was wrong about Alex. He wasn't as stupid as he looked. 'Maxim is not my sweetheart. And I don't care about him. Because of him my best friend is dead.'

'What do you want then?'

'Just to talk. I like you.'

'Since when?' After a moment of quiet observation, he moved ever so slightly closer. Lisa wanted to move away but forced herself to remain where she was. 'I'm glad you're here. I hate sentry duty. Last night I almost fell asleep. Thank God I didn't. Danilo would have killed me.'

'I have something to make the time go faster.' She reached into her pocket and showed him the bottle of vodka.

Suddenly, he only had eyes for the drink. 'Where did you get that?' Not waiting for her reply, he snatched the bottle from her and pulled the cap off. Groaning with pleasure, he inhaled the sharp vapour of the alcohol. 'Did you bring glasses? Never mind. I'll drink from the bottle. It's been months since I've had a drop.'

As she watched Alex pour the drink down his throat like it was mere water and hand it back to her, Lisa wished she had brought glasses. The thought of even pretending to drink from the bottle after it had been in his mouth made her sick.

'Want to play cards? We can play Russian Fool. You know how, don't you?' he demanded.

'Of course.' She remembered playing the game with her siblings after the war had started, passing long anxiety-filled afternoons hidden inside their house, too afraid to step outside, where the streets were teeming with enemy soldiers in grey.

'Every time you lose a hand, you drink.'

'Sounds good to me.'

But Alex was all talk. He wanted the bottle all to himself and would take sneaky sips while Lisa shuffled the cards, dealt them and made her first move, only reluctantly passing it to her when she lost a hand, which was rare. She could swear he was losing on purpose, so that he would have all the vodka. And it suited her perfectly. As she pretended to sip from the bottle, it took all her presence of mind not to smile to herself with satisfaction.

Soon, Alex's gaze became unfocused and his words slurred. 'And I asked her,' he was saying, 'how do you expect me to marry you after I caught you with my own brother? Here I am, fighting for you, and you can't even wait three months without jumping in his bed. And she said she couldn't help it. That he reminded her of me.'

'That's terrible,' said Lisa, who was barely listening. Behind a thin wall of clay and straw was Maxim. Was he sleeping? Or was he awake and waiting for the night to be over and for the partisans to come for him? As far as he was concerned, this was the last night of his life. Lisa couldn't even begin to imagine what was going through his mind right now. She didn't want him to worry for a moment longer and couldn't wait to tell him he was safe, that he had people who loved him and who would stop at nothing to help him.

'Well, I did marry her and we had the baby. The little boy looks just like me,' Alex said bitterly.

'I didn't know you were married.'

He spat on the ground in disgust. 'Problem is, he looks like my brother, too. And I'll never know if he's my son or my nephew. Sometimes I look at him and I'm convinced he's mine. Other times I see my brother in him.'

'Have you tried asking your wife?'

'Like I can trust anything she says. She probably doesn't even know. I would have left but I could never leave my baby. Even if he's not mine, it doesn't matter anymore. He's my son in every way that counts. I was the one holding him when he cried. Staying up all night with him. Rocking him in my arms. Do you want to see a picture?'

'Nothing would make me happier,' said Lisa, glancing at the branches behind him. Was it her imagination or did she see the leaves move? Just the wind, she told herself. But she couldn't stop trembling.

It took Alex a few attempts to open his pocket. The black-and-white photograph shook in his unsteady hands. As he regaled Lisa with stories of his beloved son – or was it his nephew? – his speech became slower and his eyes glazed. Soon he started yawning. Another ten minutes, she thought, and he would be asleep.

It took him five.

After he slumped to the ground, Lisa waited a minute to make sure he wasn't going to wake up and raise the alarm, then picked up his rifle, having left hers in the truck. 'This is it,' she said to herself. She was really doing it. There was no turning back. From this moment on, if she got caught, she couldn't pretend she was here flirting with Alex and having an innocent game of cards.

By stepping over the threshold of the partisan prison while the sentry lay unconscious at her feet, she was committing treason.

Softly she called out to Irina, who joined her with sleeping Sonya in her arms, and the two women walked inside the hut. It was dark but in the glint of the full moon Lisa could see his silhouette. Maxim was stretched out on the straw but something told her he was awake. Maybe it was the way his head was resting on his arm, tense and motionless, like he was contemplating, not sleeping. Or the way he was breathing, torn and sharp intakes of breath, not at all like someone who was asleep. He seemed sad and resigned, and her heart was breaking for him.

'Maxim,' called Irina, tiptoeing to his side and putting her hand on his cheek. 'Look at you. You look exhausted.'

His face lit up at the sight of his wife and daughter. He pulled them closer. 'Don't know why. I've been relaxing for days. A perfect holiday resort in the woods. Nothing but nature and fresh air.' Even in the near-darkness Lisa could see him smiling. His eyes twinkled. The night before his execution, the old carefree and happy-go-lucky Maxim seemed to have returned. 'What are you doing here, in the middle of the night?'

'We are going to get you out. Lisa is here too. We have a truck waiting. We are taking you back to Kiev.'

'What do you mean, you are taking me back to Kiev? What about the sentry?'

'You don't have to worry. Lisa took care of him. He'll sleep for a long time.'

He looked past his wife at Lisa. 'What did you do, hit him over the head with the rifle I gave you?'

'Something like that. But we have to hurry. Can you get up?'

'Wait.' He turned back to Irina. 'I'm not leaving. I did an unforgivable thing and I deserve to be punished for it. I might as well have killed forty of my comrades with my own two hands. I can't just run.'

'You were put in an impossible situation. Anyone would have

done the same in your position. You don't deserve . . .' Irina hesitated, as if lost for words. 'You don't deserve this.'

'The decision has been made by a jury of my peers. Who am I to turn my back on this decision?'

Lisa couldn't believe what she was hearing. 'Your family needs you,' she said. 'We are here to save you. For your wife and daughter.'

He remained on the straw, not moving. Irina clasped his hands, covering them with kisses. 'Please, Maxim. Lisa is right. We need you. More than you think.'

Something in the expression on her face must have caught his attention. 'What are you saying?'

'I think I might be pregnant again,' she whispered.

There were tears in Maxim's eyes as he clasped a crying Irina in his arms. 'Quick, let's go,' cried Lisa. 'You can talk in the truck. We don't have much time.'

Lisa cut the rope around his ankles with the knife she had brought with her. He rose to his feet with difficulty, stepping from foot to foot to restore circulation.

His wrists still handcuffed together, he stepped outside. The two women followed, Lisa clasping the rifle nervously. Together they walked past Alex, who was sprawled under a tree, his cards in disarray, a half-empty bottle of vodka next to him. A disturbing thought occurred to Lisa. If their mission was a success, Alex would pay for it. Would he pay with his life?

'I wish I had a pen,' she muttered.

'There's one in the hut,' said Maxim.

As fast as she could she dashed back inside, found the pen on the table – the only piece of furniture inside the small dwelling – and scribbled a short note. 'This is not Alex's fault. The drink was drugged.' Her hand trembling, she slipped the note into Alex's pocket and followed Maxim.

It was a five-minute hike to the truck. If they hurried, they could make it in three. First they would have to go through a meadow, an empty space without the safety of trees to conceal them, while moonlight played on the damp grass and reflected off every leaf. A full moon, just their luck. On the night when they needed darkness the most, it was almost as bright as day.

They crawled through the tall grass, the women on their haunches, Irina carrying Sonya, Maxim on his belly like a snake, pulling himself on his elbows. Breaking the silence, he whistled like a bird, startling Lisa. A moment later Bear appeared, whining his greeting, his wet tongue in Maxim's face. Lisa was pleased to see the dog. He would protect them and show them the way. With Bear by their side, they had nothing to fear. A small knot of anxiety dissolved inside her chest. It was as if the dog was a sign from God that everything was going to be fine.

They were almost at the truck when Lisa heard a gunshot. Freezing in the grass, she raised her head slowly, gripping her rifle and bringing it to her chest. Where did the shot come from? She glanced at Bear. He had his ears down to his head and was growling in the direction of the bushes on their left. Another shot and then another made the hair on the back of her neck stand up. In horror she saw Maxim roll forward with a groan, his hands clutching his chest. Bear was barking now, but all she could hear was the screaming inside her head.

She bit her lip to stop herself from crying out. Another shot, and the grass next to her shuddered, the bullet whistling past only a few centimetres away. Her breath almost left her body. She felt the air move when the bullet flew by. Panting, she looked up and saw a shadow gliding through the trees. Taking aim, she pulled the trigger. The shot was deafening in her ears. She couldn't see anything anymore, nor could she hear any gunshots. There was no time to lose. She had to get to Maxim.

Lisa rolled out from behind the cover of grass like a bear, conspicuous and clumsy, towards his motionless body, expecting machine guns to sing as soon as she was in plain sight, expecting a sharp pain at any moment. Was it the Nazis? Had they discovered their hiding place again? And how many of them were there?

But thankfully, miraculously, all was quiet in the woods.

Maxim was breathing heavily. There was a red spot on his tunic just below his right shoulder. Lisa unbuttoned it, shook him as hard as she could and whispered his name. He groaned and opened his eyes. 'Are you all right?' she kept repeating, not recognising her own voice. 'Are you all right?'

'I'm all right but if you keep shaking me like this, I won't be. Are *you* all right?'

'Not really, no.'

Irina crawled over to them, her face white and her hand on her chest. At the sight of her husband covered with blood her mouth opened, and Lisa knew she was about to scream. 'Don't worry. He's going to be fine,' she said quickly, putting a finger to her mouth. 'Let's get him to the truck.'

'What happened? I heard gunshots. What happened?' repeated Irina like a woman possessed.

Lisa didn't reply. It took all her strength to stop the tears from coming. At any moment, she was expecting more gunshots. Irina took the sleeping Sonya to the truck first and when she returned, they lifted Maxim and carried him with great difficulty, laying him on the floor in the back of the truck. 'We need to get going,' said Lisa. 'I can clean his wound and bandage it while we are on the move. Once we get to Kiev, we can find a doctor.'

Lisa sat in the back next to Maxim, Sonya quiet in her arms. Irina turned on the ignition. The truck shook and lurched forward, uncertainly at first, then faster. When they were passing the trees where Lisa had seen the shadow, she asked Irina to stop. Jumping to the ground, she leapt through the bushes to where a body was laying facedown.

By the faded army tunic, by the shape of his neck, Lisa thought she recognised the man in front of her. When she turned him over, Danilo's lifeless eyes stared back at her.

*

The truck navigated the forest trail slowly, as if afraid of what was hiding behind the next bend. All Lisa could see over the tarpaulin were the tops of the trees swaying in the wind. Somewhere behind these trees was the partisan battalion, sleeping peacefully, oblivious to the drama that had unfolded only moments ago in these woods. And somewhere behind these trees was Danilo, who would never see the perfect moon or the bursting waters of the Dnieper across the meadow or the sun as it painted the skies purple. It wasn't the first time Lisa had killed a man. But it was the first time she had killed one of their own. She knew that for as long as she lived, she would not forget his face.

Why was Danilo in the woods, lying in wait for them with his gun? He was the one who had come up with the plan of their escape. He had thought of every little detail. And because of that, Lisa realised, he knew every little detail – every when and where and how. Had his unexpected kindness been an act? A realisation made Lisa groan out loud. Danilo was never going to let Maxim go. He wanted to be the one to kill him. That was his revenge.

A hand on her mouth, she listened to the silence of the forest. Had she known it was Danilo shooting at them, would she have been able to pull that trigger? No, she realised, she wouldn't, not even if their lives and freedom depended on it. It was one thing to shoot a faceless enemy officer, and quite another to shoot someone she knew. What would Yulya say if she could see Lisa now?

'Does the truck go any faster?' she demanded, desperate to get away from the battalion and from Danilo's haunting face. 'My grandfather can walk quicker than this.'

'I can't see where I'm going,' complained Irina.

'Then turn your headlights on.'

'And what if someone sees us? What if we are stopped?'

'All the more reason to go faster.' It wasn't just the Nazis they had to worry about. It was the partisan sentry points, too. Irina knew their rough locations, having visited Maxim on sentry duty on a number of occasions, and she had told Lisa she would do her best to drive around them. Still, they couldn't be too careful.

Sonya was curled up on Irina's winter coat, the motion of the truck having rocked her back to sleep after the commotion briefly woke her. Maxim groaned every time the truck went over a bump in the road. Lisa cleaned his wound as best she could in the dark and put a bandage on, having watched Masha do it countless times. Then she rolled up some old army tunics she had found in the back and put them under his head like a pillow. It didn't help. He was still bouncing around, so she crawled closer and slipped his head into her lap. His stubble was dark around his lips, his hair longer than she had ever seen it. She wanted to touch the skin on his face, his closed eyes, the tip of his nose. More than anything she wanted to kiss him, even though he didn't love her, even though his wife was in the truck with them, driving them to safety.

Looking away from Maxim, she said quietly, almost to herself, 'It was Danilo.'

'What about Danilo?' asked Irina from the driver's seat, her eyes on the road.

'Danilo was the one who shot Maxim.'

'That doesn't make sense. I thought he was helping us.'

'So did I. He seemed so genuine. He said he was angry at Maxim at first but he believed in God and couldn't go through with it.'

'Let me tell you something about Danilo,' said Maxim, wheezing, stirring in her lap, not opening his eyes. 'The only thing he believed in was vengeance. An eye for an eye. He lost his wife in the attack. He wanted me dead. And not just dead, but dead at his hands. He wanted a legitimate reason to kill me. An attempted escape was that reason. No one would fault him for shooting at an escaping prisoner.'

Irina said, 'He was probably worried his prey was going to break free. Maxim had many friends at the battalion. People who would be happy to risk their lives to help him.'

Lisa said, 'And I made it easy for him. He told me what I wanted to hear, and I was so desperate, I believed him.'

'No harm done. You saved my life. I will always remember that,' said Maxim.

'Now we're even.' Lisa wanted to cry. This was the last time she was touching Maxim. Soon, they would reach Kiev. He would leave with his family to start a new life and she would never see him again.

After an hour on the road, the truck slowed down and almost stopped. Lisa could hear car horns blaring and people shouting. Somewhere, a baby was crying. A man with the hoarse voice of a lifetime smoker was playing a guitar and singing a popular Soviet war tune, a song Lisa recognised from her adolescence.

'What is happening?' asked Lisa.

'We are entering the city,' explained Irina. 'Traffic is at a standstill.'

This was not what occupied Kiev had sounded like. It had always been quiet, as if petrified into silence by Hitler's troops in their grey uniforms. How long had it been since Lisa had heard Russian singing on the streets of her city? The Kievans were too afraid to speak out loud, in case their voices attracted the atten-tion of a Nazi patrol. Soviet war songs? Unheard of.

Lisa wished she could see with her own two eyes what was happening outside. But that would mean letting go of Maxim's head in her lap and she didn't want to do that just yet.

Irina cried, 'Those are our soldiers! Ahead of us, it's the Red Army!' The truck lurched as she hit the brakes.

Lisa gently wriggled out from under Maxim and placed his head on the makeshift pillow she had prepared earlier. He had fallen asleep and didn't seem to notice. Standing on tiptoes, she peered over the tarpaulin. As morning dawned, a few cars ahead of them she saw a truck with a red star on its back, filled with soldiers. They were wearing Red Army uniforms and waving to everyone around, smiles on their faces. From every direction

317

crowds of passers-by ran towards the Red Army truck, showering the soldiers with flowers and offering them bread. One woman climbed on the side of the truck and gave the soldiers kisses. Another man ran after the truck and shook everyone's hand. Before the truck turned the corner, the soldiers waved at Irina and Lisa.

'Can you believe it?' whispered Irina, tears of happiness streaming down her face.

'I can't believe it,' replied Lisa as she thought of the Nazi soldiers marching through the same streets over two years earlier, of the dark times that followed, of the deaths of people she loved, the hunger and despair. Was it really over? It felt like a wonderful dream and Lisa was desperately afraid of waking up in her little hut in the woods, with explosions bursting overhead and German aeroplanes circling the night sky.

As they drove slowly through the streets of her childhood, Lisa was shocked at the destruction in Kiev. As far as she could see, there wasn't a single building left standing. They had all been demolished by fire or shelling. The ruins peeked out of the ground, ugly and hollow, and the bare branches of the chestnut trees that lined the streets did nothing to hide them. Under the trees were pieces of broken furniture and suitcases, toys, old boxes of photographs and torn clothes, damp and covered with frost. The Nazis must have robbed every house before they were forced out, abandoning the items they didn't want on the pavement. And there it all remained, as if a deadly hurricane had torn through the city.

Every road they passed had holes in the ground – the trenches the Nazis had forced the Kievans to dig to protect Kiev from the Red Army. The city was a ghost of its former self. But the trenches didn't help Hitler. The Soviet prayers had been answered and the Red Army was here. Instead of the hated swastikas, every window sported a Soviet flag, most of them nothing more than a red shirt or towel or sheet, swaying in the breeze for the world to see.

'What are you two whispering about?' asked Maxim. He was trying to sit up.

'You need to stay still,' said Lisa, gently pushing him back. 'At least till we find a doctor.'

'Don't be silly. I'm fine,' he groaned. 'What's happening?'

'The Red Army is in Kiev,' said Irina. 'I never thought I'd see the day.'

'I never thought I'd live to see it,' said Maxim.

Soviet aeroplanes hummed overhead. Round and round they circled, patrolling the city in case of a German attack. Lisa knew in her heart it was nothing but a precaution. The Nazis were gone, not temporarily but for good. What a feeling it was, to drive through Kiev and not be afraid. She wiped tears of joy off her face as the truck made its way through narrow alleyways and broad thoroughfares, passing Pechersk Lavra, the world-famous monastery and the symbol of Kiev. Uspenskii Cathedral, the most prominent church in all of Ukraine, had been destroyed by the Germans in 1941. It broke Lisa's heart to see one thousand years of history and faith in ruin. But the rubble was surrounded by other cathedrals that over the centuries had survived earthquakes, fire, Mongol, Tartar and German invasions. Oppressors and natural disasters had come and gone but Pechersk Lavra remained, reaching for the sky in gratitude and defiance, the golden-domed eyewitness to the indominable Russian spirit that even 778 days of occupation couldn't break.

They were 778 days of occupation that to Lisa felt like 778 long, miserable years.

When they turned onto Tarasovskaya Street, where she grew up, she could hardly believe her eyes. Most buildings on the street had been destroyed. She looked at the broken glass and the carcasses of burnt-out staircases, and cried. Even though the street was unrecognisable, if she closed her eyes, she could still see her sister sledging down the hill on fresh snow, their dog Mishka running behind her as fast as his little legs would allow, his ears like a pair of orange sails swaying in the wind. Blink and fast-forward a few years and she could see her brother bouncing up and down with excitement on this street corner because he had just delivered a hundred leaflets to raise the morale of the Kievan population and felt like a real partisan, a grown-up at fourteen. The war did that. It robbed children of their precious childhoods, forcing them to grow up too soon, to see and feel things that they shouldn't.

As they drove further down the street, Lisa saw the building of her childhood. She breathed out in relief at the sight of it. It had been spared. She had been expecting the worst but here it was, standing tall and proud among the ruins. As Irina brought the truck to a halt, Lisa raised her head to their windows on the fourth floor but even with most of the glass missing, she couldn't see anything. Was her mother inside, stirring her signature fried potatoes, her brown apron around her hips, hair hidden under a kerchief? Was her brother perched at the kitchen table, reading his favourite novel? Was her sister Natasha quietly sewing in the corner, while singing softly to herself?

As Irina stopped the truck outside the building, Lisa's head began to spin and she would have lost her balance and fallen had she not been gripping the driver's seat in front of her. And that was when she saw them. A beautiful young woman with her hair brushed away from her face in a tight bun was walking hand in hand with a tall, broad-shouldered man in a tattered Soviet uniform. The two of them held hands and looked at one another as if there was no one else around. Every few steps, they stopped and kissed in full view of the jubilant crowds, who flooded the street to celebrate the end of the occupation. And when they weren't absorbed in each other, they waved at everyone who walked past, exchanging a few cheerful words, a hug or a handshake.

At the sight of her sister, Lisa murmured a quiet 'Oh!' and her hand flew to her mouth. Suddenly, it was as if the years had melted away. All she remembered was pushing her sister on the swing, while eight-year-old Natasha, all giggles, pigtails and dimples, shouted 'Higher, higher!' and dangled her feet in the air. And Lisa pushed higher and higher, even though all she wanted was to be on that swing herself. And she remembered six-year-old Natasha teaching her how to ride a bicycle faster than any boy. And Lisa pedalled as fast as she could, even though she was afraid for her life. As she watched the pretty girl and her companion disappear around the corner, she wanted to run after Natasha and press her to her heart, telling her how much she loved her. She wanted to tell her sister that whatever disagreements they had had in the past had long been forgotten because seeing her alive again, after having witnessed so much death and destruction, was a miracle.

All the colour must have left her face because Irina reached back and shook her by the arm and asked, 'What's the matter? You look like you've seen a ghost.'

'I *have* seen a ghost,' whispered Lisa, her gaze following her sister as she disappeared around the corner.

She trembled as she helped Irina lower Maxim out of the truck. And she trembled as they crossed the road, Maxim leaning on Irina, Sonya giggling in Lisa's arms. But when she opened the front door to her building and stepped on the familiar staircase, she was no longer trembling. Here it was, the moment she had been dreaming of since the war had started. What she wanted more than anything was to run up the stairs two at a time, like she would often do as a child, knock on the door that hid so many happy childhood memories, burst into the apartment she was forced to vacate at the beginning of the occupation, leaving her heart behind, and hug her mother as tightly as she could, seeking comfort and joy in her embrace, shouting at the top of her voice that she was back, that she was home.

That she was safe.

Epilogue

9 May 1945

Her arms around a large cake box, Lisa Smirnova stood outside a cottage in the village of Taborov by the river Rastaviz. Behind the blueberry bushes that embraced the dwelling, she could hear the murmur of the water, the cackling of the chickens and the low growl of a dog. Before she had a chance to knock on the door, an elderly neighbour opened the garden gate and ran up to her, grabbing her hands and waltzing her around the front yard, cake and all. Lisa allowed herself to be whisked away into the dance, her heart soaring. On and on they twirled around a large apple tree in bloom, the scent of the blossoms stirring at Lisa's heartstrings. Finally, the woman embraced her, tears leaving streaks of dark mascara under her eyes. 'It's over!' she exclaimed. 'Can you believe it? It's all over!'

An orchestra was playing in the village square, its sounds wafting towards Lisa in bursts of joy and sorrow. A male voice was crooning a familiar war tune.

I loved you, and I probably still do,
And for a while the feeling may remain. . .

But let my love no longer trouble you,
I do not wish to cause you any pain.

The powerful tenor transported Lisa to a different time and a different life, a bittersweet memory of herself perched on a chair in the underground cafeteria and of Maxim strumming his guitar, singing this song for Lisa.

'I can't believe it,' she replied, nodding her head to the stranger as if to say, *Yes, it's over, it's finally over.*

'It's the happiest day of my life,' whispered the woman, finally letting go of Lisa and bursting into tears. 'This war took my whole family. I am all alone.'

As Lisa patted the inconsolable woman on her back, the door flew open and Irina stepped outside, a chubby nine-month-old attached to her hip. Her hair was shorter than two years before and her beautiful face was fuller. 'Maria Andreevna, why are you crying when you should be cheering?' she asked her neighbour with a kind smile.

'I am crying from happiness as every good citizen should. Today is a celebration, one we will never forget for as long as we live. This is what millions of people died for. This is what our families gave their lives for,' stated the woman, before taking her leave and moving on to the next house to share her joy and sadness with another neighbour.

When she was gone, Irina embraced Lisa. 'Happy victory day,' she whispered. 'Come in! Sonya's been talking about you all morning. Here, would you like to hold Kirill?' She took the cake from Lisa and placed the baby in her arms. Lisa smiled at Kirill, poking her tongue out, tickling him, inhaling his baby smell. The little boy giggled.

'Did you bake the cake yourself?' Irina led Lisa into the corridor and glanced inside the box. 'Looks delicious.'

Lisa gave a distracted stroke to Bear, who had recently developed problems with his eyesight but came out to greet her every week when she visited. 'My sister baked it for me. All I did was lick the spoon.' She was being modest. While Natasha was certainly the mastermind behind the cake, Lisa was in the kitchen until late the night before, stirring and mixing. Thanks to her time in the partisan battalion, she knew her way around the kitchen, and after Kiev had been liberated, both sisters got jobs at a cafeteria in Podol. While Natasha cleaned, Lisa cooked. The hours were long and gruelling but there was something incredibly satisfying about feeding the starving Kievans, especially the children, whose little faces lit up when they saw Lisa and her tray of food.

Ever since Lisa's miraculous return from the partisan battalion, the two sisters had been inseparable. They lived in their old apartment on Tarasovskaya Street, helping their mother, who after the occupation had developed problems with her heart. The doctors said it was hereditary but Lisa knew better. She was convinced it was the fear and uncertainty of war and the agony of losing so many loved ones.

'Lisa! Lisa!' A small body flew into her, while a pair of arms went around her knees. 'I waited and waited and finally you're here.' Sonya was a big girl of four and a half. As the years passed, she looked more and more like her father. Her long hair was a dark curtain down her back. Her eyes were his eyes. Every time Lisa visited, the child followed her around like an overexcited puppy.

'Of course, I'm here, little one. I wouldn't miss a victory day hug from you in a million years.' She leant down to kiss the little girl on her head and when she straightened up, Maxim was standing in the doorway, his eyes twinkling. For a moment, Lisa couldn't speak. All she could do was smile and wave.

'Happy victory day!' he said, walking towards her and pulling her into a warm embrace.

'We fought hard for this, you and I.' Their eyes locked and everything they had been through flashed between them: the weight of her rifle in her hands as she took her first aim, the heartache as she took her first life, the heat of the burning branches in her face and the sensation of his arms around her as he carried her to safety. Masha's lifeless body and Danilo's face that had haunted her since they had left the woods, haunted her for seventeen months and forevermore.

Letting go of her, Maxim smiled happily but his eyes remained sad. Personally, Lisa thought he had never got over losing his parents, who were killed by the Nazis not long before Kiev was liberated. Like Lisa had promised, her friend Yuri was able to provide Maxim with a fake set of documents. Under a different name, Maxim fought the Nazis ferociously first in Crimea and later in Lvov, as if killing as many of the enemy as possible could bring his mother and father back. Nothing could bring them back but they did win this war, and to Lisa, the man standing in front of her was the reason behind this victory. Despite everything, Maxim remained her hero.

As for Irina, it had broken her heart to see her husband go off to war and she lived from furlough to furlough, leaning on Lisa for support, sharing the good and the bad. Maxim hadn't been there for the birth of their son but Lisa had, bringing Irina what little food she could find, staying up nights with the baby and holding Irina's hand as she cried for her husband. Now that Maxim was back from the front, Irina's eyes sparkled with happiness. To Lisa, Maxim and Irina were living proof that true love existed. And if it existed, maybe one day she would find it for herself.

The tea was steaming in front of them in little cups. The cake had been cut, eaten and praised. Maxim filled three small glasses with vodka and stood up. 'Let's remember those who fought hard for this day but didn't make it. I want to drink to the partisans who have fallen.' His hand holding the vodka glass quivered but he didn't pause. Lisa knew he had ghosts that haunted him at night, just like her. 'And I want to drink to my parents.'

After a moment of silence, without touching their glasses together, the three of them took a sip.

'I want to drink to my friend Tamara. She was killed in a bombing in Kiev just before the Red Army arrived,' said Irina.

Another moment of silence, another sip.

'I want to drink to my grandmother, Alexei, Olga and Masha, and my brother Nikolai, killed by the Nazis at the end of the occupation,' said Lisa, her voice hollow with sadness. 'And to Yulya and Danilo,' she added quietly. She wanted to curl into a ball and sob her heart out. She wanted to scream in pain right here in front of her friends and their two children, scream from heartbreak, from the unfairness of it all. Here they were, celebrating the happiest day their country had ever known, the day of victory over Nazi Germany. But there were so many who couldn't celebrate with them, so many who had lost their lives fighting the evil that had descended on their country like a dark cloud. What had been the point of it all? What was the meaning behind it? What had the Nazis been fighting for all these years that made the terrible losses worth it?

And what about those who were still standing? What about Masha's husband, who had his happiness snatched away from him? When she had returned to Kiev, Lisa had sent him a long letter, telling him what had happened to Masha and what a hero she was. A reply came a few months later. In every word was heartbreak. Lisa's heart broke for Oleg. And what about Azamat, who had lost a leg at the Battle of Kiev, and Anna and Anton, who got married and had a baby but would be forever haunted by what they had been through? Yes, they had survived the terrible war, but their lives would never be the same again.

The old radio on the wall screeched and came to life. Stalin's youthful voice filled the living room. 'The great day of victory over Germany has come. The great sacrifices we made in the name of the freedom and independence of our motherland, the incalculable privations and sufferings experienced by our people in the course of the war, the intense work in the rear and at the front, placed on the altar of the motherland, have not been in vain, and have been crowned by complete victory over the enemy. The period of war in Europe is over. The period of peaceful development has begun.'

Lisa cradled her cup of cold tea, under the impression of Stalin's impassioned speech, where he had called her his sister and congratulated her on their victory, thanking her for her struggles and sacrifices. The door creaked and a tall blond man appeared.

'Lisa, meet Dmitry,' said Irina. 'Maxim's cousin.'

Lisa rose to her feet and shook the man's hand. She wanted to say something witty and flirtatious – something like: *Where have you been hiding this handsome man all this time?* – but once again she found herself unable to speak. It wasn't meeting Dmitry that made her shy and tongue-tied, although he was attractive enough. It was the expression on his face.

The war was over and a stunning Ukrainian summer was beginning, with its sun-kissed days and balmy nights, when the air was scented with apple blossoms and couples in love strolled hand in hand through the streets of Kiev. The man standing in front of Lisa with a box of chocolates and a wide smile on his face was staring at her as if she was the most exquisite thing he had ever seen.

Suddenly, the evening was full of possibilities.

Acknowledgements

I would like to thank my family for always being there for me. Thank you to my mum for her wisdom and kindness, to my husband for his love and support, and to my beautiful little boy for filling every day with joy, laughter and cuddles.

Thank you to Emily Kitchin for her amazing vision for this book and for bringing out the best in me as a writer. Thank you to Abby Parsons for her wonderful feedback and for guiding this book to publication and to Belinda Toor, Helena Newton and Michelle Bullock for their help. And huge thanks to the wonderful teams at HQ and HarperCollins360 for making my dream come true.

Finally, I would like to thank all my readers around the world, especially those who reached out to me in an email or a review. Your wonderful comments make all the hard work worth it.

**Keep reading for an
excerpt from *Sisters of War* . . .**

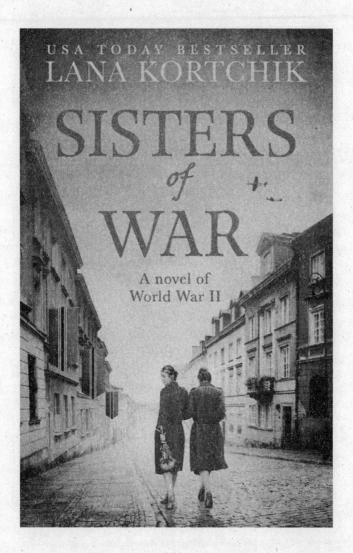

USA TODAY BESTSELLER
LANA KORTCHIK

SISTERS
of
WAR

A novel of
World War II

Chapter 1 – Black Cloud Descending

September 1941

It was a warm September afternoon and the streets of Kiev were crowded. Just like always, a stream of pedestrians engulfed the cobbled Kreshchatyk, effortlessly flowing in and out of the famous Besarabsky Market. But something felt different. No one smiled, no one called out greetings or paused for a leisurely conversation in the shade of chestnut trees that lined the renowned street. On every grim face, in every mute mouth, in the way they moved – a touch faster than usual – were anxiety and unease, as if nothing made sense to the Kievans anymore, not the bombings, nor the fires, nor living in constant fear.

Most stores were padlocked shut and abandoned, and only one remained open on the corner of Taras Shevchenko Boulevard and Vladimirovskaya Street. A queue gradually swelled with people, until they spilled over into the road, blocking the way of the oncoming cars that screeched to a stop, horns blaring and harsh words emanating from their windows. Soon, as is often the case in a line for groceries, a heated argument broke out near the entrance to the store.

'I've been standing here since four this morning, I'm not letting you ahead!' screamed a red-faced man with dull eyes. He looked angry enough to strike the intruder, a small woman holding an infant.

'I have a baby. She hasn't eaten since yesterday,' the woman pleaded, lifting her little girl for everyone in the queue to see.

'So what? You are not the only one with a mouth to feed,' said the angry man.

The woman moved towards the end of the line, while her baby screamed at the top of her lungs.

'Do we have to listen to this?' were the parting words from the man.

'Come over here, my dear,' said an old woman dressed in a winter coat with a kerchief over her head, despite the mild weather. 'You can go in front of me if you like.'

'Why are you letting her ahead? We've been waiting for hours,' complained a matronly lady behind the old woman.

'And another two minutes won't make a difference,' replied the old woman in an *I-won't-hear-any-argument* voice. And apart from a few belligerent looks, she didn't get any.

As the mother thanked the old woman with tears in her eyes, two young girls and a boy approached the store from the direction of the Natural Sciences Museum. They didn't try to jump the queue but stood quietly at the back, unsmiling and serious, as if they were attending a lecture at a prestigious university.

'What are we queuing for?' asked Natasha Smirnova, a tall, dark-haired waif of a girl.

'Sausage,' said the old woman.

'Flour,' said the woman with the baby.

'Tomatoes,' said the matronly lady. But no one seemed to know for a fact, and the line didn't move, nor did anyone leave the store with bags of sausages, flour or tomatoes.

'That's good. Tomatoes will keep,' said Natasha.

'They won't keep,' replied her companion, a petite redhead

332

with a ponytail and a sulky expression on her face. 'We'll have to eat them in a week.'

'If we pickle them, we can have them all winter.'

'Winter? This war won't last till winter,' said the young mother confidently.

'You mean, *we* won't last till winter,' murmured the old woman. 'Not if the Nazis come here.'

'Haven't you heard?' said the old man directly in front of the woman with the baby. 'Chernigov fell last week.' The old man puffed his chest out, seemingly proud to be the bearer of such important news.

'What are you talking about?' exclaimed the old woman. 'If Chernigov fell, we would have known about it. We would have heard on the radio.' Others in line had interrupted their conversations and were now listening in, their faces aghast.

'Believe me, comrades, Chernigov is in German hands,' said the man, enjoying the attention. 'I heard it from my cousin, a captain in the Red Army.'

'My daughter is in Chernigov,' cried the old woman, wrenching her arms.

The queue fell quiet. Chernigov was only a hundred kilometres from Kiev. If Chernigov fell, was Kiev next?

'Let's go home,' said Natasha dejectedly. 'We won't get anything here. The queue is not even moving. Let's just go home.' She regretted stopping at the store and overhearing the conversation. Dread like liquid mercury spread inside her, heavy and paralysing.

The three of them made their way through the crowds towards Taras Shevchenko Park, wide-eyed at the commotion around them. Those who weren't busy queuing for food occupied themselves by looting and robbing. The Red Army had retreated in July, and the government evacuated in August. In the absence of any form of authority, no shop, library, museum or warehouse was safe. Men, women, even children, moved from store to store, laden with sacks and boxes, searching for something valuable, preferably edible, to steal. Outside the entrance to the park, two men carried a piano and a woman struggled with a potted plant and a typewriter. Eventually, she placed the typewriter on the ground and took off with the plant. 'It's a palm tree,' said Natasha, watching the woman with a bemused expression on her face. 'I wonder what she's going to do with it. I'd take the typewriter if I were her.' When she didn't receive an acknowledgement from the redhead, she added, 'Lisa, will you look at that?'

'Who knows what she'll do?' replied Lisa, shrugging. 'Grow bananas? Barricade the door from the invading Germans?' She chuckled but her eyes remained serious.

When the woman disappeared around the corner, Natasha turned to Lisa. 'We should get going. If Papa realises we've left, we'll be in so much trouble.'

'Don't worry,' said Lisa. 'He's too busy searching his newspapers for news from the front to think about us. He won't even notice we're not there.'

Pulling Lisa by the arm, Natasha replied, 'He'll notice all right, especially if you don't get a move on.' At nineteen, she was only a year older than her sister but she was always the serious one, the more responsible one. Sometimes she admired Lisa's impulsive character, but not today. Not on the day when the Nazis were perilously close and their father was going to kill them.

Lisa turned her back on her sister, her long red hair swinging out to whip Natasha across the face. 'Alexei, are you coming?' Her voice was too loud for the muted street, and several passers-by glared in her direction.

Alexei Antonov, a blond, broad-shouldered boy, had stopped at what seemed like the only market stall in Kiev that was still standing. The stall boasted a great selection of combat knives, and Alexei was in deep conversation with the owner.

'Alexei!' Lisa called again. Her voice quivered.

Alexei handed the stall owner some money and pocketed a knife. 'Wait up!' he cried, breaking into a run.

'Dillydallying as always,' said Lisa, her plump lips pursed together in a pout. 'Keep this up, and we'll leave you here.'

'Nagging already? And we're not even married yet.' Pecking Lisa on the cheek, Alexei adjusted his glasses, his face a picture of mock suffering and distress.

'Get used to it,' said Lisa, pinching the soft skin above his elbow. He attempted a frown but failed, smiling into Lisa's freckled face.

They paused in the middle of the road and kissed deeply. A van swerved around them. The two lovers didn't move. They barely looked up.

'And this is why I walk five metres behind you. It's too embarrassing.' Natasha stared at the ground, her face flaming. Wishing she could run home but not wanting to abandon Lisa and Alexei in the middle of the street, she was practically jogging on the spot. 'You heard Papa this morning. Under no circumstances were we to leave the house.'

'We had to leave the house,' said Lisa. 'You know we did. It was a question of life and death.'

Natasha raised her eyebrows. 'A wedding dress fitting is a question of life and death?'

Lisa nodded. 'Not just any fitting. The final fitting.'

'The final fitting,' mimicked Alexei, rolling his eyes. 'I had to wait for you for an hour! An hour in the dark corridor.'

Lisa pulled away from him. 'You know you can't see me in my wedding dress before the wedding. It's bad luck.' She whispered the last two words as if the mere mention of bad luck was enough somehow to summon it.

'It's bad luck to be outside at a time like this,' murmured Natasha.

Lisa said, 'Don't worry. The streets are perfectly safe. And Papa will understand.'

'I doubt it. Just yesterday he said you were too young to marry.'

Lisa laughed as if it was the most preposterous thing she had ever heard. 'And I reminded him that Mama was younger than me when they got married. And Grandma was only sixteen when she married Grandpa. When Mama was pregnant with Stanislav, she was the same age as you.'

Exasperated, Natasha shook her head.

Lisa continued, 'Did you hear the dressmaker? Apparently, I have the perfect figure. Mind you, I still have time to lose a few pounds before the big day.'

Alexei ran his hands over her tiny frame. 'Don't lose a few pounds, Lisa. There won't be any of you left to marry.'

His words were interrupted by a distant rumble. Half a city away, the horizon lit up in red and yellow.

An explosion followed.

And another.

And another.

For a few breath-taking seconds, the ground vibrated. Somewhere in the distance, machine guns barked and people shouted. And then, as if nothing had happened, all was quiet again. On the outskirts of town, fires smouldered and smoke rose in a gloomy mist.

'Don't be scared,' said Alexei, pulling Lisa tightly to his side. 'There won't be much bombing today.'

'How do you know?' demanded Natasha.

'Just something I've heard. The Nazis don't want to destroy our city. They're saving it.'

'Saving it for what?' Lisa wanted to know.

'For themselves, silly,' said Natasha.

Lisa gasped and didn't reply. Natasha could tell her sister was scared because she no longer dawdled. Racing one another, they turned onto Taras Shevchenko Boulevard. It was sunny and warm, as if summer had decided to stay a little bit longer and wait – for what? The Nazis in the Soviet Union? The daily bombing? The sheer joy of nature in late bloom and its unrestrained abundance seemed out of place in the face of the German invasion. The blue skies, the whites and reds of the flowers, contrasted sharply with distant gunfire and burning buildings.

Posters adorned every wall, most of them depicting a comical figure of Hitler, his body twisted into a shape of a swastika. *We will kick Hitler back all the way to Germany*, the posters declared. On every corner, loudspeakers yelled out Soviet propaganda and occasional news from the front. Natasha wished the news were as optimistic as the posters, but it was rarely the case.

As she tried to keep up with her sister and Alexei, Natasha thought of the first time the bombs had fallen on Kiev, on Sunday 22nd June. She thought of the shock and the fear and the disbelief. Nearly three months on, they had become accustomed to the shelling, to the regular din of machine-gun fire, like a soundtrack to their daily lives. With dismay, she realised it had almost become normal. The realisation scared her more than the Nazi planes drifting overhead. She didn't want to accept the unacceptable, to get used to the unthinkable. But she knew she wasn't the only one feeling this way because there were more and more people on the streets during the bombings. Yes, they made an effort to walk closer to the buildings to avoid being hit, but they no longer slowed down, or sought shelter, or interrupted their quest for food. Even now, as explosions sounded, the queue outside the shop didn't disperse. As if nothing was happening, people continued to wait for their bread and their sausages and their flour, for all the things they needed to survive and stave off the war. What was happening to their city now, what had happened three months ago when Hitler attacked the Soviet Union, seemed like a nightmare that would never end. Natasha felt as if at any moment she would wake up only to find the streets of Kiev peaceful and quiet.

Since the day her city was first bombed in June, Natasha had waited impatiently to wake up.

In Taras Shevchenko Park, the ground was littered with shells that had once carried death but now lay peacefully at their feet. Natasha could feel their sharp edges through the soles of her boots. One of her favourite places in Kiev, the park was unrecognisable.

Anywhere not covered by pavement was excavated. In the last three months, it had transformed into what seemed like the habitat of a giant mole, full of holes and burrows. All the trenches that the Kievans had dug, all the barricades they had built, enthusiastically at the end of June, habitually in July and sporadically in August, now stood empty and abandoned. How meaningless it all seemed, how futile.

Uncertainly Lisa muttered, 'The Germans aren't coming here. Haven't you heard the radio?' Like clockwork every few hours, the radio and the loudspeakers outside screeched, 'Kiev was, is and will be Soviet.'

How ironic, thought Natasha. As if anyone believed it now.

'The Red Army will soon push Hitler back,' added Lisa.

'What Red Army?' muttered Natasha.

Suddenly, on the corner of Lva Tolstogo and Vladimirovskaya, Lisa came to an abrupt halt. Natasha, who was only a couple of steps behind, bumped straight into her sister. 'What—' she started saying and then stopped. Her mouth assumed the shape of an astonished 'O' but no sound escaped. All she could do was stare. From the direction of the river, hundreds of soldiers in grey were marching towards them.

Wide-eyed, the sisters and Alexei backed into the park and hid behind its tall fence, watching in fear.

The wait was finally over. The enemy were no longer at the gates. Surrounded by crowds of confused men, women and children and accompanied by barking dogs, the enemy were right there, inside their city, their grey uniforms a perfect fit, their green helmets sparkling, their motorbikes roaring, their footsteps echoing in the tranquil autumn air.

Dear Readers,

Thank you for choosing this book. It means the world to me to be able to share this story with you and I hope you enjoyed it.

When my debut novel, *Sisters of War*, was first published, many readers reached out to me, asking what happened to Lisa after she was taken to Germany. I knew there was a story there somewhere and it was an absolute pleasure to write it.

Just like *Sisters of War*, *Daughters of the Resistance* is set in and around Kiev (or Kyiv, as it's known in post-Soviet era) – one of my favourite cities in the world where I lived for three years as a child. Kiev will always hold a special place in my heart, and it was heartbreaking to research the period of the German occupation and its devastating effect on the city. Despite the order to hold Kiev at all costs, on 19th September 1941, three months after Hitler had attacked the Soviet Union, the Nazis entered the city. Although many people had evacuated or joined the army, 400,000 still lived in Kiev when Hitler's Army Group Centre marched through the streets. The occupation would last 778 days. It was a time of terror, hunger and persecution for the local population. Historians estimate that between 100,000 and 150,000 people perished in the tragedy of Babi Yar. Another 100,000 were forced to Germany for work. Most of them never came home. When the Soviet Army finally liberated Kiev in November 1943, only 180,000 people remained in the city.

Daughters of the Resistance is fiction but history is full of true stories just like this one, of people like Maxim, Azamat, Lisa and Irina, regular people who were faced with extraordinary challenges and did extraordinary things to overcome them, who had to make tremendous sacrifices and difficult choices to survive. While researching the period of occupation, I have read dozens of memoirs and diaries of the survivors. Three of them made a great impression on me. One was the hauntingly beautiful and disturbing diary of Irina Horoshunova, whose family had been shot by the Nazis for their connection to the partisans. Irina worked as a librarian and wrote her diary throughout the occupation, describing her daily life, hopes and fears. Another diary was that of Alexandra Sharandachenko, who worked as a schoolteacher and, later, a registrar in Kiev. These women were incredibly brave to detail the horrors of the occupation. Had their diaries been discovered, they would have been arrested and most likely shot. Finally, the diary of Ivan Genov, commander of the Second Partisan Division in Crimea during the war, provided a wonderful insight into the partisan life. The partisans were known as the Third Front and were a great threat to the Nazis and true heroes of the German occupation.

I'm always happy to hear from my readers and would love to know what you thought about the book. Please feel free to get in touch or subscribe to my newsletter at http://www.lanakortchik.com.

Dear Reader,

We hope you enjoyed reading this book. If you did, we'd be so appreciative if you left a review. It really helps us and the author to bring more books like this to you.

Here at HQ Digital we are dedicated to publishing fiction that will keep you turning the pages into the early hours. Don't want to miss a thing? To find out more about our books, promotions, discover exclusive content and enter competitions you can keep in touch in the following ways:

JOIN OUR COMMUNITY:

Sign up to our new email newsletter: hyperurl.co/hqnewsletter

Read our new blog www.hqstories.co.uk

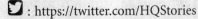 : https://twitter.com/HQStories

: www.facebook.com/HQStories

BUDDING WRITER?

We're also looking for authors to join the HQ Digital family!
Find out more here:

https://www.hqstories.co.uk/want-to-write-for-us/

Thanks for reading, from the HQ Digital team

If you enjoyed *Daughters of the Resistance*, then why not try another sweeping historical novel from HQ Digital?